She's a spy who plays by only one rule: *her own.*

D0038482

A GENTLEMAN'S GAME

"A thriller that not only grabs you by the throat—it squeezes tight and refuses to let you catch your breath."
—Brad Meltzer

GREG RUCKA
AUTHOR OF *CRITICAL SPACE*

BANTAM BOOKS

ISBN 978-0-553-58492-9

US $7.99 / $10.99 CAN

"Rucka is a **SHARP AND ORIGINAL** thriller writer." —*Chicago Tribune*

"Fast-paced action spiced with an intelligent look at the roots of radical Islamic fundamentalist terrorism and what we in the West are doing to counter it." —*Deadly Pleasures*

"A breathless battle with evil, a tribute to Rucka's established reputation as an author who **ENTERTAINS AND CHALLENGES** his readers." —*Orlando Sentinel*

"An exciting, provocative and deftly plotted novel of international intrigue." —*Mystery News*

"A rising Portland writer of international thrillers crafts another page-turning doozy, a globetrotter set in motion by the hunt for those responsible for acts of terrorism directed at London's transport system." —*Seattle Post-Intelligencer*

A FISTFUL OF RAIN

"Instantly addictive, hypnotically descriptive, witty, irreverent, disturbing, and always entertaining." —*BookPage*

"Fast-paced writing, a sympathetic Bracca, and no shortage of action right up to the dark revelation at the end." —*San Antonio Express-News*

"Leave it to Rucka to up the ante in action-suspense. . . . He still writes like Hemingway by way of Spillane and Hammett, but Rucka has progressed to something utterly unique. His voice may be reminiscent of those ancestors, but it is wholly his own, and it is something other writers should strive for. Rucka knows how to make thrillers thrilling. . . . He can write a novel that vibrates with action and genuine thrills and surprises because he knows exactly what he is doing. And he doesn't mind exploding the expectations of his readers by taking them further than they thought a thriller could go. Then there is the real danger of *Critical Space*. After you've read it, you won't be satisfied by any other thriller."
—*Salem (OR) Statesman Journal*

"Smart, high-quality action."
—*Drood Review of Mystery*

"One of the best thrillers to appear this year."
—*Mystery News*

"Compelling . . . [a] satisfying, character-driven thriller." —*Publishers Weekly*

"Cunning . . . Rucka is a fine writer, and there may be great things in his future. . . . A first-rate thriller." —*Booklist*

"Smoothly plotted and full of nail-biting suspense . . . His best so far." —*Booknews* from The Poisoned Pen

SHOOTING AT MIDNIGHT

"First-rate suspense . . . Strong writing and intelligent plotting, but best of all are Rucka's characters: edgy, complex, interesting to a one. And Bridie is a triumph."
—*Kirkus Reviews* (starred review)

"This is prime Rucka, deliberately paced and wound tight. . . . This book will keep you awake until you've finished the last page. And maybe even after that." —*Salem (OR) Statesman Journal*

"A palpable sense of danger drives the narrative. . . . A crime novel that . . . possesses a relentless and nearly irresistible force."
—*Publishers Weekly* (starred review)

"Gritty . . . true-life suspense." —*BookPage*

"Anything but traditional. Rucka creates a morally ambiguous world. . . . Rucka's deft exploration of this theme deepens and enriches *Shooting at Midnight*, raising it way above the average private-eye novel." —*Mystery News*

"A thumping good story . . . a whiplash ride . . . with more hairpin turns than an alpine highway."
—*St. Petersburg Times*

"A dark, fascinating tale of love and trust and redemption." —*Sunday Pittsburg Tribune Review*

"As grit-gray and compelling as real life . . . A-plus."
—*Philadelphia Inquirer*

"Rucka blends Spillane's 'tough-guy' private eye with Chandler's noir insights and Hemingway's spartan expression. . . . Once you've picked up this book, chances are you'll just keep going. And want more." —*Salem (OR) Statesman Journal*

"The action is nonstop." —*Boston Globe*

"If you're looking for a private eye with hard-edged skills and a soft center, try *Finder*."
—*Alfred Hitchcock Mystery Magazine*

"Fine cliff-hangers, well-executed violence, and skillfully sketched characters. Superior."
—*Kirkus Reviews*

"A fast-paced and very contemporary thriller with a plot, as they say, that will not let you go. Suspense fans will finish this in one satisfied sitting, only to find themselves impatient for Rucka's next offering." —*American Way Magazine*

KEEPER

"Impressive . . . *Keeper* is one to hang on to." —*People*

"Crisper, tighter, and tougher . . . A keeper as a novel!" —*San Francisco Chronicle*

Books by Greg Rucka

GREG RUCKA

A
Gentleman's
Game

A Queen & Country Novel

BANTAM BOOKS

A GENTLEMAN'S GAME
A Bantam Book

PUBLISHING HISTORY
Bantam hardcover edition published October 2004
Bantam mass market edition / August 2005

Published by Bantam Dell
A Division of Random House, Inc.
New York, New York

This is a work of fiction. Names, characters, places, and incidents either
are the product of the author's imagination or are used fictitiously. Any
resemblance to actual persons, living or dead, events, or
locales is entirely coincidental.

Tara Chace and others originally appeared in the comic series *Queen &
Country*, published by Oni Press, copyright © by Greg Rucka.

Library of Congress Catalog Card Number: 2004045093

Bantam Books and the rooster colophon are registered trademarks of
Random House, Inc.

ISBN 978-0-553-58492-9

Printed in the United States of America
Published simultaneously in Canada

www.bantamdell.com

OPM 10 9 8 7 6 5

To Lawrie Mackintosh,
and to the memory of his brother, Ian.
Two men who inspired, encouraged,
and made this novel possible.

Acknowledgments

Indebtedness and profound thanks to the following for their assistance, aid, encouragement, and time. Without their help, this novel simply would not have been possible.

Ben Moeling, you do good work. Please stick to your profession; the last thing I need is more competition.

TruBrit, in the form of Antony Johnston, Alasdair Watson, and Andrew Wheeler. Triple-A from NinthArt.Com, gifted wordsmiths all, who went above and beyond with every inquiry, and provided exhaustive answers, new wrinkles, and plenty of laughs. If you three can agree on anything, it's a small miracle. I cannot thank you enough for your help.

At Bantam, Nita Taublib and Irwyn Applebaum, who have exhibited patience, and perseverance, and faith in abundance. My debt to all at Bantam is great, but to you both (and that other one, what's her name?), greatest of all. Thank you for everything.

At Oni Press, publishers of the original—and on-going—comic book series featuring Tara Chace,

Queen & Country. Specifically, thanks to James Lucas Jones, Joe Nozemack, and Jamie S. Rich. I've said it before, but there quite simply is no Oni Press without these three men; without Oni, there is no *Queen & Country*. For friendship, encouragement, and inspiration, I cannot thank you enough.

Additional thanks to all the wonderful, and truly gifted, artists who have worked on *Queen & Country* thus far—Steve Rolston, Tim Sale, Brian Hurtt, Durwin Talon, Christine Norrie, Bryan O'Malley, Leandro Fernandez, Jason Alexander, Carla "Speed" McNeil, Mike Hawthorne, Mike Norton, and Rick Burchett. With every issue and every arc, you brought Tara, Paul, Tom, Ed, Angela, and all the rest to life. I am forever in your debt.

As ever, to Gerard V. Hennely, Master of the Dark Arts and Holder of the Black Bag. I'm glad you're my friend; if you were my enemy, I'd be in hiding.

To Matthew and Shari Brady, for the chemicals.

To my agents and ferocious advocates, David Hale Smith at DHS Literary, and Angela Cheng Kaplan at Writers & Artists Group International. You can put away the spurs now, this horse has run.

To the real Tara F. Chace, who snuck me into her house late at night during high school so we could . . . . watch videotapes of spy stories. "Shall we walk?"

To Bob, Roy, Ray, Elizabeth, Allan, and Jerome. Thank you for teaching me as much as Ian did.

And finally, as ever, to Jennifer, Elliot, and, for the first time, Dashiell. You make everything better.

From infancy on, we are all spies;
the shame is not this
but that the secrets to be discovered are so
paltry and few.

—JOHN UPDIKE

A Gentleman's Game

Preoperational Background
Chace, Tara F.

The first time Tara Chace was ordered to murder a man, it was in Kosovo, as a favor to the CIA.

She used a Parker-Hale M-85 supplied by the Istanbul Number Two that had been moved to a cache near what would ultimately become her sniper's nest in Prizren. She entered the country as a member of the British peacekeeping force's support staff, attached through the Ministry of Defense, then traveled as a liaison officer in an observer group past the NATO checkpoint into the city before striking out on her own. Once on-site, she hunkered down in an abandoned apartment on the third floor of an equally abandoned building to wait for her target and the dawn. The night had been cold, long, and Chace sat behind the rifle playing memory games in her head not to keep from falling asleep but to keep her mind off what she was there to do.

The target, a former Soviet general named Markovsky who had leaped gleefully into bed with the Red *mafiya*, appeared just after dawn, riding passenger in the cab of a three-ton truck laden with confiscated small arms. At first it had seemed Markovsky wasn't going to exit the vehicle, and Chace, behind the scope and with her pulse making the optics jump with every beat, half-wondered, half-hoped she would have to abort. The driver seemed to be handling the buy with the KLA, who had pulled up earlier, and all throughout the dance of "let's see the merchandise" and its companion two-step, "show me the money," Markovsky stayed put.

Then the driver turned and signaled the general to join them, and before Markovsky had set a foot on the ground, Chace had put three pounds of pressure on the trigger and sent his brains misting onto the truck's windshield.

All hell had broken loose then, as everyone back in the Operations Room in London had known it would, and Chace had run, pursued by the angry KLA and the angrier Russians. Her alpha route out of Zone was almost immediately compromised, and her UN cover blown soon thereafter. Running pell-mell through the streets of Prizren, the KLA firing wildly after her, she had caught a ricochet in the left calf and gone ass over tit, only to rise and run again. Two further near-misses with her pursuers before finally managing to steal a car, and then she'd had to keep a straight face and give a good lie past a Coalition checkpoint before finally making it to the British Sector.

At which point, safe at last, Chace permitted herself the luxury of passing out.

The mission had been considered a success, and her stock in the Special Operations Directorate of Her Majesty's Secret Intelligence Service had risen accordingly, even as she limped back into the cramped and ugly little office in the M16 building at Vauxhall Cross. Her Head of Section, Tom Wallace, had rewarded her with a glowing write-up in her AIR, the annual evaluation that all directorate chiefs were required to submit concerning their personnel. Wallace had shown it to her before submitting it—not strictly against the rules, but an unorthodox decision—and taken great delight in pointing out his recommendation for "promotion at earliest opportunity."

"You'll have my job, soon enough," Wallace had said, and his grin had been as open and good-natured as ever, the look of a proud mentor. Nothing in his words hinted at anything other than sincerity.

"Let's hope so," Chace had replied. "Then I'll get the really *good* assignments."

It had been a joke, and they had both laughed, and time passed and the glow of the job faded as other jobs came, but the memory of it stayed with her. It followed when she was sent to Egypt and nearly lost her life in an ambush and was forced to kill three men in self-defense. It trailed her to T'bilisi where a

Provisional Minder Three by the name of Brian Butler, who had been recruited into the Special Section
only four days prior, died mere inches from her side.

It accompanied her home, first to her bedsit in
South Kensington, and then later relocating with
her when she moved to a flat in Camden.

It was tenacious, and the comfort found neither
in a bottle of scotch nor in the arms of an eager
lover could break its grip.

It became part of her life; more—it became part
of her.

Wallace and she had laughed at the joke, but the
fact was, there are no good assignments when you
are a Minder; there are only ones marginally less
likely to get you killed. As Wallace had told her
when she'd first joined the Section as an eager
Minder Three, "It's not the bullet with your name
on it you have to worry about, Tara. It's all those
damn other ones, marked 'to whom it may concern.' "

There were no good jobs, and assassination was the
worst of them all. Even putting all moral and ethical
questions out of mind—and when the order came, it
was Chace's job to do precisely that—assassinations
were fiendishly difficult to execute on every conceiv-
able level. Politically, they were nightmarishly sensitive; logistically, they were almost impossible to
adequately plan; and finally, once operational, even if
the politics and the logistics had fallen in line, it would
all go out the window anyway.

Everyone involved, from the staff in the Ops
Room to the officers of the Special Section—

known in-house as the Minders—to the Director of Operations himself, Paul Crocker, understood that. Chace, as Minder Two, had distinguished herself, and Wallace had been right. One day she would have his job. One day she would be Minder One, the Head of Section.

But distinguishing herself wasn't enough. The "good" assignments didn't interest her. She wanted the bad ones, the ones no one believed in, the ones that required a Minder and, more, required *her*. She wanted to prove herself, not just that she was capable, but that she was better.

While she had done all these things, she had also murdered a man in the name of queen and of country.

No matter how she tried, it couldn't be rationalized.

And finally she understood why Tom Wallace's laughter never reached his eyes.

1

The planning was exceptional, the result of two years spent preparing for the action, an operation meant to run like clockwork. And much like clockwork, it nearly failed, simply because men are not machines, and they feel fear.

When it came upon him, it came by surprise. It stole his breath and cramped his stomach, and for an instant he was certain he would wet himself. Just inside the Marble Arch tube stop he balked, the wash of passengers flowing past him in both directions. He felt the uncomfortable pressure of the glass bottles in his backpack, felt the sweat springing to his palms. Adrenaline filled him, made the stink rising from the tunnels all the more rank, the perfumes and deodorants and colognes that much more cloying. The noise of the station, the echoes of the trains and the voices and PA, became almost unbearably loud, adding to the sudden rush of vertigo.

For a second time, he thought he might vomit.

He steadied himself against the wall, closed his eyes, fought to control his breathing. Of all the things he had practiced, of all the things he had envisioned the eleven times he had made this same trip as a dry run, he had never considered this. He had known he would be nervous. He had even acknowledged that he might be scared. But this level of fear was unexpected, and it unmanned him.

Worse, it made him question his faith, and that added a new emotion, a rising sense of shame. He willed himself to walk on, to continue through the turnstiles and onto the escalator and down to the platform, painfully aware that seconds were passing, that the schedule they had so carefully crafted was now in dire jeopardy. And still he couldn't move.

He thought of the others, ready to board trains at Baker Street and Bank, and he was certain that their faith was stronger than any fear. His mind, which had seized, as paralyzed as the rest of him, suddenly snapped into gear once more, began racing with doubt. Even if he did move, they would fail. Even if he did move, it wouldn't work. Even if he did move, he would be stopped before boarding the train, before opening his backpack, and perhaps the others had been stopped already, had been caught already. Perhaps they had talked, and even now, on close-circuit monitors, he was being watched, and the police were beginning to close in upon him.

He prayed, or tried to pray, but the battering his faith had taken was enough to make him feel insincere, and he had no hopes for it. God worked through him and others like him, and everything he did was as God's Will, and wasn't it, then, God's Will that he be weakened in this moment? Wasn't it God's Will—all praise to Him—that he stand here now, lost?

Someone laughed, and he was so certain it was directed at him, that it was mocking him, that his head jerked round in an attempt to find the source.

It was a woman, or a girl almost a woman. Perhaps sixteen, traveling with friends the same age, of both sexes. She was small and slender, with a lovely face and a mouth that, to his eyes, was impossibly large as it opened in her laughter a second time, now shrieking with glee as she batted the hands of one of her male companions reaching for her. A boyfriend, he thought, and watched as the boy wrapped his arms around her waist and lifted her through a turnstile. When the boy hoisted her, her skirt crushed between them, accentuating the curve of her maturing hip, the slender strength of her thigh. She twisted in his grip, laughing, and the cotton shirt she wore was trapped between them, the front pulling down slightly, and it revealed cleavage and, against the stretched fabric, the curve of her breasts and shape of her nipples.

Then they were through, moving toward the

escalator, and without another instant of hesitation, he followed, his prayer answered, his faith restored.

He had seen it all throughout Europe: women without men to watch and protect them. Women forced to live what was so condescendingly referred to as liberated lives. They worked as clerks and hostesses and teachers to men, their bodies and voices and every movement geared to entertain and to advertise. Even now, riding the long escalator down to the platform with the girl and the boy and their friends only a few meters ahead, he was surrounded by it. Placards and posters advertising clothes and watches and perfumes and liquors and movies. All using women as bait, the promise of their sex, of their surrender. A tease and a temptation, degrading both the subject and the viewer.

How could they not see the danger this posed? How cruel it was to treat them in this fashion? To treat women in this way, to allow them to be used and paraded and corrupted, and in so doing, to make them creatures that could only corrupt others.

It made him angry, restored his strength, made him feel righteous. All of it coming to a point in the form of this girl, at this moment. Surely Pakistani, perhaps born not far from his own home in Kashmir, now standing on the platform with her mouth pressed to the lips of that London boy, her skirt blowing against her leg with the crush of air from the approaching train.

That girl, who could have been a good girl— should have been a proper girl—raised in another place, in a proper way. That girl, who would have been content as one of many wives, protected and nurtured and honored, rather than corrupted in the arms of neglect. Perverted by a myth called liberation, an excuse for indulgence and hedonism, flying in the face of God's Will.

That girl, who could have been his sister, if his sister had not been murdered.

●

He followed them into the car, entering as close to the front of the train as he could manage, so he would be near the conductor's door and so his back would not be exposed. The train was not so crowded that he could not find a seat, and he removed his backpack before sitting, then set it on the bench beside him, claiming it as his own. He heard the muted clink of the bottles inside as the train began to move again, but he was the only one who heard it, and it did not worry him. Even if it had been heard, it would mean nothing. He was just a young man, just another tourist university student with a backpack, youth hostel–bound, nothing more.

His watch read three-twenty-three, and he saw that his fear—already fading into an embarrassment—hadn't cost him. He was still on schedule.

He prayed the others were, too.

The train squealed, began slowing into the Bond Street station. He waited until the doors slid open and passengers began to move, then used their motion to conceal his own. He opened the backpack just enough to reach inside, found the pistol resting between the two liter bottles of petrol. He wrapped his hand around the butt of the weapon, grateful for the solidity of it in his grip, anchoring him to the moment. It pleased him that his hand no longer perspired.

Doors closed. He looked to find the girl and the boy, and they had stayed aboard. The girl was touching the boy's face, speaking to him, and the boy had placed one hand on her bare knee.

The train took speed again, heading toward Oxford Circus, and as its acceleration crested, he rose, pulling the pistol free from the backpack. His thumb struck the safety, knocking it down, and he raised the gun and imagined himself as he appeared to them, moving with precision and grace, and he felt an indescribable elation.

He shot the girl first.

"Get out!" he screamed. "Get into the next car!"

Then he shot the boy, and then pivoted and shot the middle-aged man surging off a nearby bench, trying to reach him. The motion of the train and the man's own momentum carried him forward, and as the man's body slid to a stop by his feet, he stepped aside, moving his sights across terrified faces, still shouting at them.

"Now!" he screamed. "Get out!" And to urge them, like cattle, he fired again, and again, and there was screaming now, and the passengers were scrambling over each other, pulling on one another to make for the door at the far end of the car. He fired into them, hitting a woman he thought was moving too slowly.

The car emptied, and the train was still swaying, speeding toward the station.

He turned to the closed-circuit camera in the corner above him and put a bullet into it, knowing that it had already witnessed what he had done. If all was according to plan, the conductor was already contacting the station, and the station, in turn, had begun its emergency response. The evacuation would have begun, the police been notified, Armed Response Units dispatched.

All to plan.

With his free hand, he reached into the backpack and removed the first bottle, turning and throwing it down the length of the carriage. It shattered on a metal handrail, glass bursting, petrol splashing, its scent sudden and almost sweet. He took the second bottle and threw it against the conductor's door, where it smashed. Petrol spattered on his pants and arms, sloshed across the floor, saturating the clothes of the wounded man at his feet.

He heard the door from the adjoining carriage open, and he fired without looking, not caring who, or even if, he hit. The gun was almost empty, but the gun had never been the weapon, only a tool. Even the petrol was only a tool.

As he had been taught, he was the weapon.

He reached into the backpack a final time for the box of matches. He tucked the pistol into his pants and opened the box quickly. The door at the far end opened again, and he knew they were coming to stop him, seeing this moment as their opportunity, or perhaps realizing what would happen next.

He fumbled the matchbox in his excitement, the wooden sticks spilling onto the floor. He heard cursing and shouting, but it didn't matter, he had a match in his hand now, and with a stroke it was alive, and he let it fall.

The air around him moved, heated, and he saw flame race over the floor of the car, eating the petrol, taking purchase, growing hotter. The man at his feet made a noise as he caught on fire, and he glanced down to see that his own clothes had also caught, felt the fire climbing his body. He looked down the length of the carriage, saw that the flames now held the others at bay, felt the flames sear his skin as his shirt caught.

From the corner of his eye, he saw the blackness of the tunnel open to the harsh light of the station.

He pulled the gun from his waist, put the barrel in his mouth, and pulled the trigger.

●

It happened again three minutes later, on the Bakerloo Line, as the train pulled into Piccadilly Circus.

●

And again, seven minutes after that, on the Northern Line, at King's Cross.

●

When the final numbers were in, the death toll stood at three hundred and seventy-two. Very few of these fatalities came from direct contact with the terrorists, all three of whom had used essentially the same technique: the gun as the instrument of terror, to empty the car and to buy time; the petrol as the primary mechanism of attack, to set the trains aflame and to force them to stop on the tracks.

As anticipated, the Underground suffered from not one but two weaknesses, and the terrorists had exploited both. The first was that, at any given time on the tube, there were more trains in motion than there were stations to receive them. A station closure, therefore, or an instance of track blockage would result in multiple trains stacking up between stations. If those trains were then forced to evacuate their passengers, the evacuees faced walks of varying lengths through the tunnels until they could reach appropriate access back to street level. With most of the tunnels one hundred feet or more beneath street level, it made for quite a trek.

In and of itself not life-threatening, but certainly an added complication for riders and rescue teams, should the situation ever arise.

It was the second weakness that made the situation not simply life-threatening but a death trap. The Underground had no mechanical means to circulate air, fresh or otherwise. No air-conditioning. No fans. Air moved through the tunnels and the stations as a result of the movement of the trains, forcing dead air up and out at stops and other ventilation points, sucking new air into its wake.

While the cars on the Underground were constructed with fire-resistant and fire-retardant materials, gasoline can ignite *dirt*. With three trains set ablaze on the three busiest London lines, all within minutes of one another, the tube had come to a violent and convulsive halt. Cars evacuated into tunnels that swiftly filled with roiling clouds of dense black smoke, an orgy of burning plastics that in turn spawned their own toxic gases. While counterterrorist and emergency service personnel responded as best they could, as fast as they could, civilians succumbed to the lethal mixture of poisonous air and their own panic.

King's Cross, which had seen a fatal fire in 1987 that claimed thirty lives, suffered the worst, as dozens of riders were trampled to death in the panicked attempt to flee the station.

•

An added tragedy came to light in late August, when *The Guardian* ran an article citing an uncirculated report commissioned by the Home Office through the Security Services at the request of the Government. The report had been undertaken specifically to determine what, if any, exploitable weaknesses existed in the public transport systems in and around London, and it had concluded that the Underground—despite massive counterterrorism measures taken in the past—was still vulnerable to "a coordinated attack directed against those traits unique to the system."

Further investigation revealed that this document had actually enjoyed limited circulation and support, until it was killed by a senior civil servant in the Home Office, who had unfortunately given his reasons in writing. "While the report is admirable in its concern," he had written, "it fails to take into account the difficulties, both financially and in terms of public discomfort and inconvenience, that a retrofitting of the Underground would require. Given the unlikelihood of such a coordinated effort as described, and the pointlessness of the result of such speculative mass murder, the author's suggestions shall be set aside until such time as action becomes feasible."

Resignations followed immediately, culminating, in late September, with the withdrawal from public life of the aforementioned senior civil servant at the Home Office.

2

London—Camden, Regent's Park Terrace
07 August 1551 GMT

It was a peculiarity to those in Tara Chace's line of work, their habits and hobbies, the things they would obsess upon in lieu of family and friends.

Tom Wallace, for instance, had put his passion into cars, specifically into the Triumph, and more precisely into the Triumph Spitfire MK I, 1962 model year. Wallace had, in the years Chace had known him, acquired four of the vehicles. He had tenderly restored each, enjoying its comfort and power in his free time, then sold the previous to make room for the next. He hunted the Triumph online and in newspapers, engaged in long, enthusiast correspondence with others of the Triumph religion, and generally poured every pound and pence not vital to his day-to-day existence into the hobby.

The late Edward Kittering had shared Wallace's lust for internal combustion, but in his case it had been motorcycles, and like Wallace, he'd been a devotee of a particular make and model, the Buell Thunderbolt. Kittering had been in the Section almost three years before his death from an apparent brain aneurysm, and in that time she'd seen him go through five bikes, and ridden two of them herself. They were, in her opinion, nothing more than two wheels ornamented with an overactive engine and a saddle, an opinion Kittering had often mocked her for voicing. He had been a far less discriminating collector than Wallace, his only criterion that the motorcycle be built prior to 1996, when the Harley-Davidson purchase of Buell had led to a redesign of the bike, and the motorcycle had "gotten all nice and proper like," in Kittering's words.

Chace had inherited the last of Kittering's bikes, a black and yellow 1995 Thunderbolt S2T that made her feel like a wasp whenever she rode it. She didn't ride it often, traffic in London being a perpetual nightmare and public transport being more than sufficient to service most of her needs. The Thunderbolt was expensive as well; on those rare occasions when she did ride it, it would invariably break down. Whereas Kittering had the patience and interest to tinker with the vehicle, Chace could hardly be bothered.

But she kept the motorcycle anyway, because it was one of her only links to Kittering, and because in the year before he died, they had been lovers. The affair had ended badly, with Chace breaking

Kittering's heart. His death had left many things unresolved, and so she kept the bike, and hoped that in doing so it would bring more closure than grief.

Nick Poole, the current Minder Two, was a passionate cook. The kitchen of his Spice Quay flat, in the shadow of Tower Bridge, had been renovated with restaurant-grade appliances. Poole invested in only the finest cookware and tried—generally in vain, due to the unreliable schedule of their work—to grow his own herbs for seasoning. He took cooking classes, read cookbooks, and was zealous in his pursuit of "the fresh." The week after Wallace had departed the Section, leaving Chace as Minder One and Poole suddenly elevated to Minder Two, he'd invited her over for a dinner of sole paupiette with crab and smoked salmon mousseline, watching her like a hawk until she'd taken her first bite. The meal had been extraordinary, as fine as any Chace had tasted when she'd run alongside the Sloanes and their wealth, and her praise of the dinner had done more for her relationship with Poole than any interaction they'd had in the office or in the field.

As for Chris Lankford, Minder Three—Provisional, he was still too new to the Section for Chace to have discovered his particular passion, though she was certain he had one. She guessed it was something boring, perhaps philately.

Chace herself had survived the Section for a couple of years without adopting an obsession of her own, not seeing the need for one. She had been wrong and, in the wake of Kittering's death, had reached a moment of clarity. Even as a child, her desire for self-abuse had been dangerous and acute, based less in the physical than in the emotional. She had been a rule-breaker, a discipline problem, and what past lovers had charitably described as a "wild spirit," an appellation Chace herself detested. She smoked and drank and, upon entering university, had discovered sex, three things she had pursued with the same passion that Wallace, Kittering, and Poole directed toward their hobbies. But without the same rewards, enjoyment, or results to show for it.

It was after the breakup with Kittering that Chace had come to the conclusion that, perhaps, such self-abuse was counterproductive. Certainly, arriving in the Ops Room for a crash briefing at oh–three hundred carrying a hangover or, worse, a drunk wasn't going to help her career prospects. And the less said about what it would do to a mission, the better. These things, combined with a warning from the Madwoman of the Second Floor—staff psychiatrist Dr. Eleanor Callard—that should such behavior continue, Chace could find herself confined to a desk if not out of a job, served as a wake-up call.

"Find a hobby," Callard had urged her, "preferably one where you don't punish yourself for sins you haven't committed."

"May I still punish myself for the ones that I have?" Chace had asked sweetly.

"By all means."

It had taken Chace a while to find something that would engage her. As a girl, her mother had taken great pains to see her educated in a "proper" fashion, including piano lessons, ballet lessons, and riding lessons. Chace had loathed it all when she was six, and now at thirty-one, she discovered that nothing had occurred in the intervening time to alter that assessment. Unlike Poole, she had no interest in cooking, and her kitchen was merely the room where take-away was moved from a paper sack onto a porcelain plate, and even then it was most likely to be eaten straight from the container while she stood over the sink. Unlike Wallace, her interest in automobiles was entirely professional. She knew enough to break into them, to hot-wire them, to drive them much too fast, to use them to kill people without getting herself killed in the process, and, sometimes, should the situation warrant it, to travel in them from Point A to Point B.

It ended there.

Finally, she'd decided to try painting, resurrecting a dim memory from her boarding-school days at Cheltenham Ladies' College. Not with oils or watercolors and palettes and easels, as she had learned, but with great sections of canvas spread on the floor or tacked to the wall, and pails of paint to spatter, drip, drizzle, and smear. She had no aspirations to be Jackson Pollock and at best considered her work to be more Modern Accident than Modern Expressionism. She had no idea if she had any talent for painting at all, in fact, but she discovered that she did, indeed, enjoy it, to a degree that truly surprised her. It was the main reason she had moved to Camden, to have more space in which to paint. The sensuality of it, in particular, appealed to her, the indulgence of the paint on her hands and its scent clinging to the back of her throat, the feel of the canvas as it drew color away from her fingers. She could lose herself in the activity for hours, and her mind could relax as her body worked, her clothes peppered with splatters, her trainers caked with paint.

And this is why Tara Chace was up to her elbows in grasshopper green when she learned that terrorists had attacked London.

●

"Chace."

"Duty Ops Officer. Minders to the Ops Room, black, I repeat, black."

Chace adjusted the handset between her ear and shoulder, hastily swiping her hands down the front of her shirt, trying to clean the paint from them. The thought that this was a drill flickered through her mind, but it was gone before she could even entertain it, defeated in the subconscious acquisition of detail. One, there was strain in Ron's voice, and not once in four years while Ronald Hodgson had worked the Duty Operations Desk had Chace ever heard that before; two, the background noise was not the usual low murmur of voices in the Ops Room but the frantic sound of motion, of voices calling for attention, information, assistance.

And three, black meant bad. Black meant about as bad as it could get, on the scale of "we're at war" or "a royal has been kidnapped" or "we've lost a nuke" bad.

"Confirmed, twenty minutes," Chace said.

"Twenty minutes," Ron echoed, and he cut the connection, but Chace had already reseated the phone in its cradle and was halfway to the remote control. She flicked the television on with one hand, raising the volume so the sound could follow her as she pivoted back to the bedroom, already stripping off her shirt and tossing it aside. She pulled a new one from the pile of dirty laundry at the foot of the bed, struggling into it as she searched her unmentionables drawer for the keys to Kittering's bike.

She was out the door sixteen seconds later, still tucking the shirt in, and had unlocked the Thunderbolt and brought the engine to life before her mind fully processed the voices of the reporters and the coverage she had overheard. She didn't know the details, but she'd caught enough to know it was most likely terrorism, and it was London, and it was bad.

She drove with those things in mind, grateful for once that Kittering had left a motorcycle and not a dog, using the bike to snake through snarled traffic, to quick-turn from roadblocked streets, and twice to drive on the pavement.

Even with all that, it took her almost an hour exactly to reach the Ops Room.

●

Chace entered thinking that enough time had passed, surely the chaos she'd heard over Ron's call would have abated. It hadn't.

At its worst, she'd never seen the Operations Room looking like this. The monitor wall, plasma screens with a glowing map of the world that normally presented an up-to-the-minute accounting of all active SIS operations everywhere on the planet, was in schizophrenic disorder. Patches of BBC and Sky News and CNN jumped on the wall, voices from professionally calm to practically shrill seeped from the speakers, mixed in the din of radio reports and the calls of the Ops Room staff, runners crisscrossing the room, papers or maps or telephones in their hands, trying to track it all. Only the U.K. remained uncovered on the map, a bright red halo tracing the country, a gold dot pulsing on London.

At Duty Operations, Ron was juggling three phones at once, his coms headset bouncing against his chest, dangling from the wire clipped to his shirt. Sweat had soaked his collar, wilting it around his neck, and when he caught sight of Chace, he used his left elbow to indicate the map table at the far side of the room, still balancing his multiple conversations.

Helmet still in hand, Chace plunged into the room, making for the map table where Poole and Lankford already waited. She glanced back toward the plasma wall, saw Alexis at Main Communications, where she was matching Ron move for move with her own phones, then swept her gaze around farther until she realized she was looking for Tom Wallace, and that she wouldn't be finding him.

Tom wasn't Minder One. She was.

"What the fucking hell happened?" she demanded

of Poole as she reached the table, dropping her helmet into the nearest empty chair.

"We've been hit," Lankford said.

"I bloody know we've been hit, I figured out we've been hit, I'm asking what the fucking hell happened?"

"It's still coming in," Poole told her, indicating the plasma wall. "Best anyone's made out, we had three terrorist strikes within minutes of each other, started roughly fifteen-thirty, all of them on the Underground. Central, Northern, and Bakerloo, Oxford, Piccadilly, and King's Cross, respectively."

"Nerve agent?"

"No, it's not a Tokyo scenario," Lankford said.

"They bomb them, what?"

"Fire," Poole said. "In the tunnels, at the stations. Hard to tell just how bad, but there're reports of people being trampled at the stations, asphyxiating on the tracks."

Chace nodded, fixating on the wall, trying to see everything at once. Images of bodies being carried from station entrances, soot- and smoke-stained passengers with oxygen masks pressed to their tear-streaked faces, of dead firefighters and rescue workers laid out in lines on the pavement, being covered with opaque plastic sheets. Men and women, young and old, and children, in all of London's colors and diversity. Curling clouds of black smoke, so thick she thought she could see the oil in it, billowing from tube vents, rising over Oxford Circus.

A sudden perversity struck her, watching the multiple television images of the disaster, that this was happening just minutes away. She'd been on Oxford Street the night before, Selfridges and the Marks & Spencer, before heading home.

By tube, of course.

"Who's claiming it?" Chace asked.

"No one," said Poole. He looked at her with a grim smile. "Yet."

She nodded slightly, scanning the wall, searching for any new facts to absorb. There were none, and she realized that both Poole and Lankford were watching her, waiting for the next move, the next step.

"We won't have marching orders until Crocker's done with C," she told them. "And probably not even then. Crisis call, they brought us in while waiting for another shoe to drop."

"Follow-up strikes?" Lankford asked.

"Well, that's one possibility, isn't it, Chris?" she said. "Three in one go, there could be more waiting in the wings."

"Immediate panic dies down, then everyone holds their breath waiting for the next one," Poole agreed. "Could be tomorrow, next week, who knows."

"If there's more coming at all."

Lankford scowled at Chace, then Poole, then at the plasma wall. "So what do we do in the meantime?"

"Nothing," Chace said.

"Nothing?"

Lankford stared at her, and Chace wasn't certain if it was outrage or simple impatience she was seeing in his expression. She wasn't certain she cared, either. All of twenty-six, an inch or so taller than Chace's five foot ten, black hair and blue eyes that combined with a lack of distinctive features to make him a perfect "gray man," as they were called in the trade. Nothing about Chris Lankford leaped out upon first impression, or upon fifth, for that matter. But he had the energy about him, not of youth, but rather of inexperience. It charged him, made his engine race, made him want to leap into the breach, and might, Chace mused, get him killed sooner rather than later.

She recognized it, because she had arrived in the Section with it herself. With more of it, in fact. A woman in the Special Section, she had come in believing she had a lot to prove. It had taken almost a year before she understood that arriving in the first place had been proof enough.

Still, Lankford worried her, and this ill-concealed hunger for revenge only added to her concerns. He'd had one go into the field since being named Minder Three, hence his provisional status. It had been in St. Petersburg, six weeks back, and he'd gone with Chace as her backup, and had failed dismally at the outset, only to redeem himself—marginally—later in the op. Whether he knew it or not, Lankford was on thin ice with Chace and, worse, with D-Ops.

"Nothing," Chace repeated. "Unless you know something you're not sharing with Nicky and me, Chris?"

He took it in, the frustration visible, then let it go

with a shake of his head and turned back to watch the plasma screens.

"You two get down the Pit," Chace told Poole. "I'll go up to the Boss's office, wait for him there."

"Bench-warming?" Poole asked.

"You could go through the circulars these past six months, see if D-Int dropped anything that might point a finger."

"Will do."

"For whatever good it'll be worth," Lankford groused. "Bit too late to act on it, don't you think?"

"Not if there's another one coming," Chace said and, scooping up her helmet, headed for the lift and the sixth floor.

3

The SIS headquarters at 85 Albert Embankment, Vauxhall Cross, had many names, and few of them were complimentary. Five stories deep, towering over the Thames behind triple-paned glass and electronic countermeasures, crammed with fiber optics and copper wire, protected by gates and guards and more surveillance than even the most paranoid pedestrian could imagine, it was considered by many to be an eyesore, and far too ostentatious to house M16. Disparagingly referred to as Babylon-on-Thames, or the Ceauşescu Towers, or— Paul Crocker's personal favorite—Legoland, it had an interior that was a maze of white corridors and nondescript doors with only the barest departmental labeling, part of the ever-present attempt to maintain secrecy in a Service that still winced whenever it hired anyone named Guy, Donald, or, worst of all, Kim.

It worked, and more than one fresh-faced officer, new to the Firm, had found himself lost in the halls and in dire need of direction.

The nicest office, situated just below the top floor, belonged to the Chief of Service, currently Sir Francis Barclay or, in keeping with the tradition established by Mansfield Cumming in 1922, C. From the hall, it looked as nondescript as any other in the building. Inside the outer office, it had desks for not one but three personal assistants. But once one went through and into the inner office, everything changed, as if all pretension to modernity had been rejected in favor of those good old days when spying was deemed a Gentlemen's Game. Thick Oriental carpet and a mahogany desk that could keep eight afloat should the Thames burst its banks, three modestly comfortable leather-backed chairs arrayed to face it, and its larger brother positioned behind, to make certain everyone seated knew their place in the room. A separate sitting area off to the side with two couches, two armchairs, and a coffee table. A sidebar heavy with crystal glasses and decanters, and the mandatory door leading to the private washroom, which, rumor held, contained not only the toilet but also a shower and a whirlpool bath.

Paul Crocker hated the office.

Sitting on the far right as he faced the desk, with

Deputy Chief of Service Donald Weldon to his immediate left, and Weldon himself flanked by Crocker's opposite number, Simon Rayburn, the Director of Intelligence, Crocker thought the only thing he hated more than the office was the man seated opposite him.

"The bloody Harakat ul-Mujihadin?" Barclay asked, incredulous. "Are you certain?"

"The Abdul Aziz faction, we think," Rayburn replied calmly. He was a small man, slight and drawn, and his voice was the same, and Crocker often had to strain to hear him when Rayburn spoke. "But it's only a working theory. The tape offers nothing to disprove it."

"But it doesn't prove it, either?"

"Not conclusively, no, sir."

"Where did it come from?"

Weldon slid forward in his seat, saying, "The BBC, sir. Delivered to them via messenger shortly before the first train was hit."

"The BBC had advance warning, and they neglected to pass it on?"

"The timing is in question," Rayburn said. "They didn't know what they had, and before anyone could review the tape, the events of the day overtook them. As soon as they realized what they were looking at, they handed it over to the Home Office."

"It's a wonder it made it to us at all," Barclay mused, and despite himself, Crocker found himself in agreement. The Home Office/Foreign Office rivalry was well-known and ongoing and extended to an intense rivalry between the Security Services and SIS.

A rivalry that justly took a backseat in light of the day's events.

"Well, let's see it," Barclay said impatiently.

All four men turned in their seats to face the screen hanging on the far wall, above the sidebar. Rayburn targeted the screen with the remote in his hand, and a still frame of a young Pakistani male—Crocker didn't put him a day over twenty—flickered to life, standing in front of a bare white plaster wall. The man wore khakis and a blue short-sleeved button-up shirt, and dirty white sneakers. Behind him, resting against the wall, was a well-used backpack, navy blue with black straps, and beside it what appeared to be a shallow stack of cardboard sheets, propped upright.

"I'm not hearing anything," Barclay said. "Why am I not hearing anything?"

"No audio, sir," Rayburn answered. "Only the video. If you'll note, they've done an exceptionally good job staging this. The background tells us almost nothing about where this was shot, or even when."

"They? How many?"

"At least two, sir—the man we're watching, and someone behind the camera. Here, you'll see."

Rayburn moved his thumb, and the image went into motion, the young man kneeling to open the backpack, turning it toward the camera, demonstrating that it was empty. Then he rose and reached with both hands for something off screen. He returned to the backpack and set two clear glass liter bottles on the floor, then reached toward the camera a second time. A hand, presumably the cameraman's, entered the frame and handed the young man a metal funnel. The hand had a similar skin tone, and Crocker supposed it was another Pakistani, perhaps, but that was only a guess. If it was the Harakat ul-Mujihadin, their ranks were filled with Kashmiri refugees as well as Arab elements. Composition of the Abdul Aziz faction was less known, but Crocker suspected that it drew recruits from many of the same locations.

On the screen, the young man was now filling the bottles, using a red jerry can and the funnel.

"Petrol?" Barclay asked.

"Presumably," Rayburn said. "There aren't many liquids more flammable, and it's easy enough to acquire. Which may be the point in showing us this."

The young man set the jerry can aside, then screwed a cap onto each bottle. Finished, he placed the bottles upright into the backpack, then rose again and reached in the direction of the camera. The same hand presented him with a pistol, then with a clip, and then with a box of ammunition.

"The gun is an FN P-35, for the record," Rayburn said softly.

"Thank you, Simon," Barclay said drily.

Crocker frowned, looked toward Rayburn, and saw that the Director of Intelligence was glancing to him in turn. It made Crocker's frown deepen. The FN P-35 was known more commonly as the Browning Hi-Power, a popular enough firearm to those who used it, and in and of itself, nothing more needed to be noted. Except the fact that the Browning was the sidearm of choice for the Special Air Service, and while the gun itself was produced by Fabrique Nationale, a Belgian concern, and named after an American gunmaker—John M. Browning—there were many who thought of the weapon as Very British Indeed.

The young man was very deliberately loading the clip, one round at a time, to capacity. When he finished, he closed the box of ammunition, slid it away, and seated the clip into the pistol. Then he racked the slide, chambering the first round, and set the safety.

"Interesting," Crocker said.

"Yes," Rayburn murmured.

Weldon turned in his chair, looking first to Crocker, then to Rayburn, confused. Opposite him, Rayburn tapped on the desk.

"Explain."

"Very practiced, sir," Crocker said. "He knows just what he's doing with that weapon."

"One would expect as much."

"No one wouldn't, not necessarily." Crocker tried to keep his tone civil. "A suicide bomber doesn't need training, sir, he needs indoctrination. You put him in a *madrassa* and fill his head as full of Wahhabism as it can hold. You tell him he's got Allah and infinite virgins waiting for him on the other side. But you *don't* worry about training him as a fighter, because it's a waste of both your time and his. His job is to wear a bomb and die in the name of God, and your job is to make sure he does just that and doesn't have second thoughts along the way. You don't worry about training him in the proper usage of a firearm."

"You're reaching, Paul," Barclay objected. "That boy isn't older than twenty, and God knows there are plenty of ten-year-olds on the Subcontinent who know their way around guns. Pakistani, from the looks of him, too. Probably fought in Kashmir."

"I agree, sir," Crocker said.

"Then you see my point."

"And you've made mine. If he's a Kashmiri veteran, why waste him on a suicide run?"

"You'll want to pay attention to this next bit," Rayburn said, gently enough that Crocker wasn't certain who was being admonished.

The young man had finished loading the backpack, leaving it open, and now was taking up the cardboard that had remained propped against the wall. He got to his feet once more and, holding the cardboard sheets against his chest, began showing them, one at a time, to the camera. The writing on each sheet was clear, all caps, written in black marker.

The first read:

JIHAD IS THE SIXTH PILLAR OF ISLAM

"No, it isn't," Weldon muttered, annoyed. "There *is* no Sixth Pillar of Islam."

"Wahhabism at its best," Rayburn agreed.

The young man let the first card drop, turning the second to the camera. The man's expression,

Crocker noted with some alarm, wasn't much different from the look his wife, Jenny, wore when she was teaching preschoolers.

YOU, ENGLAND, WE CALL YOU KUFAR—INFIDELS

The card dropped, and the third was turned.

A NATION OF MUSHRIKUN CANNOT STAND, SO SAYS THE ONE GOD

"Mushrikun?" Barclay asked.

"Polytheists," Rayburn said.

"Since when has C of E been polytheism?"

"Since God the Father, the Son, and the Holy Ghost entered Christian dogma, sir. But it's not the C of E that's being targeted here. Wahhabist doctrine indicts capitalism as a form of polytheism, the love of money being akin to worship, etc., etc. The wealth of the West, namely the First World, versus the poverty everywhere else."

The fourth card was presented:

A NATION OF VERMIN WILL BE GASSED IN THEIR TUNNELS

"Veiled reference to Israel, perhaps," Rayburn said. "Perhaps an oil reference as well, possibly directed at our presence in Iraq specifically, the Middle East generally."

The man raised the fifth card.

WE ARE THE BROTHERHOOD OF HOLY WARRIORS

"The English translation of *Harakat ul-Muji-hadin*," Rayburn said. "Also can be the 'movement' of holy warriors."

The last card was raised to the camera.

THERE IS ONE GOD, ALL PRAISE TO HIM

The young man turned the card and kissed it, then folded it along the middle and slid it into the backpack, between the bottles of petrol. He zipped the backpack closed, then settled it onto his shoulders before walking out of the frame. The camera remained focused on the empty wall, then went to static.

Rayburn switched off the monitor, and Crocker and Weldon turned with him to face Barclay once more. Barclay remained focused on the dead monitor, brow furrowed, and Crocker wondered what, exactly, his C was thinking. Much as he detested Barclay, Crocker couldn't—and wouldn't—deny the man's intelligence.

"Why no audio?" Barclay asked after a moment. "Why not simply tell us who they are and what they're doing? Why the signs?"

"No clues," Crocker said.

Barclay looked at him sharply. "Are you editorializing, or is that an answer?"

"They didn't want to leave us anything we could use, sir."

"I agree with Paul," Rayburn said. "The whole

production is designed to give us only the barest essentials, and even then to leave several questions unanswered. There's no way to tell when the video was shot. The presumption is that it was made this morning sometime, but it could easily have been shot three months ago, and we'd be none the wiser. My people have yet to do an in-depth analysis, but I'll stake my job that they won't pull anything we can use, sir."

"No ambient noise, no way to target their safe-house," Weldon mused. "No idea where they're working from, or if there are more of them waiting somewhere in London."

Barclay waved a manicured hand at Weldon. "That's Box's problem, thankfully, not ours."

"It's all our problem if there are others set to do it again," Crocker said.

"Domestic issues, it falls under the Home Office and the Security Services. Our problem at the moment is what, exactly, do I tell the Prime Minister when he summons me back to Downing Street? I cannot go to him four hours after the fact and say we're still exploring leads. The Government is already desperate to formulate a response, and an appropriate response, and that cannot happen without a target."

Crocker resisted the instinct to wince at Barclay's words. It was a given that HMG would respond, and Crocker believed not only in the right to retaliate but in the necessity to do so. But for Crocker, any response would be as a necessity of security, would have to demonstrate not only to the enemy who had attacked them on their own soil, but to those other enemies watching and waiting in the wings, that such violence would not go unanswered. It was an issue of domain, of self-defense, not one of vengeance, and Barclay's choice of words confirmed Crocker's suspicion that his C could not discern a difference.

It was only one of the legion of problems Crocker had with Barclay, both professionally and personally.

While Crocker had entered SIS out of the Army in the late hours of the cold war, Barclay had come in through the Foreign and Commonwealth Office. While Crocker had begun his career in the Special Section as a Minder, Barclay had begun behind a desk in London, then moved to other desks, abroad, until he had become Head of Station in Prague. It was in Prague that the two men first encountered each other, though they had never actually met face-to-face during Operation: Landslide. Instead, all of Crocker's contact had been through the Prague Number Two, Donald Weldon, the man now seated to his left.

History, Crocker mused, is a hamster wheel.

Prague had gone horribly wrong, Crocker had been shot, the man he'd been sent to retrieve murdered by the Czech army as he'd tried to break through the fence at the border. Crocker blamed Barclay for abandoning not just the operation but the agents involved. Barclay blamed Crocker for playing cowboys and Indians with both the KGB and the Czech SSB.

What Weldon thought of the whole affair, he'd never said.

Crocker's largest problem with Barclay—and he was about to see it in action yet again, he was certain—was that his new C was too susceptible to the whims of Government, as opposed to the needs of the Firm. After Prague, Barclay had gone on to a position in Washington, D.C., liaising with American Intelligence on the political level, and from there parlayed his way onto the Joint Intelligence Committee and, ultimately, to a seat at the head of the table. It affected how Barclay saw SIS, its capabilities, and its mandate. At his core, C believed in Intelligence above all else.

Which left Operations to stand outside like an unwelcome guest, until all hell was breaking loose and Crocker and his Minders were asked to pick up the pieces.

But Barclay's devotion to Intelligence had come back to haunt him today. If there was blame to be laid, it was there, and not in Operations.

"How certain are we that it's the HUM-AA and not some other organization?" Barclay asked.

"Based on what we've seen on this tape?" Rayburn said. "Not certain at all. But there are signifiers that point to the organization. The phrasing and the rhetoric. Everything we've seen is extraordinarily deliberate, from the choice of words to the order in which the cards were shown, right down to the heart of the message."

"The HUM signed bin Laden's 1998 *fatwa*?"

"Yes, sir. War against the U.S., the West, Jews, and Christians. The whole package."

Barclay grunted, then swiveled his chair away from the desk, putting himself into profile. No doubt rehearsing his presentation to the Cabinet, Crocker thought.

"Who leads the HUM?" Barclay asked.

"Farooq Kashmiri," Crocker said. "But if this *is* the Abdul Aziz faction, then it's led by Sheikh Abdul Aziz Sa'id."

Barclay's head came around quickly, and he narrowed his look on Crocker. "Not the other one, what's his name? Not Dr. Faud?"

"Dr. Faud bin Abdullah al-Shimmari has no direct ties to any terrorist organization," Rayburn said. "He is still considered to be a spiritual leader and a respected *imam*, Wahhabist rhetoric aside. That said, the message as relayed was pure Faud, right down to the phrasing and, indicatively, the omission at the end."

"Omission?"

" 'There is but One God, and Muhammad is His Prophet.' Faud leaves the last bit out, in opposition of conventional Islamic belief. Again, it's pure Wahhabism, sir, the belief that naming Muhammad in prayer is akin to praying to Muhammad."

"And hence an act of polytheism," Weldon added.

"Is Faud linked to al-Qaeda?"

"The *fatwa*, nothing more," Crocker said. "At the most, the only connection to bin Laden is that the same Wahhabism factors into HUM-AA ideology."

"But isn't that precisely the situation with UBL?" Barclay asked, turning his chair back to face his deputies and now leaning forward, resting his arms on his desk. "No direct link to terrorist action other than by association?"

"No, sir. UBL leads al-Qaeda. There is no evidence that Faud has any presence in the HUM hierarchy, or any organization's hierarchy, for that matter."

"D-Int has just said otherwise."

"He's speaking of rhetoric."

"That rhetoric may have been directly responsible for what's happened on the Underground today, Crocker."

To his left, Crocker saw Weldon shift uncomfortably with the escalating tension. Rayburn stayed still, listening and reserving comment.

"We're getting ahead of ourselves, sir," Crocker said, trying to change tack. "We cannot begin to formulate an operational response before we know the facts of what's happened."

"You're normally quite eager to task Minders to the field."

"With clear conops, yes, when it is clearly identified Special Operation, yes. But at this moment, you'd have me sending the Minders to Kashmir on the hint of a whisper."

There was a moment of quiet while Barclay considered his responses, and the intercom on his desk took the opportunity to cry out for attention. He pressed the key with a manicured finger, listened as one of his assistants told him that his car was ready to take him back to Downing Street.

"I'll be right down," Barclay said, then came off the intercom, settling his attention on Crocker. "When it comes, it will be a Special Op, make no mistake. And when it comes, when the Government presents you with conops—whatever that concept of operations may be—I will not abide argument or hesitation. I will expect my Director of Operations to implement HMG's orders immediately, and to see the mission through to its completion. Are we clear?"

"Quite clear, sir."

"There will have to be retaliation," Barclay said, rising. "When the PM asks me who is responsible for this, I want to be able to answer him in no uncertain terms, and saying the Harakat ul-Mujihadin won't be enough. Whether it's Faud or someone else, I want names. If you have to go to the Brothers to get names, do it. This is priority."

Barclay adjusted his tie and coat, and the other men rose, waiting for him to lead the way out of the office. Crocker took up the rear, and before he exited, Barclay rested a hand on his shoulder, stopping him.

"I won't have you fighting me on this," Barclay said softly. "Not on this."

"We don't know what 'this' is yet," Crocker said. "Sir."

Barclay straightened, the smile thin on his bland face, his lips stretched, almost colorless. "This is your only warning. If you're wise, you'll heed it."

Then Barclay passed through the door, leaving Crocker to follow.

4

**London—Vauxhall Cross, Office of D-Ops
07 August 1807 GMT**

Normally, access to D-Ops was restricted. Those who wanted face time with Paul Crocker had to get past his personal assistant, Kate Cooke, and her desk in Crocker's outer office first, a labor most of the Intelligence staff considered not worth the result. Those who came to gaze upon Kate herself, widely considered the finest bird in SIS, left disappointed. Kate guarded her master's door with the same tenacious ferocity that the Royal Marines employed at embassy gates throughout the world.

Crocker had been assigned his first personal assistant immediately upon his promotion to Director of Operations, a fifty-six-year-old matron by the name of Gloria Bowen who had spent the preceding eleven years as lead pool secretary to the Joint

Intelligence Committee. Gloria didn't last the week, unable to keep pace with the spastic tempo of the office and, more critically, the legendary Crocker misanthropy.

None of the six assistants to follow fared any better, all chewed up and spat out over the next two months, until Personnel, housed on the fourth floor, found itself on the verge of conceding defeat.

Kate Cooke fell into the job almost by accident, jumping several more senior assistants in the process. She'd come to SIS as a clerk, working as a junior secretary on the South American Desk, where she was primarily responsible for trafficking the reports, memos, and pacts that made their way through the Intelligence infrastructure. Shortly after joining the SA Desk, she had been asked to rewrite a report delivered by the Argentine Number Two on possible troop movement in the Falklands region; she had objected. The objection turned into a shouting match, whereupon Kate had left the office, with report in hand, and walked it directly to Simon Rayburn herself.

Rayburn, about to brief the MOD on the very subject, had been grateful. Kate's Head of Section had not, and the next day she found herself transferred to SE-1168, Joint Operation Archives, housed off-site in a dismal basement in Whitehall.

It was Rayburn who had urged Kate to apply for the position of Crocker's PA, and it was Rayburn again who had prevailed upon Crocker to give the young woman a chance. Crocker had grudgingly agreed, as had Kate, and throughout their first week together the hallway leading to Crocker's office had echoed with his shouts, growls, and endless demands.

Kate had survived, primarily because she saw right through him, or thought she did. Crocker was demanding, he was overbearing, he was arrogant, he was outright rude, all these things were true. And while these traits sparked fear, loathing, and resentment in nine out of ten SIS staff, Kate didn't mind them in the least. She understood Crocker as a zealot, and her way to deal with him was to be just as zealous in her job in turn. He did not frighten her, and both understood that.

When Francis Barclay had become C, he had invited her to come work for him instead. Kate had politely declined, claiming that she preferred to work directly under a single master rather than on a team.

It was a half-truth. Kate had long ago decided that only two things would move her from her job: Crocker's own departure or a fortuitous marriage to an ungodly wealthy movie star. Since the latter did not seem to be forthcoming, she was content to stay.

"Besides," she'd told Crocker on more than one occasion, "without me, you'd fall apart."

To which Crocker had responded, characteristically, "Shut up."

●

It didn't surprise Crocker, therefore, to find Kate behind her desk when he entered the outer office after his meeting with C. Saturday early evening, God only knew how long it had taken her to make it to the office, but there she was, working away at her terminal, and the coffeemaker on the supply cabinet behind her was on, the carafe still filling.

"What are you doing here?" he demanded.

"I was bored," Kate said. "Minder One is waiting in your office."

Crocker glanced to the open door, saw Chace seated in front of his desk in the inner office, a file open on her lap. "How long has she been there?"

"She was here when I arrived." Kate stopped typing long enough to look from the monitor to him. "I made coffee."

"So you're good for something. Pull everything we've got on the HUM, Harakat ul-Mujihadin, including HUM-AA, and get it on my desk. Then get onto Cheng at Grosvenor Square, tell her we need to meet."

"She already called for you. She's with her ambassador until late, but she says she'll call when she's finished."

Crocker grunted, stepped into his office, and closed the door. Grunting again, this time in acknowledgment to Chace, he moved around behind his desk, taking off his suit coat and hanging it on the wobbly wooden stand in the corner. The inner office wasn't much larger than the outer, and spare. The desk was old, pitted beneath the blotter, its surface neat with everything in its place—two phones, one black for general calls, one red, used for urgent internal communications. With the press of a button, Crocker could reach the Ops Room, the Deputy Chief, Rayburn, C, or, should the situation warrant it, the Special Projects Team, SIS's commando unit. A terminal for use on the in-house network balanced the desk, and a small stack of folders waited in the in-tray.

Aside from the coat stand, there wasn't much more to see. A safe stood by the door, and beside it a rickety bookshelf with the latest editions of the various Jane's titles. A framed black-and-white print of a stylized Chinese dragon hung on the wall behind the desk, and two chairs sat opposite it, with a third backed into the far corner, beneath the window. Through the glass, a view of the Thames, and when Crocker looked, he could see thin black smoke still rising from Central London.

He took his seat, fishing his cigarettes and lighter from his vest pocket. He watched Chace as he lit one, and she closed the folder she had been reading and settled it back atop the stack in his tray. The folder was pink, stamped SECRET at the top with a bar code beside it, and beneath that was its title: "Impact Analysis—U.K. Commerce Zimbabwe, Q3-Current."

Crocker exhaled smoke, looking her over, frowning. "Your hands are green," he said.

"I was painting." Chace brushed hair behind an ear. "Who did it?"

"The BBC received a tape, apparently claiming responsibility. Looks like the HUM."

"HUM doesn't play in Western Europe. Certainly never has moved against us."

"I am well aware."

Chace pulled on her lower lip with her teeth for a moment. "You don't buy it?"

"I'd like to hear what the CIA has to say before we start making plans."

Chace nodded. "Lankford and Poole are in the Pit, pawing the ground like irate bulls. They want you to point them at someone."

"Not you?"

Chace shrugged, smiled by way of answer. When she smiled, she looked ten years younger than she truly was, and the weight of the job evaporated for a moment. Crocker saw the expression for what it was. Of course she was pawing the ground, of course she wanted the job. If the day's events had occurred when he had been Minder One, he'd have wanted it, too.

"May not be us, Tara." Crocker tapped the end of his cigarette into the square glass ashtray next to the phones. "Might be a military response."

Chace's smile grew a fraction, and she shook her head. "No, it won't, you and I both know that, Boss. Military action would require that another sovereign nation be held responsible, and if it's the HUM, we're not about to invade Pakistan."

"If that's where they're based."

"Farooq Kashmiri isn't anti-West as much as he's anti-India, isn't he?"

"If Kashmiri is still running the show. And that precludes confirming that it was the Abdul Aziz faction that we're dealing with, in which case we're now talking about invading Saudi Arabia, and that will *never* happen, as we both well know."

"More likely it's AA, then. Killing Londoners on the Underground, that doesn't really help to liberate Kashmir, does it?"

"No, it doesn't."

"So it's someone else. HUM-AA."

"Perhaps."

Chace shifted in the chair, brushed more hair back behind an ear. "If we're talking a job on foreign soil, I'm going to want Poole to back me up. I don't want a repeat of St. Petersburg."

"I just had this conversation with C. There is no job yet."

"But there will be."

"And again, I say perhaps." Crocker turned the cigarette in his fingers, knocked more ash into the tray, appraising her. "You're worried I won't give it to you."

The smile came back, almost sheepish.

"You don't have to worry," Crocker told her. "If there's someone we need to kill, you'll be the one to do it."

●

Chace's office, which she shared with the two other Minders, was near the end of a long and dull corridor in the first sublevel of the building. Also on the hall was a lavatory, a storage closet, three archives, and a very large, very secured room that housed perhaps one-quarter of the data-storage and computer servers used by the in-building network. As in the rest of the building, the rooms were marked in exactly the same fashion, with black plastic rectangles mounted to the left of each doorframe, declaring—as cryptically as possible—what lay within.

The plate beside the door to her office read "SB-01-213—S-Ops." Nowhere was the word

"Minder," and nowhere was the word "Pit." Once, nearly four years ago, Kittering had decided to change that. Spurred by a fit of boredom, he'd come to work with a box of wax crayons and spent the better part of a very slow morning coaxing what few artistic skills he had onto paper. When he was finished, he had a multicolored cartoon of the three Minders at the time— himself, Chace, and Wallace—in a deep dark hole, over which, in ragged and bloodred letters, he'd inscribed the words "The Pit."

The cartoon had survived on the door of the office for almost a week before the Deputy Chief, on one of his walk-throughs of the building, had caught sight of the sign and torn it down himself. He'd then delivered an angry, if brief, lecture to them all on the need for departmental security and discretion, before heading back upstairs to complain to Crocker. They'd received a memo from the latter that afternoon reiterating the point.

Chace stopped at the door, hand out, ready to open it, remembering, and felt the echo of sadness swell briefly in her chest. She hadn't thought about Ed in a while, in almost six months. No, that wasn't quite true. If she was going to be honest with herself, she thought about Ed Kittering quite a bit; what was more accurate was that it had been almost half a year since the thinking of him had caused her pain.

Standing in the empty, anonymous hall outside the office, the pain was back, and it surprised Chace with its intensity. They'd carried on the affair out of the office, with as much discretion as they could muster, knowing that Wallace knew and disapproved, afraid that Crocker would know and bring the hammer down.

On the floors above, tandem couples—personnel involved with each other—were permitted, even encouraged. It made awkward questions easier when both parties knew what the other did for a living, when both parties knew the boundaries of their secrets, of their work. If analysts were sharing a bed, well, at least Internal Security, not to mention the folks at Box, knew who everyone was sleeping with, and as a result—to beat the metaphor to death—everyone could rest easier.

Not in Special Operations. Not when the two people creaking the bedsprings at night might be called upon the next day to parachute into northern Iraq, for instance. Not when one might be required to leave the other behind or, worse, leave nothing behind at all. In Paul Crocker's book that translated to an operational liability, and the Minders had enough of those already; he wasn't about to countenance personal feelings jeopardizing the job as well.

When she'd ended it, she'd known that Ed was in love with her, and was deathly afraid that she'd fallen in love with him. She'd tried to be precise and quick, to limit the pain for each of them, and of course had failed utterly. For the three months following the end of the affair, their interactions had been confined to tepid pleasantries in the office and almost no contact outside of the job.

Almost.

Exactly six weeks after she'd ended it, Chace had

spent a Saturday in Camden, visiting the market, killing the day slowly by herself. Off Kentish Town Road she'd stopped in a pub for a pint and an early dinner, and there had been Ed, at a table in the corner, his back covered, a black-haired and far-too-young pretty thing half in his lap, her tongue alternately in his mouth and his ear, or so it seemed. Ed had seen her immediately, and for an infinite second they had stared at each other, caught in one of fate's crueler little bear traps.

Then Tara had left, and they had never spoken of it, and nine days later Ed was sent to Caracas to back up the station on a surveillance job, and two days after that he was discovered dead in his bed in the Caracas Hilton. There'd been no sign of foul play, no sign of violence, and when the autopsy was completed, cause of death was attributed to a cerebral aneurysm, to natural causes.

Chace shook the memory off, wondering why it had come back now, wondering if it was the death of the day or something else that was making her remember things she'd rather forget. She had a stack of folders beneath her arm, courtesy of D-Int by way of Kate, everything that could be scrounged up on HUM and its associations and activities, and it was brain-time now, not heart-time.

And she would be damned if she'd let Nicky Poole and Chris Lankford see their Minder One looking anything less than ready to do the job at hand.

"We were starting to think you'd been eaten," Poole said as Chace entered.

"And a tasty treat I'd be," Chase responded.

The Pit was aptly named, a cube of a room, dead-white cinderblock walls with no windows and poor ventilation, gray carpet that utterly failed to diminish the cruelty of the concrete floor beneath it. Each Minder's desk faced out from three of the walls, so that the Minder Two desk faced the door from the hall, and the Minder One desk, on the left as one entered, faced Minder Three's. The remaining space was occupied with two metal filing cabinets, a coat stand by the door, and a file safe, on top of which sat the go-bags, one for each agent. Inside each small duffel were the bare essentials—toiletries and clean underwear and socks. The only decorations were, above Minder Two's desk, an old dartboard, and above Minder Three's, a map of the world that had been printed in 1989.

Chace dumped the folders she carried onto the already cluttered surface of her desk. "The Boss was in with C when I got up there, kept me waiting for most of an hour."

"Are we on, then?" Lankford asked.

Chace began sorting the folders, speaking without looking up. "It's going to be a while, Chris, if there's going to be action at all."

"How long a while?"

"Days? Weeks? Months?" Chace finished breaking down the folders into their stacks, then picked up the stack closest to her and walked it across the room to Lankford's desk, handing it over. "Maybe never. Crocker says the response might be military."

"Then why the hell did they call us in? What are we supposed to do?" Lankford took the folders without looking away from her, and again, she could read the frustration in his gaze.

"It's hurry up and wait, you knew that was the job when you signed up. Months of sitting on your soft end punctuated by bouts of bowel-freeing panic. Just because the tragedy was local doesn't mean it moves any faster."

Lankford hesitated, frowned, then gave her a grudging nod of comprehension.

Chace gathered the second pile, dropped it with Poole, then returned to her desk.

"Harakat ul-Mujihadin, Abdul Aziz faction," she told them. "No positive ID yet, but it's the working theory. D-Ops wants anything useful, anything vaguely operational. Start reading."

Without a word, Poole and Lankford dove into the folders.

Chace took her seat, wooden and designed, it seemed, by one of England's crueler chiropractors, and began working through her own pile. Most of the information was already known to her, and the files served as a refresher course more than anything else.

The HUM began as the Harakat ul-Ansar, formed in central Punjab in Pakistan in the early 1980s by Islamic religious elements. The group almost immediately began sending fighters into Afghanistan to assist the Afghani Mujihadin in their war against the Soviet occupation. Fighters were recruited from both central Pakistan and Pakistan-occupied Kashmir, and the CIA estimated up to five thousand troops had entered Afghanistan to join the fight by 1987, with recruitment funding coming from Egypt, Pakistan, and Saudi Arabia, including the bin Laden family.

As the war in Afghanistan progressed, more recruits were drawn from Muslim communities in other countries, including Tunisia, Algeria, Jordan, Egypt, Bangladesh, Myanmar, the Philippines, and of course Kashmir. Recruits were trained in camps set up in the Paktia province of Afghanistan and run by Hezb Islami (Khalis) Afghan Mujihadin leader Jalaluddin Haqqani, who later went on to join the *taleban* leadership as Minister of Tribal Affairs.

The file noted that Haqqani was still alive and at liberty, presumably hiding in the mountains of western Pakistan.

Following its initial entry into the conflict, the HUM established its own camps in Afghan territory, and Chace found herself leafing through old satellite surveillance shots, views of tents and training courses, and clusters of men engaged in all manner of paramilitary training. The camps were constructed just across the Miran Shah in the NWFP, and declassified Russian intelligence stated that some of the Soviet army's fiercest opposition had come from HUM-trained soldiers.

After the Mujihadin taking of Kabul in 1992 and the establishment of the *taleban* government, the HUA merged with the Harakat ul-Jihad-al-Islami, another Afghani partisan organization, and took the

new name Harakat ul-Mujihadin, now directing its
energies to defending the rights of Muslims all over
the world. It expanded operations to those same
countries it had drawn recruits from, and added
Chechnya, Bosnia, and Tajikistan for good measure.

In the aftermath of the bombing of the U.S. embassies in Kenya and Tanzania, the Americans
launched cruise missile attacks at the HUM training
camps, and then again during the Coalition action
in Afghanistan, virtually destroying the groups'
training infrastructure and scattering its various elements. D-Int's assessment, and here Chace found a
corresponding CIA analysis, was that the HUM had
been driven out of Afghanistan entirely and pursued underground in Pakistan. Given the activity in
the region, and the HUM's ideological similarities
to other radical Islamist—read Wahhabist—organizations, it was likely that those HUM elements still
surviving had been absorbed into other militant
groups throughout the region.

It was out of these surviving elements that the
Abdul Aziz faction was believed to have been born,
founded by Sheikh Abdul Aziz Sa'id, an Arab of unknown origin who had been linked to Muslim ex-
tremist organizations throughout the Middle and
Far East. Abdul Aziz was suspected of supplying
material and support to al-Qaeda operatives in
northern Africa, as well as providing the Semtex
used in the recent Jamaat al-Islamiyya bombings in
Micronesia.

As with all such organizations, information on
HUM finances was hard to come by. It was known

that the HUM took donations from Saudi Arabia and other Gulf and Islamic states, as well as from individuals and organizations inside Pakistan and Kashmir. Rayburn noted that the HUM also solicited donations via magazine advertisements and through pamphlets, videotapes, and the like. The extent of the group's holdings was unknown, but since the crackdown in Pakistan in late 2001, it was assumed much of its money had been redirected into more legitimate ventures—real estate, commodities trading, and the production of consumer goods.

Chace shut the last folder and sat back, rubbing her eyes. Her watch now read nine minutes to ten, and she realized that she was both tired and ravenous.

"You find anything in the circulars?" she asked Poole.

Poole looked up from his file, shook his head slowly. He was a big man, perfect for rugby or leg-breaking, and, if he was to be believed, had spent much of his youth doing both. He certainly was adept with violence, though whether that was a result of his time in the SAS or something else seated far deeper, Chace didn't know and, in fact, labored to avoid drawing conclusions. It mattered less where the Minders were from than what they could learn, and Chace herself was living proof of that. Everything in her own upbringing and education should have led her to a good marriage and a proper job, and yet here she was.

Still, of any Minder she had ever known, it was Poole who looked most like the thugs Whitehall and the FCO and all the rest took the Special Section to be. He wasn't, of course; Crocker would suffer no bullies and no violence junkies, gourmet cooking notwithstanding. Chace trusted and respected Poole, all the more since he hadn't batted an eye when Tom had left and they had all shifted desks anticlockwise, with Tara taking the first chair. Poole treated her exactly as he had treated Wallace, and Chace was grateful for that.

"No mention of HUM, no mention of anything brewing targeted at us." Poole pushed aside the folders on his desk and pulled open his desk drawer, rummaging about. "Unless something got dropped through the cracks, this one was a complete surprise."

"I'm not sure I like that very much," Chace said.

"Suppose it could be a good sign, at least with regard to follow-ups. You have to figure if they moved more than three men into England, someone somewhere would have noticed something."

"You're putting a lot of faith in the boys at Box."

"I am a pillar of faith," Poole said, smiling now, with a rubber band dangling from an index finger and a paper clip held between two others.

"Christ, I hate this," Lankford said abruptly. "I bloody hate this."

Chace canted her head toward him, curious. "All fired up, are you, Chris?"

"If you're asking if I want a chance to hit back for this, that's a no-brainer, Tara. I'd give a year's pay for a crack at these bastards."

"And who, exactly, would you hit, Chris? Any suggestions? Unless you're planning on taking on the whole of the Harakat ul-Mujihadin? And that's assuming, of course, that it *was* the HUM and not someone else."

Lankford's chair groaned with dismay as he tilted back in it, looking to Poole, trying to conceal a growing frown. "You know that's not what I meant. I'm talking about cutting off the head, not taking pieces out of the body."

"You're talking about assassination."

He looked back to Chace, and his expression surprised her with its certainty. "Absolutely," he said.

Chace didn't respond, instead glancing to Poole, who was studiously avoiding involvement in the conversation by tilting back in his chair and trying to snatch the darts embedded in the board above him with the makeshift grappling hook he'd made from the rubber band and the paper clip. She didn't know his stories, but the action told her that Poole understood, in the same way that Lankford's certainty made it clear that the new Minder Three didn't.

After a moment, Chace said, "If it comes, it'll be D-Ops who tasks it, not us. We just complete the mission, we don't lobby for the action."

"Won't be you, anyway, Chris," Poole said, snagging one of the darts and then quickly scooting his chair back as the missile fell, point down, to the floor. "If they call for a hit, it'll go to Minder One, with me as backup."

"Because I'm the baby?"

Poole grinned at Lankford over his shoulder. "That's right."

"It's academic," Chace interposed. "It'll be weeks before anything is authorized, and that's *if* anything is authorized. They'll want to be damn sure we're going after the right people before initiating any op."

Lankford's frown deepened. "Then what the hell are we doing here?"

"Nothing productive. If you boys want to shove off, I've no problem with it."

Poole grunted and tilted his chair forward, getting to his feet almost immediately. "You'll tell the Watch?"

Chace nodded.

Poole moved past, fetching his coat from the stand.

"The Boss won't think we're ditching?" Lankford asked.

Chace shook her head. If Crocker had a problem with her turning Poole and Lankford loose, he'd bring it to her, not to them. And Chace doubted that he would have a problem. The fact was, until there was more data, until there was a mission in the offing, the three of them were just killing time. And time didn't seem inclined to die without a struggle, not while all London was still holding its breath.

Lankford hesitated, looked from her to Poole, watching the big man pull on his coat before rising to follow suit.

"For what it's worth," he told Chace, "if he asks, tell him I'll do the job."

"Of course you will, Chris," Chace told him. "That's why you're here."

Preoperational Background
Leacock, William D.

Some nights, before plummeting into his exhausted sleep, Sinan bin al-Baari would stare at the shadowed ceiling of the tent and think about names.

At twenty-two years old, he had already gone through two, not counting the odd handful that had served as covers or other deceptions, or the dozens that had been thrown unkindly in his direction throughout his youth. He had been christened William Leacock, but that name was long dead to him, and when his thoughts did stray to it—something that happened less and less frequently these days—it seemed to him the name of a boy he had known only briefly and had not much liked.

Then he had found Allah and taken the name Shuneal bin Muhammad, as was appropriate to one

who had found the True Faith. It was the name he'd
used upon reaching Egypt, during the months he'd
spent studying in Cairo. It was the student's name,
and though he would never be mistaken for an
Arab, by that name he was always known as a Muslim. It was that student who had entered his first
madrassa, had read ibn Abdul Wahhab's *Book of
Tawhid*. It was that student who had begun collect-
ing the cassette tapes sold outside of mosques
throughout Cairo, sermons by the great Wahhabi
clerics of Saudi Arabia. In his room, shared with
Aamil and six other students, they had listened to
the tapes for hours. To the sermons of the late Abdul Aziz bin Baz, to the passion of Sheikh Wajdi
Hamzeh al-Ghazawi, to the fury of Sheikh Safar al-
Hawali, and, most of all, to the faith of Dr. Faud al-
Shimmari.

It was Shuneal bin Muhammad who had first
heard jihad described as the Sixth Pillar of Islam. It
was Shuneal bin Muhammad who had nodded his
head in agreement at al-Ghazawi's words when his
recorded voice said, "Jihad is the peak of Islam."

It was Shuneal bin Muhammad who, with Aamil
and two others, had begun lurking in the mosques
and cafés of Cairo in the vain hope of making contact with some member of the Jamaat al-Islamiyya.
But although Shuneal bin Muhammad was a Muslim, even perhaps a Wahhabist, he was not, and
would never be, an Egyptian. After three months of
fruitless attempts at contact, it had been a lean and
quiet man named el-Sayd who had explained it to

him in the back of a Cairo café, off Sharia Muski, in the Islamic Quarter.

"We fight to free our country," el-Sayd had said quietly. "We fight to overthrow this government of *mushrikun*, to make Egypt a true Islamic state. That is not your fight, Shuneal, and you have no place in it."

"I want to be a *jihadi*," Shuneal had answered in his best Arabic, the tongue finally beginning to sound natural on his lips. "I am a Muslim, and I must follow all the teachings, and you would deny me the Sixth Pillar of our faith. If you will not take me, where do I go?"

El-Sayd had started to answer, then bitten it back, instead finishing his coffee. Shuneal bin Muhammad had waited, unmoving in his seat, staring. Aamil, seated beside him, seemed to barely breathe.

"Continue your studies," el-Sayd had said finally. "Be true in your faith. Allah, all praise to Him, will provide a way."

And with that, Shuneal and Aamil were escorted out of the café, to return to the *madrassa* with their disappointment.

Less than a week later, the *imam* of the school spoke to Shuneal and Aamil after *isha'*, the evening prayer.

"You are favored," he told them both. "Prince Salih bin Muhammad bin Sultan, may Allah watch and keep him, has offered to bring certain of our students to Madinah, that they may make the Hajj. You have both been chosen."

•

Sponsorship for the Hajj wasn't unusual, but Shuneal felt fortunate nonetheless. To properly perform the Fifth Pillar—to make the pilgrimage to Makkah—was to guarantee one's entry into Paradise, the desire of every Muslim. That Shuneal and Aamil had found a benefactor was remarkable; that such good fortune fell upon them at such a young age was extraordinary. There were millions who, in their lives, would never have the opportunity to see Makkah, to walk in the Prophet's shadow, prevented by either poverty or other provenance.

Near the end of January, Shuneal and Aamil flew from Cairo to Madinah in a private jet, supplied by Prince Salih bin Muhammad bin Sultan. Eighteen others traveled with them, young *madrassa* students like themselves, gathered from other schools in Egypt, Tunisia, and Sudan.

The jet was like nothing Shuneal had ever experienced, and it spoke loudly of the Prince's generosity and wealth, from the walnut-inlaid fixtures to the thick red carpeting on the floor and the marble-topped counters in the bathroom. They sat on comfortable couches and in overstuffed chairs, and Aamil drove the blood from his hands as he clutched the armrests of his seat when the plane climbed into the air, and Shuneal realized he had never flown before.

At the airport, they were met by a guide from the Prince himself. He escorted them to an air-conditioned coach, then drove them to a private home in Madinah. There they were given rooms to share and a meal to eat, then taken to Masjid al-Nabee, the Mosque of the Holy Prophet, for prayers and the recitation of *ziyrat*. Kneeling toward Makkah, so close to the Holy City, Shuneal found it impossible to clear his head, to focus on his worship. Here, where it was said that one prayer was worth more than a thousand prayers offered anywhere else, except in Makkah, he felt insincere, and the more he fought his mind to concentrate and focus, the more obsessed with his thoughts he became.

After the mosque, they returned to their lodgings, to settle in for the night. There were rumors that Prince Salih would be coming to greet them, to receive their thanks, and Shuneal imagined the encounter, practicing the different things he might say. He wanted to make a good impression, to show that he was humble and sincere, that he was grateful for this opportunity to mark his place in Paradise.

But it was not the Prince who came to visit them that night at all, but a man named Abdul Aziz. He arrived late, nearly one in the morning, and of the sixteen students in the house, all were asleep and had to be awakened. They were brought into the dining room of the home, told to sit on the floor and to listen.

Abdul Aziz was a short man, dressed in a simple white cotton *thobe* and a white-and-red-checkered *kuffiyah* held in place on his head with the traditional black wool *igaal*. His face was hard, as if set and blasted by the kiln-heat of the desert, and Shuneal studied the starburst scar on his left jaw that shone in the low light of the room. The look Abdul Aziz ran over the students as each took a seat was critical, if not nakedly suspicious.

"I am Abdul Aziz," he told them. "You have come to Madinah to reach the Fifth Pillar, and I am here to tell you of the Sixth. I am no *imam*, I can teach you nothing. You seek to secure your place in Paradise, but I tell you that my place is already ensured. You will walk with your brothers, but in your heart, look to yourself and ask if this is all that Allah, all praise Him, would have of you. What more can you give to His glory? What more can you give to your brothers, oppressed and hunted by Satan even today?

"You will stone the three Jamrah, you will strike at Satan, and when you do, see not stones, but see the enemies of Islam. See the Big Satan and the Little Satan, and ask yourself if a stone is enough, and ask yourself if there isn't more Allah, all praise Him, would have of you.

"I will be here when you return. And if you are righteous, and if I have seen that righteousness in you, I will show you the way to the Sixth Pillar."

•

On the eighth day of Dhul-Hijah, they began their pilgrimage, purifying themselves as directed, donning their *ihram*, the unsewn white garments that stripped away their status, their wealth, their identity, making them all equal before God. One of almost two million, Shuneal made the pilgrimage to Makkah and came to the Holy Mosque, the most sacred place on earth. Right foot first, he entered the Ka'bah and spoke the words, "In the name of Allah, may peace and blessings be upon the Messenger of Allah. Oh Allah, forgive me my sins and open to me the doors of Your mercy. I seek refuge in Allah the Almighty and in His Eminent Face and in His Eternal Domination from the accursed Satan."

With crowds at his sides, gently jostling him, he approached the Black Stone, the stone that was given to Adam upon his fall from Paradise, the stone that was once white but had turned black with the sins absorbed from the millions of pilgrims who had touched its smooth surface. He touched the stone and spoke as was proper, "In the name of Allah, Allah is the greatest. Oh Allah, with faith in You, belief in Your book, loyalty to You, faith to the way of Your Prophet Muhammad, may the peace and blessings of Allah be upon him."

Then he walked, keeping the Ka'bah to his left, seven times around the Holy Mosque, first with the small steps meant to increase his pace, three times, and then four times at his normal speed. Reaching the Rukn Al Yamani, he touched it, saying, "Our Lord, grant us good in this life, and good in the hereafter, and save us from the torment of the Hellfire. Oh Allah, I beg of You forgiveness and health in this life and in Paradise."

Each time he passed the Black Stone, he said, "Allah is the greatest."

He did all these things, and while he believed in

everything he did, he did not feel what he hoped he would feel, the transcendence, the oneness, the peace. Try as he might, Shuneal found his brain cluttered again, cluttered with too many thoughts, too worried about how he looked from without rather than within, and he cursed himself for squandering this opportunity.

He ran seven times between Mount Safa and Mount Marwah, giving prayers as he reached the summit of each, and they were hardly mountains now at all, mere bumps in the terrain, but he ran between them as was required, and others ran with him. He listened as the other pilgrims around him gave their thanks to Muhammad and to Allah, and he wondered at following the Prophet's footsteps in this way, wondered if they were not, perhaps, deifying the Prophet himself, and this troubled him.

The second stage of the Hajj began, and Shuneal and almost two million others made their way to those holy places outside Makkah, to Mina first, praying as was required of him, and then the next morning to Arafat, entering the Namira Mosque to hear the sermon and to pray to Allah over and over again, until his back ached from the motion and his legs felt cramped folded beneath his body. Around him others broke away from their supplication, engaged in quiet conversation, reading silent passages from the *Qu'ran*. But Shuneal found strength in his prayers, here, in the words, "There is no God but Allah, He has no equal. All dominion and praise are His, and His power is absolute over all things," and he supplicated himself until the sun had all but vanished from the horizon.

Without rest, he left Arafat the same night, making his way with a thinning crowd to Muzdalifah, and arriving just before midnight, with barely enough time to spare to pray. He offered thanks and supplications to Allah until just before sunrise, and though he had taken water on the journey, he felt himself wearied and weakened, his head felt light, and his thoughts wandered again. But this time they wandered not with his doubts but with his thoughts on Paradise and Allah and the Will of God. His worship had distanced him from his body.

Just before sunrise, Aamil helped him to his feet, and the two young men made their way slowly back to Mina. Taking the pebbles they had gathered, they reached the first pillar, the Jamrah al-Aqaba, the one standing closest to Makkah, and they threw their stones at Satan himself, and Shuneal put what strength he had left in him into his arm as he let each fly, and with each throw he said, "God is the greatest," his voice intense and cracking.

He watched the pebbles bounce harmlessly from the Jamrah, and he felt himself begin to weep.

He understood. Satan was not a pillar. Satan would not be stopped with a pebble. Shuneal looked on the Jamrah and saw instead his parents in Sheffield, complacent and arrogant in their simplicity; he saw Americans rolling into Baghdad and the British rolling into Basra; he saw Coalition bombs falling on Afghanistan; he saw Israeli rockets in Gaza.

He threw his pebbles and offered his choked
prayer, and when he had thrown the last, he bent to
scoop more, enraged, and Aamil had to stop him
then, to grab his hands and pull him away, telling
him to be calm, that he understood, that he had
seen it as well. Shuneal trembled with the anger, the
effort of self-control, and though he could once
again see the Jamrah for what it was, the image remained dancing before his eyes. Even as he ate of
the goat that had been prepared, even as Aamil and
he and the others shaved the hair from their heads,
he found himself swimming in memories of fire and
blood.

"How do you fight Satan?" he asked Aamil insis-
tently.

"With everything," his friend answered.

•

Shuneal completed the Hajj, returning again to the
Ka'bah, making the prescribed circuits once again,
finishing the pilgrimage as it had been completed
for over a thousand years. He and the others returned to Madinah, back to the house that Prince
Salih had arranged for their comfort. All of them, it
seemed, had been touched by their journey, each
feeling its effects in privately profound ways. Some
of the students, freed from the weight of their pilgrimage, began to laugh and joke again, talking of
what they had seen and experienced, speaking of
what they would do upon returning to Egypt. Their
time was almost at an end, their visas, specially ac-

quired for them by the Prince himself, soon to expire.

The impending departure filled Shuneal with a growing sense of despair. He had tried Egypt already and had been told there was no place for him there. He was not an Egyptian, not even an Arab, just a Muslim. After the past two weeks with other pilgrims, wrapped in the *ihram*, he had forgotten such distinctions mattered. But returning to Cairo reminded him, and he did not want to leave.

So when Abdul Aziz came to the house for a second time, Shuneal knew it was his only chance.

•

A cassette player rested on the dining table this time, and once everyone was seated and still, Abdul Aziz moved to it and, without a word, set the tape to play.

The voice that filled the room was immediately familiar to Shuneal.

"You who have come to make Hajj, give thanks to Allah, all praise to Him," Dr. Faud bin Abdullah al-Shimmari told them. His voice crackled, distorted through the tiny speaker on the cassette player. *"You who have come to secure your place in Paradise, know that you have spared yourself Hellfire. You have achieved the fifth pillar of our faith, but there is a sixth, and who of you dare to reach it?*

"To be muwahhidun, *to be the greatest advocates of oneness, should be your highest aspiration. Jihad is a great deed, indeed, and there is no deed whose blessing, whose reward, is that of it. For this reason, if none*

other, it is the greatest thing you, any of you, can volunteer for.

"The warrior who gives his life in a true jihad becomes shahid, guaranteed that rarest place in Paradise. You must rub the sleep from your eyes, my brothers, and rise to jihad! Find the ember in your soul, and let your breath give life to the flame! Let that flame feed your hatred of those who defile and damn us, of those Jews and Christians and infidels who would steal from you that which is yours, your future in the One True Religion! We know the Jews are the objects of Allah's avowed wrath, all praises sung unto Him, while the Christians have long since fallen from the path of righteousness. The Qu'ran tells us the Jews are a nation cursed by Allah, a nation he turned into apes and pigs, who worship idols.

"You live in great times, the days before the Days of Judgment, with civilizations in conflict, with the civilization of the corrupt West on the verge of collapse. While the West seeks to steal our youth from us, to diminish our heritage as the One True Religion, we see they are weak, immoral, and corrupt. The battle before you is not one simply of ideas, but one to be fought with bloodshed, with the rifle, the airplane, the word, the bomb. This is a new phase in our great Crusade, to accelerate that collapse, to return in kind a thousandfold what they have laid at our feet.

"Allah will take revenge against the tyrants with His sword in this world, and in the world to come. We beseech Allah to grant Mujihadin everywhere speedy victory, and forsake America, and those who help and

*are allies with her, and bring destruction upon her and
her friends. It is Allah's will, and it will be done.*

"Allah's prayers upon you, you who would be jihadi."

●

The silence after the tape ended was heavy, broken
only by the sound of their breathing, the students
seated on the floor. Abdul Aziz did not move, letting the cassette run out, and there was a shocking
snap as the button on the player popped up once
more. From the corner of his eye, Shuneal saw several of the students start at the noise, surprised.

Abdul Aziz took the cassette player from the
table, tucked it beneath his arm, and, still without ut-
tering a word, turned and walked out of the room.
Shuneal could hear him moving away, the echo of his
steps on the tile floor, and then the sound of the door
opening and closing. Around him, other students exchanged looks of confusion and loss.

Shuneal moved first, taking a step forward, then
stopping, looking back. Aamil, still seated, hesitated, then rose to follow. Shuneal heard the rustle
of cloth as more of the students got to their feet,
but he didn't wait, and he didn't look back, now
moving faster, suddenly afraid that Abdul Aziz
wouldn't wait for him. He reached the door, pushed
it open, and rushed out into the cool Madinah
night.

Abdul Aziz stood at the back of the battered military surplus truck that had pulled up outside. Canvas covered the sides and back of the bed, but as

Shuneal approached, Abdul Aziz reached up and drew it back, then pulled the latch and dropped the gate. Shuneal started forward, reached out to hold on to the side of the vehicle to help pull himself inside, but Abdul Aziz put a hand on his breast, a forceful pressure just short of a push.

"Give me your name, boy."

"Shuneal. Shuneal bin Muhammad."

Abdul Aziz's face broke into an amused smile and the shining scar on his jaw seemed to climb to reach his eye. "You are British?"

"I am a Muslim."

"Do you still have your passport?"

Shuneal couldn't understand why it mattered. "Yes, with my belongings."

"In the house?"

"Yes." Shuneal dropped his hand from where he was still gripping the side of the truck, felt a swell of desperation so acute and so sudden, he was afraid it would bring him to tears. When he spoke, he tried to keep the whine from his voice. "Please, I understand. I understand what you told us, before we made the pilgrimage, I saw it, I saw the Jamrah, Abdul Aziz. I saw it."

"I know." He said it with such flat conviction that Shuneal realized all at once that Abdul Aziz had been watching him throughout the Hajj. "Shuneal bin Muhammad?"

"Yes, the name I took when I avowed my faith."

"No, no more."

Abdul Aziz reached out and took hold of Shuneal's still newly shaven head in a surprisingly strong grip, and turned him to face Aamil and the others who had come outside.

"See your brother," Abdul Aziz said. "He has the heart of a *jihadi*, and I give him the name of one now, the name Sinan bin al-Baari. The spearhead of God."

He released his grip.

"Get on the truck," Abdul Aziz ordered.

And Sinan bin al-Baari, who had been Shuneal bin Muhammad and who had been christened William Dennis Leacock, climbed aboard and began his long trip to his new home in the Wadi-as-Sirhan.

5

London—Wood Green, North London
10 August 0414 GMT

Chace came around the back way on foot, as instructed, mounting the six steps to the apartment building, hands thrust deep in her windbreaker, head down, pretending to the walk of shame, just in case anyone who shouldn't see her coming did. She'd passed one of Box's surveillance vans almost two hundred meters back, done up to look as if it was on its last legs, and she knew they'd seen her, and that was to the good, because it meant no one would be surprised by her arrival, and that therefore no one would shoot her by mistake.

She was armed herself, an HK P2000 tucked at her waist, and that in and of itself was almost as odd as the errand she'd been sent on. It was a rule broken: Minders did not go armed in London.

But the errand itself broke another rule: SIS and Box do not work together.

It was a big, sad building, late fifties architecture that had forgone aesthetics in pursuit of efficiency, but even that had failed it, and in the cast of the electric lights over the door the masonry had the hue of a smoker's teeth. She pushed through the entrance, out of the night, and into a hallway that was even more poorly illuminated than the world outside. She stopped to let her eyes adjust before continuing down the hall, stepping carefully around the trash in the corridor, food wrappers, empty bottles. A television was playing in one of the apartments she passed and she heard the unmistakably empty passion of a porno.

She ignored the elevator and took the stairs, climbing three flights before stepping onto a landing and orienting herself. The light was marginally better, flickering from a spastic bulb in a fixture halfway along the wall. Chace slowed down, going as quietly as she could. She passed four-twelve, stopped in front of four-fourteen, and didn't knock.

The man who opened the door was dressed in black tactical BDUs, and he motioned her inside without a word. Chace stepped through, then aside, and he closed the door as silently as he'd opened it. He pointed to her, indicated toward the main room, and Chace nodded, following as he led the way.

There were three others just like him, one affixing a fiber-optic cable to the wall with strips of tape he'd stuck to the left thigh of his pants. The other two were crouched around a laptop, their faces lit in green from the light from the screen. All were armed, pistols set in holsters on their legs, MP-5s hanging from the straps at their backs. None of them looked up.

The furniture had been moved to the far side of the room, and Chace could see the naked picture hooks on the wall that adjoined four-twelve, where the Assault Team had taken down the frames. Resting in a corner of the couch, she counted four stuffed animals, heaped haphazardly atop a stack of picture books. One of the toys was a small fat panda bear, with thick, brightly colored pieces of hardened rubber stuck to its hands and feet.

A family's apartment, Chace concluded. One child, young enough to still be teething.

She wondered where they'd been relocated to, and if they had any idea why the Security Services had so covertly and unceremoniously evicted them from their home.

The man guided Chace across the room, pointing down to indicate the coiled power cables and cords, mutely warning her to watch her step, heading for a door opposite the wall to four-twelve. She heard a soft whine, cast a glance back to see that the one who'd been placing the fiber optics was now using a small electric drill to cut a lead hole into the drywall. They'd place charges next.

The man gave her another nod, then left her to go through the next door alone. She did so, stepping into the bedroom and more light than she'd encountered in the last ninety minutes. She hadn't expected it, and it blinded her for an instant, and when her vision came back she was facing a man.

"Fucking hell," David Kinney said softly, and he looked anything but pleased to see her. "You."

"Me, Mister Kinney," Chace said. "How nice to see you again."

Kinney pulled a face, then turned away from her, lifting the radio in his hand to his mouth, whispering a string of orders. He was built of a similar stock as the Deputy Chief, but a larger version, as if Weldon had been the structural test case and David Kinney the final product. In his early forties, straight black wiry hair and a mustache to match, black suit, hands like hammers, he always made Chace think of the stereotypical trade union leader, at least physically. Kinney's position was much like D-Ops's own, except at Box, where he ran Security Service operations in the Counter Intelligence and Counter Terror divisions.

This was most certainly a CT operation. It made sense that Kinney would be here.

But Chace had to wonder why he couldn't have been somewhere else instead, at one of the two other operations running, perhaps, where Poole or Lankford would have had to deal with him instead of her. But she knew the answer as soon as she posed the question; she'd dealt with Kinney before, and the bad blood of that past encounter notwithstanding, Crocker had been obliged to send his Head of Section as a courtesy. Anything else would have been an insult.

Chace waited until Kinney was finished on the radio, then asked, "How many?"

Kinney sucked air through his teeth, as if debating whether or not to tell her. It was against his every instinct to be honest with SIS, just as it was against all of Crocker's to play fair with Box. But tragedy made for strange bedfellows, and for the moment inter-service rivalry had been forced into the backseat, at least for tonight.

"Five," Kinney said. "Three men, two women."

"Armed?"

"That's what we've been led to believe."

"Explosives?"

"Suspected. Not confirmed."

"And they're HUM-AA?"

"That's what our intelligence suggests, yes." Kinney looked at her pointedly. "Unless you have anything to the contrary?"

She shook her head. "Terrorist cells operating in London are your province, not ours."

Kinney started to respond, then seemed to think about what she'd said. He closed his mouth abruptly. Chace continued before he could respond to the slight.

"So we're taking them?"

"*We* are taking them, yes."

"When?"

"When we're ready. You're here as an observer, Miss Chace, as a courtesy. This is a Box operation, not some Minder shoot-'em-up. We want them alive, for questioning."

"That's a lovely sentiment," Chace said. "Have you shared it with them?"

Kinney held her stare for a second, then turned away, speaking into his radio once more.

•

Chace moved back into the main room before dawn, settling on the couch to watch the video feed of the action coming in over the laptop. The CT team had finished placing their breaching charge, a snake of explosive that ran in a tall oblong on the wall, roughly half a meter from where the camera had been placed. The detonator sat beside the laptop, a toggle switch with a lead that ran back to the explosive on the wall.

The camera itself could be turned nearly ninety degrees in any direction, controlled by a remote with a thumbstick set in its center, and the image it sent back was remarkably clear for a device so small. Looking into apartment four-twelve was like looking into a mirror image of their own room, at least in terms of dimension and layout. But content was radically different, and there was no question in Chace's mind what all that equipment on the kitchen table was meant to do.

Four-twelve held explosives, and its occupants were building themselves a bomb.

"If there's one, there could be others," Chace said. "We don't know what else is in that apartment."

"The second team drilled through into the bedroom, from four-ten," Kinney retorted. "They've seen nothing but the two women asleep in the bed."

"Where are the men?"

"Out and about. We've got them under surveillance. We'll take them when they get back."

"Out and about at five in the morning? They're scouting locations, Mister Kinney."

"We have them under surveillance. If they try anything, they'll be stopped."

The four men on the CT team had stopped their work, listening to the hushed debate. Chace looked to the man who'd let her into the apartment, the one she took to be the team leader. He shook his head slightly, turned his attention back to the laptop.

"The point is that they're not trying anything *yet*," Chace whispered. "You wait until all of them are in the apartment, you're giving them a chance to react."

"Miss Chace, you're here as an observer—"

Chace gestured angrily at the laptop screen. "You don't even know if it's armed! For God's sake, Kinney, at least start evacuating the building!"

Kinney clamped his mouth closed, and for a second, Chace thought she could hear his teeth grinding.

"Miss Chace," he said, "if you cannot keep your voice down, I will have one of these men escort you from the scene."

"You want to get blown up?" she demanded.

Kinney leveled a finger at her. "One more word. One more word and you're out. Now, be a nice little girl and sit down, shut up, and mind your own."

Chace bit back the immediate urge to respond, feeling heat climbing down from her neck to her shoulders, feeling the eyes of the four men on the CT team on her again. Normally she could take sexism in stride, but here, now, coming from Kinney, in front of an audience, it infuriated her. She knew why he was opposed to evacuating the building, let alone the floor; it would tip his hand, give the game away, and as far as it went, he was right, it would. His targets might escape, and he wasn't willing to let that happen, especially in the wake of the disaster on the tube only three days gone.

The Security Services were taking it on the chin, and Kinney wanted the big success, to prove that they were still in the game. Hence the three operations in one night, timed to coincide; a message to say, what you did to us, we can do to you.

Chace understood it, right down to the symbolism of Box picking three targets of their own. But looking at the monitor, and on it the view of the kitchen table, of the bomb-in-the-making, it seemed an awful risk to take for the sake of soothing a bruised ego.

Kinney moved forward, bending his mouth to the ear of the CT leader, whispering. The leader glanced at Chace, then back to Kinney, nodding. Kinney returned to her, fingering the radio in his hand.

"I've informed Sergeant Hopton that if you so much as cough, he is to remove you from the site," Kinney whispered at her. "Further, should it be required, he has been directed to take whatever action is required to keep you silent. I'm sure you understand what that means."

Chace stared at him, then mouthed the word "yes" as widely as she could manage. Hopton was watching her, and she caught him looking, and he turned his attention to the laptop once more.

Kinney nodded and slunk back toward the bedroom.

She fumed, leaning forward on the couch, trying to get a better look at the monitor. Hopton shifted to his left, trying to accommodate her view, and that mollified her somewhat. She didn't doubt that he would do as Kinney had directed, but at least he didn't seem happy at the prospect.

●

At eighteen minutes to six, they blew the wall, and even then, it was almost too late.

Activity started in four-twelve at oh-five-thirty-three, with the return of the three men Kinney had been waiting on. They were all in roughly the same age bracket, mid to early twenties, two of them of indeterminate Middle Eastern origin, the third Caucasian, and Chace could hear them through the thin walls even as she watched their entrance on the video feed. They looked exhausted and nervous, and she thought that was a bad combination. They'd been living in fear since the seventh, she supposed, knowing what the inevitable response to the attacks on the tube would be, knowing that Box would be out in force, bent on finding anyone anywhere who might be a threat.

A justified paranoia, as far as Chace was concerned.

She watched over Hopton's shoulder as the three men removed their coats, dropping them onto the couch in a heap, then headed in different directions—one toward the bathroom, one toward the bedroom, the third, the Caucasian, digging into his discarded coat, where he pulled a small digital camera from its pocket.

Site selection, Chace confirmed for herself. *They've been out choosing targets.*

The Caucasian had moved to a chair at the kitchen table, and Hopton twisted the knob on his control, turning the camera to keep the man in view. Chace watched as the man opened a laptop computer of his own, booting it up, then attached a cable from the computer to the camera, preparing to upload his photographs.

Chace heard the soft click of the bedroom door opening, Kinney stepping carefully to join them. Chace glanced away from the screen long enough to look the question at him, but Kinney shook his head.

"Not yet," he murmured.

She wanted to scream at him.

"The women," Kinney explained softly. "They're too close to the wall from four-ten. If it's blown they'll get hit in the blast, and we don't want to risk losing them. I want them alive."

Chace rolled her eyes, looked back to the monitor. Hopton was getting to his feet, holding the detonator for the wall-charge in one hand, using hand signals to motion the rest of the team to prepare for their entry. All of the men were moving carefully, quietly, pulling their balaclavas and gas masks into place, swinging their weapons into their hands.

On the monitor, the Caucasian man was bent to the laptop, back to the camera, working.

Then he stopped, and Chace saw the tightening along his back as his head came up, saw him turn his chin, realized he was listening, that he'd heard something.

She felt one of the stuffed animals resting against her thigh where she sat on the couch, reached down for it, brushing the hard rubber of the teething bear with her fingertips.

It wasn't what he was hearing, Chace realized. It was what he *wasn't*.

"Now!" she hissed to Hopton.

"Chace," Kinney growled.

On the screen, the man had risen from the table, was walking toward the wall, their wall.

"Jesus Christ, do it now!" Chace said. "He knows, dammit—"

Kinney dropped a hand onto Chace's shoulder, already turning to Hopton, snarling, "Get her out, and don't be gentle about—"

She launched herself off the couch, trying to shrug free of Kinney's grip on her shoulder, pleading with Hopton. "He doesn't hear the *baby*, Sergeant! He *knows*!"

"Sergeant, get her out of here."

Hopton grimaced. In her periphery, Chace could see the man on the monitor, now at the wall, so close to the camera his image was distorting.

"Clear," Hopton said, and Chace shut her eyes,

tucking her head, trying to save her vision from the inevitable flash of the explosion, and even then she could see the light, a searing red that matched the crackling burst of wood and wall. There was a scream, and Hopton shouting, and she opened her eyes to see the CT team pouring into the apartment, stepping over the Caucasian man, twisted on the floor.

Beside her, Kinney was shouting into the radio, telling the other team to go go go, but even as he was saying it Chace heard the second detonation, muffled, and a scream.

The bathroom door opened, and the man inside surged out, pants half-raised, and Chace had just registered the pistol in his hand when one of the CT team shot him.

She pulled the pistol from her waist, stepped through the breach in the wall, coughing as she caught a lungful of atomized debris still hanging in the air. The CT team was already disappearing into the bedroom, and she heard an exchange of fire, two single shots, and the rattle of multiple MP-5s in response.

Behind her, Kinney was shouting that he wanted them alive. Chace didn't know if it was directed at her, the radio, or God above. She didn't much care.

Pistol held low in both hands, Chace followed after the CT team, peering around the doorframe into the bedroom. Blood spattered the wall and ceiling, and she saw the two women, still in the bed, each in their nightclothes, one of them now being dragged free of the sheets by Hopton as another of the CT team readied a set of plasticuffs. The other woman was pitched face forward, as if she'd been sitting and then simply toppled, and past her Chace could see the gap into four-ten, where the explosion had taken the wall. It had also taken the back of the woman's head.

The third man was slumped against the wall, legs splayed, eyes wide.

Chace stepped back and nearly slammed into Kinney as she turned.

"You bitch, you stupid bitch! Look what you've done!"

Past him, on the floor, Chace could see the Caucasian man trying to roll onto his side. The blast had caught the side of his face and chest, and blood bubbled out of him where the shrapnel of the wall had driven through his flesh.

"You've fucking ruined it," Kinney raged. "I wanted them alive! We *needed* them alive!"

"Two of them are." She indicated the man on the floor with the pistol in her hand. "Though I don't fancy his chances. Shall I put him out of his misery?"

Kinney's face lost all the color that had flooded into it, and he struck at her forearm, trying to get her to lower the pistol. She laughed, tucking the pistol back into her pants.

"You're an evil piece of work," Kinney said, raising his radio again.

"No," Chace told him, heading for the door. "They're evil, Mister Kinney. Me, I'm one of the good guys."

6

It was one of the oldest espionage clichés in the
Firm, certainly outdated, and in the current day and
age of parabolic microphones and laser-beam listening devices quite possibly tragically insecure. But
walking in Hyde Park was still Paul Crocker's favorite method of information exchange with the
CIA, and he balanced the potential of compromise
with the benefit of being able to talk out of the office, away from the alarmist eye of the Deputy
Chief and the distrust of C. Meetings like today, the
only person who knew for certain where he was and
what he was doing was Kate, and she'd run dutiful
interference should the need arise.

Cheng was waiting for him on a bench near the
Park Lane entrance, and though he was certain she

saw him coming, she didn't move until he'd reached her.

"You're late." She said it mildly and didn't bother to look at him, instead keeping her eyes on a couple picnicking with their two children some twenty feet away.

"Tube's still fouled," Crocker said, which was the only explanation he was willing to give, and truly the only explanation necessary. It had been just six days since the strikes, and even with crews working around the clock, the Central and Northern Lines were still down, and the Bakerloo had resumed service only that morning, and even that was limited. The economic impact of the closures had yet to be measured, but traffic in Central London had predictably become even more of a nightmare than it already was.

Cheng got off the bench, adjusting the linen jacket she was wearing. The jacket was navy blue, and the blouse beneath it a pearl white, and her trousers, linen as well, were black. She watched him take in the wardrobe, then looked him over in turn and cracked a smile.

"You must be burning up."

Crocker grunted, pulling his cigarettes from his pocket and getting one lit. It had turned unseasonably hot in the past week, and the air in the city had been still and heavy. Depending on where you were, you could still catch the scent of the smoke. Standing in his three-piece suit, Crocker felt as if he might spontaneously combust.

Cheng turned and began walking, heading deeper

into the park, and Crocker fell in beside her. He had almost a full foot on her, and a stride that could easily outdistance Cheng's own, but the walking was habit as much as the meetings were, and they'd long ago worked out a rhythm. Cheng had been posted to London as the CIA resident a year after Crocker had ascended to D-Ops, and though they had never interacted in the field prior to that point, they instantly saw in each other a kindred spirit or, at the least, an ally against a common foe—the bureaucrats. Cheng would always put America's concerns first, as Crocker would put England's, but the friendship that existed between them was honest, if shaped by the respective demands of their assignments.

In the main, SIS needed the CIA more than the CIA needed SIS. But not always, and Cheng was wise enough to see that, even if her bosses back in Virginia weren't.

They walked, taking in the park, the smell of the grass and the trees, the summer hour. Scattered on the lawns, Londoners sunbathed or took lunch or kicked footballs, but it was quieter than normal, and Crocker knew there were fewer people out and about. That, and the abrupt lack of tourism, gave the park a strangely empty air.

"How're Jenny and the girls?" Cheng asked.

"Fine. I'd ask how whoever you're seeing is, but you're not seeing anyone."

Cheng smirked. "Not that you know of, at least."

Crocker blew smoke from the corner of his mouth. "So what do you have?"

"You talked to Rayburn?"

"Not since yesterday afternoon."

"He'll be getting our analysis of the tape sometime today. He'll be able to tell you everything I can."

"Angela."

"You are an impatient man."

"I have an impatient C, who apparently has an impatient Prime Minister. They want action, and they can't have that without a target."

"Speaking of action. Quite the stunt your Mister Kinney pulled on Tuesday morning."

"That wasn't Kinney, that was Chace."

"Chace killed three suspected terrorists in one sitting? There are folks back home who'd give her a medal."

"Four, actually," Crocker corrected. "One of them died in hospital from injuries sustained at the scene."

Cheng pursed her lips in a silent whistle of appreciation.

"It wasn't her fault," Crocker said, far more defensively than he'd intended. "They'd been made, there was reason to believe there was an explosive on scene, they had to move."

"Was there?"

"Was there what?"

"An explosive?"

Crocker flicked his cigarette away, watching it bounce off the gravel into the grass.

"It hadn't been assembled yet."

"You can't really take chances with that, though, can you."

"Which is something I've been trying to explain

to Mister Kinney since Tuesday afternoon." Crocker glanced down at her. "The tape, Angela."

"It's definitely Harakat ul-Mujihadin, this new wing, the Abdul Aziz faction."

"You've confirmed it?"

Cheng nodded. "They've got this program back at Langley, it can take the facial characteristics off an image, a photo or a video or whatever, run it against a database, establish an ID. It's pretty neat."

"Yes, we have that program, too."

"Difference is, ours works." She shot him a quick grin. "The young guy on the tape is named Tariq Ahmad Dar. He is—or was—a HUM militant out of Kashmir. We have intelligence that says Abdul Aziz recruited him for his faction in late spring last year."

"Where'd you get this?"

"Some of it from the Khalid Shaikh Muhammad bust. You remember the mad scramble we all went on after he was taken into custody?"

"Painfully," Crocker said. Muhammad had been, at the time, the al-Qaeda military chief. His capture had netted hundreds of pages of scattered intelligence, ranging from operations in progress to hints and whispers of other plans in development, most of which later turned out to be suspect when the Americans discovered a Syrian-manned al-Qaeda link to the prisoners in Guantanamo.

"Dar was on the watch list that came out of the bust."

"Almost all of that intelligence has been downgraded as a result of the compromised source. That's not enough."

"We have other means of verification, as I said."

"I'm not going to go to C with the fruits of your blown networks. Not on this."

Cheng's expression soured and hardened. "Not everything was blown by the Syrians."

"Angela, the CIA has been relying on networks ten and fifteen years old, built by agents later exposed as doubles. Between Ames, Hansen, and Wu-Tai Chin, your HUMINT has been shit, and the Company refuses to redress the situation. Ames himself recruited the majority of your informants out of Egypt and Afghanistan, agents later linked to al-Qaeda or al-Qaeda factions, and some of whom had direct contact with UBL. Unless you can verify an alternate source, it's fucking trash, no matter what your computers are saying."

Cheng glared. "The Company has done—is doing—everything it can to restore its security."

"It could start by admitting how bad the breaches were."

"I think we have."

Crocker snorted.

"I can't compromise the source, Paul. It's not my operation, and even if it was, you know I'm not going to share that kind of intel with you. Certainly not in the middle of Hyde fucking Park."

"Then, as I say, I can't run with it."

Cheng stopped on the path, forcing Crocker to stop as well and to turn back to her. Three young men walked by, two of them arguing with the third. Crocker heard just enough of their conversation to determine that they were discussing a woman.

When the three were well out of earshot, Cheng said, "We have someone inside."

Crocker raised an eyebrow. "Since when?"

She shook her head. "No. But we trust the source, and the source says that Tariq Ahmad Dar was HUM-AA. Dar was in a group of half a dozen HUM regulars who were flown to Saudi earlier that year, recruited by Abdul Aziz for broader operations."

They resumed walking, Crocker thinking on it. When he spoke, it was sourly, saying, "C will be delighted. You've just established a link between HUM-AA and al-Qaeda."

"Yeah, but I can establish a link between the Red Crescent and al-Qaeda, and so can you. You can't take it to the bank."

"Why bring them to Saudi?"

"Hell if I know. They probably ended up in a training camp somewhere teaching new recruits."

"That doesn't explain how Dar got tapped for a suicide run on the tube."

"No, it doesn't, but it doesn't much matter, does it? He did, he's dead, there you go."

"That would have put him in Saudi a year ago."

"About eighteen months ago."

"So something happened in Saudi in the last eighteen months to turn an HUM veteran into a suicide bomber."

"Suicide arsonist," Cheng corrected. "Maybe there's a manpower shortage?"

"Not in Saudi there isn't. They've got a surfeit of

eager young men willing to blow themselves sky-high in the name of Allah."

"That's a rather broad brush you're using there, Paul."

Crocker glared at nothing in particular. "We both know who the enemy is here, Angela, and blaming HUM-AA or al-Qaeda or the Islamic Society of North America is only part of the bloody tree, not the roots. The Saudi government has spent four decades fomenting and funding Wahhabist extremism. They're not our allies, they've *never* been our allies, and all declarations to the contrary, they never *will* be our allies. It took al-Qaeda blowing up the foreign workers' housing complexes in Riyadh before the Saudi government took substantive action, and then they arrested, what, twenty people?"

"Twenty-one."

"And promptly denied us the opportunity to interrogate any of them by rushing them off for public execution. They didn't want uncomfortable questions asked, anything that might point a finger back at the Palace. The Saudis were covering their asses."

"You're in a mood," Cheng observed.

"I'm always in a mood."

"And here I was about to blame it on the heat."

"Blame it on whatever you like, it goes back to the same problem. Until Saudi Arabia changes its policies, we reap the result of institutionalized hatred."

"You ought to run for office," Cheng said.

"You know that the belief of Islam spreading

through the sword is a myth, don't you?" Crocker asked suddenly. "Not many people do, they believe the propaganda—Christian propaganda, a thousand years old. Islam is not a religion of violence, despite certain individuals and organizations doing their damnedest to paint it as such."

"Wahhabism isn't Islam."

"That's my point entirely, thank you."

"Really pisses you off, doesn't it?"

"On the scale of my daily outrage, it ranks an eleven," Crocker confirmed.

They continued walking, now past the Albert Memorial, turning south in the direction of Rotten Row.

"I heard the folks at Box found another one of the safehouses," Cheng said. "I assume Kinney has been by to rub your face in it, or if he hasn't, he soon will be."

"I won't ask how you know that."

Cheng tapped the side of her nose. "About the safehouse, you mean? I know what C had for breakfast this morning, too."

"Weetabix, to keep him regular, I'm sure." Crocker scowled. He hadn't known about Box finding another safehouse, and he didn't much relish the inevitable visit from Kinney, especially given the events of Tuesday morning.

They found a bench, took it, and Crocker broke out his pack once more, lit another cigarette.

"We're going to hit back," Crocker said after a moment.

"That's a given, isn't it? Unless the rules have suddenly changed."

"No, the same rules still apply."

"You sound uncharacteristically reluctant."

He sighed out a cloud of smoke. "I don't object to retaliatory action. I object to committing to retaliatory action with undue haste. It wasn't three hours after the strikes that C was ready to order me to send the Minders on a bloodletting."

"This is the same C who thinks the Special Operations Directorate is a waste of time, money, and a danger to the Security of the Free World?"

"That's the one."

"Changed his mind right quick when he wanted to show the PM that you boys can kick some ass, huh? Sounds like you'll be sending Minders to Pakistan."

Crocker opened his mouth to respond, then closed it again as a couple passed in front of the bench, holding hands. Cheng waited, tilting her head back against the seat, catching sunlight on her face as she watched the lovers kiss.

"*If* it is HUM that was behind this," Crocker resumed. "Those eighteen months leave that open to question."

"HUM and HUM-AA are two different groups, don't forget that. Same origins, different agendas."

"In which case it's Minders to Saudi."

Cheng chuckled. "Like that will ever happen."

"They've got their knickers in a twist, it might just get authorization."

"No, it won't. Covert action in Saudi? You'll

never get that kind of directive, even if your masters decided it was warranted. They'd go to the MOD for SAS instead, wouldn't they?"

Crocker grunted the concession. "Still presuming your intel is correct, that Dar was HUM-AA. Just as possible he fell in with another organization."

"My intel is correct."

Neither of them spoke for a time, and Crocker finished his cigarette and flicked it away much as he had the first.

"You'll let me know if anything else crops up?" he asked.

"Hey, we're in it with you," Cheng replied. "There's more than a couple of folks Stateside saying, 'Hey, that could've been us.'"

"New York."

"New York, San Francisco, Chicago, D.C., the list goes on and on." She got to her feet, waiting for Crocker to follow suit. "I'll see if we can't find out exactly what Dar was doing in Saudi."

"I'd appreciate it."

She smiled, began to turn, then stopped, struck by a memory. From her coat pocket, she removed a gift-wrapped package of blue paper with a crushed pink ribbon, which she offered to Crocker.

"It was your youngest's birthday this week, wasn't it? Ariel?"

"She turned eleven."

"Tell her I said happy birthday."

"I shall."

He took the package, waited for her to turn away.

Cheng didn't move. "You want to keep us in the loop on this, Paul."

"That's been my intention."

"All the way, that's what I'm saying."

It took him a moment to see it. "What was the final tally?"

"Eighteen," Cheng said, and she turned away, beginning her walk back to Grosvenor Square and the American Embassy. "Most of them were college kids."

Crocker watched her go before slipping the gift into his pocket and making his own way out of the park, thinking of the eighteen Americans and the twenty-three French and the seven Germans and all the rest who had been murdered in the tunnels of the Underground.

●

He was back at Vauxhall Cross at eighteen past one, passing through the security first at the gate, then in the lobby, and then at the elevators, and at each point he showed his pass to the guards, then swiped it through the reader. He stopped on the fourth floor, ducking into Rayburn's office in the hopes of finding him, and instead got D-Int's PA, a perpetually grumpy young man named Hollister, who informed him that Director Intelligence was presenting to the JIC, and would D-Ops like to leave a message.

"Yes," Crocker snapped. "Ask him why the CIA knows more about what Box is doing at any bloody given moment than we do."

Then he went to his office, to find Kate waiting

for him, and before he'd even come through the door she was up and coming around from behind her desk to intercept him.

"Bloody Box," Crocker said.

Kate cringed and motioned toward the inner office, where the door was ajar, and Crocker groaned inwardly.

"How long has he been waiting?" he asked.

"Twenty minutes."

"I assume you cleared my desk."

Kate looked indignant and didn't bother to respond.

"Coffee," Crocker told her, and then pushed his door open the rest of the way, to see David Kinney seated in one of the chairs facing his desk. He paused again, taking a breath, reminding himself that Kinney was good at his job. Kinney's people were good at theirs.

But that didn't change the fact that Crocker hated the man's living guts, and the feeling was mutual, and their encounters were always exercises in barely restrained civility. Tuesday had only made matters worse.

Interservice rivalry had existed from the word go, when the Special Operations Executive had become SIS following the Second World War. Where SIS was responsible to the Foreign and Commonwealth Office, the Security Services, more commonly known by their short-form official mailing address, or their "Box," reported to the Home Office. In issues of security and domain, SIS and Box were almost constantly tripping over each other's toes. An SIS operation in Gibraltar, for instance, would lead to Box screaming that Crocker had overstepped his bounds—Gib still being viewed in the Home Office as "home territory."

The legacy of Empire.

Kinney didn't rise and didn't acknowledge Crocker's entrance. Crocker removed his jacket, hung it on its peg at the stand, then took his seat behind the desk. The desk was bare, and he appreciated Kate's efforts. He hadn't left anything compromising out—he never left the office with anything on his desk that should be in a safe—but all the same, it gave him comfort knowing that Kinney wasn't sneaking a peek at anything he shouldn't.

"Sorry to keep you waiting," Crocker said. "If I'd known you were coming, I'd have stayed out longer."

Kinney's smile was sincere, in that Crocker saw in it the man's desire to gut him. "It's all right, I could use the pause. Been running nonstop since Chace's little bloodbath."

"Better late than never. What can I do for you, Mr. Kinney?"

"We located a flat in Southwark," Kinney said. "Where one of them staged from, looks like. We're working back from the lease, have a list of names. We're running those down but don't expect to find much on them, obviously. But there's the issue of money, how it was supplied to them, and I thought you might like to lend a hand there."

"Meaning you've hit a dead end."

"Meaning the inquiries we wish to have made need to be made in Germany and Greece." Kinney pulled a folded sheet from inside his jacket, set it on the desk at the edge so Crocker had to lean forward to take it. "We'd appreciate it if you looked into it."

Crocker took the paper, opened it, reading names and numbers.

"Normally I'd have done this through channels," Kinney told him. "But time is of the essence, I'm sure you agree."

Crocker grunted, set the paper back down, and got up from his chair. "I'll put people on it today."

Kinney rose, taking his time about it. "And you'll let us know, of course."

"I thought it went without saying."

"No, Mr. Crocker, with you, I like to hear the words straight from your mouth."

"Any findings will be delivered to your people."

"Nice to cooperate, isn't it?" Kinney said. "Nice being friendly."

"Yes," Crocker said, holding the door for him. "It's always nice to play make-believe. Kate will see you out."

As soon as Kinney was through, he slammed it closed behind him.

7

Sinan bin al-Baari almost hesitated before bashing the four-year-old's face in, but then he remembered that it wasn't really a boy, it was a pig and an ape, and that freed him. He struck the blow with all the savagery he could muster, infinitely more than was needed, and the butt of his rifle shattered the child's face with an audible and wet crack, and the boy crumpled to the floor. As soon as he was down, Sinan struck again, and this time broke through bone and spilled brains onto the linoleum floor.

The boy's father screamed with animal anguish, inhuman in its grief, and then Aamil shot him, and the man fell, eternally silent.

They stood still for a moment, each of them viewing their work, and finally Sinan said, "God is great."

"God is great," Aamil echoed, and Sinan thought his voice sounded hoarse and almost choked. He looked to his friend, trying to read the expression on his face, but Aamil was moving away already, toward the switch on the wall, and he flicked it and plunged the small kitchen into darkness.

Sinan moved out of the room into the hallway, carrying the rifle with its butt pressed between his arm and his chest. The butt was wet from the child and he felt fluid soaking into his shirt, but he didn't mind that, and he continued forward, toward the closed front door with its broken lock. Through the window, he could see the street, the fading sunlight, and as he watched an IDF armored personnel carrier rolled down the street, and when Sinan caught sight of the Star of David painted on its side, he couldn't stop himself from spitting in disgust.

He turned away from the door to see Aamil was now behind him, looking anxious.

"We should go now," Aamil said.

"We haven't finished."

"There's no one else here."

Sinan gestured with a free hand back toward the kitchen. "Father, son . . . Where's the mother? There's at least one more."

Aamil glanced over his shoulder quickly, then looked back to Sinan, as if he hadn't liked what he'd seen. "It's enough, we've done enough, Sinan. We should go before we can never go."

"You're afraid."

Aamil shook his head.

Sinan considered, then looked out the window

once more. The street was empty, the purple and red of the sky melting to a darker blue. Darkness would help their escape, but it would also lend them more time for the work. Maybe they could enter another house, put down another animal or three? The idea excited him, made his stomach tighten in anticipation. That would be wonderful, to be able to return to the camp and tell all who doubted him what they had done in the Zionist settlement, how they had proven that no one was safe there, not even in their own homes.

Then he thought of the APC and reconsidered. Aamil had fired his weapon, and it was luck, it seemed, that had kept anyone from hearing the shot. In another house, if it happened again, Sinan doubted they would be so lucky a second time. Even more, he doubted that they would be able to kill those descendants of apes and pigs in silence.

Aamil was right, but for the wrong reasons.

It was time to go.

●

They waited until full darkness had descended and the APC had passed by the house three more times, now shining its mounted halogen lights into yards and alleys. Each time it passed, Sinan could see the soldier at the spot, and each time, Sinan imagined a bullet from his gun entering the soldier's head, and his finger slid from its safe position alongside the guard to the trigger, feeling the curve of metal against the pad of his forefinger. But he kept the gun down, resisting the urge despite his craving to seize the opportunity.

At last they emerged, sprinting quick and low across the street, between the settlement houses, across a wide backyard, making toward the barbed-wire fence. Sinan led as fast as he could, but this wasn't the way they'd come into the settlement, and he wasn't entirely certain they were heading in the right direction. He tried to remember the map Abdul Aziz had shown him, tried to remember where the gap had been cut in the wire. It occurred to him that they should have left the weapons behind, in the house, in case they were spotted. He still had his passport, the passport he had used to enter the Zionists' so-called state, and if they were stopped, there was the chance he could bluff.

It had gotten him into Ma'le Efraim, after all, traveling as a man named William Leacock. It had gotten him, and two automatic rifles, and two grenades this far.

William Leacock's last act, Sinan thought. After this, the name would be dead forever, known and therefore useless.

They ran across a dirt track, a narrow patrol road running between the outskirts of the settlement and the fence that surrounded it. The fence had been described as barbed wire, but Sinan knew it was more than that, not simply lines of cruel metal but rather a sharpened grate, impossible to climb quickly without perilous lacerations. He saw the shine of the metal in the starlight, surged forward, and the terrain dropped abruptly beneath his feet, turning into a shallow slope. He stumbled, hitting his knees and falling forward, and the fence clattered as his rifle collided against it.

Sinan righted himself in a scramble, Aamil dropping to a crouch beside him, and he could barely make out his friend's expression, the anger at the noise, the fear of what it might bring. He looked away, focusing instead on the fence, where their escape passage had been cut.

Except it wasn't.

At first Sinan put it down to the darkness, the only illumination from the stars above and the dim ambience of the settlement lights. Breathless from the run and the fall, with Aamil hovering close beside, squinting at the barbed links in front of him, he realized they were in the wrong place. He quickly looked down the length of the wire in both directions, trying to find a landmark, something to place him on the remembered map, but the night had stolen all markers, and with a bubble of fear in his stomach, he realized they were lost.

"Go on!" Aamil whispered urgently. "What are you waiting for?"

"It's not here," Sinan hissed. "It's not here, this isn't it."

Somewhere behind them, a dog began to bark.

"Shit," Aamil muttered, dropping against the slope and freeing his rifle from his shoulder.

Sinan followed suit, pressing himself against the cracked earth, just as the lights began coming on in the houses they'd left behind. The dog continued its alarm, growing more frantic, and he heard another dog joining in, this one sounding closer, to their left. Halogen bounced off the ground above their heads, cracking the darkness, and in its spill he could see Aamil, the fear on his face, and he shared it. If they were lucky, the Zionists would kill them. If they weren't, they'd become prisoners, and he'd heard enough stories from others in the camp to know what that meant. Torture at the hands of the Zionists, how they used water and electricity, how they fed their prisoners the blood and flesh of Muslim children.

"They don't take us alive," Sinan whispered.

Aamil responded with an urgent, spastic nod. They could hear voices in the distance now, alarmed but cautious. From farther away, the sound of the APC's engine coming closer. And the damn dogs were still yapping, and if anything, now it sounded like there were more of them.

Sinan rolled softly onto his back, holding his rifle against his chest. The rifle was a Kalashnikov, *his* Kalashnikov, fully loaded and ready for work, and he pressed it against him with one hand, reaching into his coat with his other. The grenade in his pocket was smooth and cool and reassuringly solid as he wrapped his palm around it, pulling it free. He glanced to Aamil, waiting for his friend to do the same thing. Aamil hesitated, then licked his lips and quickly followed suit.

The APC was coming along the track now, they could hear the rocks and pebbles crackling beneath its tires, its engine so low Sinan could almost believe it was on idle. The dogs had been silenced, and he strained his ears, trying to make out voices. Lights were being shined along the fence up the road, filling the little gully where they lay, making their way closer.

Sinan watched the beams approaching, felt his heart beat so fiercely in his chest he was certain his rifle would fly from his body. He moved the grenade in his right hand onto his chest, reached over the rifle with his left, slid his index finger through the metal pin. If his throw was true, if Allah was with him, perhaps he could drop it into the APC and take the soldiers with him. It wouldn't be enough to win freedom, he accepted that. Even if the soldiers fell, the settlers were surely armed, it would end the same way. But he would have taken more of these *kufar* with him, and that was the only thought in his mind now.

"Look!" Aamil whispered, pointing past Sinan and up the length of the gully. "Look!"

Sinan snapped his head around, feeling the dirt grinding into the back of his head, and it took his eyes a moment to register what he was seeing past the light, the darkness in the fence. At its base, near one of the posts, fifty or sixty feet away, the gap that had been cut for their escape.

Aamil was already starting to move, dropping down to the bottom of the shallow gully, rifle in one hand, grenade in the other. Sinan began to push himself forward, to follow, then stopped, watching as his friend prowled farther away. Digging his feet into the earth, Sinan pushed himself up toward the road, peering over the edge of the slope.

The APC was crawling along, the spot now drawing carefully along the fence, when suddenly it stopped moving. He heard a soldier's shouted exclamation and the APC ground to a halt. The spotlight readjusted, focused on the gap at the base of the fence, where the sheeting and wire had been cut and pulled away. Sinan heard weapons being readied, orders exchanged, and the first soldier dropped from the vehicle to the ground, readying his weapon, as another moved to take position behind the mounted machine gun.

Sinan looked up the gully, saw that Aamil had realized what was happening, that there was no way out for him. He watched as his friend dropped to his knees, laying his rifle carefully at his side, and Sinan thought it was odd, but perhaps he was just preparing to throw the grenade. Then Aamil set the grenade on the ground, too, and raised his arms, folded his hands behind his head, and Sinan felt his mouth dry as if filling with sand. The impact of the betrayal was so sudden and so unexpected that, for a moment, he lost his breath.

One of the soldiers was shouting, coming down into the gully toward Aamil, another covering them both, and all under the shadow of the APC's machine gun. Aamil was shoved roughly into the ground facefirst, his rifle and the grenade kicked away. The soldier worked quickly, his knee in Aamil's back, binding Aamil's hands together with a plastic tie. Once finished, he used the cuffs as a handle, jerking Aamil upright, forcing him toward the APC.

Sinan waited until they were about to load Aamil into the vehicle before he ripped the pin from the grenade in his hand. He threw it hard, underhand, heard the soft metallic ring of the handle as it sprang away from the casing. It landed short of the APC, bounced, and Sinan brought the Kalashnikov up and against his shoulder and fired a burst from the rifle, bullets clattering against the APC, striking the armor of the soldier at the machine gun. They shouted, began to react, turning to return fire.

The grenade detonated, just to the side of the vehicle, and Sinan dropped back into the gully, sprinting half the distance toward the gap in the fence. He heard screams but no more shots, and he risked another view, leading with his rifle, and saw that one of the soldiers, bloodied and cut, was trying to regain his feet. Sinan loosed another burst from the rifle, and the soldier slumped against the vehicle, toppled to the ground.

He dropped back again, ran the rest of the way to the gap in the fence, and was about to crawl through when he thought again about Aamil, more precisely, what if Aamil was still alive? He couldn't leave him like this, not if he was still breathing, and it meant he had to check, and already he could hear the doors opening, the dogs going again.

Sinan clambered back up the slope. The lights on the APC still burned but were unfocused, without motion, and he had sufficient darkness to risk skirting the track directly as he made his way back to the vehicle. The soldier who had manned the machine gun was slumped at an almost comical angle on his side, half out of the vehicle, and another was splayed out flat, facing the heavens, at the rear.

Aamil was trying to pull himself into the APC, whimpering with the effort and with pain. Blood flowed from beneath the knee of his left leg, the flesh savaged by shrapnel, and Sinan saw that the grenade had caught his left arm as well. He slowed, cradling the rifle in both hands.

"Aamil?"

His friend started, as if surprised, then released his hold on the APC, leaving a blood smear where his palm had rested. He turned his head and Sinan saw dirt and blood mixed in Aamil's beard, an almost-vacant expression in his eyes. Aamil blinked, as if he needed to reset his eyes.

"Shuneal . . . ," Aamil said. "Shuneal, help me. . . ."

"God is great," Sinan told him, and this time he didn't bother to raise the Kalashnikov to his shoulder, just fired from the hip, two quick bursts. The first tore through Aamil's pelvis, the second hitting higher, climbing the chest, and Aamil flopped back onto the APC. Then gravity took him, tugging him to the ground.

Sinan didn't see it. He was already through the gap in the fence and making for the Jordan River.

8

Crocker hadn't closed the door to the Deputy Chief's office before Donald Weldon was offering him a red file folder.

"Read," Weldon said.

The folder was labeled "Most Secret," but the operation designation line had been left blank. A bar code had been assigned, stuck to the lower-right corner of the front of the file, and the tracking boxes along the front were empty but for four entries: C at 0723 that morning; Weldon at 0808; Rayburn at 0858; and Weldon again at 0949.

Crocker knew what it was without opening it, but he did so anyway, to be certain of the particulars. Within were two sheets, clipped together, neatly typed. The first was a directive from the Prime Minister, authorizing SIS to undertake action as described in the concept of operations following. Despite the nature of the operation, Crocker noted that the PM had omitted any reference to retaliation or retribution. Instead, he'd declared the proposed action as one of self-defense and protection vital to the Crown and its holdings.

The second sheet was the conops, as prepared by the Intelligence Oversight Committee, including the Prime Minister, C, and various other members of the FCO and Cabinet, as well as the Chief of the Defense Staff. It was, even given the vaguely legal nature of its language, short to the point of being curt: it ordered SIS Director of Operations Paul Crocker to immediately plan and execute the assassination of Dr. Faud bin Abdullah al-Shimmari.

Minor provisions were given, all of them standard. The operation was to be carried out with due care to prevent collateral damage to secondary targets, but only in furtherance of primary mission objective; requisite concealment of authorizing agency and operative(s), inclusive; declassification date declared fifty years to the day of mission completion. The mission completion date was openended, and Crocker presumed that was Rayburn's doing, considering that Faud was most likely at his home in Jeddah, and there was no way in the world they'd be able to hit him there and get away with it.

There were things that were different about this conops, though, things that it took Crocker a moment to realize. There was no equivocating, no doublespeak. It was as blunt a directive as he had ever received, in that sense, and the message was clear: Kill Faud, we don't give a damn how. Even the clause excusing collateral damage "in furtherance of primary mission objective," the Government's way of saying that if an agent had to, perhaps, machine-gun three of Faud's closest friends on the way to target, well, it was a pity, but it would be forgiven.

At the bottom of the page were the signatures of those who had authorized the action, including the Prime Minister and C.

Crocker flipped the folder shut with one hand, dropped it back onto Weldon's spotless desk with a frown.

The Deputy Chief folded his hands across his broad middle. He wasn't so much an overweight man as a stocky one, built like the support column one found in underground car parks, with the addition of a liberal head of graying brown hair. Neither of them made enough to afford the tailors that men like C did, and Weldon, like Crocker, purchased his suits at Marks & Spencer. Unlike Crocker, who stayed religiously in the black, blue, and gray spectrum, Weldon went more to the browns.

"Directive came down this morning, as you can see. You're to undertake the operation immediately."

"I'm not going to send a Minder into Saudi."

"I repeat, Paul, you're to undertake the operation immediately. According to D-Int, Faud is at his home in Jeddah. Poole can take him there."

Crocker shook his head. "I'm not putting a

Minder into Saudi to perform an assassination. I'd never get him out again."

"With proper planning—"

"It's Saudi Arabia, not Croydon, sir. Travel in the country is restricted, even to nationals. We'd have to give the Minder cover that would not only get them into the country, but get them from Riyadh to Jeddah, and then out again."

"There are other routes out of the country."

"To where? He's supposed to take a boat across the Red Sea into Sudan or Egypt? Or do you think he should tab overland to the UAE, maybe to Jordan? There are too many things that could go wrong."

Weldon's hands slipped down, then came up again to rest on the desk, now in the form of fists. "Your job is to undertake and execute a successful mission, that's all."

"Safe egress is part of a successful mission."

"Not a vital part."

"I beg to differ with you, sir, but if you'll direct your attention to the concept of operations, we've been directed to conceal the origin of issuing body. Poole dead in Jeddah becomes a very big clue as to who is responsible, don't you think?"

"Not if his cover holds."

"It won't hold after he's dead, not if they know he's the one who pulled the trigger. They'll go over his movements with a microscope, and eventually they'll find their way back to us."

Weldon's fists tightened, then relaxed.

"It's academic, anyway," Crocker continued. "Egress isn't the problem. Travel restrictions in Saudi are so tight there's a good chance whichever Minder we put into the country would never make it to target in the first place. And since I've only got three of them, I'd rather we get it right the first time."

"It's been two weeks since the attacks, Paul, and the Government is impatient. C won't suffer you dragging your feet."

Crocker glared at Weldon, biting back his immediate urge to snap a response.

"The clock is running," Weldon added unnecessarily.

"I will not initiate an operation that's been half-planned solely to appease C," Crocker said. "And begging your pardon, sir, but neither should you. You should be defending me on this, not urging me forward."

"C is of the opinion that you coddle the Minders. Stalling on this will not help alter that."

"They are not coddled." Crocker didn't bother to hide the acid in his voice. "The mere fact that I've lost two of them in the past eighteen months should make that perfectly plain. I have three Special Operations Officers, sir, three highly trained, highly committed agents, and any one of them, from Lankford to Chace, would march straight to Jeddah right now if that's what I ordered. They all know their job."

"But do you know yours, Paul?"

"I'll see that the mission is completed."

"See that you do." Weldon pushed the folder toward Crocker, then sat back in his chair.

"And to hell with the Minder who falls in the process," Crocker muttered, and taking the folder, departed the Deputy Chief's office for the safer confines of the sixth floor.

9

Chace was eating a sandwich and reading about surplus grain production in Shanxi Province, China, when the black phone on her desk started beeping for her attention. Lankford, at his desk across from her, immediately stopped what he was doing to watch her answer, then reluctantly turned his attention back to the paperwork before him as he realized it wasn't the red circuit that had rung.

Poole, who by now knew the different tones of each phone, didn't bother to react.

"Minder One," Chace answered.

"D-Ops has requested the pleasure of your company in his office," Kate said. "He asks that you come with haste, and that you bring with you those wayward young men with whom you share an office."

"He didn't say that."

"No, he said get the Minders the hell up here now, but I thought my version was more polite."

"More florid, at least," Chace said. "We'll be right up."

•

Kate ushered them into D-Ops's office, and Chace led the way inside to find Crocker standing behind his desk, surrounded by a cloud of his cigarette smoke and speaking on the telephone. With the hand holding the cigarette, he waved for the Minders to come in and then waved a second time, dismissing Kate, all the while listening intently to whoever was speaking on the other end of the line.

Kate closed the door behind them, and Chace motioned for Lankford and Poole to take the two chairs already positioned in front of the desk, then moved to the corner to push the third chair closer, for her own use. As she did, she glanced at Crocker's desk and the red folder waiting there. She could read quite well upside down—another skill acquired as a child—and solely from the labeling at the top, she knew that conops had at last arrived.

She settled into the chair, Lankford and Poole to her right, wondering what it meant that Crocker had brought them all upstairs for the news, and not her alone. The job had been promised to her, and she didn't like the idea that things had changed, and that it might now be up for grabs.

"I can't mount an operation based on that, Simon," Crocker was saying. "No, I understand that it's hard to get reliable intelligence out of the region, but until we have a confirmation on his location, I'm not committing anyone to the field."

From the corner of her eye, Chace saw Lankford shoot a curious glance her way. She shrugged, and he slid his attention back to Crocker, shifting in the chair, trying to relax.

"We'll talk about it later," Crocker told the phone, then slapped the receiver back into its cradle, harder than was necessary. He put the cigarette to his lips, drawing on it and looking over the three of them, and then, exhaling, he said, "Each of you is heading out to the School for a refresher. I don't want to drain the Pit, so you'll go one at a time, starting tomorrow, and starting with Minder One."

"Why me?" Chace asked.

"Because the last time you were at the School, Ed was still alive," Crocker snapped. "Because I bloody said so, that's why. I've talked to Jim Chester, he knows you're coming. You'll do the course over two days, first day standard, second day active drills. You're the damn Special Section, I expect your scores to be five point oh, nothing less. That's for each of you."

All three of them nodded, with varying degrees of enthusiasm.

Crocker focused on Poole. "And don't think the SAS attitude is going to help you. Last time you took the motor course, you barely passed. Not again, Nicky."

"No, sir," Poole said with such seriousness he was

clearly mocking Crocker. Chace found herself looking at her knees in order to hide her smile.

"And as for you, Chris, I remind you that despite the events of two weeks ago, your status as Minder Three remains Provisional, pending approval by your Head of Section and me. I've given Chester the quick brief on that arsing up you had in St. Petersburg, and he'll be watching you."

Lankford nodded, then added, "Very good, sir."

Crocker glared at each of them in turn, then stabbed out his cigarette in the ashtray and took his seat, drawing the chair in closer to the desk, sitting up straight. He was tall to begin with, and with them all seated opposite, it had the desired effect of making each feel like a reprimanded schoolchild, or so it seemed to Chace.

"Her Majesty's Government has today supplied me with a directive to locate and neutralize Dr. Faud bin Abdullah al-Shimmari," Crocker informed them. "The action is to be undertaken at the earliest feasible opportunity and will be carried out by a member of the Special Section. When this window opens, it'll be one of you who's going through it.

"This means, with the exception of the refresher at the School, you're to stay in London. No leave, no sick days, I don't care if your pet bunny Flossy kicks it, you're on call. Each of you is to brief on Faud, his associations, his history, his movements, all of it. Since we don't know what may turn out to be relevant, *all* of it is relevant.

"Right now, Faud is presumed to be at his home in Jeddah, though we're still awaiting confirmation of that. If he is, he's safe, and will remain safe as long as he stays in Saudi. Our window will come only when he leaves the country, for whatever reason."

"How likely is that to happen, sir?" Lankford asked.

"He's been known to travel in the region. Visited Egypt last year, and Sudan in late 2001. There's a good chance he'll be moving again shortly."

"Not if he thinks he's a target," Poole said.

"We already know he thinks he's a target," Chace said. "The question is, how much of one? Is he wearing body armor beneath his *thobe*, that's the question."

Poole grinned lazily. "Head shots all 'round, then."

"He's guarded, we know that much, has been ever since the attempt on his life in 1996," Crocker said. "It was tribal-motivated, but since then, he's never seen in public without security. Minimum of four bodyguards, sometimes as many as twice that. Whether he knows he's caught our attention now, we've no way of ascertaining, but he'd be a fool if he didn't think we were looking at him after what happened on the seventh."

"And we know he's not a fool," Chace murmured.

"He's in his seventies, isn't he?" Lankford asked suddenly.

"Seventy-three or seventy-five, depending on the source," Crocker confirmed.

"Maybe we can scare him to death," Poole offered. "Send Tara at him in a short skirt and halter top, that should cause a little cardiac arrest."

"Or fishnets," Lankford added. "Short skirt with fishnets ought to do the trick."

"That's enough," Crocker said, and Chace was grateful, because it meant she didn't have to.

Lankford and Poole went quiet.

"Does conops specify method?" Chace asked.

"At discretion, but it'll have to be precise. HMG is anxious to minimize any collateral damage, so anything short of a sniper shot or a bullet at point-blank is probably out of the question."

"Hence the refresher course."

"Hence the refresher course, yes," Crocker echoed. "So now you know what we're waiting on, I suggest you get to it. Go on, get out."

There was a clatter as three chairs moved in unison, the Minders rising, murmuring "Yes, sir," and "Thank you, sir." Chace took the time to move the third chair back to its place in the corner, fell in last behind Poole as the others headed out the door. She followed them as far as the hallway, then tapped him on the shoulder.

"I'll catch up," she told Poole, then turned back into the outer office. Kate glanced up from her terminal, her fingers still flying over the keyboard, arching an eyebrow. Chace grinned at her as she went past. Crocker had swiveled his seat to scowl at London beyond the window, working a fresh cigarette, the ashtray resting on a bony knee.

Chace rapped her knuckles on the doorframe. "Boss?"

He didn't move. "Close it."

She shut the door quietly behind her, then approached the desk. The tang of the tobacco in the air settled at the back of her throat and she felt the crawling memory of addiction. She'd quit smoking almost a year before, and still the cravings could be enough to make her want to commit a little GBH at times.

As if taunting her, Crocker flicked ash into the tray. "I don't want to hear it."

"It's mine."

"Until we know where, we don't know how. Until we know how, we don't know who. If it's going to be close quarters, Poole's a better choice."

"I can kill a man as well as the next guy," Chace said mildly.

"It's a matter of strength, Tara, and Nicky's stronger than you are. If it's neck-breaking, it'll have to be him."

"Give me a pistol and a suppressor, I can do it just as well and a damn sight quicker."

Crocker took another draw from his cigarette, let the smoke go slowly, so that it climbed along the window and curled back toward them from the ceiling. The silence spread like the smoke, but it didn't bother Chace. She could wait. She was well versed in the nuances of Crocker's moods. When D-Ops acted like this, you didn't rush him, because he was still working his angles. There was a validity to what he was saying about Poole, but she knew it wasn't the real reason. She may have lacked the upper-body strength of Nicky Poole or Chris Lankford, but she was faster than both men and, with a knife or a gun or even her bare hands, just as lethal.

"How's Lankford coming along?" Crocker asked.

"He's been hitting the books. Having a hard time learning patience, but I had that problem, so did Ed."

"Not Poole."

"That's only because he came to us wrong way 'round."

Crocker nodded, accepting the assessment. Almost every Minder had been seconded from within SIS to the Special Section, normally after serving some field time, but just as often was taken straight from the School at Fort Monkton. While some Minders came with prior military experience— Wallace had been a Royal Marine, Butler a sergeant in the Coldstream Guards—neither Chace nor Lankford had come to the job with armed services experience. It wasn't a prerequisite.

Poole was an exception, because he was homosexual. Unlike the American military, there was no Don't Ask, Don't Tell policy in the British armed forces, as a European high court decision in early 2000 had declared such policies, and indeed Britain's general ban on gays in the military, to be an unwarranted discrimination. The fact that Poole fancied men shouldn't have mattered in the least under the ruling.

But it was still the S.A.S., arguably Britain's most prestigious regiment, and when one of Poole's fellow troopers, a man by the name of Hart, had fired a bullet into Poole's body armor during a training exercise in the Killing House, events had threatened to explode into the public eye. Faced with the choice of letting the matter stand or pursuing Hart with charges—an act that would have brought yet more scrutiny upon the S.A.S., still reeling from the bad press of the last decade—Poole had instead decided to leave the Army altogether.

It would have been an extraordinary waste of the thousands of hours and millions of pounds that had been spent on his training, and fortunately, that was exactly what Poole's CO had thought as well. After some pointed inquiries through the MOD, Poole's CO had contacted the Colonel who headed the SPT, the military-trained Special Projects Team tasked directly to SIS under control of D-Ops, asking about an opening. Poole's personnel jacket was forwarded as a matter of course, with a copy to D-Ops as protocol dictated. Normally, it wouldn't have earned a second look, but Kittering's replacement, Butler, had just died in T'bilisi, and for the second time in less than a month Crocker had found himself scrambling for a warm body to fill the post of Minder Three.

Poole had caught his eye. Minders were hard to come by at the best of times; few who could do the job actually wanted to, and those who wanted to were, almost universally, the most likely to completely arse it up. The last thing Crocker wanted in the Section was an agent who imagined himself the next Jack Ryan or, worse, the next James Bond. In the face of that, an agent who was homosexual was laughably mundane, and a liability only if the agent let it be one. Crocker didn't give a damn if Poole fancied women, men, or livestock, as long as it didn't get in the way of the job.

Crocker put out his cigarette, set the ashtray back on the desk.

"It took eight months to find Lankford," he told Chace. "Took three months of additional training after we'd found Poole to get him ready for action."

He'd lost her for a second, then Chace realized what he was saying and she nodded slightly, trying to conceal her surprise. Crocker wasn't sentimental, she knew that, but all the same, it touched her. He could afford to lose Lankford, he could even afford to lose Poole, but what she was reading between his words now was that he *couldn't* afford to lose her. The needs of the Firm came first.

"You think it'll be a one-way trip?" she asked.

The scowl came back. "An hour ago the Deputy Chief was trying to convince me to put a Minder into Saudi. I held him off, but I don't know if I can do the same if it's C who's behind him on the next go-round."

"It'd be madness."

"I did point that out to the DC."

"If Faud moves, goes abroad—"

"No guarantees, Tara."

"I'll make it back, you know I will."

The look he gave her was uncharacteristically sincere, and abruptly sad.

"No," Crocker said. "I don't."

10

After prayers and sunset Sinan was called to Abdul Aziz's tent, arriving to find four others already waiting outside with the commanding officer. Since coming to the camp, Aziz had forgone his *thobe* for the more military desert fatigues the rest of them wore, so it surprised Sinan to see that Aziz was once again in his cotton robe.

"You men are coming with me tonight," Aziz told them, and gestured toward the old Russian truck, draped with camouflage netting and parked in the shadow of the wadi wall. "Get in the back."

They moved to the truck, climbing into the bed as directed. There were wooden benches bolted at either side in the back, and the canvas top had trapped the heat of the day within. Sinan heard grumbles from some of the men as they took their seats, stowing their Kalashnikovs either beneath them or between their legs.

The drive was long and uncomfortable, the truck bouncing and hopping along the almost-roads out of the camp and into the desert. With the canvas flaps thrown back, Sinan could see the desert stretching forever into the night, and the stars were brilliant, thick in the sky. There was no illumination except for what the heavens provided; the truck drove without headlights, the driver wearing NVG.

Of the four others with Sinan, three were Saudi. The fourth was an Afghani named Matteen, and he had good stories of fighting Americans and British near Tora-Bora, and to relieve the boredom of the trip, he shared them. Sinan listened to the veteran's tales with absolute attention, eager to learn from Matteen's experience.

"They tried to bomb us, you know?" Matteen told them. "For days and days they dropped bombs on us, and the whole earth shook and shuddered, as if Satan was trying to climb free. But Allah protected us in the caves, and their bombs did nothing. They tried to murder us for days, and in the end, their bombs did nothing. We were protected because we were righteous."

All of them nodded.

"Back in the camp," Matteen continued, "it's the same thing. The wadi is a good place, very safe from the air. No satellites to spy on us, and if the *mushrikun* try to bomb us, there are many places to wait and stay safe. A very good place."

"If they come on foot?" Sinan asked.

The Saudis laughed. "It will never happen," one of them said.

Matteen shook his head, barely visible in the cowled darkness of the back of the truck. "You don't know, you don't know. Your rulers allowed Americans to build bases on our holy soil. There are *mushrikun* in Riyadh, and they are cowards. Spineless, gutless . . . Don't believe for a moment that we won't be sacrificed on the altar of their greed if it comes to that."

"The Crown has always supported us in the past."

"In the *past*, yes. But even with the West in its death throes, there are still those who want to pacify the Americans. Look what happened to our brothers in Riyadh and Sakakah after the bombings last year. It was *your* leaders who rounded up those *muwahhidun* and had them executed, all to appease the apes and pigs of the West."

Matteen waited to see if the man would offer a counter, but none came.

"If they come on foot, Matteen?" Sinan asked again.

"The same thing, like we did in Afghanistan. Know the land, Sinan, and use it. Anyone who comes to us, comes to us blind. But *we* fight with our eyes open, and with clear vision, we are victorious."

Sinan thought about that, looking out at the desert lit by stars. Since his arrival, he'd spent almost all of his time in the camp, with the exception of the successful trip to the West Bank. His days, spent mostly in prayer, classes, and training, left little time for exploration of the surrounding area. But he would find the time, he resolved.

Anything that made him a better warrior, Sinan would do it.

•

Sinan felt the change, the truck's tires moving from cracked and desiccated earth to pavement, and he guessed they were soon to arrive at their journey's end. He had no idea where it might be, but he also lacked any feeling of apprehension. Abdul Aziz was in the cab, leading them, and it was Abdul Aziz who had brought him this far, after all.

The truck slowed, then stopped, but the engine remained running. Sinan heard one of the cab doors open and Abdul Aziz's voice, but he couldn't make out the words. A man's voice answered, and there was the sound of machinery, and the truck shook slightly as the cab door slammed closed again. The truck started forward with a lurch that nearly sent each of them toppling one against the other. Sinan righted himself and looked out the back to see that they had passed through a gate into a compound of some sort. The gate was closing now, and in the illumination from the guard post, he saw two men dressed like paramilitaries.

The truck stopped again, and this time the engine died. Doors opened for a second time and then Abdul Aziz appeared, lowering the gate to let them out.

"Treat our host with respect," he warned them. "No matter what he asks or what he says, he is worthy of your respect, and he is your host."

Sinan dropped out of the vehicle behind Matteen, adjusting the strap of his rifle on his shoulder. The others fell in, and Aziz motioned for the men to follow.

They were in an enormous courtyard, the size of a football pitch to Sinan's eyes, and that alone would have been amazing, but more than half of it appeared to be comprised of an immaculately maintained lawn. In the starlight all colors washed away, but from the scent of it, Sinan knew it was lush and green. Centered on the lawn was a fountain, perhaps eleven feet high, spurting water in arcs that shimmered as they fell to the pool at its base. As they walked along the tiled driveway that skirted the lawn, Sinan felt the sand and dirt in his clothes, grinding against his skin.

Following Aziz, they made their way to the front of an enormous, sprawling mansion. Marble steps led to a massive door where two more paramilitaries, wearing grenades and pistols on their belts, each holding a submachine gun, watched their approach. Sinan thought the men looked bored and wondered if they would ask for his rifle, and then wondered what he would do if they did. Much as he hated the thought of it, he decided he would hand it over, in order to show respect.

It turned out that the rifles didn't interest the

guards; they wanted their boots. Following Abdul Aziz's lead, each man removed his shoes, setting them in a matched pair on the second step, before proceeding inside.

The group moved into a cavernous entry hall, so brightly lit that Sinan's eyes began to tear from the glare. Chandeliers glowed above, and sconces along each wall, and there was more marble here, on the floor, on the walls, on the curving staircase that climbed to the upper floors. Fixtures glittered gold and silver, compounding the effect.

A young man in a black *thobe* and white *kuffiyah* came through a door down the hall, followed by a boy no older than ten.

"Salaam alaykum," the man said.

"Salaam alaykum," Abdul Aziz echoed.

The man reached for Aziz's right hand, placed his left on Aziz's right shoulder, and Aziz mirrored him. They exchanged kisses on each cheek before releasing the grip.

"Hazim will take them to the study," the man told Aziz. "But His Royal Highness wishes to see you first, upstairs."

"Very well." Aziz turned to them. "Go with the boy."

Sinan nodded, reassured. It explained the extravagance of the mansion, the mysteriousness of their journey, the guards, everything. This was the home of a prince to the House of Saud. At least now he understood where they were, if not why.

Hazim led them down the hall and through another set of doors, and here the marble floor gave way to smooth stone and a new flight of stairs, this one leading down. They descended perhaps twenty feet into what Sinan would have called a rec room but that he assumed was the indicated study.

The floor was carpeted in an emerald-green shag that felt strangely uncomfortable to Sinan's bared feet. Three large televisions occupied the far wall, spaced irregularly, two of them plasma screens, one of them a projection model. All three were on, and all were broadcasting sports, two football games, one basketball. A billiard table stood to one side, purple felt with fittings that Sinan first thought were brass but on second look decided were gold. Books and magazines were strewn on the easy chairs and couches, and he was shocked to see that a number of them were pornographic. CD jewel boxes and DVD cases littered the floor. The titles ranged from Arabic to English, pop music from the Middle East and the West.

Sinan looked to Matteen, and Matteen frowned, made the faintest shake of his head.

"Please, be comfortable," Hazim told them, and then vanished through a door off to a side.

The group stood still for a few moments longer, and then two of the Saudis propped their Kalashnikovs against one of the easy chairs and took up pool cues. Matteen moved to the nearest couch, facing one of the football matches, the remaining Saudi joining him. Only Sinan didn't move.

It was all so Western, he thought, and this made him uneasy. It had been years since he'd been anyplace like this, in a space like this, and it was a space for William Leacock, not for Sinan bin al-Baari.

He didn't like it, and he didn't like it in the home of a Prince of the House of Saud most of all.

One wall was covered with framed photographs, and Sinan made his way to it, picking his steps carefully to avoid the debris. The pictures were a mix, black and white as well as color, and as far as he could see, the only unifying factor was that the same man appeared in most of them. If there was a purpose to the display, Sinan figured it was in presenting their host the Prince in as many roles as possible.

Most often, the Prince appeared in a black *thobe* and white *kuffiyah*, with trimmed black beard and mustache, often wearing sunglasses that failed to flatter his face. There was one of the Prince with King Fahd, and another, apparently more recent, with Crown Prince Abdullah. Another, elegantly framed and dominantly placed, showed the Prince seated between Usama bin Laden and Mullah Omar, taken at a camp, presumably in Afghanistan before the Coalition had arrived. Still others showed the Prince with various holy men, Sheikh Wajdi Hamzeh al-Ghazawi and Sheikh Muhammad Saleh al-Munajjid, and Dr. Faud bin Abdullah al-Shimmari.

It wasn't all vanity. There were three photographs of racehorses, beautiful creatures at a gallop, breaking away from the pack. Another of a kindergarten graduation ceremony, and Sinan recognized it instantly, because he'd seen others of its kind before.

Beaming Palestinian children, wrapped in pretend bomb harnesses, their hands dripping with the red paint that signified the blood of the apes and pigs.

The door opened again and Hazim returned carrying a silver tray laden with small cups. The boy served the men at the pool table first, then worked his way around the room, offering coffee to each of them in turn. Sinan sipped his, savoring the flavor, the hint of cardamom mixed into the drink. By the time he'd finished the cup, the boy was making second rounds, and this time Sinan waggled the cup in his hand back and forth, indicating that he was fine, that he didn't wish another serving. The coffee had driven the taste of the desert from his mouth but had failed to do anything for his thirst.

He moved away from the wall of photographs, toward one of the couches. Matteen was still engrossed in the match he was watching, and the Saudi who wasn't playing pool was flipping through a magazine. He was one of the veterans, named Jabr, and had been in the camp when Sinan had arrived. Jabr had taken delight in mocking Sinan and Aamil, hazing them as rookies.

At least until Sinan had returned alone.

Jabr stopped on a photo spread of a pale blonde, holding her thighs apart, head back, breasts artificially full and defiant. Beneath her belly, inked into the skin above her shaved opening, was a red and black tattoo of a valentine's heart.

"Sinan, you ever had one like this?" Jabr asked, raising the magazine. "Back home, you must have fucked one like this, yes?"

Sinan glared at him, shook his head. The magazine was contraband in Saudi Arabia, it shouldn't have even been there. If any of them had been found with such a thing in their possession at the camp, they'd have been beaten, if not killed. In Riyadh, it would lead to prison, or worse.

But here in the Prince's house, it was easy and available, and the hypocrisy made Sinan want to spit.

"Never?" Jabr grinned at him, not believing the answer. "Not even once?"

Sinan shook his head a second time. The room was air-conditioned, the whole house was, heavily so, but he felt himself growing warm, heat crawling along his spine.

He tore the magazine from the man's hands, threw it down on the carpet. Jabr cursed, starting to his feet, fists turning to balls. Sinan swung his Kalashnikov on its strap, bringing the weapon up and into line, trapping the butt against his hip with his forearm, and Jabr stopped cold, looking up the barrel.

The pool game had stopped.

"Sinan, lower that weapon," Abdul Aziz ordered from the bottom of the stairs.

Everyone except Sinan and Jabr turned to look. Jabr didn't because he was still fixed on the gun leveled at him; Sinan didn't because, at first, he hadn't heard the order. Then the words penetrated, and he let his finger return to the trigger guard, and he stepped back from Jabr on the couch, lowering the weapon.

The man in the photographs on the wall was

standing beside Aziz, looking at Sinan with delight. "If he needs to shoot him, could he do it outside?"

"He doesn't need to," Aziz said. "I'm sure it was a misunderstanding. It was a misunderstanding, wasn't it, Jabr?"

Jabr, still looking at Sinan, nodded.

"Sinan?"

"Yes."

"So you see, Your Highness," Aziz said. "A misunderstanding, nothing more."

The Prince frowned. "I'm not certain they're the best men for me, for this, if there are misunderstandings of this kind, my friend. You understand my concern."

Abdul Aziz moved into the room, motioning Sinan toward him. Sinan let his rifle rest against his chest once more, on its strap, moving closer as ordered. Aziz put a hand on his shoulder, turned him to face the Prince.

"These are *jihadis*, Your Highness. They live for one thing alone, to serve Allah, lord of the universe and prayer. They are the sword in Allah's hand, the tip at the end of His arrow. You cannot ask for better."

The Prince adjusted his sunglasses, pursed his lower lip, examining Sinan. His *kuffiyah* was white, Sinan noted, but the *igaal* had threads of gold woven into the black wool.

"Tell me your name," the Prince said.

"Sinan bin al-Baari."

"Your Arabic is very good."

"There is no other way to read *Qu'ran*."

The Prince smiled. "Have you tasted blood, Sinan bin al-Baari? Have you been tested in battle?"

Sinan glanced to Aziz and saw nothing in his expression to indicate that he shouldn't answer. "Not as much as others. More than some."

The Prince's smile broadened. "I like him," he told Abdul Aziz.

"I thought you might, Your Highness."

The Prince used his right hand to indicate Matteen. "You, where are you from?"

Matteen got to his feet before answering. "Gazni, Your Highness."

"Abdul Aziz says you fought alongside my friend at Tora-Bora."

"That was my honor."

"Tell me, did you kill any Americans?"

"Three, Your Highness."

The answer seemed to please the Prince, and he bobbed his head in appreciation, then turned back toward the stairs, again using his right hand, this time to motion at Abdul Aziz. "My friend, come with me."

Abdul Aziz moved back to the foot of the stairs, bent his head to the Prince, listening as the other man spoke. Then Abdul Aziz nodded, turned to face them.

"Jabr, the rest of you, Hazim will lead you back to the truck. Wait for me there."

The three Saudis did as ordered, each bowing to the Prince as they passed him, then making their way up the stairs, following the boy. Abdul Aziz waited until they were gone and the echo of the closing doors above had faded before speaking again.

"His Royal Highness has been of great help to us in the past," Aziz told Sinan and Matteen. "He is our fiercest ally, and we thank Allah daily for his help, and pray daily for his continued health and well-being.

"Now, he asks a favor of us, and we have agreed."

"You two men, you will stay with me for a time, guests in my home," the Prince told Sinan and Matteen. "I have bodyguards, of course, but I will be traveling soon, I hope, and would welcome the company of experienced soldiers like yourselves."

"It shouldn't be more than a month," Abdul Aziz told them.

Sinan tried to keep what he was feeling off his face, certain that he was failing. The thought of remaining in the house, in this place, was a punishment, not a reward. The Prince was an empty shell, he was certain, more interested in appearing to be *jihadi* than in being one. The photographs on the wall in the same room with pornography and the trappings of Western decadence proved it, if the Prince's manner alone didn't.

Abdul Aziz was watching him, waiting for an answer. His expression left no doubt as to the answer he wanted to hear.

"Of course, Your Highness," Sinan said. "It would be our great honor."

11

Hampshire—Gosport, Fort Monkton
18 August 0611 GMT

Morning fog from the Channel still clung to the grass as Chace made her way out to the shooting range, dressed in baggy sweats and trainers, trying to shake the last sleep from her head. She'd slept poorly and not for long, opting to take the Thunderbolt from London on the off-chance that Crocker would recall her and she'd need to get back in a hurry. She'd left after work, returning home just long enough to gather her mail, change into riding leathers, and stuff a bag with essentials. It had taken her fifty-seven minutes exactly to clear London traffic, still in catastrophic disarray from the lack of tube service. By the time she'd hit the M3, she'd been more than ready to roll the throttle back and just get the hell on with it.

Which was precisely the moment the Thunderbolt chose to break down.

She managed to get the bike and herself towed to a garage in Winchester, but by the time they arrived, the mechanic had left, and no amount of persuasion, cajoling, or pleading had been enough to rouse him from his home. It was all the more infuriating to Chace because she was positive, absolutely positive, that whatever was ailing the Thunderbolt was minor at best, and certainly a quick fix for anyone who knew the first thing about Thunderbolts specifically or even motorcycles in general.

Forced to abandon the bike, she'd switched to rail, catching a train that took her into Portsmouth and then left her on the platform at half past midnight. She'd utterly failed to find a cab, and after debating her options, she'd used her mobile in an attempt to reach Tom Wallace, hoping that he would drop whatever he was doing—say, sleeping—to come and fetch her the rest of the way. But Tom hadn't answered his phone. Even when she let it ring two dozen times.

In the end, annoyed beyond the capacity for speech, Chace had gone down to the ferry and caught a ride across the harbor to Gosport, then walked the remaining two and a half miles to Fort Monkton, only to be further delayed by the guards at the gate, who found it hard to believe that London had sent an agent down on foot for a refresher. Even after finding her name on the "expected" list and double-checking her pass, they'd insisted on searching her person and her bag.

At which point she'd had enough and informed the guard reaching for her that he could try to lay a hand on her, but if he did so he'd likely draw back his arm fractured in such a way that he'd have three major joints on the appendage rather than the more traditional two.

"And get Jim Chester down here right fucking now," she'd added.

●

The rangemaster, a bitter old retired Royal Marine who demanded that students call him "The Master," remembered her, just as she remembered him. Common lore at the School was that he promoted the appellation not because of his position as the ruler of the firing range but rather because he was a dyed-in-the-wool *Doctor Who* fan. He brought her four pistols and two hundred rounds of ammunition, along with shooting goggles and ear protection.

"Still know which way to point them, do you?" he asked.

"Why don't you trot downrange and we'll see?"

"Ah, that's the lass I remember. Let's get started, shall we?"

Chace loaded the P99 first, worked through two clips, thirty-two shots, with The Master over her shoulder, heckling, correcting, and generally annoying. She moved to the Browning next, then the HK USP 9, and finally the Walther TPH. The range remained empty but for the two of them the entire time, though as Chace was finishing with the TPH, she began to see other signs of life on the campus, students emerging from the dormitories in their workout clothes, gathering for the morning physical-training regimen.

They were ready to move to the more practical drills when Jim Chester came down the slope of the lawn from the main house to join them, carrying two paper cups of coffee.

"Feeling better this morning?" he asked, offering her one of the cups.

"She can't have that," The Master said, taking the coffee for himself. "Caffeine goes straight to her hands, and she's on to practicals next."

Chace looked at the coffee longingly, then to Chester. "I could have done with more sleep and less aggravation."

"It's aggravation that keeps us safe."

"That aggravation, perhaps. I was on the bloody list, Jim."

"They're just being cautious." Chester gave her a proud smile. "Minder One suits you, I must say. You're as radiant as ever."

"You testing me on pickups, Jim? I look like hell and feel worse."

Chester laughed, patted her on the arm with unconscious condescension. Chace smiled in return, knowing that there were things that would never change, and that James Chester was one of them. In his mid-fifties, balding and fringed with gray, perpetually in tweed, he always reminded her of the don who'd instructed her in eighteenth-century French literature when she'd been at Cambridge. His sexism was bone-deep and unconscious, and manifested in him holding the women who came through the School to a higher standard than the men. Not by much, and never obviously, but enough so that when Chace had graduated with the highest scores anyone had remembered for half a century, they both had known she'd truly earned it.

He'd been heartbroken to see his prize pupil join the Special Section. A waste of her talents, he'd said.

"Well, I won't keep you," Chester told them. "Firearms today, hand-to-hand tomorrow, is it?"

"And the E&E refresher."

"Ah, yes, right. We should have lunch if The Master will release you long enough for sustenance."

"She can eat." The Master sounded almost sullen.

"Then I'll see you at twelve-thirty, all right?"

"I'll be looking forward to it," she said, and then added, "Is Tom around?"

"He'll be in this afternoon. Shall I tell him you're here?"

"No." Chace grinned. "Let me surprise him."

●

The rest of the morning was spent in the simulator, killing video projections with modified pistols that did everything real guns did, but fired light instead of lead. The Master ran Chace through multiple scenarios: take the target in a crowd, in a café, in a hallway, on a flight of stairs; take the target with no protection, with two bodyguards, with six, at a traffic stop. What to do if you miss? If the gun jams? If the gun breaks? If you snag the pistol on your draw?

After each exercise, The Master would play back the video he'd recorded of Chace, berating her for her errors, grudgingly acknowledging her triumphs. Much as she was loath to admit it, she'd begun the day rusty. It had passed, and passed quickly, and everything she'd been taught came back as fresh as ever, and it pleased her that she'd even managed to improve in the practicals.

The Master made her wait as he finished her evaluation, telling her to break down and service all of the weapons she had used during the day. When Chace had reassembled the last of the firearms, he dropped the sheet in front of her so she could read her score. Crocker would be pleased; she'd delivered on his demanded five point oh.

Wishing The Master a good evening, Chace headed back to the dormitory. She showered quickly and then, dressed once more, went in search of the only man Tara Chace was certain she had ever truly loved.

●

The Field School shared Fort Monkton with the Royal Navy, which maintained a submarine-escape training facility on the site, as well as other tactical simulators. The whole area around Portsmouth was thick with RN types, the city and the fleet sharing a long and distinguished history, of which Monkton was but a small part. The site had first seen the construction of Haselworth Castle in 1545; Fort Monkton had been erected some two hundred years later at the behest of the Royal Navy, and a companion fortification and artillery battery, Gilkicker Fort, had been raised nearby later in the eighteenth century.

Both Monkton and Gilkicker were closed to the public. Students at the School were housed on campus, but the instructors were not. Most had their homes in one of the many communities surrounding the harbor, in Portsmouth or Gosport or Fareham. Many of those same instructors chose to drive to work, and the parking lot shared by the Field School and RN staffs was thick with their cars.

There was only one Triumph Spitfire MKI among them, though, and while she'd never seen the vehicle before, Chace had no doubt who it belonged to.

The top was down, so she climbed into the passenger seat and passed the time by rummaging through the glove box, which ended in disappointment when she couldn't find anything embarrassing. She did find an unopened pack of Silk Cut and some matches and, with only some minor internal debate, decided she'd earned a reprieve.

She was smoking her third cigarette when she heard footsteps on the gravel, approaching the car.

"You always were a weak-willed bird," Tom Wallace said.

Chace flicked the cigarette away, leaned over to push open the driver's door, and waited for Wallace to settle behind the wheel before saying, "Let's go someplace where you can get me drunk and then take advantage of me."

"Fucking brilliant," Wallace said, and started the car.

●

Wallace had been in Gosport long enough to find a pub he liked, the Black Swan, and had been frequenting it enough that the pub had come to like him. While Wallace got them a table, Chace went to the bar to order the first round, two lagers. The barman was old, and old-fashioned, and when he served her one pint, presumably for Wallace, and a half, presumably for her, she sent the half back.

"No, another pint, if you please."

The barman's eyes turned critical. "Not terribly ladylike."

"I'm a terrible lady."

The barman's lower lip worked, rising up and out as he gave Chace a second appraisal before barking out a short laugh and taking the half back. He pulled a fresh pint for her, and she moved off to join Wallace at their table to begin the work of serious drinking and less serious catching up. Over the course of three pints and most of the pack of Silk Cut they traded recent history, and Wallace confirmed most of what Chace had already determined for herself. He was doing well, he told her, relaxed and recovering from a life of abuse at the hands of SIS.

Certainly his appearance supported the claim, and Chace couldn't recall when Tom Wallace had ever looked so good, or so relaxed. He had ten years and an inch in height on her, but sitting in the pub, he seemed both younger and even taller. The lines on his face had softened, and color had returned to his complexion. He'd put on some weight as well, but it was appropriate to his frame, and she thought he looked as fit now as he ever had. His black hair, streaked with gray, was still as sloppily trimmed, but the brown eyes that watched her were no longer bloodshot or red-rimmed, and the mirth in them had begun to return. With his summer slacks and white trainers he looked more like an architect or an ad executive than a spy-turned-instructor.

Most Minders left the job in one of three ways, either sacrificed on the Altar of Bureaucracy in a discharge, promoted up the ladder in SIS—as Crocker had been—or killed in action. Wallace was unique in the history of the Section. A twelve-year veteran, he'd left on his own accord but still remained in the Service via lateral transfer to the School. Now, four days a week, he lectured to new recruits in the wood-paneled and electronically secured classrooms of the Manor House, a living legend passing on his pearls of wisdom.

And if the students gathered in his classroom knew who he was, had heard rumors about this operation or that mission, about this daring escape or that piece of unbelievable luck, it was a given that Wallace, bound by the Official Secrets Act, could neither refute nor deny the story. The most he would ever say was that he'd done his job, and he was proud to have done it, and now he was doing this one, and the students had damn well better feel the same.

"You look remarkably good for a man who's gone soft," Chace told him.

"I sleep a full night. No fear of the phone waking me. You have no idea what a pleasure that is."

"Full night is right. You turning your ringer off? I tried raising you last night, didn't get an answer."

Wallace glanced away from her, toward the rest of the room, and the weathered lines creased at the corners of his eyes, giving away the smile even as he tried to hide it. Chace leaned around, to see him full on, and that did it, flushed the grin from hiding and onto his face.

"Oh, dear Lord," Chace said. "You've got yourself some bint tied to your bedposts, haven't you?"

"I prefer to say that she's got me."

"And how long has this been going on?"

"Three weeks, if it's any of your business, and I'm reasonably certain that it isn't. You don't have to fear, Tara, she's been cleared. Safe for government work."

"Is that what you call it these days?"

"I'm an old man. I can use whatever euphemism I choose."

"You're not old, Tom, you're just randy."

He laughed, drained the last of his pint, and rose, saying that he'd found a good Indian place nearby, and that they'd better get some food before they were too pissed to manage the utensils. Chace agreed, emptied the last of her own glass, followed him out. Ducking beneath the blackened crossbeam at the pub's entrance, climbing the steps into the fresh air off the Channel, she felt it again, the pang of jealousy, and it annoyed her enough that she voiced it.

"She'd better be worthy, or else I'll find her house and burn it to the ground."

Wallace stopped to light a fresh smoke, handed it off to her, then lit a new one for himself. "It's down this way; we can walk."

"Her house? But I don't have my arson kit."

"The restaurant, you daft cow. Her place is over in Portsmouth, and that's the only clue you get."

"No, tell me more about her. I find myself possessed of the same fascination I normally feel when viewing accident scenes."

"Or causing them."

"I can't say. I never stick around long enough to admire my work."

Wallace chuckled, leaking smoke. They continued down the lane, turning onto the High Street. It was a pleasant night, and the streets were alive with traffic, but not crowded, and it made walking a pleasure.

"You needn't worry, Tara," Wallace said after they had traveled several blocks in silence. "She'll never replace you in my affections."

Enough sincerity had crept into his voice that Chace wasn't certain if they'd left the realm of jokes and crossed the border to someplace more serious.

●

They found a newsagent's on the High Street and bought more cigarettes, then made their way to the Magna Tandoori Restaurant, on Bemisters Lane. The curry was devastatingly hot, the way they both liked it, and each washed the meal down with more beer, spending most of the meal bitching about everything from expense reimbursement to the bastards in the Motor Pool who wanted seventeen forms for every time you needed a car on the job. It was late and they were both drunk when they finally staggered back onto the street, and when Wallace offered to give Chace the couch at his place, she agreed without hesitating.

It was only when they were back in the Triumph, the night chill of sea air forcing some sobriety back into her brain, that Chace recognized the danger of what they were doing.

●

Wallace had found himself a two-bedroom flat on the third floor on a block of surprisingly posh-looking homes on Marine Parade Drive. He parked the Triumph in his garage, cluttered with auto parts and tools, then guided Chace through the front door and into the building. There was a videophone in the alcove, and another set of doors, triple-locked, and inside doors to two ground-floor flats, a flight of stairs, and a lift. They took the stairs as a matter of habit.

His flat was cramped and plain, with two large curtained windows facing toward the seafront. Chace dropped her leather jacket over the back of the couch, then pulled the curtains to take in the view of the water and, in the distance, the lights shining from the Isle of Wight. In the kitchen behind her, she could hear Wallace rattling around, opening cabinets, clinking glasses.

He offered her a glass of whiskey when he joined her, holding the bottle and a glass of his own, which he then attempted to juggle while opening one of the windows. It swung outward, and he stepped over the sill and onto the small balcony. Chace followed him out, and they stood together, drinking their drinks and listening to the sounds of the sea and the distant horns and clatter from below.

"What do you think?" Wallace asked.

"It's spectacular. I'm wondering who you robbed to pay for this place."

"That's not really what I was asking."

Chace took more of her drink.

Wallace sighed, refilled his glass from the bottle, then hers. "We could, you know."

"Oh, trust me, Tom, I know. I'm drunk, but I know."

"I didn't mean to . . . I mean, when I offered, it wasn't because I was planning on anything. It's the truth, I don't know if you believe me."

"I believe you."

"Then I have to ask it again, Tara. What do you think?"

Chace almost laughed. "I wish I knew."

After a moment, Wallace broke open one of the new packs, offering a cigarette to her before taking one for himself. They smoked them down in silence.

"The whole thing with Kittering," Chace said. "The thing with Ed, you know. You never told Crocker."

"I never told him, but he knew."

"No, he didn't. I mean, he knew what Ed and I were up to, but he didn't *know*."

Wallace looked away from the water to her, curious.

"It was about you," Chace explained. "Took me until you announced that you were leaving to realize it, but it was about you, Tom. The whole time, it was about you."

Wallace stared at her, and she laughed without a sound, amused by how pathetic it all seemed to her.

"Tara?"

"Come on, don't do this. You're a bright lad, you can figure it out."

"Not with this I can't." Wallace looked away, back to the sea. "I've never been good at figuring things like this."

"Neither have I. That's why it took until you were gone."

Wallace shook his head ever so slightly.

Chace looked into her whiskey, then drained the glass, feeling the raw heat in her chest. The lights from the Isle of Wight danced on the water, teasingly, as if you could walk all the way to their source.

"I didn't want Ed," she said. "I wanted you, Tom,

and there was no way in hell I was going to make a try at my Head of Section."

She turned to him, waited, and when Wallace finally faced her, she kissed him, feeling his mouth unyielding at first, then softening, answering. The taste of cigarette smoke and whiskey and curry and the ocean, all the flavors of the forbidden.

"I wanted you," Chace said.

12

Israel—Tel Aviv, Mossad Headquarters
23 August 0904 Local (GMT+3.00)

It was the second bombing in as many weeks, this time in Jerusalem, on King David Street, Friday night, when the kids were out. Another suicide to accompany the murders, an eighteen-year-old Palestinian girl who'd walked up to a crowd of teens and ended them all in fire and light. Seven dead, another four wounded, two of them critically. The eldest had not turned twenty; the youngest was fifteen.

The Israeli response came the following Sunday morning, less than thirty-six hours later, when two IDF helicopter gunships launched two missiles each into the home of Abu Rajoub, near the Gaza Strip. Rajoub, long identified as the director of the Palestinian Islamic Jihad's martyrdom division, was killed along with two lower-ranking members of the organization, his wife, and one of their six children.

The thing that bothered Noah Landau most about all of this was that it barely bothered him at all.

Wrestling his beaten Toyota through Tel Aviv traffic and listening to the news on the radio, outrage and regret and condemnation and threats, he couldn't bring himself to feel anything about it anymore, one way or another. The intellectual response remained intact, the understanding of the horror visited and revisited, the seeming futility of the cycle. He knew all the reasons, beginning with the essential principle that a government is obligated, morally and legally, to protect its citizens from violence, within and without. He still believed that a zero-tolerance policy was the only possible solution in the face of terrorist violence.

But as he cleared the security to the underground parking lot of the innocuous and frankly dull building that housed his office with the Mossad, Noah Landau realized that his emotional disconnect was complete. It wasn't that he didn't know what he should feel; it had reached the point that he simply could not feel it any longer.

He'd reached this point before, twice. Once in late 1982, fifteen years old and kicking a soccer ball in the front hall of his family home in Haifa, much to the fury of his mother. The phone had rung and she had answered and he had continued to play, and then she had screamed. It had been an extraordinary noise, and as an adult, he still heard that sound, something perfectly pure in its horror, the sound of a soul being torn from a body.

His father had been killed in action in Lebanon.

His mother's grief had so overwhelmed him, he'd been left with nothing of his own. In that vacuum, he'd felt the absence for the first time.

The second time had been when his wife, Idit, and their eight-year-old son had died in a Tel Aviv café, when a car bomb had detonated twelve feet from where they were eating.

•

"Noah."

"Viktor."

"El-Sayd is on the move."

Landau stopped in the hallway but didn't look back, wondering if this was another of what Viktor Borovsky considered "jokes."

If it was one, it wasn't funny.

"He doesn't leave Egypt," Landau said softly.

"Yeah, well, I know that, but this is out of Cairo. El-Sayd's making plans to go to Yemen sometime in September."

That was enough to earn second consideration. Landau turned around, peering at the other man over the top of his glasses. Viktor was leaning in the doorway of his office, his long arms folded across his chest like spider's legs. He shot Noah a sharp, thin smile and then, with the heel of one foot, kicked his door open farther, pushed away from the frame, and disappeared into his office, inviting Landau to follow.

So Landau followed, closing the door behind

him. Borovsky was already at his desk, flipping through stacks of signals and memos. He was almost six and a half feet tall, bamboo-shoot thin, and bony. Landau could see the rounded cap of each of Borovsky's shoulders beneath his cotton shirt.

"The Old Man hasn't seen it yet," Borovsky was saying. "Got it this morning, haven't finished with the stack that came in overnight. But I saw el-Sayd, I thought of you."

"Does it check?"

Borovsky stopped riffling through the papers long enough to blast him with a glare. "Got it this morning, I said. Haven't had a chance to do anything else with it. Still have three dozen of these shit signals to do, okay?"

"Then until it checks, you're wasting my time."

"Don't be such a cocksucker all the time, Noah. You don't have to be such a dripping-dick cocksucker."

Landau moved to the desk, set his case down beside it, not speaking. When Borovsky swore, his Russian accent grew thicker, sometimes to such an extent that it was impossible to make out the Hebrew he was using. Adding profanity into the mix didn't help, since most of the profanity in Hebrew was actually taken from Arabic.

"Fuck my dog, where is it?" Borovsky muttered. "Little piece of turd, where is it?"

Landau removed his glasses, used the tail of his shirt to clean the lenses. The lenses didn't need it, but it was something to do instead of becoming impatient. The glasses were plain, black plastic frames designed to hold thick lenses, and Landau knew they were unflattering on him and didn't care in the slightest. He hadn't cared what he looked like since Idit died.

There was a rustle of paper and Borovsky made a satisfied grunt, tugging a thin sheet free. Without his glasses, Landau wasn't sure if it was a single sheet or perhaps a couple of sheets clipped together.

"Little shit can't hide from me," Borovsky announced, then waited until Landau had his glasses back on before handing the signal over.

The message had been printed on colored paper, almost a pistachio green, the date stamp from the Signal Officer at the upper left indicating the intelligence had come in just before four that morning. Routing indicated that the message had originated with one of the Cairo cells, but nothing more specific on the sourcing. Landau skimmed it quickly, then reread it again, more slowly, then handed it back to Borovsky.

"Useless," Landau said.

"The fuck you say."

"It's from an informant, it's bought information. Muhriz el-Sayd hasn't left Egypt since the Luxor shootings, Viktor."

"You think like a train, Noah, you go only back or forward, not sides, you know? Just because he hasn't left, that's not he never leaves."

"This is not enough to act upon, you know that."

"So maybe we get more, huh?"

"It'll have to be better than some unidentified informant's intelligence. It'll have to be something verifiable."

Borovsky grinned. "Well, shit, I can do that, sure."

Landau handed the sheet back, picked up his attaché, and left the office without another word.

●

Thursday afternoon, this time heading in the opposite direction down the hall, Borovsky stopped him again.

"I think I'll make you happy," Borovsky said.

"I doubt that."

Borovsky laughed, and this time, instead of ushering Landau into his office, he stepped farther out, shutting and locking the door behind him before starting off down the corridor. Landau followed to the elevators and they waited for the second car, and then Borovsky used his passcard to access the second basement level.

"Where are we going?" Landau asked.

"SigInt."

Landau sighed.

"You are a big baby, you know that?"

"I have five operations running right now, Viktor, I don't have time for this."

"How's that thing in Istanbul? You get the fuckers yet?"

Landau blinked at him slowly, hoping his expression was enough. Apparently it was, because Borovsky barked laughter.

The elevator ground to a stop, then opened to the pleasant cool of the subbasement. The guard seated at the checkpoint fifteen feet down the hall got to his feet by the door, his Uzi hanging from its strap on his shoulder, and waited for Landau and Borovsky to approach. The guard knew them from sight, just as Landau knew him, but he asked for their passes nonetheless, then checked them against the computer before logging them in and allowing them to proceed. The magnetic locks on the door snapped back with solid thuds, felt more than heard.

They made their way down the hall, past the rooms full of computers and communications equipment, to the Signals Intercept lab. Borovsky led the way inside, and they moved through a room of cluttered tables to another door, where David Yaalon sat, headset firmly clamped over his ears, face a sculpture of concentration. He was a young man, not older than thirty, working with a pen in one hand and a cigarette in the other. The room stank of cigarette smoke and coffee and ozone, computers and various blocks of audio equipment built into banks on every wall.

Landau would have been happy to wait, but Borovsky had other ideas and, with two fingers, rapped Yaalon on the back of his bowed head. Yaalon squeaked in surprise, dropping both pen and cigarette and yanking the headset from his ears, alarmed.

"Boo," Borovsky said, and then began barking with laughter again.

Landau looked an apology to Yaalon, who returned it with a wounded face, then bent to pick up his still-smoldering cigarette and the lost pen. Once everything was back in place, he reached to the console in front of him and pressed three buttons in sequence, apparently shutting down whatever he'd been listening to.

"You didn't have to do that," Yaalon said to Borovsky.

"What were you listening to? Someone having a bit on the side?"

Yaalon frowned, moved his attention to Landau. "You don't get down here often, sir."

"I don't often have a reason," Landau said.

"Ah, but now he does," Borovsky said, excited. "You play him the intercept from this morning, okay, David? The one with el-Sayd."

"I haven't completed the translation."

"Arabic?" Landau asked.

"Yes, sir."

"I'll be able to follow most of it."

"You want the headphones?"

"Speakers will be fine, David."

"Yes, sir."

Yaalon swiveled his seat back to the control panel, began using a combination of button presses on the console and mouse clicks on the nearest computer, queuing up the intercept. Landau pulled the nearest empty stool closer, perched on it carefully, waiting. Borovsky had scooped up Yaalon's pack of Camels and was getting a cigarette going.

"This came from one of the listening posts in the West Bank this morning," Yaalon explained. "Normally, we never would pick this kind of thing up, but something must have taken a bad bounce, because we caught most of it, and it's pretty clear. I already ran the voices through the database, and the matches are ninety-nine point eight and ninety-eight point four, respectively."

Landau nodded, then looked to Borovsky for explanation. Borovsky grinned and blew out a plume of smoke.

"Faud and el-Sayd," he said.

Landau registered his surprise by raising an eyebrow.

"Play it," he told Yaalon.

The young man leaned over the console again, depressed a button, and the speakers in the room came alive with a squeal of static, high-pitched enough to make each man wince. Then the noise broke and the voices came through, split with occasional squeaks and scratches on the line, the sound of other conversations on other calls faint in the background, as if parroting what was being said.

Older voice, male, presumably Faud: "... *why do you drag your feet?*"

Younger voice, male, presumably el-Sayd: "*No, you don't accuse me. You have my respect and my honor, for you are a learned man, but you do not accuse me of failing in the fight when you yourself cannot be bothered to take up arms.*"

"*I do what Allah, praise Him, commands of me.*"

A pause on the line, and Landau was sure he heard someone complaining of stomach problems in one of the background conversations.

"*All around you, your brothers fight,*" Faud said.

"*Your brothers who are destined to become* shahid. *Would you let them do the fighting for you?*"

Brief static, and then el-Sayd: "*—more from us? I've already told you what we require, and you can make it happen. I am willing to meet you both, to meet you and your benefactor in person, but I will not risk the journey on a promise alone. I need a proof.*"

A pause before Faud answered, "*Do not worship money, my friend. You condemn yourself to Hell in its pursuit.*"

"*I fear no Hell. I am a righteous man. You asked why, I tell you why, I do not need to be given a lesson I already learned. You want more from us, we need money. You have access to that money.*"

"*I have given you my word—*"

"*And I have said I need a proof.*"

Borovsky tapped Landau's shoulder, grinning. "Sounds like you, Noah."

"*How much?*"

"*Fifty thousand, American. You know the account.*"

"*If I arrange it, that will be the proof you require?*"

"*If you arrange it, I will meet you and your benefactor in San'a', you have my word.*"

"*Very well. Look to your account before the end of the week. Then look to San'a', and we shall meet—*"

Burst of static, almost as intense as the first, and then nothing but the ghost conversations lingering on the line.

"David?" Landau asked calmly.

"I know," Yaalon said. "I've been trying to clean that last piece up all day, but I'm getting nowhere."

"He was about to give the date."

"I know, sir." Yaalon shrugged. "I'm sorry."

Of course, Landau thought. *Everything but the piece we need.*

"Keep working on it," he said, and slipped off the stool, then headed out of the lab.

Borovsky caught up with him in the hall, halfway to the checkpoint, clearly pleased with himself. "Huh? What about that, huh? Fucking gold, that's what that was, Noah, yeah?"

"There are thirty days in September," Landau said. "San'a' is a big city. San'a' is a big city in Yemen. I can't mount an operation based on this."

Borovsky clapped a hand down on Landau's shoulder, stopping him. The mirth had vanished. "You can't let this go, Noah."

"And I can't act on it. Not with this, not yet."

"Go to the Americans, they have sources. They can find el-Sayd's plans, when the fuckbagger will be traveling."

"And they'll know why we're asking the minute we ask, and they'll never give it up," Landau replied.

"Muhriz el-Sayd needs killing."

"No one knows that better than I do, Viktor."

Borovsky scowled, then seemed to remember his hand was still on Landau's shoulder and let it drop away. "Maybe there's a trade?"

"We have nothing the Americans want."

"But the British, they're looking for Faud," Borovsky said. "They hold Faud responsible for the murders on the Underground, Noah. They've been asking the Friends for any news of Faud. And Faud and el-Sayd will be together in San'a'."

Landau thought about it and the first look didn't reveal any flaws, and so he looked again and still saw none.

"Yes, they will," he agreed finally.

"They can help."

Landau nodded slowly. "Yes, I think maybe they can."

Borovsky's smile returned, bigger than ever. "Then there is no problem. We kill Faud for the British, or they kill el-Sayd for us, everyone will be happy."

"Everyone except Faud and el-Sayd," Landau said.

"Terrorists." Borovsky spat on the floor. "Let them drown in their own fucking blood."

13

It was in the dizzying race of thoughts that always seemed to come to her in those seconds building to climax that Chace admitted to herself that old habits really did die hard, and none of hers were willing to go into the grave just yet. It made her laugh aloud, and beneath, inside her, the young man named Jeremy stopped moving, his hands slipping from her hips and his face flooding with concern. Chace bit her tongue to keep from laughing again, bowed her head to his ear.

"No, don't stop, Jeremy," she whispered. "You're doing fine."

She ran her tongue along the side of his neck to prove her sincerity, tasted his sweat. He moaned, and she rocked her hips to encourage him further, and that did it, his hands returning to her, roaming once more. He opened his mouth and told her that he thought she was so beautiful, that he thought she was so sexy, and Chace didn't care what he thought, and it made her irrationally and passionately angry. To silence him, she kissed him, hard, then bit his lip, pulling on it with her teeth, taking him harder, trying to steal both his breath and her own.

She'd found him at the White Horse pub, Soho, off her normally beaten path, but she'd decided to try it for a quick drink and to check out the scene after work. There had been Jeremy, in a gaggle of his friends, all of twenty-five, skin like coal and claiming to be an editor. He'd been charming, reasonably witty, looked healthy, and been easy on the eyes. It had taken less than two minutes before Chace knew she could have him if she wanted.

Whether it had been her intent upon entering not to leave alone, she still wasn't certain. But when eleven o'clock had rolled around, pleasantly lit on Chimay White, she'd slipped one arm around Jeremy's waist and let the fingers of her free hand touch his throat, then whispered in his ear, "I hope you live alone."

"Or else?" Jeremy had stammered.

"We'll have to rent a room."

He had lived alone and, even better, nearby.

●

She was hungry and aggressive and demanding, trying to drive away her thoughts of Wallace, of what had almost happened between them. Jeremy did his best to keep up, but when Chace's pager went off at three minutes before two and she showed no signs of answering it, he took it as an excuse and withdrew from her, then collapsed beside her on the bed.

"Maybe you should get that?" he asked.

Chace slumped into the pillows, feeling her heartbeat rattling in her breast. The pager went off again, and with its trilling, the night revealed itself to her for what it was, and she felt heat rushing into her face. She pushed herself up quickly, twisting to the side of the bed, catching Jeremy in the corner of her eye, stripping off his condom. The pager was still affixed to her belt, and her belt still affixed to her jeans, and she gouged at it with her thumb until it was silent, then read the message, certain she knew what it would demand of her, that it would be the DOO calling her to the Ops Room.

But it wasn't, and the message she read was both surprising and troubling.

She began pulling on her clothes, dressing with a practiced speed that came from being naked in front of a stranger too many times before. Jeremy, lying on the bed and above the mussed covers, didn't move, watching, perspiration shining on his skin in the weak light that dripped in from the street.

When her belt was fastened and she was pulling on her shoes, Chace said, "I'm sorry, I have to go."

"Nah, it's no trouble."

"I had a lovely night," she lied.

"Me, too." He pushed himself up on an elbow, smiled. "I'd love to do it again sometime."

She had her jacket on by then and was halfway to the door.

"No," Chace said.

●

She waited until she hit Regent Street before digging out her mobile to make the call, and Crocker answered on the first ring.

"Why the hell aren't you at home?" he demanded.

"You said I couldn't leave London, you didn't say I—"

"I bloody know what I bloody said. Where are you now?"

"Regent Street."

"Where none of the tube lines are up and running as yet." She heard the whistle of his breath as he exhaled cigarette smoke. "Come in. Now."

"Am I bound for parts unknown?"

"Now," Crocker repeated, and hung up.

●

The first thing that surprised her when she reached Crocker's office was that someone had made coffee, and since Kate was presumably at home and asleep, Chace was forced to conclude that it had been Crocker himself. Unless he'd forced someone on the janitorial staff to do it, which wasn't out of the question but somehow seemed even more implausible.

The second thing was that Crocker wasn't alone, and as Chace entered the inner office, she immediately regretted stopping to fix herself a cup of her own.

The man seated opposite Crocker rose immediately when she entered. She read him as hovering near forty, tanned skin that, beneath Crocker's fluorescents, made him look almost a dusky orange. His hair was brown, cut close, the narrow shape of his face broken by a pair of broad black-framed eyeglasses of the kind favored by rocket scientists and fashionably nerdy software engineers everywhere. His suit looked both uncomfortable and inappropriate, better for fall or winter than the dying days of summer, and hung loosely on his frame. Perhaps five foot seven, maybe five eight, and when he rose, his arms dangled at his sides, loose, as if he was unsure of what to do with them.

Crocker indicated Chace and told the man, "Tara Chace."

"So I see," the man said, and the accent gave him away as Israeli.

"Noah Landau," Crocker explained to her. "Mr. Landau runs the Metsada Division of the Mossad."

"You would call it like your Special Operations Division," Landau offered.

"A pleasure to meet you, sir."

Landau barely nodded, looking her over, taking his time to do it. Chace resisted the urge to brush at her hair and hoped to God she had managed to get her clothes on right way round. His eyes were brown, Chace noted, and seemed smaller behind his thick lenses.

He maintained the survey for several seconds before returning to his seat and facing Crocker once more.

"Sorry to get you out of bed," Crocker told her. "But I thought you should hear this, as you may end up going as backup on the operation."

"Her?" Landau asked.

"She's Head of Section, Mr. Landau. She's the best I have for this kind of job."

"I would not presume to dispute that. But we are talking about Yemen, and a European woman in Yemen will attract notice."

"She won't be running deep. In and out, provided we can fix the dates of travel."

"Deep or not, she will need an adequate cover. I don't want your support for my agents to be taken into custody before the operation is completed. And an English woman traveling in Yemen alone? I think it would raise suspicion. You speak Arabic?"

The last had been directed to her, so Chace answered, saying, "Words and phrases, sir. No fluency."

Landau looked back to Crocker, shrugged.

"Tell him what you are fluent in, Tara."

"I can pass as native in French and Italian. My French is best, but the Italian is a very close second. My German and Spanish are both fluent, not native, and my Russian is passable."

"So you see we have some room to work," Crocker said.

"So I do." Landau considered, then glanced to

Chace, as if begrudging her a reevaluation. "She should sit."

"Tara."

"Thank you, sir."

Landau waited until she'd taken the seat beside him, then said, "We know that Dr. Faud bin Abdullah al-Shimmari will be visiting Yemen sometime during the month of September, Miss Chace. We know that he will be in San'a', to meet with a man named Muhriz el-Sayd. Do you know this name?"

"El-Sayd's the tactical operations man for the Egyptian Islamic Jihad. Trained under Ayman Al-Zawahiri, and like Al-Zawahiri was educated as a psychiatrist, I believe. Responsible for the murder of seven German tourists in Luxor in '96, the bombing of the Beit-Shalom school in Elat in '98, and the attempted bombing of the U.S. embassy in Albania in 2000. EIJ merged with al-Qaeda in late 2001, if I remember correctly."

Landau cleared his throat. "We also have evidence tying him to a car bombing in Tel Aviv in May of 1997."

"I was not aware of that, sir."

"Not many are, Miss Chace." Landau removed his glasses, held them up to the fluorescent lights above, examining them. "We understand that you are seeking Faud. We have been seeking el-Sayd. Both men are untouchable in their native countries, and for this reason, both men avoid travel if at all possible."

He brought the glasses to his mouth, blowing on

each lens, then using the corner of his jacket to wipe them clean.

"Both men are now exposing themselves by journeying to Yemen for a meeting," he continued. "While we do not wish to assume the purpose behind your recent inquiries into Faud's whereabouts, I have no such qualms sharing with you ours with regard to el-Sayd."

"They want him dead," Crocker told Chace.

Chace nodded, mostly because she couldn't think of anything to say to that.

"Faud is responsible for the attacks on the Underground," Crocker told Landau.

"Yes. So, you see, we have a common purpose, if not a shared target."

"Do you have the dates of travel?" Chace asked.

Landau shook his head. "No. Nor is it likely that we will be able to gather that information by ourselves. But you have paths not open to us. People who would ignore our inquiries will answer yours. And we do have other information that we would be willing to share, things we have learned about Faud's itinerary."

Chace looked a question at Crocker. "It's certainly very interesting, sir."

Crocker thought for a moment, then reached for the intercom on his desk, bore down on one of the keys as he got to his feet.

"Escort, please," he told the intercom, and then asked Landau, "How long will you be in town?"

"Only until tomorrow night," Landau answered.

"I'm staying at the Vicarage Hotel, under the name Simon, if you wish to speak further."

"I can't guarantee an answer for you before you head back to Tel Aviv."

Landau shrugged again, as if Crocker had stated the obvious. "Time is pressing, Mr. Crocker. Delays will cost us the opportunity."

There was a rustle from the doorway behind Chace, and the discreet clearing of a throat as the escort announced his presence.

"This gentleman will escort you out," Crocker said.

Landau rose, extending his hand to Crocker, and Chace got to her feet as well, to maintain respect. He offered her his hand next, and his grip was firm, the handshake brief.

"We'll do everything we can to move quickly," Crocker said. "Thank you for coming."

They waited until they heard the door to the outer office close, then took their seats again. Crocker brought a cigarette to life, then arched an eyebrow as he watched Chace do the same. Without comment, he slid the ashtray on his desk closer to her.

"He wants us to do both?" Chace asked.

Crocker shook his head. "He's offering to have one of his people do both, provided we can get him the dates."

"Why doesn't he go to the Americans?"

"I'm not sure. The White House has been putting a lot of pressure on the Israelis to play nice, maybe because they still think that peace in the Middle East will lead to the Second Coming of Christ."

"You scare me when you say things like that, because I know you're not joking."

"Not nearly as much as they scare me. There are some very strange ideas coming out of Washington these days. God only knows what they've got cooking with the Egyptians."

Chace frowned. "El-Sayd's a terrorist, a known one. EIJ is on the list."

"You know damn well none of that matters in the face of politics. And that's precisely Landau's problem at the moment. The Mossad makes inquiries into el-Sayd's travel, the CIA will know what they're up to. We make inquiries about Faud, it avoids the problem."

"How'd he know we were after Faud?"

Crocker cracked a tired smile. "Nothing nefarious. Rayburn put the word out to all the Friends as soon as conops came down that we were looking for him."

"Well, in that case Faud *definitely* knows we're after him," Chace said drily. "You trust Landau to do the job?"

"Are you asking if I think his people can take out both Faud and el-Sayd?"

"Yes."

"Without question. But he won't get a chance. If we get the dates, I'm sending you."

"Not to be contrary, but why not let them have it?"

"Are you saying you don't want it?"

"Of course that's not what I'm saying. I'm trying to understand the thinking."

"Two reasons," Crocker said. "Unless Rayburn pulls a miracle out of his network, I'll have to go to Cheng to get the information. Then I'll have to pass it to Landau. At which point Landau hits both Faud and el-Sayd, and the CIA wonders how it was the Mossad knew where and when to strike. The distance between that question and us is the distance between here and Grosvenor Square. That's one.

"Two, Faud's the target, not el-Sayd. El-Sayd is a bonus, and if we pull it off, the Mossad will owe us, and by extension, the Israélis. I can use that, and I'm not about to let the opportunity pass us by."

Chace took it in, nodded her understanding. "It's mine?"

"Yes."

"I thought I was going to have to arm-wrestle Poole for it."

"It's Yemen, it's September, tail end of the holiday season," Crocker said. "I'll get on to Mission Planning, but we can place you as an Italian tourist, one of those women who take a danger tour in hopes of being kidnapped by local tribesmen."

Chace rolled her eyes, not so much at the suggested cover as at the viability of it. Perhaps it was because she already had enough adrenaline in her life, but the thought of paying money for the chance to be abducted in some *Arabian Nights* scenario held absolutely no appeal for her. It didn't alter the fact that Crocker was correct, however; European women, and for some reason Italian women in particular, had been making such trips exactly as described. They would be cordially abducted from tourist spots outside of San'a' by local tribes, then ransomed back to the Yemeni government in exchange for various concessions such as new wells for a village or road repairs. By all reports, the abductees were treated very well by their hosts, who knew a good game when they saw one. Chace had even heard of firms that sold tours with precisely this scenario in mind.

"I should brush up the Italian, then," Chace said. "You know that Landau will be expecting us to take the job from him."

"I'm sure of it. But he came anyway, which means he can live with that, as long as the job gets done."

"Two for the price of one," Chace mused.

"Think of it as a fire sale," Crocker said.

14

London—U.S. Embassy, Grosvenor Square
2 September 1818 GMT

"**Why was Noah Landau** in to see you?" Cheng asked Crocker.

"I answered that when I made the request on Tuesday," Crocker said. "The Mossad trapped a phone call between Dr. Faud bin Abdullah al-Shimmari and another—unidentified—party, where Faud discussed plans to visit Yemen sometime this month. Mossad knew we were after Faud, they gave the information to us."

Cheng rocked the pen between her index and middle fingers faster, making the movement into a blur, scowling at him. Then she stopped and rammed the pen back into the mug on her desk that she used as its holder. The mug, Crocker noted, had the seal of the Central Intelligence Agency stenciled on its side.

"In person?"

"We had other things to discuss."

"Why didn't he go to Rayburn?"

"Who says he didn't? And after Rayburn, he came to me."

"You're a fucking liar."

"I don't need to take this abuse from you," Crocker said mildly. "I've got a C and a Deputy Chief who are more than eager to do the same thing. They're better at it, by the way."

"Give me a chance," Cheng retorted. "I'm just getting started."

"Do you have something for me or not, Angela?"

"I have something for you. It's got a point at the end, and it's headed straight for your crotch." Cheng brought her hands up to her head, ran her fingers through her hair, making it fall back in sheets, clearly exasperated. "Your opposite number in the Mossad doesn't just fly from Tel Aviv to pass over information that could just as easily have come from their resident. Noah Landau doesn't meet with you simply to drop good news in your lap."

"He felt the information should be presented in person."

"He wanted to cut a deal."

"Does that surprise you?"

Cheng shook her head vigorously enough to again send her hair into the air. "But it makes me wonder what he wants in exchange."

"That's none of your business."

"It is if it affects American interests in the region."

"How is our taking out Faud going to hurt American interests in the region? I'd think it would help."

"If that's all you do."

Now it was Crocker's turn to play exasperation. "It's all I'm planning on doing. Provided, of course, that your people have learned when Dr. Faud bin Abdullah al-Shimmari is going to be in San'a'."

The stare Cheng fixed him with was cold with her frustration. Then she sighed and opened the folder resting before her on the desk.

"We don't have anything reliable coming out of Jeddah," Cheng said. "But we've got a couple of people in place in Yemen, and there's been activity. One of our boys spread some money around and learned that a VIP from Saudi is scheduled to arrive the week of the fifth. We can't be certain it's Faud, but given the Mossad intel, it seems likely."

"That's this Sunday."

"I know," Cheng said pointedly.

"The week of the fifth? Nothing more specific?"

"We're assuming that Faud's keeping the details vague as a security precaution. Yemen is hot right now, you know the drill. You've got advisers in country, we've got advisers in country, the whole place is jumping with the black balaclava set."

Crocker frowned. "You'd think Faud would be avoiding the place."

"Why bother?" Cheng said. "He knows we don't have evidence to charge him with anything, and he knows the Yemeni authorities wouldn't dare touch him."

She closed the folder, handed it over to Crocker.

"You can read this one yourself, but it stays here. I'll have a copy sent to you via the JIC."

"I'll make sure Simon knows it's coming," he said, taking the folder and settling back in the chair. The chairs in Cheng's office were infinitely nicer than the ones in his own, and he resented how much more comfortable he found them. He flipped the folder open, read the brief assessment inside, determining that it was exactly as Cheng had described. He closed it again, sighed, and pulled himself out of the chair.

"Who're you sending?"

"Haven't decided yet."

"Stop lying to me. Is it going to be Chace?"

"Haven't decided yet."

"It should be Chace," Cheng said. "She's the best you have."

●

"Poole," Weldon told Crocker early the next afternoon.

"I'm sorry, sir?"

"Send Poole to Yemen."

Crocker clenched his fists, forced them open again, grateful that he was holding them behind his back as he stood in front of the Deputy Chief's desk. Outside the windows, London was blanketed in gray, a weak rain drifting down.

Weldon returned his attention to the proposal Crocker had brought to his desk, flipping through the three pages detailing what, Crocker hoped, would become Operation: Tanglefoot. He had spent much of the previous night drafting the document, much to the annoyance of his wife, Jenny, who was left alone to entertain his parents. He'd handed the proposal to Kate first thing that morning, and she had promptly typed it up and then submitted it for approval to the requisite department heads. When Weldon flipped to the last sheet, Crocker could see Rayburn's signature next to his own.

Two of the signature lines remained blank. One for the Deputy Chief, one for C. Without signatures from both, the operation would never happen. Or at least never happen with proper authorization.

It wasn't beyond Crocker to play out of bounds. He'd mounted operations without approval before, but it was always a risky proposition, and he never did it without a compelling reason, at least to him. But in this instance, there was simply no reason to try and circumvent the chain of command. Conops had come down with the PM's blessing, and unless things had radically changed in the last three weeks, there was no reason to think that HMG had changed its mind about the fate of Dr. Faud.

Weldon let the sheets drop back atop one another, then tilted back in his chair to look Crocker in the eye.

"Send Poole," he repeated. "You don't know how long it will be before Faud shows, and you'll want your Minder in country by tomorrow, latest. Could be a week whoever it is finds himself left there, twiddling his thumbs. Poole can go with military cover, it circumvents the weapon issue, and it will make it easy for him to stay unnoticed and to deploy. Should make his egress easier as well."

"I disagree, sir. Military personnel working in Yemen are almost universally being surveilled by one force or another—"

"It shouldn't matter. They won't know who he is."

"They'll know he's British, and if he's spotted around the scene after the assassination—assuming it goes off—it'll splash back on us."

Weldon's mouth twisted. "That's a valid point."

"I certainly thought so."

"There's no need to get testy, Paul."

"I don't appreciate being second-guessed in this fashion, sir. I am the Director of Operations, operational planning is my purview, not yours."

"And mine is oversight. Something you could stand a little more of, I daresay."

Crocker continued to stare over Weldon's head, out the window, watching the rain fall.

"If you send Chace, she's going alone?"

"As detailed in the proposal, yes, sir."

"Why no backup?"

"Conops specified concealment of origin. Two Minders are that much more likely to be made."

It was a lie, but Crocker had no intention of letting Weldon know that he was relying on Landau's people for backup. The thought of working with the Israelis on an assassination of a Saudi religious figure in Yemen would cause the Deputy Chief to break out in hives.

Weldon grunted, reached for his favorite fountain pen, black lacquered with mother-of-pearl inlay, and slowly unscrewed its cap as he reviewed the proposal a final time. When he reached the last page, he laboriously signed his name, then capped the pen, replaced it, closed the folder, and handed it to Crocker.

"You should take it up to C."

"Very good, sir," Crocker said, leaving Weldon to his fears, and the rain at his window.

●

Barclay, like Weldon, kept Crocker waiting, his chin resting on his steepled hands while he read the proposal. He read it slowly, very slowly, as Weldon had, and Crocker was certain Barclay did it to annoy him. When he was finally finished, he lowered his hands and gazed levelly at Crocker.

"Now tell me what you've neglected to include in this proposal," Barclay ordered.

"I don't follow, sir."

"Of course you do." Barclay tapped the pages before him. "I know you, Crocker, I know every one of your little tricks, and all of your back-alley games. You don't meet with the head of the Metsada in my building at three in the morning and not cut yourself a deal on the side. Now, I want you to tell me what the Israelis wanted in exchange for their information, and I want it now."

"Landau asked for the meeting as soon as he arrived, sir. As he was leaving for Tel Aviv the next day, I couldn't exactly ask him to call again later."

"Don't lie to me," Barclay snapped. "Landau left on El-Al flight thirty-seven at seventeen-twenty hours on Tuesday the thirty-first. He could have met with you at any point during the day, and he didn't. I don't like it when you're here in the small hours, I never have. It means you're in your kitchen, cooking something likely to make me ill to the stomach."

Crocker fought off a smile at the thought of his C doubled over and vomiting in the executive lavatory.

"Either you tell me about the deal you cut with Landau, or I withhold my signature," Barclay said.

"If I may remind you, sir, the proposal for Operation: Tanglefoot has been prepared in response to HMG's issuance of conops, dated Tuesday, seventeen August—"

Barclay slapped both palms down on his desk violently, half-starting out of his chair. "Who the hell do you think you are? You stand there and condescend to me, telling *me* about conops issuance when I've been fielding calls from the Prime Minister twice a day for the last month, demanding to know what we're waiting for, telling me to get on with it?"

"All you have to do is sign off on the proposal and you'll have his answer," Crocker said.

Barclay, now on his feet, glared at Crocker in what could only be described as a mixture of amazement and fury.

"Every time I believe I've seen the limits of your arrogance, you delight in proving me wrong," Barclay said. "Yes, Crocker, I know how to make my Prime Minister happy. But I'm not about to offer him hollow comfort, not if it's liable to come back and bite this Government in the ankle, or somewhere higher.

"You think you can trump me, that I will bow to pressure from above. You're wrong. I assure you, I will happily weather any dressing-down Downing Street delivers, rather than authorize an operation the scope of which I am unaware."

The two men glared at each other, until Crocker slid his eyes away, looking past Barclay's shoulder.

"Very well." Barclay closed the folder, all but tossing it back at Crocker. "Tanglefoot is denied. Come up with something else."

"There won't be another opportunity for months, if not years."

Barclay, already settled again behind his desk, reached for the stack of papers awaiting his attention to the left of the blotter. Without looking up, he said, "Pity."

Crocker turned the folder in his hands, thinking. Barclay's head remained bowed as he began reading the latest needs projections from the East Asian desk.

"That's all," Barclay said, still engrossed in his reading. "You're dismissed."

Crocker sighed, dropped the proposal down once again in front of Barclay. "Muhriz el-Sayd."

Barclay took his time, leaning back in his chair. He kept the look of satisfaction on his face in check, but enough of it survived the process to make it plain they both knew who had won the round.

"Go on."

"He's EIJ, commands tactical operations," Crocker

said. "The Mossad wants him dead. He's the man Faud will be meeting in Yemen."

"Landau wants us to do the job on both men. Is that it?"

Crocker shook his head. "Landau had the itinerary, but not the dates. In exchange for us providing him with the dates of travel, his people would take Faud when they hit el-Sayd."

"Much to the chagrin of the Americans."

"I'm sure."

"So Chace is going as backup to a Mossad hit squad?"

Again Crocker shook his head. "Chace is going to assassinate Faud, that's all."

"You expect me to believe that she'll leave el-Sayd alone?"

"She'll be ordered to take no action in the pursuit of el-Sayd," Crocker said, picking his words carefully.

Barclay gave him a look of thinly veiled suspicion. "So you're just going to forget that the Mossad expected something in return for their information?"

"I made no promises to Landau, sir. If he assumed we had an arrangement in place, that's his error, not mine, and not the Firm's."

"He won't like it," Barclay mused. "If he realizes what you're up to, he's liable to send in people of his own to go after el-Sayd. That could foul the attempt on Faud."

"It is a possibility," Crocker said.

Barclay fingered the proposal, considering, then

plucked his pen from its holder and scribbled his signature on the last page.

"You should tell him that Chace *will* be going after el-Sayd," Barclay said. "He doesn't need to know that we've no intention of pursuing it, and it could keep the Mossad off our backs."

"That was my plan, sir."

"Then for once we're in agreement." He handed the proposal back to Crocker. "Copies to Downing Street and the FCO by close of day, if you please."

"Very good, sir."

"Don't leave just yet."

Crocker tucked the folder under his arm, waiting for the rest of it.

"I want a success on this, Paul," Barclay said softly. "You've just been handed an opportunity to prove the worth of your precious Special Section, not just to me but to the Government. This is an assassination, nothing less, and anything less than Faud's death will result in mission failure. Whatever it takes, Faud doesn't leave Yemen alive."

"There are limits to what even Chace can do."

"She's the leader of the Special Section," Barclay said. "I think it's high time she proves just how special she is."

15

**Saudi Arabia—Tabuk Province,
Residence of Prince Salih
bin Muhammad bin Sultan
3 September 1404 Local (GMT+3.00)**

For Sinan, it had been two-plus weeks of growing disgust and frustration, watching the Prince pay lip service to everything they believed, everything they had been taught, only to swiftly pivot and shamelessly bury himself in behavior that should have cost him his head, literally. That Abdul Aziz had condemned both Matteen and him to bear witness made him feel further betrayed, and bewildered.

Had he not proven himself in the West Bank? Had he not gone to act with Hamas as ordered, and had he not further culled the weak from their pack with the removal of Aamil? Abdul Aziz had told him, in front of the camp, that he had done well, that he had acted as a *jihadi* should. He had, in front of the camp, declared Sinan bin al-Baari a True Warrior in the name of Allah, all mercies upon him.

Had Abdul Aziz lied? Was he still condemned as an outsider—a Muslim, yes, even a Wahhabist, yes, but not an Arab—and therefore never to be fully trusted?

It had occurred to Sinan that this might be a test. If so, he reflected, it was a particularly grueling one. The Prince seemed eager to violate every prohibition in Islam short of eating pork, and Sinan suspected that, at some point, the Prince had probably violated that prohibition as well.

After Abdul Aziz had departed with the others from the camp, the Prince had ordered Hazim to show Sinan and Matteen to their rooms, wishing them both a good night and a pleasant rest under Allah's watchful gaze and inviting them to join him for breakfast the next morning. Hazim had guided them to "modest guest rooms," which had been anything but. Sinan's bed had been the largest he had ever seen, and with a water-filled mattress, to boot. The bathroom had been larger than the admittedly small house he'd been raised in near Sheffield, and after enjoying the luxury of a shower, he had tried to sleep for the few hours that remained of the night. After months of his cot in the camp, the bed had seemed a tempting proposition.

A false temptation, much to his surprise. He'd ultimately wrapped himself in a blanket on the carpeted floor, sleeping in that fashion until he'd been woken by the muezzin's call to prayer, played through speakers outside the mansion. He had roused himself, dressed, and prayed toward Mekkah, then donned his Kalashnikov and cautiously emerged from his room.

Matteen had emerged at the same time, and together the two men had gone in search of their breakfast, not wishing to insult the Prince by appearing tardy. Hazim was nowhere to be found, but another servant, Hazim's age and just as attentive, had offered to guide them. While the boy led them through the maze of the house, Sinan and Matteen had talked of how they would approach their duty.

"We are not guards," Sinan had muttered. "This is not our work."

"I don't believe we'll have to worry about that," Matteen had replied.

●

Matteen had been correct.

From the moment they sat down to dine on a breakfast of dates, figs, pastries, and tea with the Prince, the Prince made it clear what he wanted from them.

"Your battles! Tell me everything," he said. "I want to hear it all, every detail! I want to hear your stories as if I was there, beside you. I want to hear them so that your memories become my own. So that we will be brothers, truly."

Matteen and Sinan had exchanged looks then, and Sinan had known they both thought the same thing. Sinan was proud, very proud, of what he had done, and had hopes for what more he would do. But what he had done, he had done in the name of

jihad, to fight for *tawhid*, for the belief in the Oneness of God, as Wahhabism required.

It was not done for bragging rights, for gloating,
for anyone or anything. It was done for Allah, praise
Him, and that any man, beggar or Prince of the
House of Saud, would want to lay claim to it as well
bordered on blasphemy.

He was relieved when, at the Prince's insistence,
Matteen began telling him some of what had happened in Tora-Bora.

"You saw the picture?" the Prince interrupted.
"In the study?"

Both men knew exactly the one the Prince
meant, and Matteen nodded.

"That was in '98," the Prince said, and the practiced nonchalance with which he said it made Sinan
want to spit out his meal and toss the mess across
the table. "I brought Usama a check, stayed with
him at the camp outside Asadabad, in Kunar
province. We flew falcons together. He's a gifted fal-
coner."

The Prince smiled at them, waited for an acknowledgment.

"I didn't know that," Sinan said.

"Oh, yes. Loves falcons, ever since he was a boy."

"Do you keep falcons, Your Highness?" Matteen
asked after another painful pause.

"I do. Would you like to see them?"

"If it wouldn't interfere with our duties for you,
yes, please."

"No, no, don't worry about that. I have bodyguards, they are the best, you know. No, that's not

why you're here. You're here so we may get to know one another, so that we may become friends, brothers in arms."

Sinan had nodded, finishing his tea, and thinking that if Allah were truly merciful, he would strike the Prince down very soon indeed.

●

So for two-plus weeks, Sinan and Matteen had been the Prince's friends. They had stayed with him in his palace. They had enjoyed his hospitality at royal insistence, sharing their stories again and again. Sinan discovered that the Prince seemed never to tire of hearing about Ma'le Efraim. They prayed five times a day, dined on lavish meals, played football on the remarkably green lawn in the incredible heat of the afternoon, accompanied the Prince as he flew his falcons, and watched sports and movies in the Prince's study.

Sinan hated all of it, but especially the time in the study, and the films. Action films with explosions and gun battles and special effects, where American heroes laid low all who opposed them, then returned home to sleep with some eager whore who had spent most of the movie half-dressed at the most.

But the Prince had other films as well, and after their first week, he broke those out. These were home movies, videos shot in Monaco and Beverly Hills and Marbella, where the Prince and other members of the royal family went to pursue all those things forbidden at home. That the Prince would show these films to them troubled Sinan, until he realized the Prince's thinking.

Sinan and Matteen were not Saudi, after all. Sinan, in particular, had come from the West. Whether the Prince mistakenly took that to mean that Sinan had shared in the things he was showing them, Sinan didn't know, but it was clear that the Prince felt that not just he but they, Sinan and Matteen too, were held to a different standard.

In the home movies, the Prince rode Jet-Skis and played roulette and purchased Rolexes and danced with blondes who wore little more than the jewels the Prince himself had given them. So did the other princes and their families. One of the videotapes was nothing but footage of the women the Prince had taken to his bed in these places, alone or two or three at a time.

Sinan knew the Prince was married, and had three wives, and ten children by those wives. He knew that the Prince believed himself to be righteous, even as he showed them these movies, twisting in his leather chair to hide his erection.

If Allah were merciful, Sinan vowed again.

●

In early September—Sinan wasn't sure of the date—the Prince presented Matteen and Sinan with gifts. This wasn't new. He had already given them new Kalashnikovs, and new pistols, too, Glocks that could weather almost anything the desert would throw at them. But this time he presented them each with a small white box, not much larger than Sinan's hand, nor much thicker, and wrapped with a green silk bow.

Inside, each of them discovered a passport for the Kingdom of Saudi Arabia.

The documents were real, not forgeries, and Sinan's had his name, his *true* name of al-Baari, and the surge of gratitude he felt when he saw that confounded him. That the Prince would do this for him, after all he had thought of the man, gave him guilt.

"We are taking a trip," the Prince told them. "We are going to Yemen."

16

Chace beat Crocker to the Ops Room by a minute, was getting a light from Ronald Taylor at the Duty Operations Desk when he entered.

"D-Ops on the floor," Ron said.

Crocker made a beeline to them, dropped the folder in his hand into Taylor's lap, saying, "Designation is Tanglefoot, Minder One allocated."

"Operation: Tanglefoot," Ron echoed.

"Lex? Put it up."

At the MCO desk, Alexis tapped on her keyboard, and the plasma screen representation of the world redrew itself, now with a lime-green halo surrounding Yemen. The call-out appeared beside it on the map, and Chace watched as the letters, one by one, appeared.

"I hope that doesn't mean I'm liable to be tripped up," Chace said. "Tanglefoot."

"It was either that or Lemontree," Crocker said. "I hate that fucking computer."

Chace chuckled. Contrary to popular belief, mission names were chosen entirely at random, from a computer-generated list of suggestions. It was a mystery to her exactly for what criteria the computer searched, and she suspected—as did most of the Ops Room staff—that the nameless technician who had written the program in the first place had done so with a Pythonesque relish of the absurd. She had, in her time, been associated or instrumental in such operations as Shoebox, Tanlines, Eyefire, and, personal favorite, Laceboy.

Tanglefoot was positively tame in that light.

Crocker turned from the plasma wall, apparently only marginally satisfied by Lex's execution of the order, and glared at Ron. "Mission Planning's delivered the brief?"

"Right here, sir. Minder One departs Heathrow oh-seven-fifteen tomorrow the fourth, BA flight 902, arrives San'a' via Frankfurt twenty-three-twenty local, same day."

"Long flight," Chace observed.

"At least you're going first class."

"And coming back steerage."

Crocker's look was icy. "Continue, Ron."

"Arriving San'a', Minder One checks in to the Hotel Taj Sheba. It's on the outskirts of the old city, ten kilometers from the airport, but it places her centrally, and it's popular with the tourists, so she'll fit right in."

"Five star, is it?" Chace kept the sarcasm mild.

"Actually, yes."

Crocker snapped his lighter closed, jetted smoke from his nostrils. "Cover?"

"Given the nature of the mission and the possible length of stay in country, Mission Planning felt it would be best for Minder One to be working with fresh papers." Ron sorted through a briefing file on his desk, settled on a new sheet. "Diana Kelsey in Documents is doing the passport right now, going with the Italian romance-novel cover."

"I'll pack my most billowy blouses."

"You're traveling as Adriana Maribino, from Como, in the north. Should help explain your looks some."

"And I thought I'd have to dye my hair."

"That's enough," Crocker snapped. "You're as bad as Wallace ever was."

Chace doubted that. There had been times when Wallace so completely undermined the seriousness of a briefing, he'd reduced the room to stitches, leaving Crocker glaring at a sea of faces, all trying to stifle the giggles. It had earned Wallace a dressing-down by D-Ops on more than one occasion.

"Sorry, sir," she said, unrepentant.

Ron hesitated, glancing from Crocker to Chace, then back again, before resuming. "Miss Maribino is single and works as a waitress at one of Como's finer dining establishments, the Trattoria del Gesumin. Restaurant favorites are the salmon tagliatelle, saffron risotto, and osso buco. This is a big trip for Miss Maribino, and she's splurged, registered with FST Arabia for a fourteen-day 'Roads of Arabia' package. The first week is centered in and around San'a', with trips to Ar-Rawda and Wadi Dhahr, so it'll support your cover."

"Procedure," Crocker demanded.

"The Yemen Number Two, Andrew Hewitt, is the pointer. As soon as he can confirm that Faud has arrived and can provide a location, he'll contact Minder One by phoning her room at the Taj Sheba between oh-seven-ten and oh-seven-twenty."

"My wake-up call," Chace murmured.

"He'll only call once, and only after he has the information, so it's vital you be in the room at those times."

"Understood."

"Hewitt will ask how Minder One slept. If she replies that she slept well, he'll come around immediately and deliver the gun and what intelligence on the target he's been able to gather. If Minder One feels that she has been compromised in any way, either by local security or opposition forces, she will respond that she slept poorly and needs to go back to sleep.

"In that instance, fallback is three hours plus seven minutes from the time of call, at a teahouse on Az-Zubayri Street, just south of the medina wall and east of the Sa'ila." Ron checked another of the sheets arrayed before him on the DOO desk. "Incidentally, there's a chance of rain, so the Sa'ila may be running. Otherwise your weather is in the low twenties."

Which meant the nights would be colder, Chace told herself, and reminded herself to pack a sweater.

"Failing the first fallback, the Station Number Two will load a dead-drop in the Qat Suq, in which Minder One will find the weapon and a briefing on the target's location and movements. Details on the drop are still being worked out, but we'll have them before her departure."

"Is there a selection to be had, or has someone made the firearm decision for me?" Chace asked.

"Chester reports that you rated highest with the P99 and the TPH," Crocker said. "Assuming that you'll be working close, we're arming you with the TPH and a Gem-Tech Vortex suppressor."

"Twenty-five or twenty-two?"

"Twenty-two," Crocker said. "Quieter."

Chace nodded. The smaller round meant less noise, but it also meant even less damage, especially with the addition of the suppressor. Not only would she have to be close, she'd have to make each shot count and most likely need every one of them. With six in the clip and a seventh in the chamber, it wasn't a lot to work with if things went wrong.

"If it all goes off," Ron said, "Minder One will have no other contact with Hewitt or the Station after the meeting at the Taj Sheba. If there's trouble or if Minder One is blown, she's to make her way to the safehouse on Maydan al-Qa', running through the old Jewish Quarter. Clay house, basement access, there's a map to it in the briefing. Minder One goes to ground, waits for the Station to contact her. There's a waterpipe on the northern corner of the building, street-side, little bit of rope around it. She removes the rope to indicate the house is in use. If the rope isn't there when she arrives, Minder One is to avoid the safehouse altogether and take whatever action she then deems necessary to complete or abort the mission."

"The basement?" Crocker asked.

"Unlike the rest of San'a', homes in the Jewish Quarter have basements," Ron explained. "There was an imamic declaration forbidding them to build any structure taller than nine meters."

Crocker grunted.

Ron looked to Chace. "Any questions?"

"Think that covers it. I'll nip home and get my things sorted, start practicing my Italian."

"Be back here by oh–three hundred," Ron said. "Gibbons will be on the desk then, but he'll have your documentation and tickets."

"Go over it again." Crocker ground out his cigarette in the cracked ashtray on Ron's desk. "Make certain you have it cold. I want drop-loaded and drop-cleared signals for the Qat Suq, as well as two alternate escape plans for Minder One to get out of the country if for some reason it goes to hell."

"There aren't many places for her to go," Ron said. "North and she's in Saudi, west she's in the Red Sea, east she's in Oman, south she's in the Gulf of Aden—"

"I know the damn map. Two alternates."

"Yes, sir."

"When you're finished, come see me," Crocker told Chace, and then whirled and blew out of the Ops Room much as he had entered.

Both Chace and Ron watched him go without comment.

"Right, going over it again," Ron said. "You'll be traveling as Adriana Maribino, from Como. . . ."

•

"Close it," Crocker said.

Chace did as ordered, then took one of the seats in front of the desk and helped herself to one of the cigarettes remaining in Crocker's pack, resting atop the red operations folder. He remained standing, staring out the window. Night had descended, and London's lights flowed past, much like the Thames itself.

"You've got it?" Crocker asked.

"*Perfettamente*," Chace answered. "*Signorina Maribino è molto eccitata di visitare lo Yemen. Lei spera di essere rapita e stuprata fino allo sfinimento da uno stupendo indigeno.*"

"You won't have time."

Chace grinned, then said, "I noticed the briefing had no mention of el-Sayd."

"You did, did you?"

"I'm not all thick. Does that mean I don't pursue?"

"If the Mossad intel is correct, el-Sayd will be meeting with Faud. If, by chance, that's when you hit, then el-Sayd becomes collateral and an unavoidable secondary target." Crocker moved back to his chair, focused on Chace. "Am I clear?"

"Perfectly."

"The primary target is your concern. You take the secondary only if the opportunity presents itself. I don't want to burn Landau on this, but I want this blown even less. El-Sayd is a bonus, that's all. You take what you can get, and then you get the hell out of Yemen."

"Yes, sir."

Crocker leaned forward on his desk, and the stare he gave her now was as intense as any she could remember from him. "Understand something else. The security on Faud's going to be tighter than Weldon's wallet, and you're not going in armed for a gunfight with his bodyguards. If you can't get to target, if you see *anything* that makes you cranky, you abort. Don't be reckless, Tara, it'll get you killed, and I can't afford to lose another Minder, not right now."

"Understood."

Crocker scowled, as genuinely unhappy as Chace could ever remember having seen him.

"Go," he said.

17

Israel—Tel Aviv, Mossad Headquarters, Office of the Metsada Division Chief 6 September 1956 Local (GMT+3.00)

Borovsky sat with his gangly legs crossed at the ankles and propped on Landau's desk, oblivious to the folders he toppled every time he moved his feet. The desk lamp threw long shadows on the cinderblock walls of the office.

"You know, the Arabs think by doing this, with my feet like this, I'm saying you're like the dirt on which I walk." Borovsky grinned. "They would say it was an insult, Noah, that I'm saying you're less than dirt."

Landau, still on the telephone, glared at Borovsky in the hopes that the look alone would shut the man up. It seemed to work, but not until Borovsky had barked another of his laughs. He didn't move his feet, however, until Landau was off the phone.

"That was your new friend at SIS?" Borovsky asked.

"Crocker, yes."

"They're going to do it?"

"They've already started. Their agent arrived in San'a' Saturday night."

Borovsky's face seemed to grow even narrower as he pondered this. "We have no intelligence that Faud's even left that fucking desert he hides in as yet. And fuck only knows if el-Sayd is on the move."

Landau didn't speak.

Borovsky shook his head. "They don't have a date. They're shooting in the dark."

"No, Crocker would not allocate an agent on a hunch. Not even for Faud."

"You're sure?"

"I wouldn't. He won't."

"Who did he send?"

"He did not say, but I think it would be Chace, the head of his Special Section."

"He any good?"

"*She* is the head of his Special Section, Viktor."

Borovsky's surprise was apparent but short-lived. "That's smart, that's clever. We need more women, you know that? The women, they can be fucking vicious."

Landau ignored him, pinched the bridge of his nose above his eyeglasses, trying to think.

"You think Crocker just told us to grab our ankles?" Borovsky asked.

"I don't know. I'm not sure. It was always a possibility."

"I think we're about to grab our ankles."

"Why?"

"We're Jews, Noah. If history has shown us anything, it's that we get screwed in the ass at every opportunity. You gave the British a gift, a chance for *revenge*, in exchange for which we asked for the opportunity to *defend* ourselves. What do you think will happen?"

"The decisions are political, not personal."

Borovsky shook his head, looking at Landau sadly. "Killing Faud is purely personal. It will not prevent another attack like they suffered. Faud is not the planner, he is the cheerleader. They've already cut us out, Noah. They sure as hell aren't going to expose themselves to take el-Sayd, too."

"No, we know Faud and el-Sayd are going to meet. That's the logical time to strike."

"You put too much faith in the British."

"Faith has nothing to do with it. You're Intelligence, Viktor, look at it logically."

"No, logic is for planners. I don't plan, I interpret, and that is something else." Borovsky folded his hands behind his head, sighing up at the ceiling. "We're going to get screwed."

Landau nodded slightly, conceding what Borovsky had said. He'd known when he'd gone to Crocker that there was the possibility the Mossad would be left out of the loop, and he'd understood that risk. El-Sayd would never be London's priority the way Faud was, and Landau could hardly fault the people at SIS for that. Each group ostensibly did what its commanding government felt was in its best interests. He bore Crocker no ill will.

But just as SIS had to serve England, Landau and the Mossad had to serve Israel.

"It'll have to go past the Chief," he said after a moment longer.

"What will?"

"Action." Landau reached for his phone again. "Put together a briefing, Viktor. I want our man in Yemen by tomorrow night."

18

"Ciao?"

"Miss Maribino?"

"Sì?"

"How did you sleep?"

"Fine, fine. *Grazie per chiedere.*"

"Glad to hear it. Enjoy your stay."

●

Seventeen minutes later Chace heard two firm but gentle raps at her hotel room door. She rose from where she had been seated on the bed, cross-legged, going over her tourist map of San'a', and moved to the short entry hall, pressing herself against the wall as she reached its end, to keep out of the line of sight from the peephole. It was a Wallace move, and in a situation like this, pure paranoia, but, she rationalized, paranoia keeps you alive a few minutes longer.

Not that she had any reason to be paranoid. She'd been in Yemen for four days, and so far the greatest dangers had come from the potential of nonpotable water and the rather unsubtle advances of a young Frenchman from her tour group who had insisted on using her to practice his Italian.

"Sì?" she called through the door. *"Chi è?"*

"Miss Maribino? Mr. Hewitt. We met at the Al Dobaey restaurant last night?"

Chace reached out, silently turned the deadbolt on the door back, pulled the lockbar, and then rotated the doorknob just far enough to dislodge the latch. Finished, she slid back, stepping into the doorway of the bathroom. It wouldn't buy much time, but if it wasn't Hewitt, the extra time would give her the initiative should it turn out to be needed.

"Entra," she said.

The door opened, and Andrew Hewitt stepped into the room, searching for her behind his thin glasses. When he saw her watching him, he smiled in cheerful greeting, then stepped the rest of the way inside before closing the door after him. Chace waited until he threw the locks before she moved back to the bed, retrieved her cigarettes from the nightstand, and then resumed her previous posture and position. She lit a smoke, watching as Hewitt stepped out of the small hall, taking stock of the accommodations as she took stock of him.

She put him in his early thirties at the most, and better-looking than his file photograph had made him out to be. Five foot eight, broad from the shoulders down, light brown and curly hair, eyes so light blue as to have moved on to gray. His skin, which back in England had probably been quite fair, had acquired the tan and character that come from exposure to strong sun for extended periods. He wore a tan linen coat over his lightweight suit, the shirt white, the tie blue, the belt black, as were his shoes, though a thin coating of dust clung to the latter. He carried a small briefcase, oxblood-colored leather, in his left hand.

When he'd finished taking in the room, he smiled cheerfully at Chace a second time, then laid his briefcase on the foot of the bed and quickly worked the locks until they released. He lifted the lid, then turned the case to show Chace the contents. Inside, restrained with elastic straps to keep them from rattling about within, was a box of ammunition in .22, a Walther TPH that could easily have been the very same gun Chace had trained with at Fort Monkton, a Gem-Tech Vortex suppressor, a box of surgical gloves, and a rolled-up poster.

"I trust you've been enjoying Yemen?" Hewitt said. "You're still clean, I take it?"

"Pristine." If anyone had been going through her room or her things aside from the maid while she'd been out and about, they were better at hiding that fact than she was at spotting it. It wasn't a real concern; there'd been no sign whatsoever that the Yemeni authorities even knew she existed, and a random wiretap on an Italian tourist visiting San'a' was out of the question. They could speak freely here.

Cigarette in her mouth, Chace reached into the case. She took two of the gloves first, setting them aside, then removed the Walther, the box of ammunition, and the suppressor, laying them out on the map before her. English was common enough in Yemen that the switch in languages didn't throw her too much, but nonetheless, it took an effort not to answer him in Italian.

"You're certain?" Hewitt asked.

"Positive," she told him as she began checking the weapon. "No trouble at the airport, no shadows on the way to the hotel, nothing since. There's a Frenchman in the group named Billiery; at first I thought he might be a plant. He's not. He's a student."

"Keeping his hands to himself, I hope?"

"He is now," Chace said. "I think it's safe to say that the only people who know I'm here are the two of us and a handful of people in London."

"And another handful in Tel Aviv."

Chace looked up from the gun in her hand. "That suspicion or something more?"

"Straight from D-Ops. I don't know why he wanted it passed along, but there's a lot I don't know. Presumably it means something to you."

The cheerful grin came back, and Chace wondered if it was affect or sincerity. It didn't much matter to her, and she wasn't inclined to answer, so she shrugged and went back to examining the

Walther. Content that it would do its job when called upon, she set it aside and moved onto the task of loading the clip.

"What's the word on Faud?"

"Normally we'd lay down a bundle of riyals and buy information," Hewitt said. "But London told us to go softly, so it proved a little more difficult. He arrived yesterday with his bodyguards, six of them. He's staying with Saleh Al-Hebshi, in the Old City. Al-Hebshi is one of the louder resident Wahhabist *imams*, normally works out of the Al-Jami' al-Kamir—the Great Mosque—but seems to be favoring the Qubbat Talha Mosque a little more of late. Hebshi was linked to one of the Yemenis who rammed the USS *Cole* in 2000."

"When yesterday?"

"Did he arrive? Late afternoon. Arrived on a private jet from Jeddah, landed fifteen-forty, was met by Al-Hebshi at the airport. Taken by four-wheel-drive convoy to Al-Hebshi's home."

"How large was the convoy?"

"Three vehicles. Al-Hebshi had two guards of his own." Hewitt's look was full of sympathy. "I'm afraid you're going to find it very hard to get Faud alone."

Chace finished with the clip, set it aside, and put out her cigarette in the ashtray on the nightstand, then gave Hewitt a reappraisal. Number Twos were the legmen for London, while the Number Ones maintained cover and attended the day-to-day running of the Station. Most every One, and quite a few Twos, viewed a Minder's arrival in their terrain with hostility or loathing or both. Minders were trouble for a Station, sent in to do a job, to get a result, and then to depart once more. For the Station, that quite often meant the residents had a mess to clean up, a politically sensitive, potentially law-breaking mess.

So Chace was used to dealing with recalcitrant Twos and bitter Ones who wanted nothing more than for her to leave them alone.

Hewitt didn't seem to be one of those, and while she didn't show it to him, she appreciated the fact.

She swept the box and suppressor from the map, saying, "Show me where Al-Hebshi lives."

"I'm ahead of you there." Hewitt removed the poster from the case, slid the elastic off its end and onto his wrist, and then unrolled it in front of her, revealing a detailed map of the Old City. He used the gun and the box of ammunition to weigh the ends down. "Think you'll find this a bit more useful than that one provided by the General Tourism Authority. You'll see I've already marked the key spots."

She stared at him. "All of them?"

Hewitt seemed confused for a second, then shook his head. "No, not all of them. The place you're thinking of, I think, would be right about here."

He set an index finger on the map, indicating a block well outside the walls of the Old City. There was no other indication of the safehouse aside from the pressure of his finger on the paper.

Chace nodded, and Hewitt retracted his finger.

She studied the map, noting the streets and the street names, and particularly how the same street seemed to switch identities several times within the space of only a few blocks. The Great Mosque was marked, as was the Qubbat Talha. She stayed focused on the map for several minutes, long enough for Hewitt to realize that no questions were immediately forthcoming, and so he moved to one of the two chairs in the room, beside the television, and settled himself.

It wouldn't do, Chace decided. She had to get into the Old City away from the tour, learn the lay of the land herself. She'd have to see Al-Hebshi's place, to verify what she already suspected: there was no way she'd be able to get to Faud as long as he was inside. And if Faud's travel in San'a' was, as she suspected, going to be conducted via four-wheel drive, she wasn't likely to get a crack at him in transit, either. At least not a crack at him where a twenty-two-caliber semiautomatic with seven shots would make a difference.

So far, almost every excursion she'd made had been within the confines of the tour group, an act to maintain cover more than anything else. The thought of wandering through San'a' alone didn't bother Chace; this wasn't Saudi, and while women here still lived very different lives apart from the men, the same rules simply did not apply to foreign women, seen as a strange kind of "third sex." As long as she remained culturally sensitive, traveling alone through the Old City wouldn't be a problem, and she had packed the wardrobe to do just that. A long skirt that fell to her ankles, a loose top that fell almost to midthigh and would remain unbelted to hide her shape, and a scarf to conceal her hair were all that modesty demanded.

Yemeni women, on the other hand, moved through their days hooded in their black *baltas*, shapeless cotton coat-slash-cloak combinations that effectively hid any body beneath. Almost all of them wore veils as well. It was deception of an entirely different sort, a public modesty in the face of a private vanity. Chace knew for a fact that most of the women she'd seen on the streets wore midriff-baring tops and tight designer jeans beneath their *baltas*.

Chace rolled the map once more, offered it back to Hewitt. "Anything else?"

"Sorry, that's all. When I left it this morning, Hebshi and Faud were still at the house, though I suspect they went to the Great Mosque for their morning *ziryat*."

"Why the Great Mosque and not the other one?"

"I would think its name would tell you everything you need to know. It's truly spectacular, what little I've seen of it, and I've seen very little, and I've been here two years, now. It was built sometime around A.D. 630, when the Prophet was still living, just after Islam had come to Yemen. Man like Faud, I can't imagine him being content to worship anywhere else."

Chace considered that, then nodded. "You're a perceptive fellow, Mr. Hewitt."

He lifted the case in his hand, smiled again. "Perceptive enough to know that I'm desperately hoping I won't be seeing you again."

"It's mutual, I assure you." Chace followed him down the hall, unlocked the door so he could exit.

"Best of luck," Hewitt said.

Chace locked the door again after he'd left.

●

She started the walk through the Suq al-Milh, literally the salt market, though as far as Chace could ascertain, salt was a very small part of what was for sale. In truth, the *suq* seemed comprised of dozens of other, smaller markets, with vendors selling everything from silks to jewelry to uniquely curved tribesmen's daggers called *jambiya*. It was warm but not uncomfortable, and Chace assumed the sky was blue, but Ron's projected rain hadn't come, and as a result, clouds of dust hung endlessly in the air, kicked up by foot traffic or, worse, vehicle traffic.

Chace made her way through the noise, jabbered conversations, and blasts of music played from boom boxes, bootlegs sold by vendors. Men sat in the shade at the sides of the streets, talking, smoking, chewing *qat*, others walking hand in hand, showing their friendship. A few were armed, sporting antique carbines and rifles, weapons left over from the Ottoman occupation that had ended in 1911, as well as the modern Middle Eastern mainstay, the Kalashnikov AK-47.

She drew the eyes of everyone, some briefly, others longer. Chace found it necessary to remind herself that she was a curiosity, even in her modest dress. Near Bab al-Yaman, two very excited young boys ran up to her, shouting in Arabic, "Welcome to Yemen!" and then repeating it in English before darting away again.

"*Shukran*," she called after them, then paused on the street, trying to reorient herself. From the hotel, the minarets and structures of the city were clearly visible. Standing in the Old City, however, the houses were crammed together, built five and six stories high, and blocking any view of the horizon. From where she stood, the Great Mosque could only be a few hundred meters to the west of her, but looking around, she saw no sign of it.

An older man, in *futa*, shirt, and jacket, passed on her left. "*Haram*," he growled. "*Haram*."

Chace glanced down, couldn't see what had caused the offense. Her skirt fell to her boots, the only skin she was showing at her face and her hands.

"*Ismahlee*," she said, trying to apologize, not certain why.

The man stopped, gestured roughly at her face with the back of his hand, then moved back into the crowd. Chace reflexively put a hand to her head, felt the scarf in place, ran her fingers along its edge. Some of her hair had crept loose at her temple, and she quickly tucked it back into place.

Crisis averted, she thought, and made the turn north out of the square, and instantly became certain that she was being followed.

The street narrowed, and the air thickened with a collision of spices: cinnamon, cardamom, ginger, pepper, mint. Chace passed a group of three women, clad in black, and she identified them as San'ani from the red and white eyes marked on their black veils. She offered them a smile, saw the lines curve at the corners of their eyes as they answered the expression with smiles of their own, and then continued moving north, threading through the stalls and shacks. Over the sounds of the market, she heard a speaker blaring the muezzin's call, glanced down, and pulled back her sleeve enough to read her watch. Noon call to worship.

Almost immediately the flow of traffic altered, and Chace moved along with it until she saw the walls surrounding the Great Mosque. Traffic was flowing through the main doors, mostly men, but she noted several women wrapped in *baltas*, veiled in the traditional black *shar-shaf* or the painted *lithma*, moving with them, unmolested and mostly ignored. She took it in as best she could without pausing and, alongside the main entrance, from across the street, stole a glance at the revealed interior, glimpsing the colonnaded inner hall and beyond it the fountain and ablution pool. She looked away before anyone could take offense, moving on.

Three Toyota SUVs were parked on the street, six men standing with Kalashnikovs by the vehicles, posture bored while trying to remain watchful. From their dress, Chace picked two of them as locals, wearing the *futa*-jacket combination most Yemeni men favored. The others stood in drab and worn fatigues, their heads covered with white and checkered *kuffiyah*, either leaning against the cars or watching the street.

She didn't break stride, looking past them, continuing north. In her periphery, she saw them mark her passage, one of them gesturing, a couple of them speaking. The irrational fear that they knew who she was, what she was doing, why she was there, raced through Chace's mind before she shoved it aside.

The thought moved, but reluctantly. There was always the possibility that she had been blown, that somehow, some way, Faud or someone else knew she was coming. A weakness in the local network, a wrong word, or something more politically motivated perhaps, a scuffle higher on the food chain in London, Tel Aviv, or Washington, D.C., and that could be all it would take.

She was still being followed.

She crossed Talha Street, made her way past the strangely empty front of the Center for Arabian Language and Eastern Studies, stopped at a sidewalk café that was nothing more than three rickety tables with cracked wooden chairs outside a storefront. There were three men settling at another table, and the owner emerged and went to them first, taking their order before giving Chace his attention. It was the hierarchy, men first, women last, and tourist women somewhere in between.

"Is-salamu 'alaykum."

"Wa 'alaykum is-salam," Chace responded. "Mumkin sha'i talqim."

The owner smiled, showing crooked and clean

teeth, delighted with her attempts at the language. "You speak English?"

"A little. *Ana italiya.*"

"No, no *italiya*, but English *tammam*. Tea?"

"*Shukran.*"

He moved back inside, and Chace smoothed her skirt, making certain that nothing more offensive than her ankles could be seen before looking over the street. The three men were watching her, as interested as the proprietor, if not as friendly, and she avoided eye contact and did not smile. It was the appropriate response, and they turned their attentions back to one another.

Her shadow was across the street, bartering with a vendor for a bottle of water. Male, mustached and bearded, by his dress Yemeni, but Chace didn't trust that. Certainly not European, and nothing in his appearance linked him to the group she'd seen clustered at the SUVs.

The proprietor brought her tea, took her riyals in exchange. She sipped from the small glass, the tea hot enough to burn her hand if she held on for too long, and incredibly sweet.

Her shadow had moved down the street, back toward the Center, drinking his water. He wasn't clumsy and he wasn't obvious, but now she was sure he was tailing her, simply because he wasn't doing more than waiting. When he raised his bottle, sunlight reflected off the watch at his wrist and she noted that he wore it face-out rather than face-in.

She considered, the thought that she'd been blown again rearing its head, and this time she had to give it more attention. There was no London backup, and there was to be no further contact with the Station. Either the tail was local, perhaps part of the Faud-Hebshi connection, or he was another player, maybe Mossad.

Or he could be neither and is just looking to kidnap me, Chace thought, and for the first time became aware of the Walther tucked beneath her shirt. She'd left the suppressor in the room, wedged into the hollow of one of the bedposts, but the gun was so small and so light she'd felt safer bringing it with her than leaving it behind. Its shape made it harder to conceal, and there had been the chance, however remote, that the opportunity to kill Faud would drop in front of her.

The opportunity clearly hadn't, but all the same she was glad she had brought the gun.

The proprietor returned, cutting in front of her to clear the now-empty cup. *"Kayf halik?* You are fine?"

"Fine, yes."

"More? Another tea?"

"No, thank you."

The proprietor seemed disappointed, but the smile remained as he again left her alone.

The tail had disappeared.

Of bloody course, Chace thought, and she rose from the table, moving back onto the street, resuming her way north to the Handcraft Center, and in particular, to the Women's Branch within to do some needed shopping.

19

Israel—Tel Aviv, Mossad Headquarters, Commissary
8 September 1919 Local (GMT+3.00)

"She went shopping?" Borovsky demanded. "The British agent went shopping? Doesn't she know Yemeni silver has been shit since Operation: Magic Carpet?"

"Yosef doesn't think she was after silver." Landau switched the gas on beneath the burner, waited to hear the flame ignite. It took three clicks of the ignition before the gas caught. He moved away from the kettle, began searching the kitchen for Nescafé. "He thinks she was making a walk-through of the *suq*."

"The *suq* is fucking huge, Noah, you don't just walk through the *suq* in a day. Hell, you can't cover the *suq* in *ten* days, and even if you could, the stalls change."

Landau found the instant coffee in the cupboard above the sink, along with powdered nondairy creamer and sugar. There was also dishwasher soap, a stack of paper plates, and a can of condensed milk.

"Doesn't anyone ever clean this room?" he asked.

"Write a fucking memo."

Landau sighed, found a clean spoon in the sink, began loading coffee, sugar, and creamer into his mug. "I don't see why you're getting so worked up."

"I'm getting worked up because she doesn't have the time to waste." Borovsky began pacing the cramped break room. "El-Sayd will only allow a small window, it'll be a fucking cunt hair wide, that's what it'll be, it'll be *nothing*. And if this British bitch is out trying to get a deal on silks, she'll miss it."

"But that's not what she was doing." Landau frowned at the kettle, readjusted its position on the burner. His wife had hated it when he'd done that, always telling him it would take twice as long the more he fiddled, but he couldn't help himself. There was an optimum place to sit on the flame, and until the kettle was there, he wouldn't be happy.

"You keep saying that. So you tell me, what was she doing?"

"She's going to hit them in the Great Mosque," Landau said, and readjusted the kettle's position.

Borovsky stared at him, then tapped his temple.

"No fucking way, *we* wouldn't even do that, and we're fucking desperate."

"She's going to hit them in the Great Mosque," Landau repeated. "Or at least she'll try to. It's the only place where she knows Faud will be without armed protection."

"They still have bare hands, Noah. They'll tear her to pieces."

Landau shrugged and said nothing. The kettle was finally beginning to creak, the heat accelerating through the metal.

"Crocker, you think he would have her do that?"

Landau shrugged again.

"Stop being a fucking cipher! I work with you, you can share a little insight."

"You're Intelligence." Landau grinned. "Be intelligent."

"Fuck off."

"Has el-Sayd left Cairo?"

"As of thirteen-ten today, yes."

"Then he'll be in San'a' by morning at the latest, presuming he goes direct. He'll want the meeting with Faud as soon as possible thereafter."

"At the mosque."

"That's what I'm thinking, and I'm certain that is what she is thinking as well."

The kettle began to whistle. Landau flicked off the heat, filled his cup with water, watched the freeze-dried grains blossom into something approximating coffee. He stirred the water with his finger, ignoring the pain.

"Either she's a genius or she's fucking insane, Noah. If you're right, she's one or the other."

"Perhaps we should ask Yosef to find out?" Landau said, and tasted his drink, and wasn't surprised to find that, despite all the sugar, it was still bitter.

20

Chace returned to her room to find that the maid service had been and gone. She checked her tells on the bedpost and on her luggage, saw that both were still in place, and only then stowed her purchases in the closet. She put the Walther beneath one of the pillows on the king-size bed, grinning at the cliché, then took off her long skirt and draped it over the back of the desk chair.

She'd purchased two liters of water in the *suq* before returning, and a can of Canada Dry Ginger Ale, and spent the rest of the afternoon working her way through them and her second-to-last pack of Silk Cut, watching the television. The Taj Sheba had a satellite link, and the channel selection was good. She caught up on the news with CNN, then switched to Al-Jazeera, trying to follow their broad-cast. When she'd had enough, she surfed until hit-ting one of the few Yemeni stations, which was showing a local boxing exhibition. The audience at the event was enthusiastic, men and women.

At seven she turned off the television and got back into her skirt but decided she would forgo the head scarf. Again hiding the Walther beneath her shirt, she headed down to one of the Taj Sheba's two restaurants for dinner, the cafélike Bilquis, where they were offering, bizarrely, an Italian-food theme night. Chace took a seat away from the en-trance and the kitchen, where her back was covered by the wall and that allowed her a view of the room.

She ate a passable mushroom risotto, thinking that, if anyone asked, she could claim to be compar-ing it to the one they served back home at the Trattoria del Gesumin in Como. Music from the Bilquis's companion restaurant, the Golden Oasis, was just audible through the walls, the band playing a mix of Mediterranean traditional and pop.

Chace was on to the coffee when her shadow from earlier in the day entered and was seated at a table three up from her, along the same wall. She didn't make him as the tail until he'd put his order in with the waitress, who was one of the only non-Europeans she had seen going uncovered. No *balta*, no veil, just a long black skirt and an off-white top, hair drawn tightly into a bun behind her head. When the man returned his menu to the waitress, the sleeve of his shirt crept past his wrist, showed his watch face out, and Chace remembered and gave him a second look.

Definitely Mediterranean, but now in more European dress, casual but nice. A rather plain face, and his beard and mustache were thinner than Chace had thought at first, and neatly kept. She watched as a glass of Coke, no ice, was delivered to his table, and when the man raised it to drink, he inclined his head toward her in a mock toast.

Chace grinned, put out her cigarette, and finished the rest of her much-too-sweet coffee. She signed the bill Adriana Maribino, separated her copy from the original, folded it down twice, and then pinned it against her palm with her thumb. She rose, thanking the waitress as she began clearing the table and, when she passed her shadow, dragged her hand along the edge of his table, leaving the copy behind.

Then she went to her room and waited.

●

He took thirty-seven minutes, and when he knocked on the door, Chace repeated the same process for letting him inside as she had with Hewitt, with a minor variation. This time, as soon as he entered, she quickly stepped from the bathroom and jammed the suppressor, now securely affixed to the barrel of the Walther, against the side of the man's neck while kicking the room door closed with one foot.

Gun still in place, she pushed him against the

wall, then held him there as she threw the locks again.

"You dropped your receipt," he said. He said it in English, and his accent was American. He raised his right hand slowly, showing Chace the flimsy sheet pinched between his index and middle fingers.

"*Grazie,*" she said. "Who the fuck are you?"

"Simon Yosef. We have a mutual friend."

"I have lots of friends."

"This one lives in Tel Aviv."

Chace moved directly behind him, pressing her left thigh between his legs, forcing his stance wider. She moved the barrel of the gun from the side of his neck to the base of his skull, then reached around his front and began running her hand through his clothes, over and then inside his shirt, then around his waistband, then into his pants. She found a billfold, a pack of Camels, and a green plastic lighter. All three were tossed to the floor. She moved the search lower, up one leg to the crotch, then down again. On his left leg she found a snub revolver in an ankle holster, and she took that as well.

When she was done, she stepped back, pulling the Walther away from his neck.

"Have a seat," Chace said.

Yosef turned into the room, moving for the chair at the desk. "May I smoke?"

"Go ahead."

He picked up the pack and the lighter but left the billfold on the floor. While he was lighting up, Chace opened the cylinder on the snub and dumped its bullets onto the bed. She ignored the billfold. If it was anything like her own wallet, it was one grand lie anyway.

Yosef smoked from the corner of his mouth, looking her over. His expression seemed to say that he would have done the same thing to her had their positions been reversed, and Chace took that, more than anything else, as proof that he was who he claimed he was.

"I made you in the Suq al-Milh," Chace said.

"I hoped you would. I didn't want to alarm you."

"How'd you pick me up?"

"I was told that you would be either French or Italian, with one of the groups. It didn't take long to find out where you were staying."

Chace considered, then made the Walther in her hand safe and set it on the edge of the bed.

"Make it fast," she said.

"They will be meeting tomorrow," Yosef answered. "El-Sayd should arrive in San'a' by morning. Our assessment is that he will want to limit his exposure as much as possible, so he'll press to meet Faud at some point during the day, then depart for Cairo by evening. I've been told that our assessment and yours are in agreement."

Her eyebrows arched. "You don't know my assessment."

"No, I don't. I am only relaying to you what I was asked to relay."

"I see. And that's all? You're all finished now?"

"I'm to offer you support, if you require it. Backup, nothing else."

"I don't need it. I don't *want* it. And if I see you anywhere—and I mean *anywhere*—tomorrow, the whole thing's off. I don't want you compromising me. And you can tell your people that, too."

Yosef exhaled another stream of smoke, watched it fold and curl, then met Chace's gaze and nodded, once. He rose, scooping the billfold and replacing it, then indicating the revolver on the bed.

"May I?"

"Well, I sure as hell don't want it," Chace said.

He picked the cartridges up, dropped them into his pocket, then took the revolver and secured it back at his ankle. Then he motioned to the Walther. "Little."

"It doesn't take much."

"No," Yosef agreed, heading for the door. "No, it doesn't."

21

It was the first time Sinan had prayed in the air, since the Saudia flight didn't land them in Yemen until just before nine in the morning. When he'd finished his *ziryat*, he'd looked out the windows to see that the endless desert had transformed to ragged mountains, and he'd stared in delight at the view of San'a' from above, the houses built tall on the high rocks, the minarets of the city's more than one hundred mosques.

When they landed, they were met by an airport official who walked them, Kalashnikovs on their shoulders and carrying the Prince's bags, past the long lines waiting for customs. An SUV awaited them at the curve, one of the Prince's American-trained security men behind the wheel, and they climbed inside and drove the eleven kilometers into San'a', to the Sheraton Hotel, where the other member of the Prince's security detail had already booked them into their suites.

The first thing the Prince did when they reached the suite was point Sinan to the menu on the coffee table near the largest couch, the one facing the television.

"Order food," the Prince said. "Whatever you want, lots of food. We'll have a meal and then go to the medina to meet my friends."

"Your friends?" Matteen asked.

"Men like us," the Prince answered, disappearing into one of the bedrooms and then reemerging with a frown. "That one is for you two. I'll take the room on the second level."

Sinan nodded, opened the menu. He wasn't hungry, though whether it was a result of the travel or the Prince's company, he wasn't certain. The resentment he'd been fighting had returned on the plane, as the three of them had sat in a cabin that could have seated eighty and instead held only seven, including four flight attendants who had been solicitous to the point of obsequiousness.

The menu was very Western, and Sinan scowled. Bad enough to stay in a Western hotel, but now to eat the food? There was alcohol available on the menu, and Sinan suspected that the Prince would want him to order some, but unless he was asked directly, Sinan wouldn't do it.

The Prince came back down the stairs, apparently satisfied. "Not Mirabella, but it will do," he told the two of them, then took the menu from Sinan and proceeded to make the room service order himself.

The meal came quickly, and Sinan was surprised at the Prince's restraint. The meal was mostly fruit and rice, served with a local flatbread and hot tea.

"Lunch is the big meal here," the Prince explained. "After we meet my friends, we'll have lunch."

Sinan nodded, ate another fig. The Prince was watching him with a grin.

"Your Highness?"

"You're curious, I know. You're wondering who these people are we're meeting, why I've brought you two here with me."

"I am curious, yes."

"You know both of them, I have heard. One not well, but you have met him. The other, you know him well and have not met him."

Sinan couldn't hide his confusion.

"Before you came to my friend Abdul Aziz, you studied in Cairo."

"Yes, I did."

"You met this friend there, in Cairo. He told Abdul Aziz about you, and Abdul Aziz told me, and that is how you were chosen for the Hajj." The Prince refilled his tea, chuckling at the look on Sinan's face. "You should remember him. You made an impression on him."

Matteen was dipping a piece of his *khubz* in some honey. "What about this other friend?" he asked. "Anyone that I would know?"

"Dr. Faud bin Abdullah al-Shimmari," the Prince said. "Yes, I think you *should* know him, Matteen."

Sinan gaped, and the Prince saw his reaction and laughed, then reached out and grabbed his right hand, giving it a solid squeeze of friendship. "Yes, I thought you might react like this. The doctor is a very good friend of mine. He taught me when I was in school, and I listened to his sermons all throughout my childhood. I have supported him and his work for years."

"We're going to meet the *imam*?" Sinan asked. "We'll actually meet with him?"

"My business comes first, but, yes, you will meet with him, dine with him, pray with him, talk to him. You will enjoy his company as I have."

The Prince released Sinan's hand, chuckled, resumed his meal. He talked about past visits to Yemen, told them about the riot less than a year ago that occurred outside the Great Mosque on a Friday, after prayers. The faithful had been incensed at some news or other from Iraq, had poured onto the streets screaming Death to America and Death to Israel. *Jambiyas* had been drawn and blood had been spilled, and the San'a' police had responded brutally to the unrest, killing four and hospitalizing dozens.

Sinan listened with half an ear, mind running with the possibilities of meeting Faud, trying to imagine what he would say to the great man, what questions he would ask of him, how best to make an impression. He wanted desperately to make a good impression, to receive Faud's blessing.

It surprised him how much he wanted it.

•

A little before noon they left the Sheraton, taking the SUV into the Old City, kicking up clouds of dust with their passing. It was in the low eighties Fahrenheit, and the air conditioner kept them cool as they drove past the Qubbat al-Mahdi Mosque and dipped into the wadi, still dry enough to be used as a street, then onto Talha Street. Sinan caught glimpses of the remains of the city wall that had given San'a' its name—the Fortified City—but he was disappointed to see that the segments still visible were made of stone and were clearly new patches, not part of the original mud that had made up the ancient fortifications.

The going was slow the farther they went, the SUV practically crawling through crowds at some points, and the guard who was driving was liberal with the horn, and with his gestures and curses. The Prince was uncharacteristically quiet, and when Sinan caught a glimpse of the man's reflection in the side mirror, he thought he saw nervousness. It surprised him and once again made him reassess his opinion of the Prince. Clearly, meeting with Faud meant a great deal to the Prince as well.

They parked on the north side of the Great Mosque, and there were four other vehicles already there, all of them Toyota Land Cruisers like their own, and Sinan counted eight men standing by the vehicles, smoking and chewing *qat*, leaning on their Kalashnikovs. He and Matteen got out of the car, waited for the Prince to join them, and the Saudis in the group recognized the Prince, if not for who he was then for what he was, and they immediately offered him greetings, asking Allah, the Most Gracious, the Most Merciful, to watch over him. The Prince returned the courtesies in kind, and then the muezzin's call crackled out over old loudspeakers, and all of them made their way to the entrance of the mosque.

Inside was as beautiful and sacred a ground as any Sinan had seen, second only to his visit to Mekkah. Along with the others he removed his shoes, setting them with his Kalashnikov in the growing pile against the wall. There were already some thirty or forty of the rifles there, and at least five times as many pairs of shoes, and once again Sinan rejoiced in the fact that theft was unheard of in places such as this. He listened to the voices all around him, the sounds of conversations ending as men turned their minds to worship. Once or twice he thought he heard women's voices, but he could not see where they had entered, or where women would be going to worship. A mosque as old as this one would have clearly segregated areas, and his chances of encountering the women were next to none.

With Matteen and the Prince, he made his way to the ablution pool, cleaned himself in the water from the fountain. Again, he felt the comfort in sharing ritual with so many others, all of a like mind. Young boys ran past his legs, trying to catch up with their fathers, laughing.

They found places on the field of wool and silk

rugs that covered the floor, facing the *mihrab* wall, facing Mekkah. Sinan felt a rush when he saw the old man at the *minbar*, black-robed and bespectacled, for it was Faud himself who was leading the congregation, accompanied by another man, similarly dressed but younger.

So Sinan prayed with Faud and a thousand others in the Great Mosque in San'a'.

●

There was an immediate bustle when *salat* ended, people moving with everything from reluctance to enthusiasm as they headed back to work, or to lunch, or to a thousand other tasks that needed attending. Sinan tried to keep an eye on Faud but quickly lost sight of him as he moved away in the opposite direction, disappearing into the mix of nooks and half-rooms that peppered the sides of the mosque.

The Prince saw him straining to look and grabbed his hand again.

"Soon, my friend," the Prince said. "My business first, and then you will meet him."

Sinan felt, for a moment, embarrassed. Not by the hand-holding—it was a Western bias that made the act of two men holding hands shameful; to Arabs, as he had learned, it was a sign of true friendship, and not at all an uncommon sight. Rather, it embarrassed Sinan that he was so nakedly eager, that the Prince could read him like a small child.

They made their way back toward the entrance,

and one of the Saudis they had seen outside moved to meet them.

"Your Highness, His Eminence is hopeful that you will meet with him now. If I may take you to him?"

"Of course. I know his friend has very little time to waste."

"Yes, I think that is the concern," the man said. "Please, if you'll come with me?"

The Prince turned to Sinan and Matteen. "If you wish to wait outside at the car, that will be fine. As soon as we're done here, we'll all go to lunch."

"All of us?" Sinan asked, despite himself.

"Sinan! Have faith!" The Prince laughed, then moved off, escorted by the Saudi.

Matteen chuckled. "Careful, Sinan. You don't want to be called *mushrikun*."

Sinan shot him a glare. "That's not funny."

"It was a joke. You seem to have some hero worship, that's all that I am saying."

They sorted through the piles of shoes, finding their pairs, then recovered their rifles and put them back in place at their shoulders.

"His words speak to me," Sinan said as he was pulling on his boots. "More than the others', I don't know why. From the first time I heard him—it was on a cassette, I bought it at the mosque I attended in London—it was like he talked straight to me."

Sinan glanced at Matteen, to see if he understood. From Matteen's look, Sinan guessed that he didn't.

"Here," Sinan said, and tapped his heart. "He spoke straight to here."

"I've had enough of words," Matteen said dismissively. "I've heard all of them before, Sinan, and if you last long enough, you will, too. The words become nothing in the face of the deeds. Remember that."

"The words give rise to the deeds."

Matteen gestured with his elbow, roughly indicating the way the Prince had gone. "And with him? With him, the words come in place of the deeds. Not even, they excuse his *lack* of deeds."

"He acts. Without his money, where would we be?"

"He could give more money. He *should* give more money, and since when have you found it necessary to defend him, Sinan? I've seen you these past three weeks. There have been times when I've wanted to unload your rifle just to make sure you didn't lose your temper and do anything stupid."

Sinan hesitated, caught, and honestly a little surprised himself that he had been so willing to come to the Prince's defense. They got to their feet again, stepped out of the mosque into the bustle and noise of the street. One of the guards from the SUVs offered them each a can of Coca-Cola.

"Allah, All Knowing, All Merciful," Sinan said. "And being All Knowing, he knows what is best for each of us, how we can serve Him. We do not decide how best to serve, that is for Allah alone."

"Perhaps some are not meant to serve at all, Sinan," Matteen replied.

Sinan wasn't sure, but for a moment, he wondered if Matteen was talking about him.

He turned away abruptly, opening his can of soda

and taking a long drink. It was warm, and too many bubbles filled his mouth, and he was considering spitting it out when he heard shouting and laughter, and he looked back to the entrance of the mosque in time to see a woman in her veil and *balta* hurrying out and onto the street, arms folded over her middle, head down.

An old Yemeni man was leaning out of the doorway, the yellow *kuffiyah* on his head wobbling as he hollered at her.

"Your husband should beat you!" he shouted.

Matteen and a couple of the others laughed, then laughed harder as the old man stepped out onto the street, brandishing his *jambiya* at the woman. She continued on without glancing back, and Sinan was about to turn away when he realized that she wasn't wearing shoes but black stockings. He stared, thinking he had to be wrong, that it was a trick of the light, but as she hurried along, he saw it again. Rushing without shoes over the dirt street, a hole had opened in the heel of her stockings, and the foot that was visible was white, as pale as his own had once been.

The sight shocked him forward a step, and then she had turned away again, weaving through the crowd and then around an ironmonger's stand, vanishing.

"Addled," Matteen commented. "She shouldn't even be out alone."

"Did you see that?" Sinan asked.

"Of course I saw that. Whoever her husband or

brother is should beat her, the old man's right. Letting her wander around alone like that—"

Sinan didn't hear the rest, he was already running back into the mosque, and the panic he felt was such that he didn't think to remove his shoes or drop the Kalashnikov. The Saudi who had spoken to them before was sitting on a rug near the fountain, reading his *Qu'ran*.

"Where are they?" Sinan shouted. "Where are they meeting?"

His shouting drew attention, shocked the man, and he started up, pointing back toward the *mihrab*, in one of the shadowed corners. Sinan ran, hearing people shouting at him to take off his shoes, to show respect, and Matteen calling after him to slow down, asking what was wrong. Sinan didn't stop, running through the pools of light that fell through the magnificent windows above, to the shadows of the alcoves near the back. He rushed from one to the next, seeing lone men prostrated in prayer or deep in study.

Then he found them, and the sight of their bodies, on the floor, side by side, their blood staining the colors of the silk rug beneath them to red, struck him like a physical blow. Faud was on his stomach, his head turned, and Sinan could see where one bullet had entered the old man's eye and made blood flow from his nose. The Prince, beside him, lay on his side, the hole at the base of his skull still leaking.

Sinan felt his air go and almost lost his legs, and had to steady himself with a hand on the wall.

Voices behind him were asking what was wrong, what did he think he was doing, what had happened, and Sinan turned away, and then they saw, and went silent as well.

"What . . . ?" Matteen looked from the bodies to Sinan, then back again. "How?"

Sinan shook his head, feeling grief and guilt clamoring in his chest. He sounded breathless and hoarse when he said, "It was that woman."

That stunned Matteen as much as the sight of the bodies.

"Kufr," Matteen murmured.

"Kufr," Sinan agreed.

Blasphemy.

22

She'd worn the *balta,* *hijab,* and veil, checking herself in the bathroom mirror to make certain nothing would give her away before venturing out of the hotel. In the lobby, no one gave her a second look; in fact, most of the people there actively avoided looking her way altogether, afraid of giving offense. Vision behind the veil was remarkably good, even on the periphery, and Chace was relieved. One less thing to worry about.

Only three million, seven hundred thousand, and twelve remaining, she thought.

Beneath the *balta,* Chace wore her trainers, black stockings, her long skirt, and her long shirt, but this time she'd tucked the shirt in instead of letting it hang out. In the front of her bra she had stuffed the surgical gloves Hewitt had given her when he'd delivered the weapon. She hadn't bothered with a different head scarf; the *hijab* she wore with the *balta* was common, and she had confidence that, if something was going to betray her, it at least wouldn't be that.

The Walther she taped to the inside of her upper left arm, the silencer to the inside of the upper right. If she walked modestly, there was no possible way they could be seen, and that concerned her more than being able to access them quickly. The plan, such as she had, would require her to wait for Faud, and she intended to use that time to prepare the gun.

She had debated taking another handful of rounds from the ammunition box but in the end had rejected the idea. They would be hard to carry, they could conceivably collide and jingle in a pocket, calling attention to her, and it would take too much time to reload the weapon. If the six in the clip weren't going to be enough to do the job, then the job wouldn't be done, it was as simple as that.

●

She made her way through the Old City unmolested. Her worst fear was that someone, most likely another woman, might try to strike up a conversation or in some other way delay her, force her to speak. Her intention, if that happened, was to continue on her way without responding and hope that her rudeness would be enough to dissuade further contact.

As it happened, it didn't come up, and when she reached the Great Mosque, the muezzin was just finishing. She came from the north side this time, and again she saw the SUVs parked as they had been the day before, but instead of three there were five of them, with the fifth just then pulling up. Behind the veil and virtually anonymous, she stopped long enough to watch two men emerge, and one of them she immediately recognized as Muhriz el-Sayd, from his size as much as from a remembered file photo. El-Sayd was an unusually large man, six foot two, long in the torso and thick around and, depending on which source you believed, either thirty-eight or forty-one years old. The other man with him, comparatively much shorter, appeared younger, too, and Chace didn't recognize him.

She waited until both men had passed through the main entrance of the mosque before she made to follow them. The expected doubts were doing their best to clutter her thoughts, in particular the fear that Faud wouldn't, in fact, be at the Great Mosque today but rather worshipping in one of San'a's hundred others—one hundred and four others, at last count. But el-Sayd's appearance reassured her, because she agreed with Yosef's assessment. El-Sayd would want the minimum exposure possible.

She walked the block once, to give prayers time to get fully under way, then entered herself, moving quickly, as if late. She passed through the doors, her eyes falling on the rows and rows of rifles and boots set along the wall. She stepped out of her shoes, reassuring herself that the stockings were doing their job, concealing her Caucasian ankles, then quickly looked around. The service was well under way, and all eyes were on the *mihrab*, and Chace had hopes that they would remain there.

The tension in her stomach contracted, cramplike, and she blew a steady breath out her nose to drive it back, wishing for the millionth time that she'd been able to find some sort of map or diagram of the mosque's interior. But of course, there had been none to be found: from here on out, she'd need a combination of luck and skill.

She began moving slowly, staying against the wall. The mix of shadow and sunlight helped and hindered at once, but with the noon sun, the shadows were in her favor, and the *balta* certainly didn't hurt. The most important thing was to keep moving, she told herself, to look like she knew where she was heading, even if she didn't. She had time to find a position, at least until the service ended, but after that, it would be extremely hard to move about.

She wished she knew where she wanted to go, but she remained confident that she would know it when she saw it.

Turning along the western wall, toward the north, she looked down past the colonnades and caught sight of el-Sayd again, far enough away that it was his height rather than his face that identified him. To her right, beneath the elegant arches, the mosque opened wide, voices softly mixing in prayer. To the left and continuing along to the northern wall, smaller arches opened, and as Chace worked her way from colonnade to colonnade, she could see inside semiprivate spaces, sunlight dappling onto the worn rugs spread over the floors.

El-Sayd was moving away, turning right at the end of the hall, and Chace saw him slip through a shaft of sunlight, then disappear into the dimness of one of the almost-rooms. She licked her lips behind the veil, tasted the vaguely metallic flavor of her fear and excitement, the adrenaline driving up another notch, and continued forward.

She reached the corner, looked right in time to see el-Sayd's shadow spilling from the small room, moving back. She knew instantly what he was doing simply from the silhouette of his motion, that he was checking his back, searching for the searchers. Chace stepped lightly left, turned, pressing her back against the wall of an alcove all her own, then knelt on the carpet and lowered her head to the floor, imitating *salat*. Sunlight from the windows touched her *balta*, heating it.

She had no idea if she was being watched, and she knew that if she were seen, there would be an uproar. Certainly, women weren't permitted in this section of the mosque. But perhaps the sight of her in devoted worship would silence any objections, at least until she was finished with her prayers.

She could hear her own breathing, and then even that seemed to fade as other noises rose, the sound of bare feet moving over stone and carpet, voices mixing, louder.

Service over, time to get on with the day.

Time to get on with it.

Still bent, she worked her hands up her sleeves, to her top, and tugged the gloves free, feeling them peeling from her skin. She fought them onto her hands, the rubber closing around her fingers, then straightened, still in her imitation of faith. Reaching up the voluminous sleeves of the *balta* again, she found the Walther and its suppressor. She bowed a second time, biting her lip, and pulled each free from her skin, feeling the tape pull. It would hurt less to do it quickly, but she was afraid of sudden movement and so used steady tension, until she thought her skin was tearing along with the tape.

When the gun and the suppressor were free in her hands, she bowed again, let each rest in the nest of her sleeves, and quickly cleared the tape from them, then reattached the strips on the inside of the fabric. Straightening a final time, she fingered the end of the suppressor, feeling the threads on its end through the gloves, positioning it against the barrel of the Walther, and then swiftly screwing it into place.

She held the gun in her right hand, resting against her left forearm, inside her sleeve, as she got to her feet and turned, fighting the desire to hold her breath.

There was no one behind her. She hadn't been seen.

Chace backed against the wall of the alcove, into the small protection it afforded, listening hard. Most of the foot traffic seemed to have died down, and the voices she was hearing now seemed to float out of the air in every direction, whispering.

She edged forward, peering around the lip of the arch into her alcove, looking toward the one she'd seen el-Sayd enter. There were no shadows to give anyone inside away now, either because it was empty, the sun had moved, or the occupants were being cautious. She glanced back down the way she had come, saw only a lone Yemeni man at the end of the hall, facing away from her, lying on a square of rug.

Chace guided the Walther out of her sleeve, pressed it against the front of her *balta*, concealing it with her other arm. With a deep breath, she slipped around the corner, took ten steps, and turned into the shadowed alcove to the north.

There were two men inside, both kneeling in prayer, one in a black *thobe*, the other in white, and neither was el-Sayd, and one of them Chace didn't recognize at all. Either the one in black saw her from the corner of his eye or heard the rustle of her approach, but whichever it was, it was enough. He raised his head, turning to her, and Chace saw with murderous clarity the heavy lines of age in his face, the cataract blur of his right eye, the gray beard peppered with black.

Faud.

His mouth began twisting in outrage, and he opened it to speak, and Chace already had her left hand supporting the Walther, her right index finger ready on the trigger, and she had the shot, and the Walther popped softly, and the first bullet entered

Faud's brain through the right eye. She fired again immediately, and the second bullet hit lower, splitting his upper lip and driving into his mouth.

She pivoted to her right without pausing, saw the astonished look on the other man's face, the man who wasn't el-Sayd and was simply in the wrong place at the worst possible moment. She shot him twice, two more pops from the Walther, sounds like a child's clapping hands, and hit him in the left eye and left ear. The man collapsed, still astonished, and Chace fired a third time, at the back of his neck, where it met the skull.

Then she pivoted back and put the remaining bullet from the Walther into Faud, also at the base of the skull. She dropped the Walther onto the rug, not hearing it land, and with her foot shoved it beneath Faud's body.

Chace turned and walked from the alcove, head down, stripping the gloves from her hands and tossing them aside into the shadows. She made her way back along the colonnaded walk, trying to keep her pace steady and normal, fighting the urge to run, mind whirring through the last minute of events. El-Sayd had to have already departed, he couldn't have known the hit was coming, or else he would have warned the others. Which meant that whatever the business el-Sayd had come to conduct, it had been brief, or postponed, perhaps.

The Israelis wouldn't be happy, but that wasn't her problem. It would be Crocker's and would remain Crocker's whether or not Chace could make it home. At least she'd hit Faud.

At the corner, turning toward the entrance, Chace heard a shout of alarm and felt her insides turn to ice. A man shouting, and then again, but the tone wasn't what she expected, not a cry of outrage but one of anger, and she heard someone rushing up behind her and lowered her head farther. The old Yemeni she had seen before moved to her side, shouted at her, and she nodded, understood, and he gestured sharply toward the entrance, and Chace moved faster.

Not fast enough, and the man shouted at her again, cuffing her along the back of her head. Others were sitting up, looking to the spectacle, and when Chace stopped to try and retrieve her shoes, the Yemeni man cuffed her again, then reached for the *jambiya* tucked at the sash on his belt.

Fuck the shoes, Chace thought, and she moved quickly through the doorway and onto the street. The bodyguards were to her right, waiting, bored, and she turned left, moving into traffic, feeling the ground grinding the stockings at the soles of her feet. The Yemeni man was still shouting at her, and she heard others laughing, and she dropped her chin all the way to her chest, fighting the urge to break into a sprint. Something dug into her right foot, a sharp pain that made her gasp, and she was sure it had drawn blood, and she wondered when she'd last had a tetanus booster.

Then she was past an ironmonger's stall and down into an alley, and there was no laughter and no shouting, and she slowed, heading west, then turned south down another narrow street, past the

San'a' Palace Hotel, one of the old tower buildings that had been converted to accommodations, the first few floors built of basalt, with brown brick for the higher levels. Chace doubled back, taking the ground-floor entrance to the restaurant, then headed for the stairs.

On the second floor she found one of the shared bathrooms, empty. She locked the door, stripping off her veil, *hijab*, and *balta*. There was no wastebasket, and she bundled the whole kit together, slipped it behind the back of one of the few Western toilets she'd encountered outside of the Taj Sheba. She untucked her shirt, took a moment to check her foot, and discovered that a shard of glass had embedded itself in her heel. Blood and dust had caked over the wound enough to slow the bleeding, and she cursed silently, debated, then decided there was nothing for it.

She limped back downstairs and caught a cab back to her hotel.

●

She departed Yemeni airspace three hours and twenty-seven minutes later. She'd removed the glass from her heel before checking out of the Taj Sheba and rose twice during the flight to Frankfurt to change the bandage. It looked worse than it was, and it felt even worse than that, and Chace wondered idly if she could convince Crocker to give her a couple of days off.

After all, she reasoned, job well done and all that.

23

Paul Crocker had snuck into each of his daughters' rooms, first Ariel's and then Sabrina's, part of the ritual he performed every night he was home, and wished them each a whispered good night. Neither woke, but that was hardly the point, and convinced that both were safely asleep, he turned to his own bedroom, where Jenny had fallen asleep, book open in her hand, the television murmuring nonsense.

He was as far as putting on his pajama bottoms when the phone on the nightstand rang, and he lurched for it, trying to catch it before his wife woke, an exercise doomed to failure. Jenny sat up with a start, glanced at the alarm clock, and frowned.

"It's bad," she said. "It's always bad when it's this late."

Crocker nodded, answering the phone, and expecting the Duty Ops Officer.

Instead, he got Angela Cheng.

"How's Chace?" Cheng asked him.

"Not on this line."

"See, I know how she is," Cheng continued, as if she hadn't heard him. "That's just to give you a taste of what I know. And I know something else, Paul. What I know is that you need to get your ass into your office in like, say, the next hour, and have an escort meet me in the lobby so I can come up to see you."

"Your President decided to invade some other oil-rich country, that it?"

"Ha ha, you're funny, you're a very funny guy. One hour, Paul, I mean it." Cheng hung up.

Propped on her pillow, Jenny's frown deepened. "There was a time when we would make love at night."

"Did we?" Crocker moved to the closet, pulling down a fresh suit and laying it out at the foot of the bed, then going back for a shirt and tie.

"Must've done. There are two proofs asleep in their respective rooms below us."

"Who are almost, but not quite, as lovely as their mother."

Jenny retrieved her book, marking her page before closing it, then scooted forward beneath the bedclothes, toward her husband. He had his pants on by then, and the shirt, and he stopped buttoning the front to reach out and run his fingers through her dark hair.

She didn't move, then kissed his hand as he moved it back. "Tie doesn't match."

"The shirt is white, Jenny. Any tie goes with white."

"Your shirt is not the problem." She threw back the covers, grinning as he looked at her bare legs, then disappeared into their closet. "The suit is the problem."

Crocker sat on the bed, pulling on his socks and shoes. "You're the only person who cares about these things."

"Someone must." She returned with a simple navy silk tie, draped it around his neck, then kissed him on the forehead. "See you tonight?"

"God, I hope so," Paul Crocker said with a sincerity that surprised him.

●

"Who died?"

"Funny you should ask," Cheng said, and then slapped the folder she'd hand-carried from Grosvenor Square onto Crocker's desk.

He finished lighting his cigarette, then flipped the folder open. The routings along the top of the paper were CIA standard, but the subheading declared "U.S.–U.K. Eyes Only," and it reassured Crocker somewhat that Cheng wasn't sneaking him anything he shouldn't be privy to in the first place.

As he read, he said, "Chace is fine. Suffered an injury to the right foot, impaled herself on a piece of glass. No tendon damage, had it stitched up as soon as she was back."

"I know," Cheng said flatly.

Crocker stopped middraw on his cigarette, staring down at the paper.

"Ah, just go to the juicy bit."

"This is confirmed?" he asked.

"From three different sources."

"Why am I finding this out from you?" Crocker glared at Cheng, but only because she was the only one there. "Why the hell didn't I learn this from Simon?"

"I don't know how you run your stations, Paul." Cheng gave up on waiting for an invitation and sat, tucking her legs beneath her seat. "All I know is what I get from Langley, and Langley says that two people were murdered in the Al-Jami' al-Kamir in San'a' yesterday, each of them shot at point-blank multiple times. Dr. Faud bin Abdullah al-Shimmari and Salih bin Muhammad bin Sultan."

Crocker closed the folder in disgust, rocked back in his chair, almost spitting smoke. "What the hell was he doing there?"

"Chace didn't say? Did she even file?"

"Her after-action was filed immediately on her return," Crocker replied angrily. "Before she went to the bloody hospital, she came in here and filed her after-action. She said she missed the window on el-Sayd but was able to take Faud and had to take one other as collateral. She couldn't shoot Faud and leave the other one just kneeling there."

"Kneeling there?" Cheng sat upright. "Oh, fuck

me, Paul, don't tell me they were *praying* when she killed them."

"According to Chace, yes."

Cheng stared at him, then sank back, shaking her head.

Crocker flicked ash, missing the tray and scattering it on his desk. It did nothing to help his mood.

"You're going to take it straight on the chin," Cheng said after a moment.

"Go to hell, Angela," Crocker growled.

●

"She killed *who*?" Barclay demanded. He was on his feet behind his desk, both hands planted in fists on his blotter, and Crocker decided the shade his C had turned was probably most accurately described as cherry.

"Salih bin Muhammad bin Sultan," Crocker answered. "One of the almost seven thousand princes of the House of Saud."

"In a *mosque*?"

Crocker thought that Barclay was actually shaking with his fury.

"All of this is detailed in Minder One's afteraction report, sir." Crocker motioned to the report resting on the stack of "Immediates" on Barclay's desk.

"Oddly, no, it isn't. Chace nowhere writes 'I shot a Saudi prince in the back of the head as he was kneeling in prayer.' In point of fact, there's no mention of royalty of any kind. So you may, perhaps, understand my displeasure at finding your agents committing regicide!"

Crocker closed his mouth, deciding that now probably wasn't the best time to point out that Chace hadn't, in fact, killed a king but only a prince. To his side, also standing, Weldon shifted uneasily, then stopped as Barclay moved his glare to the Deputy Chief.

"How in the name of God did this happen, Donald?" Barclay shoved the copy of the after-action away from him. "You authorized Tanglefoot, why didn't you put a stop to this?"

"Tanglefoot didn't specify location or means, sir," Weldon said tightly. "It simply undertook to fulfill HMG's order, to effect the assassination of Dr. Faud—"

Barclay waved a furious hand and Weldon went silent.

For several seconds, none of the men moved and none of them spoke. Weldon shifted again, then straightened his tie and looked past Barclay, out the window. Crocker kept his hands behind his back, watching as the color slowly began fading from his C's face. It left his ears last.

"I have been summoned to Number Ten," Barclay said softly. "I have been asked to explain how it was that an SIS officer murdered two men in the holiest site in Yemen."

"Then you should tell them it was done with efficiency and precision," Crocker said.

"I beg your pardon?"

Crocker hesitated, then elaborated. "SIS fulfilled

HMG's request to the letter of the concept of operations, sir. Exactly as requested, and in short order
of the request. While they may not like the result,
Operation: Tanglefoot is a complete success.
Minder One did exactly what she was sent to do,
and did it brilliantly. Something I hope you will
convey to the Prime Minister."

"Oh, I shall convey it, Crocker." Barclay's glare
superbly mixed outrage with incredulity. "Oh, yes,
absolutely. And when the PM asks just what it is
we're supposed to tell the Saudis, I'll direct his inquiry to you, shall I?"

"If Prince Salih bin Muhammad bin Sultan was
meeting with Faud in San'a', sir, the Prince was involved in Faud's organization and activities, most
likely as the source of their funding," Crocker answered seriously. "If the Prime Minister wishes, I'm
certain the Deputy Chief and D-Int would be
happy to brief him on the Saudi royal family's donations to organizations that promote and foster
terrorism, not just in the Middle East but in the
U.K. as well. Further, I'm sure Mr. David Kinney at
Box would be happy to join them in the briefing, to
provide the Security Services' point of view on the
situation."

"Do you think this is a joke, Crocker?" Barclay
snapped.

"I think very little is a joke, sir."

"Then you must think the Prime Minister a fool,
or an idiot, or worse that he isn't already aware of
these things."

"Certainly he is aware of them. The question is to

what extent, and to what extent politics dictates action rather than matters of security or intelligence."

"Politics has always pulled the sled. As well it should. Left unchecked, you would have your Minders putting bullets in half of the leaders in the Middle East."

Crocker's jaw tightened, sending the start of a new headache climbing along his skull. "This Service exists to protect the British people, not to serve any elected official's political agenda."

"You assume that the Prime Minister's agenda isn't the same as yours. And you further—arrogantly—assume that you are in possession of more facts at any given moment than the PM and the Cabinet."

"From what I've seen, sir," Crocker said, "that conclusion is self-evident. The PM asked SIS to undertake retaliatory action. Operation: Tanglefoot was approved by me, Director Intelligence, the Deputy Chief, and yourself before presentation to the Cabinet. If the Cabinet was worried that Chace might track blood onto the carpet, they should have rejected the proposal. Now it's done, and it's far too late to wish it undone."

"All true, and ultimately all bloody irrelevant when we're asked to mollify the Saudis."

"I'm not interested in mollifying the Saudis," Crocker replied. "Neither should the Prime Minister be. For that matter, neither should you."

"As I have stated time and time again, we follow our Government, we do not lead it, certainly not in policy."

"Then we're no better than the Americans chasing after Saudi oil." Crocker paused, took a breath, trying to calm himself. Barclay's gaze was unblinking, still enraged, and Weldon was still alternately interested in his necktie and the view just past Barclay's shoulder of the window.

"Oil we depend upon, too, I would point out."

"Halliburton doesn't have a desk at SIS yet, do they?" Crocker said before he could catch himself.

Barclay's scowl was of a quality to wither limbs.

"Look, sir, it is unfortunate that the Prince was in the wrong place at the wrong time," Crocker said after a moment's pause. "But if he was clean, he wouldn't have been there."

Weldon cleared his throat. "The Saudis will claim that Salih was in the mosque to worship, and we won't be able to prove otherwise. It looks like a cold-blooded slaughter, an affront not simply to the Saudis but to all of Islam."

"Of course that's how it bloody looks," Crocker retorted, feeling his temper starting to slip. "That was the whole bloody point, and if the PM and the Cabinet didn't see that when they ordered us to assassinate Faud, they damn well should've done. There was no way the assassination of a prominent *imam* could be interpreted as anything else, and that was the obvious goal of the operation."

"You know damn well it wasn't!" Barclay snarled. "The goal was the retaliatory killing of Faud for the attacks on the Underground, not to start a bloody war with the Saudis!"

"We haven't started a war, sir. We're trying to fight one."

"Not by attacking two men in a mosque, not by murdering them that way!"

Crocker stared at Barclay, wondering how a man with so much similar experience, of so many shared years, could be so blind. When he answered, it was with a bitterness he hadn't heard from himself in years.

"Perhaps when you speak to the Prime Minister, sir, you can inquire of him as to exactly which way he would rather we *had* murdered them?"

Barclay grimaced in disgust, poked at the intercom on his desk, and curtly called for his car.

"Are we still clean?" he asked both men coldly. "Did she at least get out clean?"

"Chace was at no point compromised, sir," Weldon answered. "There's no reason for the Saudis to think we had any hand in what transpired."

"How certain are we of that?"

"Director Intelligence is still looking into it, but so far the Saudis seem to be following their usual response in incidents of this nature."

"Their usual response?"

"They're blaming the Israelis," Crocker replied.

Barclay considered, then nodded, pulling on his overcoat.

"Well, that's good news, at least," he said.

$$\boxed{\textbf{24}}$$

I love her, I want to send her flowers," Borovsky said. "Even if they are screaming for our blood—as if that was anything new—I adore her, and I want to show her my affection."

Landau, facing his computer and trying to compile his notes for the latest in the series of reports the Chief had demanded, ignored him.

"What is her name again?" Borovsky asked. "Her real name, not the work name, not that Italian name."

Landau didn't look up. "She's head of their Special Section. I'm sure you have it on file."

"I looked. Her name is Chace, Tara Chace."

Landau's hands hovered over the keyboard for a moment. "Then why are you asking me?"

"It's more fun this way. There was no picture of her, I think it was removed. Did you remove it?"

"Yes."

"Why?"

"To keep you from drooling over it."

"Is she beautiful? Is she beautiful, this woman who assassinates Saudi princes?"

"Go away, Viktor," Landau said, resuming his typing. "I'm sure you have researchers requiring your guidance."

"They're all working, trust me. Every desk, all of them hard at work."

"You see that I'm typing here? I need to have this finished for the midmorning distribution, Viktor. Please go away."

Borovsky wouldn't leave. "She fucked up on el-Sayd, though. I can forgive her that, perhaps. No woman is perfect, you know, they all have their flaws. Some talk too much, some are like ice in the bedroom, some cook food you wouldn't feed to your enemies. This one didn't kill exactly who we wanted, but I think I will get over that."

Landau threw up his hands, swiveling his chair around from the computer to face Borovsky. "Viktor, why are you here?"

Borovsky showed him a big grin. "I wanted to talk about beautiful British agents with you."

"I don't want to talk about beautiful British agents with *you*."

"I'm joking." Borovsky opened the folder he was carrying, set it carefully in front of Landau. "This camp here, you see? It's in Saudi, the Wadi-as-Sirhan."

Landau looked at the satellite photos Borovsky had brought, slid through them one at a time, giving each image a cursory examination. The images were clear—at least as clear as satellite images ever were in this sort of thing—but Landau didn't see anything immediately alarming. There were satellites that had resolution down to eighteen inches from orbit, the American Keyhole and post-Keyhole generations, where you could make out faces and features with superb quality. The images were so good, in fact, that Landau knew for a fact the Americans had submitted them for evidence in the trials of various terrorists.

These were not those, however, and although Borovsky's team had tried to clean them up, the best Landau could discern was that, yes, as Borovsky had indicated, he was looking down on a camp of some sort. Three large tents, ten-men size, he guessed, and some detritus on the field around the location, boxes, crates, three or four fifty-gallon drums for fuel or something else.

"It's a camp." Landau closed the folder and shoved it back at Borovsky.

"Yes, that's what I said. Training camp."

"I don't see training facilities."

"They're cleverer these days, you know that. They cover everything they can, right down to their firing ranges, these days. This, it's in a wadi, they've put a canopy over it, netting, like that. The satellite thinks it's seeing terrain."

"Then how do you know?"

"Because I am a devious motherfucker, and I know their tricks. It's a camp, Noah, and not just training the *jihadis* anymore, I think it's moving to indoctrination."

Landau reluctantly reached for the folder again, gave the pictures a second look, longer this time, conceding Borovsky's point. The terrain was wrong in places, or so it appeared to him, too uniform and then, abruptly, too broken. But none of the pictures showed people; there was no sign that the camp was even occupied.

"Why no IR?"

"Since when has our infrared been any good? Wouldn't matter. They stay under the netting as much as they can. Maybe they know the satellite's orbit, maybe not, but we can't get a good shot."

"So you can't guess at numbers?"

"I don't like guessing, you know that."

"I'm not seeing anyone on these shots, Viktor. The place looks abandoned."

"It's not. The barrels here? They're new, they were moved in on Sunday, Noah. And this tent here, this one is new, too. Went up between Saturday night and Sunday morning. It's not a good sign. They've been very careful to hide things from us; why show us this?"

"Someone slipped up."

Borovsky shook his head. "You know better, my friend. You know better than to ever call the enemy a fool, or to accuse him of acting without care. We can see these because they could not hide them.

And I will bet you when I see the shots tonight, they will show nothing, they will have found more netting to conceal it all."

Landau adjusted his glasses, sliding them back up his nose. "What are you trying to say?"

"I'm saying the camp is growing, Noah. From maybe sixty men to double that."

"What was it before?"

"Training and staging that splinter HUM group."

"So they've stepped up recruitment. Hardly surprising after Faud's death."

"Yes, in response to Faud's death." Borovsky leaned forward, more intent. "But indoctrination. We have intelligence coming out of the West Bank and Gaza that Hamas is doing something new with the bombers, with the suicide bombers. They're not just keeping them in the mosques and brainwashing them with dreams of being *shahid*, they're sending some of them away, out of country.

"Now we see this camp, and it's adding tents, adding fuel for its generators, growing so fast they can't hide themselves. I think this is where some of those kids are heading, Noah. I think they're going for indoctrination, heavy shit, maybe even basic training, to get them into countries other than Israel. I think it's going to start again, and I think if we don't shut this place down soon, we're going to be very, very sorry."

"It's in Saudi, the camp?"

Borovsky nodded. "Wadi-as-Sirhan. Eighty-odd klicks from the border with Jordan, Tabuk province."

Landau nodded, thought, then closed the folder and swiveled his chair back to face his keyboard.

"We can't touch it," he said.

"Okay, you didn't hear me because you're deaf or there's shit in your ears, I said—"

"We can't touch it, Viktor. Impossible." Landau found his place in his notes, resumed transcribing into the computer.

"Give it to the Chief, he'll hand it to the IDF—"

"A military operation inside Saudi Arabia? You're Head of Research, where's your brain, Viktor?"

Borovsky was glaring at him, Landau could see it reflected in his monitor. "We've done such things before."

"Not in the time frame you're looking for." Landau flipped the page on his notepad and had a momentary pause while he tried to decipher his own handwriting, then began typing some more. "If the Americans get a whiff, just the slightest hint, that we're considering a move against Saudi, they'll wet themselves, they will go insane. They'll say we're destabilizing the region, and that we're going to provoke a war. Israeli troops on Saudi soil? Would light a fire to make what's been going on these past five years look like a match. It's not going to happen, Viktor. Especially after the way we've been blamed for what the British did in Yemen."

"Damn you, look at me," Borovsky growled.

Landau stopped typing and looked at him.

"You say this and you say that." Borovsky spun the folder angrily, nearly ripping its cover off as he opened it once more, revealing the photographs.

"And I'm saying to you that this camp—*this camp*—right here is now actively brainwashing young Arab men and women to think it's better to strap explosives to their bodies and to kill Jews than it is to live their lives working for peace! We have to act, we have to act to protect ourselves first, our allies second, and these children third!"

There was a pause and Landau stared at Borovsky, held it until the other man looked away, sinking reluctantly into a chair.

"I know how you feel, Viktor," Noah said. "I know the frustration. But we cannot act on it. There's no way."

"You know what they do, right? They find these kids, these kids who are angry and scared because we've made them angry and scared, and they tell them, Hey, you're sixteen, you're eighteen, you're twenty, your life is shit, isn't it? But you die like this, you die a martyr, you go to Paradise, and your family, we'll give them a big check. You just need to kill some Jews and yourself along with them, we'll take care of your family."

"I know."

"This camp, this camp isn't going to be only for us."

"I know that, too."

Borovsky held out his hands, palms up, as if out of words. The air conditioner in the room clicked off, and the only noise came from Landau's desktop, the computer humming, waiting to be used again.

"Our job is to protect Israel," Borovsky finally said, putting his hands down on the armrests of the chair, helping himself back to his feet. "I am always stunned when you tell me we can't do that."

"I'm not telling you that," Landau said. "The Americans are telling us that. The United Nations is telling us that. The European Union is telling us that."

"They're going to get hit, too." Borovsky picked up the folder, brandished it like proof. "And when there's more blood in the street, they'll ask us why we didn't do anything to prevent it. This is how you lost your wife and your boy, Noah, and you sit there and do nothing."

"It's not up to me."

"A coward's defense," Borovsky said, and left the room.

25

"This is Nia," Abdul Aziz told Sinan. "Nia is *shahid*."

Sinan tried to hide his displeasure. It had nothing to do with the woman's desire to be *shahid;* he held the martyrs in the highest regard and remembered them always in his prayers. It had nothing to do with her manner, or her bearing, or even her appearance, veiled and garbed as was appropriate. He could even forgive her presence in the camp without a blood relation to watch over her. She was proper and respectful and Abdul Aziz called her *shahid*, which perhaps was overzealous, since the woman had not martyred herself yet, but otherwise there was nothing wrong with Nia that

Sinan could see, nothing he could articulate to himself.

But Sinan did not like her here, and he didn't like the fact that Abdul Aziz was presenting her to him like this.

Nia bent her head slightly. The sunlight falling through the camouflage netting that ran in great swaths above them played with the eyes, made the bright brighter, the shade murkier. Sinan couldn't tell her age but guessed she had to be younger than twenty. She was small, too, and carried herself small, so the ultimate effect was that of a black-cloaked, vaguely female-shaped ghost, floating just beyond Abdul Aziz's shoulder.

"*Salaam alaykum,*" Sinan said.

"*Wa 'alaykum is-salam,*" Nia answered, and it was almost inaudible behind the veil.

Abdul Aziz said, "Sinan and Matteen were at the Great Mosque, outside, when the murders took place. It was Sinan who realized the evil that had been done, and it was Sinan who raised the alarm."

Nia raised her head slightly. Above the veil and below the cowl of her *abaya*, Sinan could see her eyes, large and expressive, the soft brown of warm wood. When she realized that he was looking at her in return, she hastily dropped her gaze.

"They should die for what they have done," she whispered.

Sinan thought the sentiment devoid of any venom, as if the girl were only repeating a line as it had been taught to her. It probably had, at that. There were some thirty other recent arrivals since

Saturday, mostly men, but a handful of women just like Nia. Palestinians who had been undergoing instruction in the various Hamas-controlled mosques, all of them learning the glory and purpose of becoming *shahid*.

Sinan didn't know how their travel had been organized so quickly, or who Abdul Aziz had contacted to bring it to pass, and he didn't care. Once upon a time, Matteen had explained to him, this camp had held a splinter of the Harakat ul-Mujihadin, but then Abdul Aziz had asserted his control. Now, instead of training them to fight in their own lands, Abdul Aziz had decided to take the fight into the homes of their enemies.

It was a sentiment that Sinan embraced, and one he was eager to support.

The presence, then, of this *shahid* only served to confuse him, and Abdul Aziz's need to introduce Nia to him compounded that.

As if sensing the discomfort, Abdul Aziz grunted. "Wait for me here," he told Sinan, then moved off, escorting Nia back to the women's tent.

Sinan felt the tension leave him as he did. He turned to the small tent he shared with Matteen and four others, sat on his bedroll, laying his rifle beside him. He was tired, a deep fatigue that had sunk to the bone and that had come from the flurry of activity in the wake of the Prince's murder.

They had raised the alarm at once, Sinan and Matteen, shouting in their grief and alarm, until other voices joined theirs, echoing their outrage and disbelief. Sinan had shoved his way through the crowd, desperate to find the barefoot killer, to choke the life from her with his bare hands. With Matteen at his heels, they had raced out of the Great Mosque back onto the street, searching for a glimpse of the *kufr* woman, just a hint of the animal who had committed this incredible blasphemy. They had run down the maze of streets in the Old City, shouting for help, fueled by their grief. But the search was immediately impaired, none of them willing to accost the women they saw, to rip the veils from their faces, and each woman they approached would look away, and it was universal behavior, modesty rather than guilt, and Sinan's frustration had been so great he had actually screamed aloud with it.

It was Matteen who had seen the blood trail, and they had followed it as best they could, losing it every few dozen feet in the dust before finding another thin line of it and pushing forward again. Near the San'a' Palace Hotel they had lost the trail entirely and begun searching stall to stall, house to house, only to be refused entry at most. A Western woman, they had asked, have you seen her?

Yes, we've seen Western women, they were told. I sold a *jambiya* to one, a rug to another, a scarf to a third.

Then Sinan had found a group of men, seated on crates and stools, chewing *qat* in the shade, and one had said, "There was the limping woman. . . ."

"Where?" Sinan had demanded.

The man had smiled, the bulge of *qat* in his

cheek the size of a tennis ball, and indicated the entrance to the hotel across the street.

"When?"

"Not long ago. She had blond hair. Modestly dressed, but her hair was uncovered."

The other men had laughed, nodded, remembering, and Sinan had left Matteen to further the questioning, rushing into the hotel, reinvigorated with the news, anxious in his search. When he saw the dirty smear of blood and dirt outside the bathroom threshold on the first story, he'd taken his Kalashnikov off his shoulder and made it ready in his hands. He had burst through, into the room, already certain what he would do. He wouldn't kill her, no, he would wound her, wound her so that she would live, so he and Matteen could drag her back, so proper justice could be delivered.

But the bathroom had been empty, and he had found the discarded veil and *hijab* wrapped in their *balta*, and that was all. He had snatched them up, run back onto the street, nearly colliding with Matteen there.

"She's gone," Matteen had reported. "They say she took a taxi. They know the driver, they gave me his name."

Sinan had shown Matteen the clothes, and together they had searched them right there in the street, much to the amusement of the men who watched them, chewing their *qat*. They'd found nothing but two pieces of adhesive tape stuck inside the *balta*'s arms. Eventually the two men made their way back to the Great Mosque, rejoining the others, who had summoned the police. A crowd had gathered, was continuing to swell, bubbling with outrage and anger at the murders, and more police were coming in response. Matteen started the SUV and Sinan climbed in, and they had to go in reverse to get clear. As they were turning, Sinan looked back in time to see a young man in the crowd hurl a rock at one of the police, others bending to do the same.

They left as the riot began.

•

Abdul Aziz ducked under the flap of the tent, gesturing for Sinan to stay seated, joining him on the rug.

"Zulfaqar says you are good with your hands, Sinan. He says you learned the explosives quickly, that you understand how to make a bomb."

"Zulfaqar is generous," Sinan said. "He is a good teacher, and Allah, in His wisdom, makes me a good student."

"The woman. You still don't think she was Israeli."

"American," Sinan said firmly. "Or English."

"No one else thinks as you do. They believe it was the apes who did this."

"She had blond hair."

"There are Israelis with blond hair."

Sinan shrugged. "She was pale."

"You hardly saw her skin."

"I saw her foot. It was pale, Aziz. No Israeli would be that pale."

Abdul Aziz seemed to consider this for a few

seconds, then shook his head slightly, making his *kuffiyah* rustle. "No matter. We will act the same."

"Why did you bring that . . . that girl to meet me?" Sinan asked.

"Not you to meet Nia, Sinan. Nia to meet you. You will help her become *shahid*."

Sinan tried to keep the confusion from his face.

"You and Matteen together," Abdul Aziz continued. "Nia will wear the bomb. You and Matteen will make certain she delivers it, and delivers herself to Paradise."

"Delivers it where?"

"Cairo."

This time, the confusion could not be hidden, and Abdul Aziz smiled thinly at Sinan's bewilderment.

"The British Embassy will be the primary target. The American Embassy is only a block away from it. That is the secondary target. You and Matteen will take Nia to Cairo, and you and Matteen will help her on her journey to Paradise."

"When?"

"Soon, Sinan." Abdul Aziz got to his feet. "Soon. We will talk more of this later."

"I look forward to it."

"God is great."

"God is great," Sinan agreed, and watched as Abdul Aziz stepped back onto the field of shadow and light outside the tent. He lay back on his bedroll, looking up at the canvas ceiling, feeling the day's heat wrapping itself around him, its weight and the stillness of the air inside the tent. If he listened hard, he could hear the serious voices from the classroom tent, the teachings, the lectures.

Now he heard Dr. Faud's voice, crackled and distorted through the speakers as one of his sermons played on cassette. Sinan knew the words of it by heart, having played it many times himself. Once the *imam*'s words had roused him, inflamed him, spurred him to action.

Today they sparked flames of a different sort. Maybe it had been the Zionists who had murdered Faud, as so many believed, or maybe it had been the Great Satan, the Americans, or their dogs, the British. It didn't matter.

Nia would be the start, just the start.

Whoever it had been, he'd make them burn.

26

Kate stuck her head into Crocker's office and said the three words that never failed to make a good day bad and a bad day even worse. He'd just finished vetting the last reports for the final in-house distribution of the day, and was shoving the little paperwork he had remaining into his document bag, wondering how bad his commute home would be tonight. The Bakerloo Line had returned to full service Sunday night, and with it running again, he'd allowed himself to imagine reaching his family before they'd moved on to dessert.

"We have trouble," Kate said.

He froze in midaction, looking instinctively at the files in his bag. "Trouble" could mean many things in this office. If it came from the Duty Operations Officer over the red phone, it meant something, somewhere, had gone horribly wrong. An operation had been compromised, an agent had died, a spy plane had gone down, a bomb had blown up. Something that required adrenaline.

When it came from his PA, it meant it came from one of the floors above him, from the Deputy Chief or C, or outside of the building, from Whitehall or the FCO or Downing Street. On some occasions it could even come from the Ministry of Defense.

He preferred it when the red phone brought the news.

Crocker slid his hand from the bag and looked at Kate, standing just outside his door. Her expression sold it; whatever it was, it was political, and he felt his stomach sour at the thought of it.

"Are you going to tell me or just stand there like some David Blaine stunt?"

She stepped inside, closing the door behind her. "There's an inquiry that came across my desk from the Security Services, clearing permission for internal surveillance."

"Who are they vetting?"

"Minder One."

Crocker scowled. The Security Services performed irregular checks on all personnel holding positions deemed "sensitive" in the Government, anyone who could pose a security breach. It was a safety measure, another of the legion that had been instituted in the days after Philby and his brethren. The checks were fairly subtle and lasted anywhere from twenty-four to seventy-two hours, with the subject placed under constant surveillance. Sometimes Box would peek at his or her mail or listen in on the telephone. Crocker suspected that, where he could get away with it, Kinney even sent his boys into the subject's home, in search of anything incriminating.

In and of itself, internal surveillance wasn't unusual, and neither was the request; protocol demanded, and courtesy required, that Kinney, under standing order of the DG at Box, notify the subject's direct superior. In Crocker's or Rayburn's case, it meant that Weldon received notification; in Poole's or Lankford's, that Chace would. If the Head of the Special Section or the PA to D-Ops was being put under surveillance, Crocker had to be notified.

So that wasn't the problem.

The problem was that Chace had already been given a clean bill of health in July, less than two months earlier.

"They did her end of bloody July," Crocker said. "She's clean."

"I know," Kate said. "So I called over to Box to double-check, thinking it was a mistake, perhaps."

"And?"

"And they said they would have to get back to me."

"Which they did."

"Which they did." Kate fingered the ring of keys at her hip, the ones used for the safes in the outer and inner offices, and for Crocker's document bag. "David Kinney himself called to tell me it had been an error and to discard the request."

"He called you? Directly? Not his PA?"

"He called me directly, Paul."

"Where's the Deputy Chief?"

"I believe he's already left the build—"

"Bloody well find out if he has or not, and if he hasn't, tell him I'm coming up."

Kate nodded impassively and reached for the house phone on Crocker's desk, punched two digits, and waited. Crocker took the moment to shrug out of his overcoat and toss it back into his chair, then to light a cigarette.

"Oliver?" Kate said to the phone. "Kate. Has DC left the building?"

Crocker stowed his lighter in his vest pocket, gouted smoke at Kate, impatient.

"No? Could you tell him that D-Ops is on his way up, please? Yes, it is urgent."

He was already through the door even as Kate completed the call, and was moving through the outer office when he called back to her, "And find Minder One, tell her to stay in the Pit."

"I'm staying, too, am I?" Kate called back.

"Forever," Crocker snarled.

●

"Why is Box putting Minder One under surveillance?"

With hat and raincoat still in place, Weldon sighed, then set his document bag on the edge of his desk. He didn't bother to sit.

"Can this not wait until tomorrow, Paul?"

"I want to know why Kinney's putting Chace

under the microscope again, sir. Were you aware of this?"

"I seem to recall receiving something to that effect, yes."

"Kinney told my PA that it had been a mistake."

"I suppose it must have been, then."

Crocker tried to drill two holes through Weldon's skull with his eyes, and when that failed, he said, "David Kinney doesn't call my PA to address an error. He has his PA do it."

"Perhaps he's trying to foster greater cooperation between the houses?"

It didn't deserve a response, so Crocker didn't offer one.

Weldon sighed again, very much put-upon. "You'll have to talk to C."

"Then let's go up there right now."

"He's left for the day."

"Let's call him, I'm sure he's available."

"You're overreacting, Paul. Box is putting Minder One under surveillance, that doesn't mean they're looking to arrest her for violating the Official Secrets Act."

"You confirm she's under surveillance, but you won't tell me why."

"I don't know why!" Weldon shook his head. "C informed me that the DG at Box had been on to him, and that it was understood. You weren't to receive a copy of notification, for reasons C did not make clear to me, reasons of his own."

"Then I'll ask him."

"You will not!" Weldon looked appalled. "This

can wait until tomorrow, surely? For a routine surveillance?"

"No, it can't," Crocker shot back. "Kinney goes behind my back to put a watch on Chace, then the surveillance isn't routine, it's extraordinary. It means they don't want me to know, it means they're concealing their motives, so it's not a spotcheck, it's not vetting. They're keeping track of her, and I want to know why. I *should* know why, she's my Head of Section, the Minders are my direct purview, no one else's."

Weldon's hand began working the handle of his document bag. "If the Director General was given an order to place Minder One under surveillance, he received that order at the request of Downing Street. Regardless of the reason, he is most certainly acting on a direct order from HMG. Last I checked, we still *work* for HMG."

"This is about Yemen, isn't it?"

"I honestly cannot say." Weldon frowned, then seemed to resolve that he'd said all he was prepared to say and hefted his bag from the desk. "I have a train to catch, Paul. Now if you'll excuse me . . ."

Crocker stared at him, and Weldon, uncharacteristically, not only met the stare but bounced it straight back.

There was nothing more to be gained here, Crocker realized.

"Very good, sir," Crocker said, and he stepped back, and even went so far as to open the door of Weldon's office, holding it for the Deputy Chief. "Sorry to delay you."

"Not at all. I shouldn't worry about it, Paul. It's probably nothing."

"Let's hope Minder One agrees with you."

Weldon stopped halfway through the door. "You're not going to inform Chace? Bad business, Paul. I wouldn't."

"I won't need to," Crocker said. "She'll spot them herself."

"They do know their jobs, Paul. I wouldn't get overconfident."

Crocker shook his head.

"She did the last time," he said.

27

Soaked from the rain, Chace limped through her front door, bumped it shut with her hip and locked it, shucked her coat to the floor, and dropped onto the couch. She took her left shoe off, tossing it away toward the television, and then gingerly unlaced the right, easing it free, before stopping and taking in her flat once again. Lights burning the way she had left them; dishes piled in the sink; mail scattered on the end table; cans of paint haphazardly stacked in the corner; canvases rolled and propped against the wall, waiting for abuse; latest letter from her mother crumpled and still resting where it had landed on her bookshelf, dangerously close to the never-been-used aromatherapy candles a rich schoolmate had sent for her most recent birthday.

She got to her feet, wincing at the pressure on her still-injured foot. The staples or stitches or whatever had been used to close the wound itched almost constantly, and Chace had to remind herself to not drag her heel, to not scratch at it.

She made her way into the bedroom, taking in the unmade bed, the dirty clothes heaped in the corner. Kittering's SAS beret was still hanging from the bedpost, her masochistic reminder that she would never be the woman he had wished her to be. Shoes half under the bed, closet door half open, bathroom door half closed. . . .

No, she thought. Couldn't be that, could it? Nothing so elementary, nothing so bloody fundamental. Didn't they think to take Polaroids before searching the place?

It was so obvious, in fact, that Chace had to wonder if she hadn't left the door half open herself.

She went to the nightstand and searched for the penlight she kept there, digging past matchbooks, condoms, an old and uncapped lipstick, a bottle of aspirin, a notepad, and several cheap pens before finding it. She flicked it on, saw the beam was still strong, flicked it off. On her belly, she shined the penlight beneath the fraction of a gap at the bureau's base and saw in the dust there flakes of white.

With a deep breath, she blew beneath the bureau at an angle, then sat up in time to watch the thin wisps of flour, like vapor, curl from the far side.

Turning the penlight off a final time, Chace sat back, resting against the footboard of her bed, tongue poking slightly over her lower lip as she thought. The white powder on the floor was the clincher, and she didn't need to open the bottom drawer for further proof. There were six drawers in her bureau, two side by side at the top, accessories and what little jewelry remained in her life. First down, lingerie, stockings, socks, the like. Second, shirts, seasonal. Third, sweaters, scarves. Bottom, nothing worthwhile. Bottom was a tease, holding only her old rugby shirt and the sweater her father had worn the Christmas before he'd died. She never went into that drawer except to move it enough to coat its rails with a dusting of flour.

Someone had been in her bureau.

Someone had been in the bloody flat.

It occurred to her that, had it been someone with murder in mind, she'd have been in a lot of trouble, the way she'd come home. It had been sloppy of her, London eyes, not field eyes, an entry she'd never have made during a job. But concerned with a sore foot and a desire to get out of the rain, she'd forged ahead, and been fortunate.

It has to be Box, she thought, and she almost said aloud something unkind about Mr. David Kinney and his also-rans, then thought better of it. If it *had* been Box, they'd tried to go carefully, and they may have planted listening devices during their visit. Maybe cameras as well, but if there were cameras, it was too late for sneaky; whoever was watching would know she was on to them.

She used the footboard to get to her feet, strode

into the front, heedless of the pain, and began pulling on her shoes once more.

Only one way to find out.

●

It took her most of three hours to confirm—or more precisely, reconfirm—and to move suspicion to fact. But when she returned to her flat, dumping the CDs and books she'd bought during her foray, Chace was certain she was being watched, and that it was Box doing the peeking.

More, it wasn't routine surveillance. It was a targeted operation, at least four teams, at least sixteen people, on foot and motorcycle and automobile, and they had done everything they could to avoid detection. This worried her. She knew she'd been checked recently, and that had been a completely different game. One team, on foot, total of four people, working in shifts. Nothing on this scale.

She couldn't see a reason for it. There *was* no reason for it. She'd looked at it from every direction she could conceive and still saw no logic to it.

But there is a logic, Chace told herself as she watched herself brushing her teeth in her bathroom mirror. There's always a logic, you just don't know it yet.

She undressed, climbed into her bed. Maybe it was a training exercise? Not impossible, Kinney using a Minder to hone his people's technique. Stranger things had happened. If that was the case, it would have to have been cleared by Crocker; at the least, D-Ops would have been informed.

Wrapping the covers around her shoulders, burrowing deeper into her pillows, Chace told herself that had to be it. Training exercise, Kinney trying to one-up Crocker: Hey, mate, my men followed your gal, rifled her flat, she never noticed. Not so special as all that, hmm, your Special Section?

She'd ask him in the morning, she decided, and relaxed, sleepy, feeling the bed too big to occupy alone. She'd ask in the morning, and Crocker would tell her, she had no doubt.

That was the rule. All the world could turn on them, but D-Ops would always defend the Minders. At the cost of prospects, career, friends, liberty, life, Crocker would protect them. He would sacrifice everything for them, because that was what he expected in return, that was the agreement. He would order them over the hills and far away, then demand the impossible of them upon their arrival. And Chace, and Poole, and perhaps one day Lankford, too, would give it to him without hesitation, without questioning the reasons or the merits or the causes; they would do as ordered, as they were expected. They would go, and they would even die, if he demanded it.

And in return, Crocker sheltered them, guarded them, fought for them, lied for them. All of Whitehall could turn on the Special Section, but Crocker would remain, lone against the tide, to give cover to his Minders.

Crocker would protect her.

She fell asleep.

28

Kate was behind her desk and had thankfully made coffee when Crocker blew in that morning, and he acknowledged her cheerful hello with a grunt, then moved straight through the outer to the inner. She rose immediately to follow him, and he didn't look back, dropping his document bag on the desk before shrugging out of his raincoat and hooking it to its place on the stand. He ran a hand through his wet hair, watching as Kate set the stack of folders she'd carried in a neat pile on his desk, scowling. His mood was already declining, due in small part to the nightmare of his commute, but mostly in annoyance at what the day ahead undoubtedly held.

"Morning distribution." Kate pulled one of the keys from the tether at her waist, set about unlocking and then unloading Crocker's document bag. "Three items of interest."

"I'd like coffee," Crocker said.

"Philip Heller, on his famil as the KL Number Two, is down with malaria," Kate continued, as if she hadn't heard. "The Number One, Elizabeth Conrad, is binning him back to London, requesting a new Two with all speed. Notes that diminished Station capacity will hurt current operations in the Philippines. VCNS at MOD has submitted a request for operational surveillance of the Chinese naval exercises set to commence on the twenty-third in the South China Sea, and C and the Deputy Chief have both authorized action. D-Int wants ten minutes this forenoon to discuss."

"Coffee," Crocker said again.

"I heard you the first time." Kate closed the document bag, replaced the key on her hip, and then carried the bag to the cabinet safe beside the door, laying it flat on its top. "David Kinney has a message in to speak with you this morning, in person. Earliest convenience."

"I want some—"

"I'm getting it," she said, and stepped through the door to the inner office.

Crocker swiped at the rainwater in his hair a last time, then dried his hand against his vest, moving to his chair and picking up his pen. The stack wasn't nearly as intimidating as it was annoying, mostly memos and other FYIs requiring his initials. He'd already gone through half of them by the time Kate returned with his coffee.

"Shall I ring Mr. Kinney back?" she asked.

"Did he say what he wanted?"

She shook her head. "But presumably it pertains to the notification folderol of last night."

Crocker reached for the cup, nodded. "Ring him back, arrange it. Before noon, if at all possible."

"Right away."

He drank his coffee, considering. His intent had been to go to C first thing this morning and demand an explanation for Box's behavior toward Chace. But Kinney's desire to meet changed the priorities; if he could get an answer that way, it was infinitely better than having another go-round with C. At the same time, Kinney's request only made him more suspicious of the whole affair. Kinney was as territorial as anyone in the Home Office: he'd never make a request of SIS unless he had no alternative.

Or something to gain.

The intercom on his desk emitted its strangled cry for attention.

"What?"

"Minder One to see you, sir."

"She's out there now?"

"Yes, sir."

"Wheel her in."

He put down the cup and lit his first cigarette of the day, watching as Kate opened the door for Chace. Chace already had coffee, Crocker noted, as well as a smile.

"Morning, Boss," she said.

"Anything you two need?" Kate asked.

"Privacy," Crocker said.

Chace seemed mildly amused by this, watching over her shoulder until Kate had shut the door, before sitting, coffee in both hands. Her smile grew as she studied Crocker across his desk.

"Someone's been in my flat," she told him.

"Several someones, according to your personnel file."

"All lies. I never take them back to my place."

"You're sure?"

"Oh, yes."

She said it with the kind of certainty Crocker normally heard used for pronouncements of death.

"There's more," Chace said.

"Do tell."

"I'm being targeted, full job. Four teams on me last night when I nipped out to do some shopping. They've been at my mail, my phones, all of it." Chace's smile got even bigger, and it gave the chill in her eyes that much more of an edge. "I'd be willing to bet they've put cameras in my home."

"They?"

Chace drained her cup, set it on Crocker's desk, fished for her cigarettes. "Well, I'm hoping it's Mr. Kinney and his lads, though I wouldn't object to the PRC trying to honey-trap me."

"Not very likely, though, is it?"

Her lighter clicked closed, and she slipped it back into her pocket, blowing smoke at the ceiling and flopping back in the chair. The smile was still in place.

"No, it really isn't, is it?" Chace said sweetly.

She's livid, Crocker thought.

"What do you want me to tell you?"

"Oh, I know you can't tell me anything, Boss," Chace said. "Box going through my unmentionables for the second time in two, three months, you're not allowed to say if I'm being checked. Again. Defeats the purpose of them trying to catch me being a rotten apple if you warn me that's what they're doing. Trust me, I understand that. You're certainly not allowed to say if Box is suddenly twitchy with me in the wake of the slaughter in San'a', or even if I should return all those Biros I stole from Kate's desk. I know that."

Crocker waited. Chace gave him the gleeful smile for five seconds longer, then took another drag off her cigarette, leaned forward again, and jabbed it out in his ashtray. She rose, taking the empty cup.

"I just wanted *you* to know that I know," she said cheerfully. "I'll be in the Pit."

●

Kinney arrived at seventeen minutes past nine, Kate ushering him in, and Crocker liked that even less. Seventeen past nine, it meant that Kinney had come straightaway, that he'd been waiting to hear from Kate, waiting to come over for the meeting.

Crocker didn't bother to get up but decided it would be pushing things too far not to offer the other man a seat. He waved at the chairs.

"Please," Crocker said.

"Not necessary," Kinney said. "Wanted to look in on you, apologize for any confusion."

"I'm not confused."

"Clerical bloody error, Crocker. Should have my PA's hands cut off."

"They happen."

"Wanted to say it's nothing for you to worry about."

"I'd like to determine that for myself."

"And I'm here to say you don't have to bother."

They stared at each other.

Bastard, Crocker thought. *Bastard, you're scared now, you blew it, whatever it was, and you're trying to get the milk back in the bottle now.*

He kept it from his face. If Kinney didn't know that Chace had made the surveillance, it wasn't going to be Crocker who corrected Kinney's error.

"No need to worry Chace about it," Kinney said finally. "No need to worry anyone, really."

"You seem to think I'm a bundle of nerves, David," Crocker said. "I was concerned last night, but the Deputy Chief set me straight. Besides, you wouldn't dare put surveillance on one of the Minders without notifying me first. You wouldn't break that rule."

"And risk starting another Home Office–Foreign Office battle for supremacy?" Kinney's laugh was short and thick, much like the man from which it emanated. "No, never. My concern was only that you might take it the wrong way. You do tend to overreact."

Crocker shook his head slightly. "You came crosstown to tell me this?"

"We've had difficulties in the past. I didn't want this to turn into anything ugly."

"Why should it?" Crocker evaded. "You vetted Chace in July, and she cleared. You'll vet her again, and she'll clear again. As long as I'm notified when you're putting the lens on my people, you're free to spy on whomever you desire. Within your boundaries, of course."

Kinney's expression flickered, as if caught for a second in a strobe, and Crocker could see him thinking. Each of them was lying to the other, and Crocker suspected now that each of them knew that was the case, and still Kinney was trying to make like they were friends. If the stakes weren't so very high, it would have struck Crocker as ridiculous, even laughable, that they were so committed to their deceptions. But it wasn't funny, if for no other reason than that David Kinney was as much of a zealot in the Security Services as Paul Crocker was at SIS.

"Well, then," Kinney said finally. "I won't take more of your time."

"Kate will show you out," Crocker said, and he keyed his intercom, waited, and then watched as Kate entered and led Kinney from the room.

Once the door was closed, Crocker sat back in his chair, turned it to look out the tinted window, past the leaded curtains, at the rain drifting down on London.

He didn't come here to try to cover it up, Crocker realized. *He's not that stupid. He wasn't here to try to convince me of anything.*

He came to see exactly how much I know.

It bothered Crocker that he didn't seem to know anything.

He reached back to the desk, keyed the intercom again.

"Master?" Kate said from the speaker.

"Call Cheng," Crocker said. "Find out if she's free for lunch."

When in doubt, Crocker thought, coming off the intercom, *go to the CIA.* Even if they don't know the truth, their lies are always better than our own.

29

London—Mayfair, the Hole
16 September 1226 GMT

Crocker assumed that Cheng picked the restaurant because it was unrelentingly strange. Wedged on a side street six blocks south of Grosvenor Square, in a house that had been built in the 1660s—and with all the low ceilings, cramped quarters, and exposed beams that that implied—the Hole was, as best as he could tell from the menu, a Scottish/Polish/Mexican restaurant, specializing in pierogi, salmon, and fajitas. The walls bristled with antique weapons and black-and-white framed photographs of American movie stars from the 1930s, 1940s, and 1950s, and a boom box behind the bar on the ground level played Big Band tunes much too loud for the speakers'—or the patrons'—comfort.

Cheng was already seated and working on a plate

of smoked salmon when he arrived, and she had to get up from the table to give him room to pass. He was tall enough that contortions were required before he could adequately seat himself, and even then he had to watch his elbows for fear of alternately ramming them into the wall or clipping glassware and sending it to the floor.

"I hate this place," he told Cheng.

She nodded around a mouthful of fish, chewed, swallowed. "I love it."

"You're a bloody tourist, Angela."

She shrugged, as if denying the accusation wasn't worth the effort. "You're paying."

"Yes, I am." He raised a hand—carefully—and flagged a surly young man, asking for a soda.

"No argument?" Cheng poked at a caper on her plate with her fork. "No let's go halvesies, no you've got the bigger budget?"

"No."

"You must really want something."

"Why's Box going through Chace's unmentionables?"

"Because they're like the FBI?" Cheng offered. "They suffer from the same intelligence equivalent of blue balls?"

"They know how to get themselves off," Crocker said. "That's what I'm afraid of."

The surly young man came back and placed Crocker's drink on the tiny table, hard enough that soda slopped over the sides, then lingered to take his order. Crocker asked for the pierogi and another napkin, lit a cigarette as the waiter departed.

"Come on, not while I'm eating."

"Especially while you're eating. What do you know?"

"What makes you think I know anything about why *your* Security Services—meaning Britain's—are looking at *your* people—meaning *you* specifically?"

"Because at last count the CIA was supplementing the income of roughly a quarter of the staff at Box."

Cheng grinned and pointed her fork at him. "You can't prove that. And even if you could, I'd deny everything."

"I'm serious, Angela. They've got her under close watch, it's not a check, it's something else. David Kinney came to me this morning trying to figure out what I know and left smug in the knowledge that the answer is nil. We're talking about my Head of Section. Anything happens to Chace, I lose one-third of my ops capability. Bad for me, bad for you, bad for the special relationship between our houses."

"You lose Chace, you lose more than a third," Cheng remarked, now using a small slice of rye bread to make an open-faced sandwich. "Lankford's untested."

"No, he's tested, he's yet to pass."

"Making my point."

She took a bite from her sandwich, then bent back in her chair to make room for the waiter's return. The young man dropped Crocker's plate on the table with the same finesse with which he'd delivered his drink, spilling more soda. He then dropped a napkin on Crocker's lap before departing again for the bar.

"You're sure he's not Russian mob?" Crocker remarked.

"No, he makes porn," Cheng said. "This is his day job. His mother runs the place. Came over during the war, her husband was with the Polish exiles."

"You checked?"

"Sure. Didn't you?"

"About Chace."

Cheng shook her head. "You should talk to your own people, not me."

"I've tried. They are being unusually reticent."

"Meaning you couldn't bully it out of Weldon?"

"Meaning Weldon has suddenly developed a spine. Meaning Rayburn is out of the loop, whatever it is, and meaning that I can't get in to see C."

"C's avoiding you?"

"Kate's been trying to get me in to see him all morning, keeps being told that he's out of the building or in meetings."

Cheng stopped eating, used her napkin to wipe the corners of her mouth. The gesture was deliberate and slow, and Crocker knew she was using the time to collect her thoughts, and he knew the thoughts weren't pleasant ones. The mirth was draining from her face much the way ice melts under running water.

"You need to start looking for a new Minder," Cheng told him softly. "You're about to be one short. Again."

Coming from anyone else, Crocker would have

dismissed the statement as hyperbole. But for all the banter between them, all the jokes, Cheng didn't make cracks like that, not about the lives of his people or hers.

"What in the hell is going on?" Crocker asked.

"They're giving her to the Saudis, Paul."

"What?"

"They're giving her to—"

"I heard you. What the bloody hell does that mean, Angela? The Saudis have no reason to be looking at her, they've no reason to be looking at us. They were looking at the Israelis for what happened in Yemen."

"I know."

"What changed?"

"The world." She folded her napkin beside her plate, pushed back from the table, rising. "Let's go to my office. That way you can scream and shout and break things."

•

"It's in the Wadi-as-Sirhan, somewhere south-southeast of the Jordanian border." Cheng turned the photographs on her desk, facing them toward Crocker, standing opposite. "Complement anywhere from forty to eighty terrorists, mix of veterans from campaigns in Iraq, Afghanistan, Kashmir, and Chechnya, along with new recruits, mostly pulled from the *madrassa*-and-mosque crowd in Saudi, Egypt, Yemen, Sudan . . . you get the idea."

"Who claims it?"

"You don't know?" Cheng looked genuinely surprised. "It's your pals in the Harakat ul-Mujihadin, Abdul Aziz faction. Same gang that set fire to your lovely subway system. The camp's equipped for the whole nine yards, Paul—firing exercises, CQC, bomb-making, rhetoric. Word is it's higher education for the *jihadis.*"

Crocker bent, giving the photographs a close examination. They were remarkably clear and uncompromising, and he guessed they had come from the latest-generation satellites the CIA now employed. In a couple of photographs, he was able to make out faces, gestures, even expressions, all of them captured from orbit.

"How recent are these?" he asked.

"These came in this morning, requested by the White House yesterday. There's another batch coming, the satellite's making a pass every seventy-nine minutes, and for the time being, it's a hot spot."

"Wadi-as-Sirhan." Crocker chewed on it, trying to connect the location with the facts in his memory. "That's Tabuk province, isn't it? Prince Salih was on the magistrate's council in Tabuk."

"Salih was the main source of income for the camp."

"But the camp hasn't dried up now that he's dead?"

"On the contrary, it's doing booming business. Maybe they were stashing away money for a rainy day, God only knows. The Mossad has hard intel that HUM-AA is liaising with Hamas and Al-Aqsa, bringing in bombing recruits."

Crocker, mildly alarmed, moved his look from the pictures to Cheng. "They're teaming the bombers with the regulars?"

"Mossad thinks that's the plan. Your pal Landau apparently pushed a rather strongly worded pack up the chain to his Chief, and his Chief in turn presented it to his Prime Minister and select members of his Cabinet. Mossad Research believes that the bombers are being paired with trained *jihadis* to act as their cutouts and handlers. The *jihadis* move the bombers to their target locations, assemble the explosives, wire up the bombers, and turn them loose."

"And from the Wadi-as-Sirhan . . . ," Crocker said.

"Yeah, from the Wadi-as-Sirhan, they've got access to the whole Middle East. With the mess in Iraq right now, the White House is more than a little antsy that we're going to be seeing more dead soldiers on television, and that's the last thing the President wants. Not to mention what it could do in places like Egypt, Lebanon, Jordan."

"Why stop there? If they're willing to give it the effort, they could strike a lot closer to home."

"There's that, too."

Crocker made a face, discarded the photograph in his hand with a flick of the wrist, turning away from the desk. On the far wall of Cheng's office was a framed photograph of the President of the United States, and beside it, another of the Director of the Central Intelligence Agency. An American flag hung limply from a pole in the corner, between the couch and a bookshelf.

He heard Cheng moving, then the rattle of a cap coming off a bottle and the whiff of alcohol splashing into a glass. When he turned back, she was standing by the sidebar behind her desk, offering him a cut-glass tumbler of scotch.

He hesitated, then took it.

Cheng poured a shot for herself, then moved to the couch, settling in, smoothing her skirt with one hand, drink balanced in the other. She waited until Crocker had taken a seat and a sip before tasting her own.

"The Israelis are viewing this as a direct threat to their security and the lives of their citizenry," Cheng said.

"With good reason."

"Yeah. But they can't move against Saudi. If they launch a covert and it goes bad, they've wandered into *the* worst-case scenario. Israeli commandos on Saudi soil? It'll make what Chace did in San'a' look like Up with Islam Day."

"So they're pressing the White House."

"Not exactly. They double-teamed, sent their Foreign Minister to speak to the U.S. Ambassador, and at the same time the Head of Research, this ex-KGB guy—"

"Viktor Borovsky," Crocker said. "I know who he is."

"Right, Borovsky sent his findings to the Company, claiming it was a courtesy."

"But looking for verification."

"Which we provided."

"You have the same problem the Israelis have, you can't launch a covert inside Saudi."

Cheng drained her glass, set it down. "Nor can you."

Crocker thought, took another taste of the scotch. It was a blend, and not a particularly nice one, and he made a face.

"I save the good stuff for my ambassador," Cheng explained.

"So I see." He pushed his glass away. "White House spoke to the Saudis?"

"That's the only move."

"And?"

"And the Saudis said that they would happily roll up the camp in the Wadi-as-Sirhan, in the spirit of goodwill and international peace and friendship, and as a show of solidarity in the war on terrorism. They have one of their new antiterror teams standing by, apparently, and this is supposedly one of the good ones. Meaning, one of the ones where the members aren't actually foaming Wahhabists themselves."

"But."

"But they feel that the murder of Prince Salih bin Muhammad bin Sultan is a crime that must be answered, both publicly and politically. They're refusing to move on HUM-AA until the perpetrator has been rendered into Saudi custody."

The apprehension that seized his stomach took Crocker by surprise.

"They realize there's a good chance that Abdul

Aziz will launch a bomb at one of them soon enough, just like UBL, don't they?" he asked.

"If the Saudis do—and they probably do, but I never try to gauge a government's capacity for self-deception—they clearly feel it's worth the risk. Gets worse, though. They've made it real plain that any incursion whatsoever into the Wadi-as-Sirhan will be viewed as a direct challenge to their sovereignty, and they will respond accordingly."

"Meaning they'll cut off the oil."

"They know how to hit the Administration where it lives, let's put it that way. Doesn't do great things for you guys, either, I might add."

"It doesn't have to be her," he said after a moment. "It doesn't have to be Chace."

Cheng picked up her glass, examining it, as if hoping she'd missed a few drops of her drink. "Maybe not, but they know they're looking for a woman, and they know she's from the West or an Israeli."

"How do they know that?"

"Apparently there's a witness, or three or four, and while the witnesses didn't see the actual assassination, they saw a woman leaving, and they've identified her as non-Arab."

"I won't just hand over Chace."

"You're talking like you have a say in it, my friend, and you and I both know that you *don't*. The Israelis aren't going to hand over an innocent; they've already responded that, if forced to do so, they'll take matters into their own hands."

"It doesn't have to be her."

"Then you're going to have to find some chick who's willing to be rendered to the Saudis to have her head snicked off in Chop-Chop Square, Paul. Because the Saudis are locked on this, they're not backing down. And if Box is closing in on Chace . . ."

"The Government has already made its decision," Crocker concluded softly.

Cheng nodded, but didn't add anything.

The tension in Crocker's stomach shifted, moved upward into his chest. His immediate thought was that there had to be a dodge, some way to get Chace out of the situation, some way that would satisfy all the parties involved. But when he looked to Cheng, he could see the resignation on her face, and he knew its source.

"They'll execute her," Crocker said. "God knows what they'll do before that, but they'll end up executing her."

"Trust me, I know. Look, Paul, you don't have to convince me how much this sucks ass. I know exactly how much this sucks ass, I am painfully aware of the degree of ass-suckage present in this scenario. But it's the rules of the game. Chace doesn't matter one goddamn, and you know it. Neither do you, neither do I. It's the institution that matters, it's the politics, and right now there's one agency and three major governments, and they're all in agreement on this.

"As far as they're concerned, you can always get a new Minder One."

"Not like her."

"You think they care?"

Crocker bit back a response, trying to grip the anger as it surged forward. Cheng didn't deserve it; Cheng hadn't earned it.

He rose, heading for the door. "Get someone to see me out."

"I'm sorry, Paul."

"The hell with that, I need an escort, I've got to get back to my office." He stopped abruptly, veered toward Cheng's desk. "Let me use your phone."

"What're you doing?"

"I need to call my office."

"I can do it for you."

Crocker glared at her. "No. You can't."

Cheng shook her head. "I can't let you, Paul."

"Then get me a fucking escort out of here now!"

She rose, moved to the office door, and leaned out, calling for her PA. "Margo, Mr. Crocker needs an escort out and a cab." She told him, "Let me know what I can do."

"You've done quite enough, thank you," Crocker said, and left.

30

The red phone rang on Chace's desk, and she answered it before the tone had faded from the air, grinning at Lankford seated across the room, who once again had exhibited his Pavlovian response to the bell. Poole, without looking up, chuckled.

"Steady, Chris," Poole said.

"Minder One," Chace said.

"Minder Three, my office, now," Crocker's voice snarled in her ear, then he hung up.

Chace blinked, listened to the dead circuit, then replaced the phone. Poole glanced up, then did a double-take, seeing her expression.

"Well?" Lankford asked.

"Boss's office," she told him. "You."

"Me?"

"Him?" Poole asked.

"Him," Chace confirmed.

Lankford stared, then all at once seemed to realize that he wasn't moving. He sprang up, sending his chair banging back against the wall, nearly clipping his hip on the corner of his desk as he came around its side. He hustled to the door, opened it, closed it, doubled back, grabbed his suit jacket off the peg, then went to the door again and disappeared into the hall, still struggling to get his arms into the sleeves.

Chace and Poole exchanged grins, then she rose and closed the door.

"Think he's cleaning out his desk, then?" Poole asked.

"I'd like to think I would have been informed."

Poole tilted his chair back, folded his hands behind his head, watching her. "I've got a mate out Portsmouth way."

"I feel sorry for him," Chace said.

"You and me both. Does work at the School, handles the night exercises, teaches one of the tech courses."

"My sympathy grows."

"Yeah, well, he says that when you were out there on your refresher, you and a certain recently retired Head of the Special Section went out for dinner and drinks and the like. And that you failed to return to your dormitory that evening, but instead returned to the School in the very wee hours of the next morning, driven by the self-same recently retired Head of the Special Section, and that the both of you were looking considerably the worse for wear."

"Does your friend remember what I was wearing, too?"

"I can call and ask him. He is a trained intelligence officer, you know."

"So are you."

"So I am."

"And you have drawn conclusions."

"I have." Poole nodded slowly. "I have indeed."

"Do you wish to share those conclusions, Minder Two?"

"It is my conclusion, Minder One, that you and the former Minder One got blasted and then shagged like giggling teenagers when their parents are away on holiday, that is my conclusion."

Chace grinned. "Do you have any evidence to support this conclusion?"

"Aside from that cum-drunk grin you've got on your face, no, I do not."

"Cum-drunk?"

Poole shrugged apologetically. "Regiment talk."

"Lovely, that."

"But descriptive."

"Evocative, at the least."

"You have not refuted my conclusion, oh Head of Section."

"No, I haven't, have I?"

"Nor have you confirmed it. You have yet to answer conclusively one way or the other."

"That is correct, you are quite correct, Nicky. Do

you want an answer, is that what you're hoping for here?"

Poole smiled, pleased with himself. "Yes, very much."

"Right, then," Chace said, and she flipped him two fingers and showed him her best fuck-off smile. "Mind your own."

Poole laughed, dropping his hands back to his desk, returning to his work.

"I always do, don't I? It's in my job description," he said.

•

Lankford returned fourteen minutes after he'd left, and both Chace and Poole looked up from their work as he entered, curious as to what had happened in Crocker's office. The look on Lankford's face was pinched.

"You on your bike?" Chace asked him.

Lankford shook his head, took off his coat, hung it on the rack.

"What then?"

"He wanted to talk about my prospects." While he said it, Lankford dropped a folded square of paper onto her desk. "Wanted to know how it was working out down here, if I was ready to make a go of it full-time."

Chace looked at the paper, then to Lankford, quizzical. Over at the Minder Two desk, Poole's chair was scraping back on the floor as he got up to join them.

"What'd you say?" Chace asked, taking the paper.

There was nothing special about it whatsoever: copier paper, white, plain, folded in a square.

"Well, that I was enjoying the work very much," Lankford said. "That I recognized I had a long way to go until I was at your level, or Nicky's, but that I felt certain I would rise to it, and do so quickly."

"I agree," Chace said, opening the sheet. "You're coming along nicely."

"Thank you."

Chace looked at the note, handwritten by Crocker, blue ink on white paper.

Leave. Do not return home. Lose Box. 0210 Imperial Age, VIP, clean. Minders will support.

Chace found it suddenly hard to breathe, had to force herself to inhale. She turned the note in her hand, showing it to Poole but looking at Lankford. He was watching her, his expression blatantly defying the banality of his words, drawn with tension.

For a moment, she honestly couldn't think of anything to say, her mind still spinning from the note, trying to fathom it, straining to understand. Trouble, obviously big trouble, and she was at the heart of it, but she was damned if she could see the why of it, or even the how. She had known it wasn't a spot-check by Box, she had known it wasn't simply a security viewing. But this . . . This was beyond anything she had imagined, if for no other reason than that she had not, in her wildest dreams, thought it would lead to something like this.

Box wanted her, Crocker's message made that

clear. Why, she didn't know, but if Crocker was telling her anything at all, he was telling her that Kinney was going to try to put the arm on her and she'd better get moving, and fast.

The clock on the wall told her it was fourteen-thirty-three. Just under twelve hours until she was to be in the VIP room at the Imperial Age, then. Provided she could keep her liberty for the duration.

Poole had finished reading the note, and now he was looking at her, too, much the way Lankford was.

"Is there anything else you think I should be working on?" Lankford asked her. "To improve my performance?"

She still couldn't trust her voice with a response and so she shook her head, drawing the note back from Poole and crumpling it tight in her hand, then dropping it into her jacket pocket. Then she rose from her chair.

"No, Chris," she told him. "I think you've definitely demonstrated that you're ready to be Minder Three."

Poole took the cue off her, went to the stand, grabbed his coat.

"I'm off for a pint," Chace told them, and left the Pit.

•

She had a moment of apprehension, showing her pass to the warden on the door on her way out, but he didn't stop her, just gave her a nod of recognition and waved her through. She stepped out into the courtyard of the building, into the slight mist that was doing a weak imitation of rain, following the walk to the door by the gate. The gate was opening, and Chace recognized C's black Bentley as it glided into the yard. She looked away from the car, kept her stride steady.

There were more guards on the gate and they showed no signs of wishing to detain her, just checked her pass again, logged her out. Chace took the opportunity to glance back toward the entrance, saw C's driver opening the rear door, saw Barclay climbing out of the car, far enough away that she couldn't read his expression. She turned away before he could return the look, stepped through the door beside the gate, tucking her pass back into her inside pocket.

Wondering if she hadn't just left Vauxhall Cross for the last time.

31

Sinan watched as Matteen moved to the entrance of the tent, closed the flap, then slipped and turned the four wooden toggles through their frogs, trying to ensure against interruptions. Finished, he returned to the small table, propped his rifle against it, and sat on the rickety stool. On the table was a blue and black knapsack, a knockoff of a popular Western design, with several pockets and flaps and zippers. Matteen opened the pack and began loading it with boxes of ammunition, to weigh it down.

Sinan didn't sit and, after confirming that Matteen was getting the weights correct, turned his attention to Nia. They were in one of the smaller tents, and there wasn't a lot of room, and among the smell of the canvas and the heat and the dust, Sinan was sure he could smell her, too, and he cursed his imagination, willed himself to focus on the task at hand.

"We are your brothers in this," he said to Nia gently. "And you are our sister."

She nodded, hesitant, but the gesture was clear enough, even under her cloak and veil.

"You are *shahid*, and our purpose is to see you attain Paradise."

Another nod, and Sinan was suddenly uncertain if he was trying to reassure Nia or himself. Behind him, he heard the sound of the zipper running over its teeth as Matteen closed the knapsack.

"Show us," Sinan told Nia.

The woman hesitated again, then turned away from him, toward the wall of the tent. She reached up, unfastening her veil from her cowl, removing the *abaya*. Sinan looked away at first, when her bare arm revealed itself, and saw that Matteen was watching Nia's movements with a decided disinterest. He envied his fellow the ability, wondered how he could manage it.

Sinan couldn't.

But he couldn't *not* look, either, and when he forced his eyes back to Nia, she was pulling the *abaya* away from her body, and he saw her bare legs. They were smooth, their curve gentle, her thighs slim but strong, and when she shifted her weight, he saw the muscles move, disappearing up beneath the shorts that were too short, the kind of shorts the Zionist girls wore. Her skin reminded him of her eyes, the eyes he'd caught himself thinking about too many times. Warmth seemed to emanate from her and, for the first time, Sinan wanted to touch her, to feel it for himself.

And he knew he was too weak, then, and he prayed to Allah, the Compassionate, for mercy.

She folded the *abaya* carefully, then shyly turned back around to face him, her eyes on the dirt floor of the tent.

Sinan looked, and even though he was supposed to look, even though it was his job to look, he felt guilt and shame surge through him, seeing her like this. She'd been given one of the Western tops to wear, powder blue to match the dark blue shorts, and there were three thin white stripes on the top, running around the center, and they made her breasts seem bigger, more defined. Her arms, like her legs, were slender and graceful, and her black hair fell thickly below her shoulders.

When he looked at her face, he was certain she was beautiful, and he thought, for the first time, that he must be very ugly to her eyes.

It was Matteen who spoke first. "Good, I believe the clothes. But your hair will have to be cut, you understand?"

Nia's left hand started toward her head, then stopped, fell back, and she nodded, still looking at the floor.

How old is she? Sinan wondered, still drinking her in, unable to stop himself. *Eighteen? Nineteen?*

"Come sit here," Matteen said, and he got to his feet, making room for Nia at the table.

She did as he instructed, and when she moved, she glanced to Sinan, and he knew she saw how he was looking at her, and still he couldn't stop it. She knew it, it was in her eyes, and he expected displeasure or contempt.

But he saw none.

"Sinan?" Matteen asked. "You want to do this?"

Sinan looked at him quickly, but Matteen appeared just as bored by their activities as before.

"We have scissors?"

"I thought I brought them, they're in our tent," Matteen said. "I'll be right back."

He opened the flap just enough to slip out, leaving them alone, before Sinan could offer to do it himself.

Nia shifted on the stool slightly, hands in her lap. Sinan tried to find something else in the tent to look at, settled ultimately on the main support for the roof.

"Is it heavy?" she asked softly. "The bomb?"

"Ten pounds," Sinan said. "Maybe more. When we're finished with your hair and your clothes, you will try on the knapsack. Matteen's weighted it down, so you know what it will be like."

"I thought there would be a belt. In Gaza, they showed us pictures of the belts."

"The knapsack is easier to make than the belt," Sinan explained.

"Ten pounds." After a moment, Nia added, "That's not too heavy. My books were heavier."

It took him a second. "You were a student?"

She nodded.

"Why aren't you a student now?"

"They killed my friend."

Sinan moved to the tent opening, peered out between the flaps. There was no sign of Matteen, no sign of anyone about, really. From one of the larger tents, he could hear the sounds of a recording playing a sermon, Dr. Faud's voice.

"Your friend," Sinan began. "Your friend . . . you were close to him?"

He heard Nia shift again on the stool. "I am a Muslim woman."

He turned back to her then, feeling utterly like an ass. "I did not mean to insult you. I know you are a good woman and that you are proper. I didn't mean to say otherwise."

"He was my friend," she repeated, and she looked up at him, and Sinan thought her eyes were colder now. "In Nablus, and he was shot, and he died, and he didn't do anything to them."

"I understand."

She turned her head away, the gesture angry, and Sinan felt even more an ass. He looked to the tent flaps again, wondering what was taking Matteen so long.

"You aren't an Arab," she said. "You're English."

"I am a Muslim."

"But you are English."

"No, I am a Muslim. What I was before I found the Truth is nothing. It is what I am now that matters."

Nia seemed to think about this, then shook her head. "Why are you here?"

"I want to help my brothers."

"Did they kill someone close to you? Did you lose a friend to them?"

Sinan thought about Aamil.

"No," he said. "Not like you mean. But I have seen my brothers dying, my sisters dying, and that was enough for me. The *imam* in my mosque, before I came here, he taught me about what it meant to be a Muslim, he taught me that there were six pillars, not five, and it was he who helped me find a *madrassa* that would take me."

"So you came here?"

"I was in Cairo first. For many months, and then I was sponsored on the Hajj by the Prince, Allah have mercy on him. And on the Hajj, I saw . . ."

Sinan faltered, afraid to share what he had seen. Aamil had been there, and Aamil had understood, but only barely. There had been times, since then, when Sinan had wondered if his vision of the Satans, of the suffering they brought, hadn't been the result of hunger, or dehydration, or exhaustion, or all of those things combined. It did not matter; he had seen what he had seen, and he had known what he had to do, as a man, as a Muslim, but mostly, as a Wahhabi.

"What did you see?" Nia asked softly.

She was looking at him again, curious and beautiful. He opened his mouth to answer and then felt the sunlight splash him as Matteen slipped through the tent flap.

"Yassir was using them," Matteen explained, handing the scissors to Sinan. "Sorry it took so long."

"It's all right," Sinan told him.

Nia straightened in her seat, pushed her tumbled hair back off her shoulders, and none of them said anything as Sinan began to cut it.

When he was finished, Nia wiped at her eyes, and he realized she had been weeping.

32

The pub was only half a mile from Vauxhall Cross, an easy enough walk, though in the fifteen minutes it took Chace to cover the distance the mist turned to more sincere rain, surprisingly cold, considering the time of year. She cut through Vauxhall Park, then south on Meadow Road, and when she made the dogleg off Dorset onto Bolney, she stopped abruptly to light a cigarette, hunching her head against the rain, cupping the flame with her hand, then looking back the way she had come, counting to fifteen.

No one came around the corner in a hurry to catch up.

She blew out smoke, frowning as she moved to the entrance of the pub. Bad sign, she thought. It wasn't an elaborate flush, to be sure, but still, it would normally have been enough to force Box to tip their hand. That it hadn't worked meant that Kinney was playing cautious and, worse, that he knew she was on to him.

Once inside and out of the rain, she ran a hand through her hair, looking over the room. It was almost entirely empty, which, for the time being, wasn't a bad thing. The maid at the bar recognized her and had a lager pulled before Chace even reached her.

"Jacket potato?" she asked.

"Just the lager," Chace said, paying.

"You're on your liquid diet again?"

"What was it the man said? 'Beer is food, Lewis'?"

The maid grinned and banged the register, handed Chace her change. Chace took her glass to the table in the corner, put out her cigarette in the ashtray, and promptly lit another. The door opened, and Lankford came in with Poole, and they each hit the bar. Lankford's manner was easy with the maid, and before they had their drinks, he'd gotten her laughing, twice, and each time honest, and it occurred to Chace that maybe he was better than she'd given him credit for being.

Poole led to the table, parked opposite her, and stole a cigarette from her pack while Lankford was getting settled. They each took a moment to lower the levels in their glasses.

"Well, I'm fucked, boys," Chace told them.

Lankford nodded, and Poole said, "That was the rumor at the School."

"What'd you see?"

"Counted six," Lankford said. "Two in cars, radios, maybe controllers. Four on foot, even split men and women, and they were so blasted focused on keeping you from spotting them, they forgot about us."

"Two more on motorbikes," Poole said. "Those are the ones we did see, Tara. Probably double that working you up right now."

"Probably," she agreed, and cleared the smoke from her mouth to make room for more of her lager.

"Want to explain this, then?" asked Poole.

"I can't. Chris?"

Lankford shook his head. "I got into the office, he told me to park and started scribbling the note. Handed it to me, then said that Nicky and I were to follow, to do what you said, and to lie low otherwise. And that we were on no account to talk to the DC or C or anyone about what was going on."

"There you go, Nicky."

"You shag Harry or something?" Poole asked. "Why this sudden attention from Box?"

"Why are you so concerned with my sex life, Nicky?"

"Might be because you have one," Lankford observed.

"Not for much longer," Chace said. "All right, finish your beer and then shove off. Back to the Pit, do your thing. Assuming Box doesn't try to grab me between now and darkness—"

"Not a safe assumption," Poole observed.

She continued without pause, glaring at him.

"—find me at Paddington at twenty-hundred, and be ready to play. That's where I want to lose them, and I'll need you both to run interference."

"There's going to be hell to pay when Kinney realizes what's going on," Lankford said. "He'll start screaming about SIS operations in London, infringement, all of that."

"He'll be screaming about something else, we do it right." Chace looked at Poole. "I need my go-bag, can you bring it?"

"Easy peasy."

Chace rolled her eyes, and Poole chuckled. "You want docs? Cash? We're assuming you're going to ground here."

She thought, then shook her head. "No, too risky. I'll handle that myself if I have to. But I will take whatever you two have in your wallets."

"Don't you have a bank card?"

"And let Box find me via ATM? Not on your fucking life, Chris."

Both men reached for their wallets, dumped several bills onto the table. Chace counted them up quickly, two hundred and eighteen pounds. With her eighty-seven, enough to buy her way around almost any obstacle. She tucked the bills into her pocket, then came out with the note Lankford had brought from Crocker. She handed it back to him.

"Get rid of this."

"Thought you'd have already done it."

"No place to ditch it that Box wouldn't grab it themselves. Make sure it's destroyed."

Lankford finished draining his glass, rose, nodding. "Right."

Poole got to his feet. "Anything else?"

"One thing."

"Yes?"

"Wish me luck?" she asked.

Poole stared at her for a moment, unsmiling, and the full seriousness of the situation settled on them all then.

"I would, Tara," he said. "But I don't think luck'll do it."

33

"Where's Chace?" Weldon demanded.

"She's not in the Pit?" Crocker said.

"You damn well know she's not in the Pit. Where is she, Paul?"

Crocker scratched at his jaw, finding a spot of stubble he'd missed with his morning razor. "I really have no idea, sir. Perhaps you could inquire of David Kinney? I'm sure he knows."

Weldon's frustration ran through his neck, turning it crimson.

"It is after six, sir," Crocker added. "She may have headed home."

"Wardens clocked her out at half-past two. She never came back."

Crocker nodded thoughtfully. "She did say something to me about visiting her mother."

"Her mother lives in Geneva. Do you expect me to believe you allowed her to leave the country without registering the departure? That you've sent Chace on vacation without the proper authorizations?"

"I long ago abandoned hope of guessing what you might or might not believe, sir."

Weldon's hands opened and closed several times, and then he pivoted and slammed the door to the inner office. The gesture was uncharacteristically violent, and Crocker started slightly with surprise.

When Weldon turned back, his expression had drained of any readable emotion, including fury. His shoulders slumped, and his head lowered, and Crocker felt he was looking at a defeated man. Weldon wasn't a bad liar, but he wasn't the expert that Crocker himself was or, for that matter, that most of the Ops Directorate were. His words were good, but his body language had the tendency to give him away. He couldn't control it, at least not before it could be read.

This was not an act.

Weldon slowly took the chair facing the desk.

"You had lunch with Cheng," Weldon said. It wasn't accusatory.

"At the Hole."

"What did she tell you?"

Crocker didn't answer.

Weldon shook his head ever so slightly, as if he'd expected as much. "There's a directive from Downing Street coming, Paul. Probably arrived, though I haven't seen it."

"Directives are supposed to come down from C to you before distribution for action."

"I'm included in distribution after the fact," Weldon said. "This is coming from C to you."

"And this directive says what?"

"That Tara Chace is to surrender herself to David Kinney and the Security Services. Immediately."

"What's she done?"

Weldon just looked at him, clearly too tired and too defeated to play along.

"You've been fighting it," Crocker said, realizing.

"The last two days, since it was first proposed." Weldon looked away, to the sole decoration on the walls, the Chinese dragon print that Crocker kept framed behind and to the left of his desk. "Obviously to no effect."

"Why didn't you say something to me last night?"

"Because it wasn't your place, or mine! We serve, Paul, that's what we do, and we do not have the luxury of picking and choosing which directives to pursue. Every effort, every argument, was put forth on Chace's behalf. But the decision has now been made, and it is our obligation to follow our Government's orders."

"At the cost of Chace's life?"

"Regrettably, yes," Weldon said. "She's one person. For what's at stake, that's a reasonable sacrifice."

"I disagree, sir."

"I know you do. But your agreement, your disagreement, your cheerful acceptance, it's all irrelevant now. You will receive the directive, and you will implement it, or it will cost you your job."

Crocker stared at Weldon, saw in his expression that it wasn't a threat. Just another statement of fact.

"I don't know where she is, sir," Crocker said.

"But she's running."

"Perhaps."

"Did you speak to her?"

Crocker shook his head.

"I'd like to hear you say as much."

"The last time I spoke with Minder One was this morning," Crocker replied. "She was in the Pit until two-thirty, then left the building. I do not know where she went, nor do I know why."

Weldon frowned, measuring Crocker's words, probing their truth. "What did she say to you this morning?"

"That she was being targeted. That she suspected Box."

"That was all?"

"That was all."

"Did you confirm it?"

Crocker scowled. "Of course I didn't."

"Then why did she bring it to you?"

"To let me know she knew."

"I beg your pardon?"

"She was confirming it was Box."

"But you said you didn't confirm it!"

"That's correct. Chace knows that I'm to be informed if any of the Minders are under security check. She also knows I can't confirm it if they are.

And since I didn't leap to my feet and start screaming that she was the target of a hostile party, she reasonably concluded that the check was in-house and routine, performed by Box."

"Routine, you say?"

"Elaborate but, yes, routine."

Weldon's thick fingers played absently with the tail of his tie. "She wouldn't believe that, would she? Not after being vetted so recently?"

"It's possible. She's my Head of Section, I'm inclined to grant her a modicum of sense."

"So she's running."

"I really can't say. I haven't heard from her."

"You're her D-Ops, no one in the world knows her better."

Wrong, Crocker thought. *One man knows her better.*

"I can't say, sir."

Weldon expelled a breath, frowning, obviously and deeply troubled. He smoothed his necktie, got to his feet. "When the directive arrives, you will follow it."

Crocker allowed himself the glare, both because he wanted to and because it was what Weldon expected of him.

"She's to be detained for Box," Weldon continued.

"She'll resist."

"Then steps will have to be taken to subdue her."

"You're authorizing violence against one of our own officers?"

"It won't be us who initiates violence, Paul, if

that's what it comes to. If that's what it comes to, she'll be bringing it on herself."

"You'll destroy this Service, you realize that?" Crocker said, and all the anger he had been fighting against began erupting, and he heard his voice gaining volume and decided he didn't care. "We sell her like this, we'll never come back from it, we'll never regain what we lose. Sacrificing an agent in the field, on a mission, for a goal, that's one thing, that's something they all acknowledge, something they come to terms with as part of the job. But you bastards sell her to the enemy, condemn her to humiliation and death, all for the sake of a political expediency that's only required because she did exactly what you asked of her!"

"The Saudis, as I have said again and again to you, are *not* our enemies," Weldon retorted.

"How can you say that? You read the same packs from D-Int that I do! The Saudis harbor, supply, and provide comfort to our enemies, and *that* makes them *our* enemies! For Christ's sake, the camp in question is in the bloody Wadi-as-Sirhan, not in fucking Chipping Norton!"

Weldon became absolutely still, his look as jagged as broken glass. Raised voices approached the line but didn't necessarily cross it. Admitting that he knew the whys and the wherefores after denying them was perhaps insulting but expected. It was Crocker's profanity; that was another matter entirely.

"How can I say it?" Weldon repeated tightly. "Because it's what Downing Street says, Paul. It's what C says. And it's what you're going to say as well."

Crocker closed his mouth, breathing through his nose, feeling his heart pounding about in his chest as if it had been kicked free. Too much, he knew that, he'd pushed it too far, but the anger was righteous to him, and he didn't want to let it go.

He tried again, calmer. "You'll destroy the trust that exists in this building, in this service. You'll destroy the Special Section. None of them will ever trust any of us—me, you, C—again. It will kill us."

"Don't be dramatic. We will survive. We have survived worse, much worse."

"Betrayal from outside isn't the same as betrayal from within. This won't be seen as a Philby."

"No, it will be seen as a rogue SIS officer being taken in by Box."

"She's not rogue."

"If she doesn't report tomorrow morning, she damn well will be." Weldon stabbed a finger at Crocker. "If she isn't in the Pit by oh–nine hundred, you're to flash-signal all stations that Minder One is AWOL. One way or another, Paul, Chace is coming in, and she's coming in to Box."

34

London—Bayswater, Paddington Station
16 September 1959 GMT

Poole and Lankford had been wrong. There weren't eight of them following her, there were at least sixteen, and those were only the ones she'd been able to make in the hours since leaving the Royal Albert pub. They cycled quickly as well, and she was having a damned time keeping up with the changes and long since had passed the point of being able to track them all.

They dogged her in cars and on motorbikes where they could, alone or in teams of two or three on foot where they couldn't.

She hadn't made it easy on them, but she'd yet to make it hard, so their cautiousness bothered her, because she felt it was unwarranted. Aside from the dogleg she'd made before entering the pub, she hadn't tried any other moves to flush or shake them. She'd remained on foot the entire time, walking back toward Vauxhall Cross upon departing the Royal Albert, passing Century House along the way, the old home of SIS, then turning east to follow the Albert Embankment along the Thames, taking her time, growing steadily colder and wetter in the rain.

She'd crossed Lambeth Bridge, turned north on Millbank, passing the Houses of Parliament, deep into the heart of government, which Chace was sure had confused the hell out of them. She'd had minor amusement scaring them as she mixed through a group of tourists at Westminster Abbey, certain that her multiple shadows were all scurrying, waiting for her to jump.

But she played it straight, turned north again, now in the direction of Whitehall with the FCO, the Treasury, the MOD, and then turned left again at the north side of Parliament Square, making toward St. James's Park. There was a small pub off Birdcage Walk, and she ducked inside to dry off and have a quick dinner, a jacket potato washed down with two pints of lager. The day's work had ended, and the pub was at capacity and spilling out onto the street when she left, the drinkers oblivious to the dreary weather, far more concerned with the task of washing away the remains of their day.

She cut north through St. James's into Green Park, but veered farther west, realizing that if she continued on her original path she might force their hand; north would take her to Grosvenor Square, the American Embassy, and if they thought she was reaching out to the Americans, they would have to move.

Which made her wonder again why they hadn't already. What were they waiting for? Sixteen plus people all acting as her shadows, they had to be planning a grab. But something was staying their hand, and there was simply no way for her to discern it. She didn't even know why she was doing what she was doing in the first place now, except that Crocker had ordered as much of her, and really, that was all it took.

Put your faith in yourself, Tom liked to say. And when that fails, put it in D-Ops.

She still had faith in herself.

But it was a comfort in the rain and in the falling darkness to have some of it in Paul Crocker, too.

●

Chace entered Paddington Station at a minute to eight, passing Poole just inside the western doors, not stopping and not looking at him. She wished she had a radio, an earpiece, so she could hear the babble of traffic now flowing over the Box surveillance net. They'd be switching on, full alert, certain that she was about to rabbit. They'd be arguing as to whether to collapse on her or let her run awhile longer, to see which way she was going to jump—or even if she was going to jump at all.

She was banking on them taking the wait-and-see approach. It had been their guiding principle thus far, and unless she forced their hand, she was relatively certain it would last at least a little longer.

But it wouldn't change the fact that she was now making them very nervous, and as she moved farther into the station, toward the café and kiosks clustered by the ticket booths, she began to see the evidence to prove it, glimpses of her various shadows moving to different posts, trying to cover all of her possible escapes.

Chace kept herself from smiling.

Their numbers had made it near-impossible to lose them on the street, to ditch them from block to block, in the open. There were just too many of them, and each could respond quickly, ahead of her or behind her, she wouldn't be able to shake them.

But in Paddington Station she could use their numbers against them, stretching out their coverage in an attempt to watch her every possible exit. And Paddington gave them too many choices; for every train that was preparing to depart, a man had to be positioned on the platform, just in case she sprinted to board at the last moment; each of the station exits had to be covered, inside and out; the tube entrances had to be covered, the escalators, and the entrance to The Lawn, the sprawling shopping addition beyond the glass walls; even the ticket booths, in the hopes that, should she move to purchase a fare, they would be able to discern her destination.

It would make them nervous, and it would put their eyes on her as they tried to understand what she was thinking, what she was planning. As they tried to guess what she was going to do.

Chace loved it, she admitted it to herself. This was her pleasure, more than booze or sex or smokes, the moments like this, when she knew the stakes and felt the adrenaline. When she saw the test coming, and measured the chances of success and failure, and rolled the dice regardless.

They were all waiting for her, waiting to see what she was going to do.

What she did was this:

Stopping halfway to the block of shops that stood between the main platforms and the ticket booths, Chace removed her jacket and folded it beneath her arm, for no other reason than to give them something to talk about. Was she getting ready to rabbit? Was she armed?

She moved to the kiosk at her right, adorned with stuffed bears in red hats and powder-blue coats, all clutching their tattered valises in one paw, tagged with their earnest request to be looked after. The man working the stand was Indian, and he smiled at her but let her browse without comment, perhaps seeing that she wasn't a tourist.

Chace looked at the bears, examining one of the larger ones, turning it in her hands, as if considering its relative merits.

"How much?" she asked.

The vendor looked surprised. "Twenty pounds."

"Robbery," Chace told him, smiling, and she paid him with some of the bills from her wallet, then accepted an opaque plastic bag to carry her purchase.

She ducked into the WHSmith's and bought copies of *The Guardian*, *The Telegraph*, and *The Mirror*. She also bought a Lion bar and then examined the display of disposable lighters at the counter. There were seventeen of them, molded plastic, cheap things.

She bought all of them, imagining the consternation on the net.

With all the purchases in the bag with her bear, she worked her way around one of the information points, giving the appearance of heading toward the platforms before curving back and making for the glass doors that marked the entrance to the Yo Sushi eatery. At another newsagent's, she stopped and bought all of his disposable lighters, bringing her total to thirty-one. She also purchased a new pack of Silk Cut, and that went into her jacket pocket rather than the bag.

The eatery was mostly empty, and Chace took a seat, draping her jacket over the back of a chair and setting her bag on the table, turning to look out through the wall of glass back into the station. She looked around, making no bones about it. There was no one in her immediate vicinity. She nodded to herself and rested the bag on its side, removing the bear and the newspapers, setting them beside it. Then she took out the Lion bar and ate it.

Next, she fashioned a paper hat for the bear and put it on his head. It was too big to fit properly, falling over his felt hat, but she did it anyway, just to annoy them. They'd see it and swear and call her unkind things, convinced she was mocking them. As that was precisely what she was doing, she didn't mind in the least.

Taking *The Guardian*, she opened the paper and draped it over the bag, still on its side, to create a makeshift privacy screen. Then she put her hands into the bag and began playing with the lighters, doing nothing more than sliding them back and forth, mounding them into an unstable pile, spreading them out and doing the same thing again. Most of the time, she looked in the bag at her hands, as if watching her work, then looked up and around, as if concerned she was being watched. She saw a woman she was certain she'd seen on her earlier walk hovering outside the doors, watching as she moved to enter, then thought better of it and fell back.

Good, Chace thought.

If they had been switched on before, they were boiling now, certain she was planning something big, and most likely with flames. Some of them would be agitating to move, but Kinney—if it was Kinney running this show—would be snarling at them to stand down, to stay at their positions. He was probably with the station security, watching it on the surveillance monitors, having commandeered the post for the time being, trying to keep his people in line from there. And much as Box might want to move on her, they hadn't yet, which meant they were waiting for something. And if all Chace did was annoy them, well, that wasn't enough reason to grab her. After all, she wasn't running; she was sitting at a table, playing with a stuffed bear and some lighters. And even the lighters wouldn't overly concern them. Sure, there were thirty-one of them, but that much lighter fluid wouldn't create an incendiary of merit. They'd have concluded she was creating some kind of distraction, and so thinking, they would then plan to ignore it.

They'd wait until they were sure she was running. That's when they'd move.

But they couldn't risk ignoring her entirely, and that was part of her plan, too.

Chace finished fiddling with the lighters, took the copy of *The Telegraph*, and crumpled several of its pages, stuffing it into the bag. Then she stuffed the bear, hat and all, inside after it. She got to her feet, slipped back into her jacket, then bent and stuck her hand into the bag a final time, as if reaching around. She counted to five, then withdrew her hand and started resolutely toward the doors back out to the station, taking her time, passing the woman still lingering at the wall without a glance. Chace paused at the newsagent's again, glancing back in time to see the action in the eatery, six of them all descending on her table, anxious to extinguish the conflagration they were certain was about to erupt.

She turned toward the platforms, making a purposeful beeline toward the second from the left, to where the London-Heathrow Express was waiting, accelerating, almost jogging now. A man emerged from the train, from the doors nearest to her. He was an inch or so shorter than she, broad at the neck and shoulders, and she thought she recognized him from earlier that day, but it could have been from the night before, or from a pub a year ago, or never at all.

When he emerged and turned toward her, she saw his earpiece, almost flesh-colored, and he was already raising a hand to stop her.

"All right, Miss Chace," he said.

There might have been more he had to say, but she never gave him the chance. Without breaking stride, almost plowing into him, she smiled and raised her right hand as if in greeting before driving it down, index and middle fingers jabbing into the notch beneath his Adam's apple. She felt the soft skin crush into the thickness of his collarbone, and he gasped, crumpled, already choking, while she put her left hand on his shoulder to guide him down to his knees.

He gagged, pitched forward, and she was past him now, and only then did she pivot left, sprinting for the edge of the platform. She leaped, landing between rails, nearly twisting her ankle on the ties, caught the opposite edge, pulled herself up on the next platform, then repeated it all again until she had vaulted onto the last one and righted herself. She saw the exit forty feet away, and Nicky Poole was there, standing over two men from Box. One of them was flat on his stomach; the other was on hands and knees, vomiting.

"Rabbit!" someone was shouting, and in the noise and echo of the station, the word seemed even more absurd. "Rabbit, she's gone *rabbit!*"

Chace ran, flying up the steps, passing Poole again, touching his hand as he held it out to her, taking the radio and earpiece he was holding. She burst through the doors, stuffing them into her pocket, felt the wet air slap her skin. She turned, looking for Lankford, saw another of the boys from Box coming at her, wincing at the lone headlight shining down on her. The man from Box turned, hearing the bike, trying to step out of the way, and Lankford clubbed him alongside the head with the helmet in his hand plus twenty miles per hour, sending him sprawling, before lobbing the helmet her way.

She caught it, swung onto the back of the bike as it pulled up, noting that they'd remembered her go-bag, trapped against the back of the seat with elastic netting. Chace had to sit half on it to fit, wrapping one arm around Lankford's waist while jamming the helmet down on her head with the other, and he sped them away so quickly, it was as if he hadn't stopped at all. The bike jolted, hopping down the curb, and the rear tire slid as Lankford drove the wrong way through traffic, slicing between cabs and cars, speeding them away from the station.

Over the engine and the traffic, Chace heard herself, muffled in the helmet, laughing with joy.

35

The council-flat heavy on the door of the Imperial Age was as sincere a bruiser as any Crocker had met in his time as a Minder, with a head shaved bald that sat low on a thick neck. It was twenty-six minutes before the club closed, and he gave Crocker the once-over at the door, head to toe, before speaking.

"We're closing up, mate," the man said. "Don't waste your money, eh?"

Crocker offered him a tenner, ostensibly the cover charge, but potentially a bribe. "I can do a lot of looking in the time that's left."

The man looked at the note, looked at Crocker, then shrugged and stepped out of the way of the door. The door was painted metal, black, but the neon above advertising what was available inside gave it a noxious pink shine. Crocker pushed through, into a ten-by-ten curtained darkness, and was instantly assaulted by the bass and treble that pounded throughout the club. He continued on, through a gap in the hanging fabric, emerged on a broad landing that afforded him a complete view of the club, of the bar running to the left, and the tables on the main floor, arrayed around the base and runway of the stage. The woman currently dancing was naked, white, with black hair, and doing her best to convince the audience that she found her dance pole a fulfilling sexual partner. Smoke and chatter tangled through the music, and most of the tables were occupied with a mix of lads out on the piss and businessmen out for a thrill.

Along the main floor, halfway down on the walls, were mirror flights of stairs, ascending to the first level, a railed gallery with more seats and more individually attentive dancers. Crocker took the flight on the left, feeling hot in the sudden warmth of the club. He removed his raincoat at the top of the stairs, then turned back to look down and check the entrance. He gave it a minute, saw no one else entering and two of the patrons leaving, and took it as confirmation that he was still running clean.

Another set of stairs was back against the wall, with a highly polished brass plaque set on the wall beside it. The sign had an arrow, indicating upward, and the words "VIP Level." He ascended the stairs, coming to the second floor, and three doors and three more signs. The placards on the doors in front of him and to his left all read "Available," and the one to his right read "Engaged."

He opened the one to his right without knocking, stepped into a mock office set, complete with fake windows on two walls that gave the appearance of looking out from a City office building into a London sunset, the sky purple and orange. An executive's desk was positioned at one wall, its surface empty but for a cardboard computer and telephone set, its chair large, black, and leather. An executive couch, also black leather, was angled to face the "windows," and its companion coffee table was low and over-sized, wider and longer than the real thing. A drinks menu stood on the table, for convenience. There was music playing in here as well, not the raucous bass-driven madness from below, but classical, and Crocker recognized it as Rachmaninoff.

Chace was seated in the executive chair, tilted back, with a naked redhead writhing on the desk in front of her. The redhead had one leg resting on Chace's shoulder, the other bent beneath her in what Crocker could only imagine was an incredibly painful position, arms braced back to support her. When she arched, her head came back, vivid hair spilling onto the desktop, and she met Crocker's eyes and gave him a huge and unself-conscious grin, then brought her head up again, whipping her mane around and nearly knocking the cigarette in Chace's mouth free in the process.

"This is Billy," Chace told him. "Not with an *i* and an *e*, but with a *y*."

"Tell him why, Jane," Billy said to Chace, freeing

her leg from Chace's shoulder and deftly turning on the desk, to present Chace with her rear.

Chace looked at Crocker, her smile thin. "Because once she dances for you, 'y' would you want anyone else?"

"Why indeed," Crocker said.

Chace slapped Billy's ass with her palm, saying, "Right, shove off, Billy."

Billy squealed and laughed, swaying her beautiful backside for another moment before slipping off the desk and moving past Crocker to the couch, where her clothes—such as they were—had been scattered. Crocker kept his eyes on Chace, but he noted that Chace wasn't so concerned and was watching Billy dress with apparent interest. When the woman was finished, Chace produced her wallet and offered her a handful of bills.

Billy took them, kissed Chace on the cheek, and said, "Come back anytime, Miss Jane Smith."

"May do," Chace replied, grinning.

Billy headed for the door in a cloud of jasmine perfume. "We're closing in ten, so you'll need to be fast."

"Don't worry about us," Crocker assured her.

Then Crocker and Chace were alone with the music, which had switched to Stravinsky.

"Don't look at me like that," Chace said. "You're the one who picked the rendezvous, not me."

"You should have been alone."

"They wouldn't give me the bloody room alone. As it was, I'm tapped, so I hope you brought some money along with an explanation. All I've got now is this."

She held up a small radio, its leads dangling free, one to the com button, one to the earpiece.

"Clever," Crocker said.

"It was Poole. They switched on me at twenty-one forty-two, when they realized I had one of their radios, but for a while there I knew everything they were doing."

Chace tossed the radio to him and Crocker caught it with both hands, carefully wrapped the leads around the unit, then stuffed it into his raincoat pocket. He tossed the raincoat onto the arm of the couch, went into his suit jacket, came out again with an A4 envelope in his hand. Chace hadn't moved from behind the desk, and it occurred to him that she was having fun with the role reversal. He dropped the envelope in front of her, beside the hollow telephone.

"You came clean?"

She pointed her chin at his raincoat, indicating the radio. "Last I heard, they were looking for me at Heathrow, Gatwick, and Waterloo. I've been clean since I left Paddington."

He nodded, frowning, watched as Chace picked up the envelope, then put her cigarette in the ashtray, which looked to be the only real thing on the desk at the moment.

"What the hell is going on, Boss?"

"Open it."

He needn't have said it; she already had, dumping the contents of the envelope onto the desk and quickly going through them. There was a British passport, a Gold American Express card, and two thousand pounds in twenties and hundreds. Chace flipped open the passport, her expression clouding, then checked the name against the one on the Amex.

"So I'm Dorothea Palmer, am I?"

"It was the only set I could grab without being caught," Crocker said. "And when I'm asked about it by the Deputy Chief, I'll tell him you stole it."

"He'll cancel them immediately."

"Which is why you need to be out of the country no later than noon tomorrow."

Chace replaced the bills and documents in the envelope, then dropped the envelope in the small brown duffel that was resting beside her chair. It gave Crocker a minor satisfaction. At least Chace had her bag.

"My suggestion? Tel Aviv, make contact with Noah Landau."

"To what end?"

"To be briefed on a terrorist training facility in the Wadi-as-Sirhan, Tabuk province, Saudi Arabia."

For the first time, Chace looked confused. "Why?"

"Because you need to destroy the camp."

"Alone?"

"Unless you can find some support, yes, alone."

"Well, support, that would take the challenge out of it."

The joke wasn't worth the courtesy laugh, and even if it had been, they didn't have the time.

"So how large is this camp, then?" She tried to force the smile again, and again it didn't convince.

"Sixty plus, half veterans, half raw, give or take another two dozen Palestinian recruits working on their martyrdom degrees. It's the HUM-AA faction, Tara, the same lot Salih was funding, the same lot Faud was inciting."

"The same lot that hit us here."

"Yes," Crocker said. "It's complicated and it's political, but the short form is this: that camp has to go. The Saudis won't touch it unless they get you. And Downing Street has decided that sacrificing one SIS officer to achieve that end is the most expedient way to do that."

"Box was going to give me to the Saudis?"

"Correct."

She looked away from him, out toward the fake skyline. "What were they waiting for? They could have taken me anytime today."

"They didn't receive authorization until half-nine," Crocker said. "Otherwise they'd have picked you up earlier."

Chace bit her lip, thinking. "Blind luck," she said.

"What?"

"I lost them at eight. Any later, I'd not have lost them at all."

"Blind luck," Crocker agreed. "You're going to need more of it. The only way out I see for you is to remove the Government's reason for rendering you to the Saudis in the first place. That's the camp."

She turned her head, studying him. The mask was slipping again, and he could read on her face the conflicting emotions at work: the anger and the fear. "And if I don't?"

"Then you'll be pursued."

"I could disappear."

"No, Tara. I've been ordered to list you AWOL if you don't report for work tomorrow. You'll be PNGed in the Service, you'll have no access to SIS or any of its assets. Further, I'll be directed to find you. As will the CIA and, most likely, the Mossad."

"I stay at liberty until this camp of yours is rolled up—"

"You'll still be a rogue SIS officer." Crocker shook his head. "No, you've got three choices, that's it. You can stay, and end up in the loving arms of Saudi Arabian justice. You can bolt, and spend your life running persona non grata. Or you can take the camp yourself. That's it."

Chace stared at him, and it seemed to Crocker that he'd never seen her like this, suddenly naked and vulnerable. The mask was gone, and the betrayal and hurt in her eyes made him feel that he'd failed her all the more.

"I've taken the liberty of sending a signal to Landau through channels," he added softly. "He'll expect you on Monday the twentieth."

She didn't say anything, didn't even acknowledge with a nod or a look, just stared at him.

There was a knock at the door and a voice, male and South London, called, "We're closing it up."

"We'll be right out," Crocker said.

"You were supposed to protect me," Chace said.

"I am protecting you," he snapped, stung. "If Weldon or C knew I was here, they'd roast me alive. They've tied my hands, Tara. This is all I can offer."

"I can't do this, Paul," she said softly. "Eighty men in that camp? I can't take them alone, there's no way I can do that. You need SAS for that, not me. Give me Lankford and Poole, I can make a go of it, but alone—"

"Lankford and Poole are out of it now. SIS is out of it. You're alone, Tara." He glared at her, repeating himself. "You're alone."

He'd hoped to spark her anger. It didn't come.

Instead, Chace looked away again.

"I've done everything I can, Tara," he added more gently.

She nodded, then rose from the chair, straightening her jacket. She checked her watch and he saw her making a calculation of some sort in her mind. Then she moved to the door.

"I trusted you, you bastard," Chace said to him without looking.

"You still can."

She whipped around, shouting at him, her cheeks flushed with heat and her eyes shining with fury. "You were supposed to *protect* me!"

"I am doing everything I can."

"Do more!" She spun back, yanked the door open. "You'll hear from me, one way or another. You'll hear from me."

He watched her start out, moved slowly to follow.

"Good luck," Crocker offered, and even he heard the weakness of the wish as he said it.

"Fuck you," she told him, and disappeared down the stairs.

36

Nia's hair had been soft and thick and had flowed over Sinan's stomach and thighs like a whisper, and where her skin had touched his a warmth had blossomed so gently, so different from the jagged heat of the desert that he'd heard himself gasp with the pleasure of it. She had put fingers to his lips, closing his mouth, silently urging him to stay silent, and her lips had grazed his throat, and then he had felt the other heat of her, the grip of her as she mounted him. The rush came all at once, flooding out of him, and it was only then, feeling his seed cooling on his belly, that he realized he was dreaming and forced himself awake.

Matteen snored on his cot, visible in the wash of

predawn light seeping into the tent. From outside, Sinan could hear the steps of the sentry as he passed.

He shivered, feeling cold and ashamed, then threw back his blanket. The earth was hard beneath his feet, still warm from the radiation of the day. He pulled off his shirt, then found his canteen and spilled water onto the sleeve. He used the wet cloth to wipe himself clean, then set about changing, wishing for the first time in months that he could shower. With the Prince there had been hot and cold running water, bathrooms with marble and gold, and he had hated it. In the camp, the only water was for drinking.

He would have done anything to be clean then.

Matteen coughed in his sleep, rustling, and Sinan grabbed his boots and his Kalashnikov, slipping out of the tent. The sentry who had passed him by was on his way back and stopped at the sight of him, and Sinan raised his hand in greeting. The sentry nodded and continued on his rounds.

Standing, Sinan pulled on his boots, then made his way from beneath the canopy of camouflage netting, out into the wider base of the wadi. The walls of the little canyon were shallow here, and he scrambled up the side, then settled himself on the ground, sitting with his rifle across his lap. To the east, the sky was beginning to glow with the sunrise, and the stars were already beginning to fade.

He hated himself for the dream, for the weakness it exposed. It wasn't real, of course, it hadn't been real, but that his head would indulge his body while he slept, tease him with a dream of what he could not have, made him angry. At Nia, first, for making him think these thoughts, feel these things, and then at Abdul Aziz, for bringing her to the camp in the first place. But these faded, because he saw them for what they were.

Excuses.

This was nobody's problem but his own.

He had never considered taking a bride, had never thought it would even be a possibility. What man would give his sister or daughter to him, in this place? Abdul Aziz was known to have three wives of his own, all living in Jeddah, and Matteen had spoken of a bride who now lived in Pakistan, but most of the men here were single, wed only to their cause and their war. For a soldier to take a wife would be a cruelty, for he could never be with her, never protect her and provide for her.

Sinan was sure he wasn't cruel, and he didn't want to be selfish.

Sunlight had begun to bleed over the horizon and Sinan sighed, getting to his feet. It was time for prayers and work, and nothing could get in the way of those things. Not sex, not loneliness, not love.

He slung his rifle and dropped back down into the wadi, resolved.

Nia was *shahid*. She would die a martyr and go to Paradise. He would honor her for that, respect her, even aid her.

But he would not, he told himself, fall in love with her.

37

She woke him with the phone, saying simply, "I'm outside," and hoping that everything in her voice was enough.

"I'll let you in," Tom said.

Chace hung up the security phone, stepped back off the porch, looking up at Wallace's flat. It was still dark out, and fog had come in off the Channel, and she was cold and wet, and she needed to see his light come on, she needed to know that he would let her in and make her safe.

The light didn't come on, and for a terrible moment Chace wondered if Box had beat her to him, if she'd missed them in her three circuits around the immediate area, in all of her attempts to flush any possible pursuit. She hadn't seen anyone, still certain she was running clean, if for no other reason than, if she wasn't, they'd have fallen on her like buzzards on a corpse.

Then she glimpsed him behind the glass of the foyer door, shirtless, in baggy pajama bottoms, still bleary from sleep.

"Still dreaming, am I?" he said as he let her in.

Chace thought the wave of relief she was feeling might swamp her.

"If so," she said, "it's a bloody nightmare."

●

He gave her first a kiss, and then a hot shower, and, once Chace was dressed in clean clothes from her go-bag, offered a cup of very bad instant coffee, loaded with sugar and milk. Then he listened as she laid it all out to him, all the secrets he wasn't supposed to know any longer, what she'd done in Yemen, what had happened with Box, what Crocker had said.

"How are you fixed?" Wallace asked when she had finished.

"Crocker gave me what he could manage, but it was all in-house documentation. That and two thousand pounds."

"What about that?" Wallace indicated her go-bag, resting open on his couch.

She actually managed a smile. "You taught me well. I've got another five thousand American in the lining, and my good papers, the ones you told me never, ever to use."

"For which you should be damn grateful, because you'll need them now. What're they?"

"French national, Monique DuLac. Everything on her is current, and nobody but the man who made them knows she exists, and he's in Athens and not terribly talkative."

"Plastic?"

"There's a Visa, but I don't know if it'll hold. I'd rather stick to the cash."

"You'll need the Visa for the flight."

"You're assuming I'm going to go on this little suicide mission. As far as I'm concerned, D-Ops can fuck himself, and Weldon, and C, and then move on to Whitehall and slip it to the rest of them."

"He *is* protecting you," Wallace said. "You have to see that. He's doing everything he can."

"Then why am I running?"

"Are you? You're just here to say good-bye?"

Chace scowled at him, brushed wet hair impatiently back from her cheek. "If that was the case, I'd have jumped you already."

"Then it's not good-bye. So what is it?"

It was the whole reason she had come, and now, in the face of it, she found the words hard to say. It wasn't as if she hadn't made the decision back at the Imperial Age, looking out those fake windows, listening to Crocker's plea of not guilty.

But it took effort, and a strength she wasn't certain she still had, to actually say the words to Wallace. "I can't do it alone, Tom."

"Right," Wallace said. "I'll get my things."

●

They took his Triumph, speeding along the A3 and then the M25 and then the M20, racing to Ashford, with the intent of catching the Eurostar all the way to Paris. She'd been leery about taking his car, but the only other routes available to them were by rail—which would have taken them back into London first—or by fishing boat across the Channel. Although they could have caught the Eurostar at Waterloo, it had seemed like a bad idea because Chace felt—and Wallace agreed—that Box would be covering every international route possible. There would certainly be some kind of coverage at Ashford, but it wouldn't be nearly as severe, and she was confident they would be able to handle it.

With Wallace at the wheel and traffic light for much of the journey, they reached Ashford well before nine, parking in the multistoried lot that had been built to serve the terminal. The station itself was quite new, constructed for the Eurostar, modern and, to Chace's eyes, bland. Even the car park was bland, and fairly empty.

"You stay here," Wallace told her. "Give me thirty minutes to clear the terminal, see what there is to see, get the tickets. I'll need your passport."

Chace dug it out of her go-bag, handing him Monique DuLac as he stood beside the Triumph. She was suffering a headache that was the result of tension, exhaustion, adrenaline withdrawal, or all of the above.

"Seats together?"

"Might be best."

"First class, then."

"Oh, absolutely." Wallace grinned, hefted his bag, and headed for the covered walkway into the terminal.

Chace sat in the car, smoking, checking the clock. She saw the second hand sweeping past the twelve on her wrist, saw that it was precisely nine in the morning.

Rogue, she thought.

Fucking hell.

She thought about Wallace, got out of the car, stretching, looking around, seeing the rain fall outside the shelter of the car park. There were certainly cameras about, but Box would be focused on the terminal, waiting for her to board, probably thinking that she wouldn't be coming there at all.

She wondered how long Jim Chester at Monkton would wait before reporting Tom's absence back to Crocker. Or if Chester would go through Crocker at all rather than the Deputy Chief. Going through Crocker offered a flicker of hope; even if Chace had decided he was a worthless bastard, she knew he'd try to slow down their pursuit. It wasn't likely, though. Personnel issues went to the Deputy Chief, and as soon as Weldon heard that Wallace had gone missing, he'd waste no time informing Kinney to be on the lookout for him as well as for her.

Wallace had taken it in stride, had been immediately ready to go once he committed to the action. Eight minutes to change clothes and stuff some extras into his go-bag—still kept at the ready in the closet by the door—and another two to switch off the lights and lock up the flat. Coat and gloves, bag in hand, they'd been out the door before twenty past six, in the Triumph and on the road before half past.

He'd never hesitated, never questioned, and Chace wasn't really surprised when she thought about it. She'd have done the same for him.

Her watch told her it had been twenty-six minutes, and she thought that was enough and took her bag from the boot, locked the car, and made her way across the walkway into Ashford International. It was bright and airy and nouveau dull, and there were phone boxes near the walkway as she came out, and she stopped at them with an idea, wondering why she hadn't thought of it earlier.

She picked up the phone, dropped in what coins she had, and eventually was connected to British Airways reservations. Using Dorothea Palmer's Amex, she bought herself a ticket, one way, to Geneva. When she hung up, she threw the Palmer passport and plastic into the trash, then continued down to the floor of the terminal.

There was a scheduled departure in thirty-nine minutes, and a minor bustle in the terminal as passengers gathered themselves, waited in the lounge, made for the first-class/business parlor, or passport control, as their mood and their means moved them.

She didn't see Wallace.

She did see, however, a woman emerging from

the first-class lounge, wearing trainers and jeans and a navy-blue parka. She had black hair and a young face, and Chace tried to avoid meeting her eyes, but it was too late, and confusion and surprise were stamped on the woman's face with the same clarity as Elizabeth's profile on a coin.

Fucking hell, Chace thought, and she turned immediately away, keeping the motion and movement casual, scanning for a direction, seeing the sign for the women's lav. She made for it, knowing that she was trapping herself, and hoping that the woman behind her wasn't certain enough of what she'd seen to call it in.

The bathroom was like the rest of the terminal, modern and too bright, white walls and chrome fixtures, and as soon as Chace was through the door, she kicked it closed behind her, working her way down the line of stalls, trying to read which were occupied and which were open. The fear, and she knew it for what it was, was struggling to get loose inside her, and she felt her head go light and her stomach weak with the new surge of adrenaline.

None of the stalls were occupied, and Chace reversed, heading back to the entrance just as the woman came through, and again they were face-to-face and close enough now that Chace saw that she truly was fresh to the game. She had one hand in the pocket of her parka, the other out, holding the black cylinder that would become the baton, and Chace saw the outline of the wireless earpiece in her ear and knew there wasn't any other choice about it.

With her right hand, Chace brought her go-bag up at the woman's face, catching her in the chin and knocking her back into the already closing door. Her impact slammed it home, and Chace dropped the bag on the follow-through, driving her left fist at the other woman's neck, trying to put her down.

The woman saw it coming, jerked her head right, brought her free hand up to parry, and Chace saw the com button dangling from her sleeve, and it became the focus of her existence. She couldn't let her hit the button, she couldn't let her transmit. If this bird from Box got the word out, neither Chace nor Wallace would make it out of the terminal.

Chace snapped her left arm back, turning her hand, trying to grab the woman's wrist, and she felt the impact at the side of her knee, the baton connecting with soft flesh and timid cartilage, and she heard herself swearing. She knew she hadn't been hit hard because the knee hadn't abandoned her, but the pain was extraordinary and brutal, and it made her vision swim.

But she had the wrist, and then the thumb, and she trapped the digit between her own thumb and fingers, closed her hand, sweeping it down. The woman grunted, trying to turn with it and swing at Chace again, and failed at both, and Chace drove her into the door, slamming her head forward with her right before reaching down to the trapped hand and wrenching the lead free from her palm. The wire snapped and she tossed it away, and then Chace's breath was gone and the world was white, and she was tasting bile and blood in her throat, aware that she was having trouble standing, that somehow she'd lost her grip on the woman.

She came back to herself in time to see the woman spin, drawing back to jab the baton at Chace's stomach a second time, and somehow Chace got out of the way, slamming into the door of one of the stalls and crashing hip-first into the toilet. She righted herself, and the woman was coming at her again, baton raised, and this time there was nowhere to go, and Chace lurched forward, bringing her left arm up to block and taking the blow high on her forearm.

It took everything she had not to scream.

Chace continued forward, now under the woman's arm, ramming into her, fists working. She hit her four times, all with her right, all jabs along the left side of the woman's chest, trying to hurt her, to cause her as much pain as she could. The woman slammed into the sinks with her lower back, gasping, and Chace heard the baton clattering to the floor, felt the dull impact of a fist that somehow missed her neck and landed on her shoulder instead. Chace dropped her chin instinctively, felt the woman clawing at her hair, trying to get her head back, to get another shot at the throat.

Chace punched low with her left, feeling her arm scream in protest, already going numb, making it as vicious as she could, almost screaming herself. She landed the blow just above the pelvic bone, felt the punch sink, felt the woman slacken, groaning. Chace turned out of the clench, grabbed her with her right, jamming her thumb into the woman's nose, yanking her forward. The woman staggered, flailed, but her legs were going, and her breath had already gone, and she had nothing left.

Chace pitched her face-first into the stall, throwing her against the toilet, then bashed her head against the porcelain. The woman moaned, flailed weakly, and Chace bounced her again, and she stopped moving.

Wheezing, Chace got to her feet, her lungs crackling, her right knee throbbing, a hand on the side of the stall to steady herself. Over her own breathing, she barely heard the muffled announcement from the terminal PA, a call for boarding for the nine fifty-nine train. She glanced down at her watch, realized that she'd been in the bathroom now for perhaps all of a minute.

The woman groaned again, slid farther between the toilet and the wall of the stall.

Chace leaned down, caught her beneath each armpit, and hoisted her onto the toilet seat, leaning her back. She ran her hands over her quickly, finding the radio secured at her hip, pulling it free and then turning the squelch all the way up. Now, instead of no response, whoever radioed would hear distortion and static, and it was possible that could be mistaken as network trouble rather than an agent down.

Somehow, Chace didn't put much stock in that happening.

She unfastened the woman's belt and trousers, yanked them down around her ankles, righted her once more on the seat before turning and shutting the stall door, locking them both inside. The clearance at the bottom was slight, and Chace had to squeeze through, her left arm all but dead, her knee making her wince in protest. If someone came in now, she'd have a hell of a time explaining things.

But no one did, and she grabbed the baton as she got back to her feet, collapsing it and dumping it into the refuse bin. She checked herself in the mirrors over the sink, brushing her hair back into place with her fingers, straightened her clothes. *She looked*, she thought, *fucking awful, but not like a woman who'd been in a fistfight, and that was about as much as she could ask for at the moment.*

Taking her go-bag once more, she stepped back into the terminal to find Tom Wallace searching for her. Frowning slightly, already turning toward passport control, he handed over her passport and ticket as soon as she reached him.

"Stomach trouble?" he asked.

"Thought you were taking care of it."

"Mine's in the men's room," Wallace said.

●

They arrived in Paris just before one in the afternoon, at the Gare du Nord, and before they left the station, Chace found a phone and made the call to Air France reservations. The next available flight to Tel Aviv was the following morning, departing ten-thirty, and she booked seats in their false names, Monique DuLac and Richard Kent, and then paid with the credit card Wallace supplied her in Kent's name.

"Done?" he asked when she hung up.

"French is an easily acquired Romance language, Tom," she said. "You should have picked it up by now."

"Merde," he told her.

"It's done. All we have to do now is occupy ourselves for the rest of the day."

"Fancy a trip to Disneyland, then?"

"I'm knackered."

"Or we could find a room and get some rest," he amended.

"Yes, please," Chace said.

●

They spent the night at a Holiday Inn in Roissy, about a mile from Charles de Gaulle Airport, and as soon as they were in their room, Chace kicked off her shoes and jacket and fell onto the bed, utterly exhausted. The numbness in her left arm was abating, leaving radiant pain to mark its passage, and her right knee throbbed. She managed to stay awake long enough to hear Wallace tell her that he'd be back shortly, that he was going to grab some food and cigarettes, and she heard him leave the room, heard the door lock, and then she dropped away into sleep.

Wallace woke her when he returned, and she cursed him for it but took the six aspirin he offered, chasing it with half a liter of water.

Then she fell back into the same sleep, and a darkness that held no dreams.

●

When she awoke next, it was to the sounds of the television, to the smell of Wallace's cigarettes. She opened her eyes to see him seated beside her, propped against the headboard, a bottle of beer in one hand, watching the television, something in black and white and poorly dubbed into French. He gave her a grin, and she looked at the clock and saw it was fourteen minutes past one in the morning.

"Why aren't you sleeping?" she croaked at him.

"I tried, but you kept stealing the covers," Wallace said.

She nodded, accepting that as a reasonable excuse, if not an honest one, then rose and limped to her go-bag, idly wondering if her foot had healed only to be replaced by her knee and if she would ever be walking right again. She found her toiletries, then moved into the bathroom, where she brushed her teeth, stripped, and showered. She stayed under the water longer than she needed, soaking the heat, breathing the steam, examining her bruises. The baton's impact on her left forearm had left an angry, swollen ball, yellow and green that was painful to the touch. She shut off the taps, toweled dry, and went back into the room without bothering to dress.

Wallace was still on the bed and he'd removed his shoes, but that was all, and she laughed.

"You're a daft old man, Tom Wallace," Chace said, and she climbed onto the bed, took his face in her hands, and kissed him with all the hunger she'd been holding in for six years.

●

They made love twice before dawn, the first time with the clumsiness of desire, the second time with purpose and passion. They dozed together until the wake-up call shocked them back to consciousness at half-past six, and made love a third time before heading to the shower again. Her knee felt better, and the green and yellow on her arm had become yellow and blue, which translated as progress. They dressed, packed what little they had unpacked, checked out, and made it to the airport by eight.

"Three times, one night," Wallace murmured to her in the taxi. "You're trying to kill me."

"I'd have stopped with two," Chace said, "but you seemed so insistent."

"I'm not complaining. I'm just surprised. I'm an old man."

"Not so old."

"Old enough."

"They say sex keeps you young."

Wallace feigned thoughtfulness. "Guess I should be having more of it, then."

"Guess so," Chace said.

"Speaking of young."

Chace looked at him, not understanding. "I'm not that much younger than you."

"You're young enough, but that's not what I am referring to."

It took a moment's thought, then Chace grinned

and tapped her upper left arm with the fingers of her right hand.

"Depo-Provera," she said. "Every twelve weeks."

•

They flew coach on Air France flight 1620, departing Charles de Gaulle at ten twenty-five, landing at David Ben Gurion International Airport four hours and forty minutes later exactly, at sixteen-oh-five hours local. They came off the plane and into the heat of the day, cleared customs quickly, and were arrested the moment they stepped outside the terminal.

38

Crocker found Barclay in the small sitting area away from the desk, in his armchair, loading the bowl of his pipe. On the table before him were a tea service, china and silver, and a short stack of reports that he'd apparently been going through. Crocker approached, waited respectfully, folder in hand, to be acknowledged.

Barclay took his time about it. He finished filling the bowl, then set the pipe, short-stemmed and stubby, on the table. He closed the jar of tobacco, placed it back on the stand at his side, then took up his book of matches. He retrieved the pipe, put it to his mouth, sucked experimentally, gauging his work thus far. The match flared and the flame jumped higher as he drew it down into the pipe. The clouds of smoke that rose were blue and smelled of latakia and Cavendish.

When the pipe was going, Barclay discarded the match in the wide ashtray beside the service tray, then extended the same hand to Crocker, waiting to be handed the report. Crocker gave him the folder, a blue one marked for internal distribution.

"You may sit," Barclay said, opening the file against his knee, beginning to read. He didn't look up. He'd yet to look at Crocker at all, in fact. "Help yourself to tea."

"Thank you, sir."

Crocker took the couch, fixed himself a cup, dropping two sugars in, stirring. Pages rustled as Barclay turned them, drawing on the pipe. It didn't take him long to finish, to close the folder and set it beside the others on the table.

"All Stations notified?" Barclay asked.

"As per the Deputy Chief's directive, as of oh-nine-oh-one this morning."

"You listed her as AWOL, not rogue."

"All we know is that she failed to report for work today," Crocker explained.

"I know what you did, Paul." Barclay took the pipe from his mouth, examined it in his hand. It was black briarwood, aged and well used.

Crocker didn't say anything. A denial was possible, he supposed, a flat-out defiance to C's face, but Crocker knew Barclay well enough to know that it wouldn't work here.

"She's put one of Kinney's in the hospital," Barclay said. "Were you aware of that?"

Crocker wasn't, and it surprised him; he'd have expected the number to be much higher. "Then Kinney's been lucky."

"Certainly the woman receiving treatment doesn't think so. She cracked two of her ribs, Paul, and may have caused internal injuries as well as a concussion."

"She restrained herself," Crocker said.

"I know," Barclay said. "So did Wallace."

Crocker nearly showered tea all over the table. "I'm sorry, sir?"

"You didn't know?"

"She's with Wallace?"

"Apparently, yes. The Deputy Chief received a call from Jim Chester at the School. Apparently, Wallace has gone missing, failed to turn up for his classes this morning. Chester sent a man round to his flat in Lee-on-the-Solent, found his car gone and the flat locked up tight."

"According to his last Personal and Intimates, he was seeing a woman in Portsmouth."

"Chester contacted her. The woman informed him that her relationship with Wallace ended three weeks ago."

"May only be a coincidence."

"Yes, I considered that as well. But the gentleman from Box in the room next to Chace's victim positively identified his assailant as Tom Wallace."

"Where did this happen?"

"Ashford International. They took the Eurostar; they could be anywhere in Europe by now."

Crocker nodded, agreeing. Germany or France, most likely, but that would only be their first stop. "I dispatched the Geneva Number Two, Alasdair Gerrard, to the residence of Minder One's mother, Ms. Annika Bodmer-Chace, this morning. Gerrard reported back that Ms. Bodmer-Chace hasn't had any contact with her daughter since the winter of last year. Gerrard has the residence under surveillance. It's possible she's headed there."

Barclay shook his head, sucking on his pipe thoughtfully. After releasing three more plumes of smoke, he said, "What did you tell her?"

"I'm sorry, sir?"

"No more nonsense, Paul." Barclay glanced at him, then away. "You're extremely clever, and that's the reason you're still in this job and not packing up your office or opening a station in Iceland. I cannot prove, of course, that you ordered her to run, nor can I prove that you directed Poole and Lankford to assist her. Both shall claim, if asked, that they were acting on orders from their Head of Section, rather than from D-Ops, and that they had no idea that what they were doing might be against the best interests of the Service. Neither can I prove that you removed travel documents for Chace under the work name Dorothea Palmer. Or that you supplied her with two thousand pounds from the Ready Fund. I cannot prove any of it."

Barclay moved his gaze back to Crocker, and the stare was vicious.

"That does not mean, however, that I do not know those things to be true."

Again, Crocker didn't respond. There was nothing to say to it anyway. He wondered if, despite C's words, he wasn't going to be wandering Whitehall before the end of the day, trying to find new employment.

"Now," Barclay said. "What did you tell Chace?"

"Nothing, sir. She came to me yesterday morning. She said that Box was targeting her for some reason, and did I know why. I assumed she was under another random security check and therefore could neither verify nor deny it. She left my office, and that was the last time I saw her. It wasn't until last evening that the Deputy Chief informed me of the reasons for the surveillance, and by that time, she'd already gone rabbit."

"You're saying the CIA didn't inform you?"

"Why would they, sir?" Crocker asked. "As I understand the situation, it's in the Americans' interests that Chace be rendered to the Saudis as much as it is in ours and the Israelis'."

Barclay's eyes narrowed as he thought on that, then he nodded slightly. "Why indeed. But why go to Wallace? What is she planning?"

"I wish I could tell you."

"Do you?"

Crocker stared at Barclay. "She's the Head of the Special Section, sir. She's one of the best, if not *the* best Special Operations officer working in the world today. My Minder Two has just over a year's experience under his belt, and my Three is still so new there's packing material stuck to his clothes.

Without Chace, our covert action capability is crippled. It's bad for the Service."

"So you're saying, had she stayed, you would have rendered her to the Saudis willingly?"

"Of course not. I'd have done everything I could to keep her."

"At the expense of the Government's agenda?"

"As I tried to explain to the Deputy Chief, the Government's decision is grotesquely flawed. And the problem still remains, sir. If Chace is apprehended and delivered to the Saudis, no agent working for us anywhere in the world will ever trust us again. Once they find out—and they will find out—our credibility will be shattered. How can we expect our agents to put their lives at risk, knowing that, when expedient, we'll abandon them to their enemies?"

"That expediency is part of our mandate," Barclay said.

"Not at the risk of cutting our own throat."

"Where's she heading?"

"I have no idea. She knows how to run, we'll have a damn hard time finding her. And with Wallace it'll be twice as hard, because he's as good as she is. Whatever she's up to, we won't know until we get the after-action distribution."

"I see." Barclay sucked on his pipe, realized it had gone dead. He leaned forward, tapping the bowl into his palm, then dumping his palm into the ashtray. The pipe went back in its stand beside the tobacco jar. "Is that all you have to say on the subject?"

"There's nothing more I can add, sir."

"Very well." Barclay settled his stare on Crocker again. "Then let me say this: HUM-AA is planning an offensive, an offensive that we could very well bring to a halt before it begins by delivering Chace to the Saudis. There appears to be no mean average of fatalities for suicide bombings, but assuming that HUM-AA knows what they're doing—and from our personal experience, that seems a safe assumption—they will certainly target critical services and installations. There will be people murdered, probably dozens, perhaps hundreds. Men, women, children. British, American, Israeli. Civilians, civil servants, soldiers.

"Lives we could have saved, had we delivered one person," Barclay concluded. "Had we delivered Chace."

He leaned forward, took up the papers on the table, settled back in the chair. He waved his free hand at Crocker, not bothering to look up.

"You may go, Paul," Barclay said.

39

The boat was small, with a cramped cabin that, out of respect, Sinan and Matteen had surrendered to Nia for the duration of the voyage. The crossing from Saudi to Egypt wasn't far, at least not considering the distance they had already covered to reach this point, but it was slow going, and the captain of the vessel, a small Egyptian named Kasam who seemed interested only in the money to be made from this venture, had no desire to hurry.

There were quicker routes into Egypt, to be sure, but none as safe, at least according to Abdul Aziz. Going west from the Wadi-as-Sirhan would have allowed Sinan and the others to travel through Jordan, then down through the Gaza and the Sinai, into Egypt. But Gaza would have been a problem, and Abdul Aziz had been quite clear with Sinan before they had departed.

"Succeed," he had told Sinan. "For the Prince's memory, for Nia's place in Paradise, but most of all, for Allah."

Rocking on the waves of the Red Sea, looking at the star-filled sky and the empty night all around them, success seemed very far away. Kasam ran his boat without lights—Sinan wondered if, in fact, the boat even had lights—and with roughly another hundred kilometers to go before reaching the shore, there was nothing to see. The only noises came from the diesel engine belowdecks, wheezing and grinding, and the slap of the water against the hull.

Sinan turned from the prow, squinting to see through the darkness. He could barely make out Kasam at the wheel, behind the cabin, moving every so often, adjusting their course. Matteen had settled on the deck only a few feet away, was already asleep, and Sinan marveled at his friend's ability to steal rest whenever and wherever it presented itself.

Sinan couldn't, knew that he wouldn't be able to do it, not until they were safely in Cairo.

He looked to the cabin, wondering if Nia was sleeping, thinking how extraordinary it must be to know the hour and moment of your death was approaching, and to know, in your heart of hearts, that this was a good thing, as it should be. Was she impatient, anxious to be on her way to Paradise?

They hadn't truly spoken since leaving the Wadi-as-Sirhan, not even in the interminable ride in the truck to Tabuk before taking the plane to Jeddah. Crammed in the cab of the vehicle, Matteen at the wheel, with Nia wedged between him and Sinan, the drive had been silent, each of them in his own thoughts. When Nia had nodded off to sleep, she had rested her head against Sinan's shoulder, and through her *balta* he had felt the warmth of her, smelled the fragrance of her, and his dream had returned to him.

Sinan moved to the door of the cabin and knocked lightly. When he heard no response, he opened it and stepped inside. It was even darker in the cabin than out, and he stood for several seconds, trying to find Nia in the room, feeling the gentle sway of the boat.

"Sinan?" she asked hoarsely. "Is that you?"

"Yes."

Only when she moved did he see her, the outline of her shape as she pushed herself up from where she'd been lying on the floor.

"I wanted to see if you were all right," Sinan said.

"I can't sleep."

"Neither can I."

"I want to. I've been trying to."

"We'll be ashore soon, and then we'll go to Cairo, to the hotel. There'll be a bed there, you'll be able to sleep then."

Nia shifted, sitting upright. "Would you sit with me?"

Sinan hesitated.

"Please?"

He moved closer, took a seat on the floor. He

could see her smile, and it seemed a look of gratitude to him.

"Are you all right?" he asked.

The smile faded and her look took distance. She turned her head away, as if trying to see through the walls all the way across the water to their goal.

"Nia?"

"I'm just tired, Sinan."

And then she shifted and lowered her head into his lap without a word, resting it upon his thigh and closing her eyes. He felt her hand, small and warm, take his, her fingers closing around his own.

"I'm glad you're here," she whispered.

He put his hand lightly to her head, surprised himself by gently beginning to pet her hair.

"I'm glad I'm here, too."

"I'll miss you, Sinan," she murmured. "When I go, I'll miss you."

"We will see each other again."

"I know," Nia said. "In Paradise."

He felt the weight of her head grow against his thigh as she relaxed, falling asleep.

In Paradise, Sinan thought, and he continued to stroke her hair.

40

As far as safehouses went, Chace thought they could have done a lot worse, even with the four Mossad heavies keeping them under lock and key.

There was a sliver view of the Mediterranean through one of the apartment windows, lights shining off the water. There was food and beer in the refrigerator, including two steaks. The furniture was used, not terribly comfortable, but entirely serviceable. The bedroom had a queen-size mattress on a companion box spring on the floor and the bed had been made up. There was soap, shampoo, two disposable razors, a tube of shaving cream, and towels in the bathroom. The air conditioner worked, even if the radio and television didn't.

She assumed they were bugged to the gills, certainly audio, probably video, and she guessed that was why those particular appliances wouldn't function. No background noise, nothing to hide a conversation behind.

When they'd been arrested, the policemen hadn't offered any explanation, and neither Wallace nor Chace had offered any resistance. Their arrest hadn't been expected, but it wasn't directly alarming, and when they had been driven to the safehouse rather than to the police station, both had been reassured.

Once inside, two of the heavies handled the physical search, going through their bags, then their clothes. They'd been polite enough about it, careful, and had avoided the extremes in that neither Chace nor Wallace had been asked to undress. The other two had kept watch, and nobody had said anything. Then the four had left, locking them inside, and Chace was certain they were at positions next door and in the hall.

There was nothing to do but wait.

So they cooked the steaks and had them for an early dinner, then went to the bed and lay down side by side. Why squander the time pacing when sleep was available? Wallace didn't touch her, and Chace thought he was trying to be discreet, not wanting to reveal anything more to the watchers than was already known, but after lying like that for most of a minute, she decided what the hell and reached around for Tom's arm, pulled it around her waist. He rolled toward her, slipping his other arm beneath the pillow where she was resting her head, and she could feel his breath on her neck, calm and steady, and it transferred to her, and that was how they slept.

●

A knock on the bedroom door woke them.

"Come out, please," a man said.

They did, Chace walking stiffly, her knee giving her trouble. She hoped running wouldn't be required anytime soon.

When they emerged, Noah Landau was seated at the small square table by the kitchen, and another man, tall enough to be gangly, hair wiry and unkempt, was plugging in an old coffeepot to percolate. One of them, Landau or the other, had put an ashtray on the table, and two unopened packs of cigarettes, and a plate of dainty cookies, what looked like chocolate chip.

"Please." Landau swept an open hand, indicating the empty seats. "Join us."

"Oh, that's very nice of you," Wallace said.

They took seats, and the man making the coffee turned from his task and gave Chace a looking-over, grinning. Then he looked to Landau, said something in Hebrew, and Landau shook his head, as if the words were expected and not particularly original.

"Rude," Chace said. "Speaking like that when we can't understand."

"You wouldn't like the translation," Landau told her. "He thinks he's in love with you."

"If his coffee's any good, tell him I'll marry him."

The man laughed.

"It's Wallace, isn't it?" Landau asked Tom. "Yes?"

Wallace nodded. "Crete, seven years ago? Or is it eight?"

"Eight and a half, Mr. Wallace." Landau smiled. "I understand you retired."

"Well, I thought a holiday was in order, came to see the Promised Land."

"Hmm, sadly I think that will not be possible."

"Oh?" Wallace looked to Chace. "I told you we should have booked a package, but no, you had to insist on the Rough Guide."

"You like it rough," she said.

"I like snuggling, too."

The other man spoke again, laughed, then began pouring the coffee.

"He's still being rude," Chace said.

"He is very rude," Landau agreed. "Viktor, introduce yourself."

"Viktor Borovsky." The man set one of the cups in front of Chace and gave her an enormously amused smile. "And if you like my coffee, I will go search for a ring for you."

"Needs to be a big one," Chace said. "I'm a size queen."

Borovsky laughed. He joined them at the table, taking one of the cookies and dunking it before eating. Wallace reached for one of the packs of smokes, tore the cellophane free, then knocked two free. He handed one to Chace, took one for himself, and his actions seemed to provide some sort of permission, because by the time Chace had her lighter to her cigarette, Landau and Borovsky were smoking as well.

"Regular kaffeeklatsch, this," Chace said.

"Nothing regular about it," Wallace said.

Landau smiled at them both for a moment, then said to Chace, "You blew it."

"To which 'it' do you refer, Mr. Landau? I've blown so many things in my time."

"El-Sayd."

"Ah."

"Yes."

Wallace shot a quizzical look to Chace. "Muhriz el-Sayd, he means?"

"That's the one."

"You blew it?"

"I was supposed to kill him. He left before I could take the shot. Killed Prince Salih instead."

"You neglected to include that part," Wallace said.

"I've had a lot on my mind."

Borovsky ate another cookie, feeding himself with the same hand that held his cigarette. When he smiled, chocolate was visible on his teeth. "Please, don't mistake Noah's gruffness for disapproval. We're quite happy with the way things turned out."

"So this is about giving me a medal, then?" Chace asked. "That's why you're holding us?"

"Viktor speaks out of turn," Landau said softly. "I neither approve nor disapprove of Salih's death. If he wasn't an enemy of Israel, he certainly supported Israel's enemies. It is relevant to the discussion at hand only because Salih's death impacts your current situation dramatically."

Chace rolled the end of her cigarette along the edge of the ashtray, watching the embers. "Impacts how?"

"Come now, you know the position in which you have been placed as well as I."

"You're not going to hand me to the Saudis," Chace said.

It wasn't a question, but Borovsky took it as such, answering, "Fuck me, no. No, no, never, never in a million years, no."

She looked at him and he smiled broadly, and Chace motioned with her free hand at her own mouth, indicating crumbs. Borovsky swiped at his chin with the back of a hand, unashamed.

Landau said something softly to Borovsky in Hebrew, and Borovsky looked at him, surprised, responding curtly. Landau answered, as quietly as before, but longer this time, and Borovsky listened. Chace watched his smile evaporate, to be replaced with a decided scowl.

To Chace, Landau said, "Our options are as limited as yours."

"What does that mean?"

"It means that the HUM-AA camp in the Wadi-as-Sirhan must go, Miss Chace. Unequivocally, the camp must be neutralized, destroyed. One way or another."

"Then please get on with it," Chace said tartly. "The sooner you take care of it, the sooner I can go home."

"You know our dilemma."

"No, actually, I don't. I'm told that you've been blocked by the Americans, but the Americans have blocked you before and you've gone around them before. A clear and present danger to the State of Israel has always required the same response from your lot—you take care of the problem. Why not this time?"

"This time the Americans are threatening to suspend four billion dollars in aid," Borovsky said. "And since the problem can be solved without direct intervention, our Government is content to allow things to run their course."

"Which brings us back to you," Landau said. "I understand that SIS has listed you as rogue, Miss Chace. Certainly, you suspected that would be the result of your flight from England. Of all the places in the world you could run to, you came here."

"And you were waiting for me at the airport," Chace said. "Which means you knew I was coming. How is that? Crocker tip you?"

Landau shook his head. "So you are here because you want our help, because you feel you must neutralize the camp by yourself or else run for the rest of your life. You are here because your own Government will not aid you, and so you turn to us."

"And you're eager to help," Chace said. "That's why you've held Tom and me here for the last twelve hours?"

"You left the job undone," Landau said.

Chace stared at him, for a moment stunned by his arrogance. "I beg your pardon?"

"El-Sayd is still alive, Miss Chace. Until you fulfill

our last agreement, I see no reason to enter into another with you."

"You're fucking joking."

"No, I'm not."

Wallace crushed out his cigarette. "You're seriously saying that we've got to go kill el-Sayd before you'll help us take care of the camp?"

"No," Landau said.

"Thank God."

"Miss Chace will go kill el-Sayd. You will remain here."

Both Wallace and Chace stared at him, and for a moment Chace wondered at the world's insistence on making her its bitch. She shook her head stubbornly, but Wallace spoke first.

"The hell I will. If she's off to Cairo, she'll need support."

"But if you go with her, there's no reason to assume she'll complete the mission. If we hold you here, as our guest, she will be motivated to take care of el-Sayd with the same efficiency she brought to the assassination of Faud."

"You're a staggering bastard," Chace said to Landau after a moment.

"Perhaps, but no more of a bastard than your D-Ops." Landau removed his glasses, checked the lenses for smudging. "Surely you didn't think we'd want nothing in exchange for our help, Miss Chace?"

"Actually, since it's your problem as much as it is ours and the Americans', yes, I sort of did."

Landau replaced his glasses. "That was surprisingly naïve of you."

Chace sighed.

"You're telling me," she said.

●

Landau and Borovsky briefed her in the apartment, with Wallace listening, until just before dawn. Shortly after sunrise, they drove her back to the airport, leaving Wallace behind with two of the brutes to mind him. Her tickets were already arranged, a flight to Athens, and from there to Rome, and then from Rome to Cairo. They gave her five thousand dollars for her expenses and a number to contact when the job was done, to arrange her return trip.

They stayed with her until it was time to board and waited until they saw she was on the plane.

She appreciated the fact that neither Landau nor Borovsky wished her luck.

41

Sinan watched Nia through his binoculars from the window of his room in the Shepheard's Hotel, knapsack on her back, guidebook in her hand, dressed in T-shirt and shorts and sunglasses, just another visiting sightseer, exactly as they had rehearsed. He smiled when she stopped at the corner, asking a passerby for directions. She was very good, very convincing, and it made him proud and happy to know that she would soon be *shahid*. The sunlight glittered on the cross she wore on the chain around her neck, the final touch to her disguise, a Christian woman looking to take in the Coptic sites.

"Where is she?" Matteen asked.

"Turning from the marina, about three hundred meters to go," Sinan said.

"Let me see."

They swapped places at the window, Matteen putting his eyes to the binoculars on their tripod, Sinan stepping back to the desk, where the cellular phone and the remote were lying. Neither would be required: Nia would telephone only if something were wrong, and he would use the remote only if she were going to be apprehended. There was no danger of that, he was sure. He had faith in her.

He loved her.

And she had told him last night, as he saw her to bed in the adjoining room, that she loved him.

He didn't think about the opportunity that her death would deny them, and he didn't mourn her for what she was about to do. Rather, it gave him a powerful sense of pride that their bond was so deep, so profound, that they had come together in this wonderful way, Nia making the journey to Paradise, Sinan there to see her on her way.

If he had been able to articulate it, he would have gone so far as to describe the situation as romantic.

●

While Matteen had taken Nia to the hotel, to settle them into their rooms, Sinan had returned to the café on Sikket al-Badestan that he and Aamil had visited so long ago—a lifetime ago—to meet their contact, a man named Hafiz, and to acquire the components for the bomb.

But instead of Hafiz, Sinan had found Muhriz el-Sayd waiting for him, and for Sinan, it was a triumphant homecoming indeed. To be face-to-face with the man who had turned him away, and in so doing turned him toward Salih and Abdul Aziz, to meet him as an equal, was yet another moment of pride.

"Sinan," el-Sayd said. "A better name than the last time we met."

"I am a better man now, Allah be praised," Sinan had replied. "A change you helped to make happen. It is good to see you, my brother."

"I saw a boy who would be a *jihadi*. Now I see a man. Our friend speaks well of you, Sinan. He says that, with time and Allah's blessings, you will achieve great things."

"If Allah wills it."

El-Sayd had clapped a hand on his shoulder, kissed his cheeks in greeting, and Sinan had returned the gesture, relishing the acceptance. They had moved to a room in the back of the café, and el-Sayd had given him the knapsack, already prepared, and the remote, and the two mobile phones.

"The bomb is a good one," he'd said. "Like the ones Hamas uses on the Zionists. Eight kilos of explosive, PE9, another four of nails, all of them coated with rat poison. This is a big one, Sinan, it will kill many."

Sinan had hefted the knapsack experimentally. It was heavier than they had planned for by about three kilos, but he was confident Nia would be able to carry it without difficulty. It had been well packed and made no noise when he moved it, the shrapnel packed tight around the charge. Coated with poison, the nails would create hideous wounds that would hemorrhage uncontrollably.

El-Sayd took the knapsack back from him, showed him the padded straps. "The *shahid* arms it here on the right strap and detonates it here with the left. The buttons are hidden and ride high, so it looks like he's adjusting the pack, nothing more."

"She," Sinan said. "Not he."

"Really?"

Sinan nodded. "A great woman. Pure and strong. She deserves Paradise as much as any man I have ever met."

El-Sayd gave him a look, as if surprised by Sinan's words, then nodded. "She has to turn away from the target for maximum effect. Make sure she understands this, Sinan."

"She will do it correctly."

"Sometimes they get excited, they detonate early. Tell her to be calm, to focus on the words of the *imam*, on what awaits her. Make sure she understands that she will feel no pain, that there is only the decision, the action, and her arrival in Paradise, in the place that awaits her."

"She knows these things already, my brother."

"Tell them to her again, Sinan. I have seen too many *shahid* lose their nerve at the last minute, and it has cost us dearly in the past. They panic. Do stupid things. Some simply run, try to get rid of the bomb, return home. Others, they turn themselves in, Sinan. They go to the Zionists and ask for mercy."

"As if they would receive it."

"This girl of yours, she's seen a lot, she's been

with Abdul Aziz, with you, with your comrades. If she were to lose her nerve and surrender herself to the British or the Americans, she could compromise all of you."

"I understand."

El-Sayd set down the knapsack, then handed Sinan the remote. It was a squat plastic box, shorter but thicker than a package of cigarettes, with two buttons set into its face and a single small lightbulb above them. The antenna was stubby, wrapped in black plastic.

"This is the insurance," el-Sayd told him. "Right button arms the bomb, left button detonates it, same as with the backpack. In open terrain, its range is almost a kilometer, but near the embassies it will be half that, if you're lucky. Once she closes on the target, you'll have to follow her."

Sinan looked at the remote in his hand, frowned. It was heavy and crude, and he felt that, just by holding it, he was committing to betraying Nia in some way.

"Which button does what?" el-Sayd asked him.

"Right arms, left detonates, like the backpack," Sinan said, moving his frown from the remote to the other man. "I understand."

"I know you don't like it, that you don't think this necessary, Sinan. But trust me, insurance is a good thing to have."

Sinan's nod was reluctant.

"You like this girl."

"I do. I want her to have this thing, to be *shahid*."

El-Sayd's eyes narrowed and he looked hard at

Sinan. "Then don't fail her. Don't let her bow to her fear. Make certain she remembers what awaits her, that is where her mind must be. Not on what she is doing, but on where she is going."

"I will, as I have said."

El-Sayd hesitated, and Sinan wondered why he seemed so suddenly unsure.

"May I offer you some advice, my brother?" el-Sayd asked.

"Please."

"Don't tell her about the remote. Only if she balks, if you have to use the phones. Tell her then, but not before."

He didn't like that and knew it showed on his face. "I will not lie to her."

"It is not a lie if you do not speak of it. It is not a lie if, as you say, it is unnecessary. Only if it *becomes* necessary should you tell her, that is what I mean to say."

Sinan looked at the remote again, then back to el-Sayd, before nodding, accepting the logic.

"It won't be necessary," Sinan promised.

●

"She's stopped," Matteen said.

"What?"

"She's stopped." Matteen moved back from the binoculars, to let Sinan look. "Across the street from the embassy grounds, facing the river. She hasn't moved in almost a minute, she's just staring at the damn river."

Sinan rushed back to the window, pressed his eyes to the binoculars.

Nia stood motionless, staring at the Nile, morning traffic streaming along the Sharia Corniche el-Nil behind her, pedestrians and tourists making their way quickly along the eastern bank of the river. The guidebook was still in her hand, but held loosely against her thigh, as if forgotten.

Sinan cursed softly. The binoculars were good, but not so good that he could make out her expression, that he could tell what she was thinking and, more, what she was feeling.

"Move," he whispered. "Move, Nia."

"She's frozen."

"No," Sinan snapped. "Give me the phone."

He heard Matteen moving to the desk, but he didn't look away from the view through the binoculars, just extended a hand back to him, waiting to be handed the mobile. Nia hadn't moved, not a fraction, not a muscle.

Matteen put the phone in his hand, and Sinan tore his eyes away long enough to make certain he hit the right button, then pressed the mobile to his ear, hearing the hiss, then the ringing. Through the binoculars, Nia still hadn't moved, apparently watching one of the many faluccas on the river floating past, even though he was certain she could hear the telephone ringing in her pocket. Then, as if pulling her limbs through glue, she tucked the guidebook beneath her left arm, reached into her right pocket, and produced her phone.

"Sinan?" Her voice was almost lost in the sounds of the traffic around her.

"It's me, Nia."

"I've never seen the Nile before. Last night, when we arrived, I didn't get to see it."

"Nia, what's going on?"

Her answer was lost in the sounds around her, coming into his ear.

"I didn't hear you, Nia, please, say it again."

"I said you should see it. You should come down and see it, close by."

"I've seen it before. When I was here before."

"Oh, yes. When you were a student."

"That's right," Sinan said. "Nia, what are you doing?"

"There are guards, Sinan. They're outside, something's happening. I can't get close."

Sinan panned the binoculars, trying to get a glimpse of the British Embassy through the gaps in the buildings below him. The Shepheard's Hotel had been chosen because it had the best vantage point for their purpose, but even so, construction in the Garden City of Cairo had thrown up buildings of irregular height, all of them with rooftops covered with aerials, advertisements, and other signs of life.

It wasn't any good, he couldn't see.

"What the hell is she doing?" Matteen asked.

Sinan moved the binoculars back to Nia, or to where Nia had been, but she was no longer standing there, and feeling rising panic, he began panning his view around, trying to spot her.

"Nia?" He tried to keep his voice calm. "Nia, where are you?"

There was no answer and again Sinan was assailed by the sounds of traffic.

"—*to the north side of the block, then around that way.*"

"What?"

"*I'm going to go around the block and try to come down Sharia Amerika al-Latineya.*"

"Hold on," Sinan said. "Stay on the phone, don't hang up."

"*I won't hang up. I like hearing your voice.*"

"I like hearing your voice, too." He turned the binoculars on the tripod, trying to find Nia in the traffic walking below, but the angle was too steep from the room and he couldn't see her. He pulled back from the tripod, glancing at the phone long enough to make certain he was pressing the mute button, then looked to Matteen.

"What is she doing?" Matteen demanded.

"She says there are guards, that she can't get close to the embassy. She's heading north to circle around. I think she's going for the secondary target, the American Embassy."

"You *think*?"

"I can't find her. She's heading in the wrong direction, our angle's no good."

Matteen swore, turned away, swiping the remote from the desk as he headed for the door.

"Wait!" Sinan said.

"She's *shahid*, Sinan!" Matteen barked at him. "Our job is to ensure she remains that."

Then he was out the door, and after a moment, Sinan was scrambling after him, out into the hall, running to catch him at the elevator. Matteen was already inside, glaring at him angrily, one foot holding the doors open, and he yanked it clear as soon as Sinan was in with him.

"Keep talking to her," Matteen said. "Find out where she is."

Sinan put the phone back to his head, heard Nia saying his name, but dropping out, the signal suddenly weaker in the elevator.

"—Sinan? Are you—ere, I cou—oice ight now."

"I'm still here, Nia," he said. "I'm still here."

"—inking about—ared—inan, it's not right."

He realized the mute was still on, switched it off as the elevator reached the lobby and Matteen rushed out, heading for the street. Sinan raced after him, trying to keep himself from shouting into the phone.

"Nia? Nia, can you hear me?"

"When did Allah tell Muhammad that there were six pillars, Sinan?" Nia asked. "You've studied, you're smart. I looked all through my Qu'ran, and I couldn't find where the Prophet says it is the Sixth Pillar."

"It's not in the Qu'ran, not like that." They were out on the street now, Sinan chasing after Matteen's wake as he threaded through the crowds on the sidewalk, heading north.

"But that's what I mean, Sinan. It's not there, that's what I'm saying. The Prophet told us to love and to honor and to respect. He told us to live in peace, even with those not like us. He told us to pray, to be pious, to

*be charitable, to honor Allah, the One God. He told us
to make the Hajj, that we might see the world as he
saw the world, and to fast during the days of Ra-
madan. But he never told us that* jihad *was the Sixth
Pillar, Sinan. He never spoke those words."*

They'd reached the corner, turned east, heading
toward the Midan Simon Bolivar, with its monu-
ment and roundabout. Matteen was still ahead of
him but slowing, scanning both sides of the street,
straining to find her through the traffic.

"Nia, think about what you're saying," Sinan
urged. "The Prophet was a great man, he taught us
many things, but to raise him, to elevate him too far,
that's idolatry, that's *mushrikun.*"

*"Why was it so frowned upon in the camp to speak
of Muhammad, Sinan? When did acknowledging the
Prophet become a sin?"* Her voice was clearer now,
her words spoken with more volume, with more
certainty, and Sinan could hear her thoughts crys-
tallizing.

"The Prophet was a servant, Nia, just as we are
servants. Glory is to Allah, praise Him, not His servants."

*"I don't think Allah is so hard-hearted, Sinan. I
don't think Allah who taught Muhammad the True
Religion thinks so poorly of His creation, of His children. Even the children who do not share the Truth,
even them, we are taught to respect the People of the
Book, to honor Jews and Christians, not to kill them."*

"The Jews were turned to apes and swine, Nia,
because they turned away from the Truth. The

Christians forsook the One God and now worship many, their money, their possessions—"

"But they aren't, Sinan! They aren't pigs or apes, they're not animals! They don't worship their money, they only have money!"

Matteen, ahead of Sinan, turned south, now heading down Sharia Amerika al-Latineya. Sinan tried to spot her, looking about frantically, and he saw the grounds to the American Embassy down the block, the guards and barricades, and he slowed as he reached Matteen, trying to conceal his anxiety, lowering his voice again.

"Nia, listen to me," Sinan said. "You trust me, right?"

"Of course I do, Sinan."

"You had a friend, you told me about him. You loved him. Think about him, Nia, think about what happened to him, and what he would want from you."

There was silence, and Sinan thought that maybe he'd reached her.

Then Nia said, *"He wanted peace, Sinan. More than anything, he wanted peace. As all Muslims want peace."*

Matteen had stopped, looking at him with anxious curiosity. The remote was still in his hand.

"Where are you, Nia?" Sinan asked.

"I'm on the corner."

"Which corner?"

"Sharia Maglis Ash-Shaab."

"I can't see you."

"I know." Nia's voice quavered. *"I can't do it, Sinan. It's wrong. I'm sorry, but if I am going to go to*

Paradise, I want to earn it through good works and good words, not like this. Not as a martyr. I'm sorry, Sinan."

"As am I," he said, and he reached out to the remote in Matteen's hand, and he pressed the two buttons in quick succession, the right, then the left.

They heard the explosion, and then the screams, and Matteen stared at Sinan, dumbstruck, as Sinan lowered the phone, turning it off. He felt his eyes beginning to burn with tears, saw frantic people running past him, crying and yelling, heading both toward and away from the site of the explosion.

"What did you do?" Matteen asked him hoarsely.

"I saved her," Sinan answered, and started down the block again, to see who Nia had claimed on her way to Paradise.

42

There'd been a bombing in the Garden City, near the American Embassy, and, ironically, that was what allowed Chace to kill Muhriz el-Sayd.

She'd arrived in Cairo late the night before, taking a room at the Semiramis Intercontinental Hotel, known for its opulence in catering to Westerners and its hopping casinos. She was still running on the DuLac identity, and it made her nervous, because she didn't know how much longer it would last. Box would have gotten the passenger list for the Eurostar train she and Wallace had caught, would have gone over every name with a microscope, then put out a watch, seeing if any of those travelers appeared anywhere else. If they suspected she had headed to Israel, it wouldn't take them long to find Monique DuLac on an Air France passenger list.

So she was quite possibly running blown.

After waking early, Chace bought two city guides from the hotel gift shop and a copy of the *Cairo Times*, an English-language weekly, more an over-sized magazine than a newspaper. She spent her breakfast poring over the guidebooks, ignoring the paper for the time being. Borovsky had given her three possible locations to look for el-Sayd, places he was rumored to frequent, all of them in the Islamic Quarter, cafés and restaurants where he hid among sympathetic owners and employees, shielded from the Cairo police. None of the locations appeared on her map, and with a resigned sigh, Chace resolved to check each by foot.

Finishing her meal, she went to the desk and checked out of the hotel, then tossed one of the guidebooks in the trash on her way out—the weaker of the two—sliding the other into her hip pocket.

The newspaper she rolled loosely and tucked inside her jacket.

●

It wasn't yet nine in the morning, and Cairo was already accelerating to full bustle. She threaded through the thickening pedestrian traffic to the nearest Metro station, then took the subway into the Islamic Quarter. When she came aboveground again, it was just past eight-thirty, and the streets were much quieter than in downtown. She took in the medieval architecture, orienting herself to the Mosque of Mohammad Ali, its silver domes shining in the morning light, atop the Citadel, then made her way on foot toward the Khan al-Khalili, the commercial heart of the quarter.

Vendors were already laying out wares, beginning to line the streets and alleyways, selling everything from spices to souvenirs. Chace passed a stand of beautifully crafted glass bottles, another of handcrafted waterpipes, a third of children's toys, cheap plastic robots with flashing red eyes and mechanical shouts that urged her to halt. It was growing noisier, voices raised to be heard over the traffic.

Chace stopped on the east side of the market, opposite the Mosque of Sayyidna al-Hussein, checked her guidebook. A passerby stopped, a man in his late forties, asking her in French if she was lost, if she required any assistance. She answered him in English, and he surprised her by asking the question again, also in English.

"The carpet bazaar," Chace said. "Which way is it?"

The man smiled, pointed back toward the west and south. She thanked him and wished him a good day.

"*Inshallah,*" the man said with a smile, and continued on his way.

Chace started in the indicated direction, heading for the Al-Ghouri Complex, the combination mausoleum-and-*madrassa* with its red-striped minaret. Across the street from it, on Sharia Azhar, she found the first of the possible locations Borovsky had proposed, a narrow café, just opening for the day. She stepped inside and ordered herself some tea, sitting at a narrow table on an even narrower bench to drink it, while taking in the location.

There was no sign of el-Sayd, but she hadn't expected there to be. She had serious doubts about her ability to find the man at all. Cairo was one of the most densely populated cities in the world, and even with her choice of three possible locations, the chances of el-Sayd being in one at the same time as she was seemed ludicrous at best. Worse, he could be present, in the back or on a floor above, and she would never know it. Asking the staff if they had seen the man wasn't likely to be of much help, either.

She finished her tea, then checked her watch, saw it was only half-past nine. She headed back out onto the street, up to Sikket al-Badestan, heading west, stopping occasionally to peer at the items on display in windows and at stalls. If she'd exposed herself by stopping for tea, there was a chance she'd acquired a watcher, especially if Borovsky's intel was to be trusted, and the locations were hot spots for the EIJ.

But Chace saw no one who alarmed her.

The next stop was an Internet café, surprisingly busy, eighteen terminals in two rows of nine, all of them occupied by young men gulping down coffee, tea, soda, snacking on chocolates and nuts and fruit. Every last one of them seemed to be doing two or three things at once, chasing hyperlinks as they carried on conversations with their neighbors, tapping away at e-mails as they listened to the pop music playing from the radio behind the cashier's counter. Chace chose a seat near the door, ostensibly to wait for an opening at one of the computers, took out her copy of the *Cairo Times*, pretending to read.

There was no sign of him here, either.

Chace tried to keep her thoughts productive, tried to formulate a plan, but the sad truth of the matter was that *this* was the plan, and she didn't think it was a very good one. There was a reason el-Sayd had managed to survive for twelve years on the Mossad's hit list, and it wasn't by accident. If Borovsky had truly known where the man was, Landau would have sent one of his Metsada boys after him long ago. That they hadn't, meant that what Borovsky had given Chace was their best guess, but for all any of them knew, el-Sayd could have been holed up at Heliopolis or Giza or somewhere else entirely, perhaps even out of the country.

These were her thoughts and they infected her mood, and she was beginning to brood when she realized that the music had stopped and a man's voice was now speaking somberly on the radio. At every workstation, hands became idle, heads turned to better hear the sound. One of the young men present called out to the man behind the counter, and Chace's weak Arabic couldn't keep up, but she guessed he'd asked that the radio be turned up, because that was what happened next.

She leaned forward to the nearest person, a man no older than eighteen, trying to sport a mustache. *"Min fadlak, law samahti. Hal tatakalam engleezee?"*

He turned from the direction of the radio, reluctant, still listening. "English? *Naam*, a little."

"Has something happened?"

The teen frowned, shook his head. "They are saying a, what is it? A bomb? A bomb has gone off near the American Embassy."

"Oh, no," she said, convincingly horrified. "That's awful."

"Yes, the police, they are looking for the ones who did it."

"Good, that's good."

Chace sat back in her seat, taking in the room with new eyes. The reactions seemed to be much along the lines of the young man she'd just spoken with, but not all of them, and it struck her that if, in fact, el-Sayd had connections to the owner or employees here, the news might force them to move. Not the bombing itself, but perhaps the threat of the police. Cairo thrived on tourism, and the EIJ attacks on the tourists at Luxor in 1996 had hurt.

The police would respond quickly, trying to keep that financial disaster from happening again.

But none of the men at the workstations seemed to be looking to leave. If anything, they were at the computers with renewed enthusiasm, trying to glean news from the Internet. Chace looked past them, saw that the man behind the counter was speaking on the telephone. Beyond him there was a door, presumably to a back room, and Chace wondered if there was a back door as well.

She got up and stepped outside, crossing the street and buying a pair of very cheap but surprisingly good-looking sunglasses from a vendor, all the while keeping one eye on the café door. One of the young men from inside emerged as she was haggling on the price and headed west along the street. Chace handed over an Egyptian five-pound note and started off in pursuit, taking her time, sticking to her side of the street.

Her initial uncertainty vanished when she realized she was having to almost jog to keep up. The man was clearly in a hurry to get someplace, and although he didn't seem to be even remotely concerned with possible tails, his haste and the traffic, both pedestrian and vehicular, were enough that Chace twice lost sight of him altogether, before he veered south off the street into a narrow alley crammed with stalls.

She lost sight of him for a third time around a bend that made her think back to the dogleg in Lambeth, where she'd tried to flush Box. She stopped abruptly, turned, feigning vague interest in a collection of bootleg CDs offered at the nearest stall, counting the seconds in her head.

He didn't come back.

Chace continued around the bend, hoping she hadn't lost too much time, hadn't lost him, and nearly cursed when she couldn't immediately find him. The alley dumped out onto Sharia Muski, heavy with traffic.

She couldn't see him and swore aloud.

Then she heard sirens, turned to look up the street, seeing three police cars, blue lights flashing, attempting to make their way in her direction through the clutter on the road. Chace looked back to the storefronts, seeing shops, restaurants, cafés, stall after stall, and people were looking at the oncoming cars, staring and wondering, and among them she saw her man, his reaction giving him away, moving while others stood still, ducking through the narrow door of a tattered shop.

Chace hurried forward to follow, feeling the pain in her knee return with a gentle thrum, as if cautioning her. As she had done with every other warning she'd received in recent memory, she ignored it.

The café was easily the most cramped and smoke-filled establishment she had ever been inside in her life. Perhaps a foot of clearance ran between the tables on the one side and the wall along the other, and with patrons seated, the room to move was halved again. Two sets of doors stood at the rear of the room, one on the far right wall, the other directly ahead of her.

As soon as she entered, every eye went to her, staring, and most of them were overtly hostile. The door at the back opened and a middle-aged man shaped like a tree stump emerged, carrying a tray, and at almost the exact same time the other door opened, on the right, and the man she'd been following emerged, looking much relieved.

The sirens outside were very loud, the cars coming to a stop.

That was what did it for her, what threw the switch, made Chace certain this was the place. Somewhere on the other side of that door on the right was el-Sayd, but he wouldn't be for long, and she had to move, and she had to move now.

She couldn't go through, so she went over, stepping on the thigh of a very startled man to get atop his table, and then half-running, half-hopping, knocking over cups and glasses, splashing drinks and spilling food, making her way to the door. Everyone seemed to be shouting at her at once, and as she came down off the last table, driving her good knee into the chest of the man she'd tailed, she heard new voices and new shouting as the police came through the entrance.

Her Arabic was good enough that, even in the confusion, she understood they were shouting for her, for everyone, to stop. She didn't.

Crashing through the door, she found herself at the base of a narrow and rickety flight of stairs. She started up, craning her head, reaching into her coat for the newspaper. Above her, the air swirled with disturbed dust, and she thought she heard footsteps, heavy, a man's, but, with the noise coming from the café behind her, couldn't be sure.

She ascended, two, three steps at a time, her eyes fixed above as the stairs turned at the landing, continued climbing, only glancing down to be certain of her footing. In her hands as she went, she began rolling the newspaper tightly, the wrong way, from the bottom instead of the side, trapping and compressing the spine on one end, hardening its edge.

On the third floor, she heard a door bang open, and new daylight flooded the stairwell, and she caught a glimpse of a shoulder and head disappearing onto the roof. It was el-Sayd, she was sure of it now, and she remembered how he'd looked to her in San'a', how big a man he was, and she wished the damn Mossad had given her a gun.

She sprinted, and her knee hated her but supported the weight, and when she burst out on the roof, he was there, thirty feet away, at the edge. She started toward him, but he'd already made the jump, disappearing, and when she reached the edge, he was already halfway to the next roof. The gap was short, no more than five feet, and the drop was at least that far, if not a couple more, and without hesitating Chace leaped after him. She landed on her feet, and he had already jumped to the next, and she raced after him, hurdling the ledge, sprawling this time, rolling back to her feet, the newspaper in her right hand.

He heard her tumble, and maybe because she hadn't said anything yet, maybe because the sound of her hitting the rooftop wasn't the sound he had expected, el-Sayd glanced back, then stopped cold, surprised. He'd been expecting a cop, Chace realized, not this blond Caucasian woman brandishing a newspaper instead of a weapon, and el-Sayd said something to her in Arabic, curt, and Chace understood he was insulting both her lineage and her anatomy, reaching around behind his back.

There were fifteen feet between them as he started to bring his gun around, and she closed it before he had his shot indexed to her, both hands on the rolled-up paper, now holding it low, to her right. She brought it up hard, the cruel edge of the hardened spine scything at his wrist, and el-Sayd screamed in surprise. The gun went off, wide, frighteningly loud, and he dropped the weapon, jerking his hand back reflexively. For an instant, he just gaped at her in wild disbelief.

Chace grinned. Anything could be a weapon, it was just a question of how one used it. There'd been no way the Mossad would arm her, certainly not with all the travel she'd had to do, and trying to locate a gun in Cairo would have been more trouble than it was worth. But a copy of the *Cairo Times*, with its tabloid format and stapled spine, worked well in a pinch. Rolled in, essentially, the wrong way, the spine became hard as steel, and its edges potentially as sharp. With the right force directed at the right soft tissue, it was as lethal as a knife.

El-Sayd lunged at her, and Chace dropped beneath his arms, thrusting the paper up into his throat. She heard him gag, stagger back, and she came out of her crouch, turning, scything the newspaper backhand, jabbing at his right temple. His eyes snapped wide, and she punched with the newspaper a third time, again going for the throat, and this time she felt his trachea give as she crushed his windpipe.

As he was falling, she hit him again, forehand this time, left temple, for good measure.

El-Sayd landed first on his knees, then toppled onto his face, his eyes still open wide.

Chace dropped the newspaper and ran, not looking back.

43

**London—Vauxhall Cross, Office of D-Ops
21 September 1621 GMT**

"Director Intelligence to see you, sir," Kate said over the intercom.

"Send him through."

"Minder Two is out here as well."

"Fine, unless D-Int has a problem with it."

The intercom clicked silent, and Crocker finished reading the memorandum he'd been double-checking, scrawled his signature at the bottom, above his neatly typed name. When he looked up, Simon Rayburn was entering, with Nicky Poole close at his heels. From their expressions, Crocker had a good idea what this visit concerned.

"Simon."

"The CIA intelligence was good, Paul. In addition to yesterday's attempted bombing of the U.S.

Embassy in Cairo, MOD informs us that they've prevented another suicide run in Basra."

"Not that good," Crocker said. "Cheng said we were the target."

"The primary target." Rayburn smiled thinly. "I suppose the heightened security warned the bomber away. Word out of Cairo is that the Egyptian police are rather vigorously rounding up any and every suspected member of the EIJ they can get their hands on."

"It'll be a half-dozen students with *madrassa* membership cards," Poole said.

"Perhaps." Rayburn looked at him, then back to Crocker. "Perhaps, but there's word coming out that Muhriz el-Sayd is dead, killed while resisting arrest sometime yesterday morning."

Crocker set down his pen, then reached for his cigarettes, frowning. "Is that confirmed?"

"It's been confirmed that he's dead. How he got that way is still open to speculation. But the Egyptian authorities are claiming it, whatever happened."

Crocker grunted, lighting his cigarette.

"There's one more thing I thought you'd like to know, Paul. Monique DuLac flew into Cairo night before last via Lufthansa flight 592, from Rome."

"You find that yourself, or did that come from Box?"

"No, all us. I assume you'll want to notify Cairo."

"You assume incorrectly, but I'll do it anyway." Crocker exhaled smoke, ignoring Poole's look of confusion, reaching for the red phone on his desk.

Before lifting the handset, he asked, "What're the details on the Iraq attempt?"

"MOD reports they identified the bomber and his vehicle before he could reach the security checkpoint. When they tried to warn him off, he accelerated and they opened fire. The bomb detonated shortly thereafter. Other than the bomber, no other casualties."

"Twice lucky," Crocker said.

"Whatever it is, be sure to thank Cheng for us, will you? They did us a good turn, tipping us. I don't know where their intelligence came from, but for once it seems worthwhile."

"I'll be sure to ask her, if she ever returns my calls," Crocker said sourly.

Rayburn's smile widened slightly, and then, nodding to Poole, he stepped out of the office, shutting the door after him.

"Monique DuLac, that's—" Poole began.

"Shut up, Nicky," Crocker said, and lifted the handset, keying the Ops Room. "Who's on the desk?"

"Ron's off, it's Ian Morris."

Crocker nodded, heard the line answered, Morris's voice identifying himself. "Duty Ops Officer."

"Ian, D-Ops. Flash to Cairo Station, copies of signal to DC and C, as follows: 'Minder One possibly in Cairo traveling under identity Monique DuLac stop. Apprehend and detain stop.' Have confirmation sent up as soon as you get it."

"Right away, sir," Morris said.

Crocker hung up, put his cigarette in his mouth,

and motioned Poole to the chair. "Lankford in the Pit?"

"Still doing his penance," Poole confirmed. "I just finished with mine. The next time the Deputy Chief wants to punish us, sir, perhaps you could ask him to let us clean the toilets. Be marginally more exciting than spending two days helping Records move dead files from one end of the building to the other."

"I'll be sure to pass it along."

"We'd appreciate it, sir." Poole scratched at his chin, then asked, "You don't think Cairo's going to grab her, do you?"

"Doubtful. If she did el-Sayd yesterday, she's well out of the country, probably back in Israel. Until that's confirmed, I won't order Tel Aviv to move. I'm not ordering any Station to move until Simon comes in here and gives me a reason to."

Poole thought about that, knitting his brow. "D-Int's in our corner, then?"

"Was there something you wanted, Nicky?" Crocker asked, annoyed. "Or is this simply a social call?"

"Lankford and I were wondering if, perhaps, there's a Special Operation in the offing, that's all."

"Were you?"

"Thinking maybe someplace like, I don't know, Jordan?" Poole's smile was hopeful, friendly. "And if we had to pass through Tel Aviv, well, maybe we could give someone a hand, if they needed it."

Crocker almost smiled. Almost.

"Not at the moment."

"Well, maybe one will come up," Poole suggested.

Crocker shook his head.

Poole sighed, rose from the chair.

Before he reached the door, Crocker said, "We'll get her back."

Poole gave him a smile. "Oh, yes, sir. Never doubted that for a moment."

He left Crocker to wonder if he'd been lying.

●

At twelve past eight that evening his intercom went off again, and it surprised the hell out of him, because he thought Kate had left for the day.

"Angela Cheng is coming up from Reception."

"Why are you still here?"

"Wanted to see if you needed anything."

"You, rested. Go home."

"What about Cheng?"

"Send her in as soon as she arrives, *then* go home."

"I obey, master."

Crocker glared at the intercom, then got up, pulling on his jacket. He moved around the desk, paced, thinking. Cheng had been dodging him—and he was sure that was what it was, dodging—for the last five days, ever since they'd met for lunch and she'd returned to her office at Grosvenor Square. Five days, more than enough time for Crocker to go over everything that had happened and question the motives of everyone involved. Some of them were transparent, nothing more than they had appeared at the outset—Kinney's, C's, Weldon's.

But Cheng, he had realized, was playing him.

It had been a nagging suspicion since his meeting with C the previous Friday, three days earlier, and it had continued to dog him over the weekend, even as he was scuttling around the house, trying to catch up on the legion of chores his wife had left to his care. It was just possible that Cheng had given him the warning about Chace out of altruism, that everything she had said about her concern for the Special Section was true.

But it was far more likely that Cheng was pursuing an agenda of her own.

That, in and of itself, wasn't nearly as upsetting as it was annoying. They both had their loyalties, and they both understood completely that working together—as they did most of the time—was done for expedience and mutual gain. But there were always going to be times when the gains at stake weren't mutual and would require one using, distracting, abusing, or bypassing the other. Never with malice, and rarely with glee, but it happened, and it was one of the reasons why, as much as Paul Crocker respected Angela Cheng, as much as he actually liked her as a person, their friendship would always be a limited one.

What bothered Crocker now was that he still couldn't see why he was being played, and he wasn't entirely certain how. He'd been working the puzzle for three days now, harder and harder, and there was no answer, and he suspected that was because he was missing a piece.

He'd be damned if Cheng was going to leave his office without giving it to him.

•

"Paul, sorry I've been so hard to reach." Cheng grinned at him, slipping off her raincoat, then looking back to Kate as she closed the door to the outer office. When it was shut, she turned to Crocker, adding, "Been dancing on my Ambassador's strings."

"Better than dancing with your Ambassador. He's a happily married man."

"There's no such thing as a happily married man."

"Spoken like a confirmed bachelorette."

"You're not a man, Paul, you're a machine." Cheng dropped into the nearest chair, smoothing her skirt, and her grin blossomed into a smile. "I hear our two tips paid off for you boys big-time today."

"Iraq and Cairo, you mean?"

"No, Arsenal and Aston Villa. Yes, Iraq and Cairo."

"Marginal payoffs," Crocker said. "We weren't able to take them alive."

"Then you're just too slow. We caught two ourselves, both in Baghdad, and the Israelis caught another trying to get in through Gaza."

"Five for five, Angela?"

"When the network works, it works well."

She continued to smile at him, and suddenly

Crocker could see through it, and he wanted to kick himself for taking so long to do so.

He turned to his desk, smiling in return, and said, "If you have anything more along those lines, Simon would love to hear it."

"Oh, I think we've done our part." Cheng grinned at the joke, then shifted in her chair, uncrossing her ankles and leaning forward, and Crocker watched the mirth give way to concern, and he almost believed it. "Any word on Chace?"

"She was in Cairo yesterday, funnily enough," Crocker said.

"Cairo? Strange place to go if you're trying to lie low."

"She wasn't trying to lie low, she was trying to kill Muhriz el-Sayd."

Crocker thought she did a good job of acting surprised, almost as good as her job of trying to pump him for information.

"Jesus fucking Christ, she didn't?"

"Hadn't you heard?"

"Do I look to you like I had?"

Crocker chuckled. "Egyptian authorities are claiming he was killed while resisting arrest. But since Chace was in Tel Aviv with Wallace as of the eighteenth, I think it's more likely she did the job. I haven't asked Landau yet. I suppose I can wait until I hear from Chace herself."

A flicker crossed Cheng's face, and Crocker saw it, and saw they were getting close now.

"Chace has got Wallace with her?"

"She was in Egypt alone, as far as we know. Not

sure where Wallace is now, but they're certainly working together."

"You're in touch with her?"

"I wouldn't confirm that even if I could, Angela, you know that. I've declared her AWOL, we're doing everything in our power to bring her in."

"Liar."

"Professional, too."

"You know what she's doing? What she and Wallace are planning?"

Crocker shrugged.

"What're they planning, Paul?"

"I suppose you'll find out, along with the rest of us."

And then Crocker smiled at her, to let her know that they were once again on the same playing field. He might not have figured out exactly the how and the why, but he was certain enough, just as he was now certain he held information Cheng wanted.

How badly she wanted it was the next question.

Cheng's expression went to neutral and she sat back, inhaling through her nose, looking away from him to the blank walls of the office. Crocker thought that she was asking herself the same question.

"Can you get a message to her?" Cheng asked after a moment.

Crocker didn't answer, waited.

Cheng waited, too.

He won.

"They run at the camp, it's suicide, Paul. Please

tell me they're not going to try to take the camp by themselves."

"All right, they're not going to try to take the camp by themselves."

"Dammit, Paul!"

"Why do you care if they want to fall on their swords, Angela?"

"Because I don't want to see you lose more people. Maybe you haven't noticed, but your Special Operations capability has taken a hit two or three times in the last couple of years. I'd like to see you stay in the game."

"So it's concern, is that it?"

"Self-motivated concern, yes."

"That's why you showed me the pictures of the camp, told me why Box was closing in on Chace? So I'd warn her, so she could go to ground until this whole thing blows over?"

"Yes."

"Bullshit."

Cheng raised an eyebrow at him. "What'd you say?"

"Bullshit, that's the word, isn't it? Or is that too American coming from me, would you have preferred I said 'utter twaddle'?"

"What the hell are you talking about?"

"I'm talking about the fact that the Company has a man inside HUM-AA, in the Wadi-as-Sirhan. That's where your intel's coming from, why you're suddenly coming up with gold after offering nothing but lead for the last several months. That's why you tipped me to Box's intentions, so I'd spark

Chace to run. And if Chace runs, she can't be handed to the Saudis; if she isn't handed to the Saudis, the camp—and your mole—stay secure. That's what I'm talking about, Angela."

She stared at him, and Crocker took the opportunity to light a cigarette and, for the first time in quite a while, actually enjoy it, rather than simply feed his addiction.

"Christ, Paul," Cheng said finally. "You have any idea how long it's taken us to get someone in position? How hard it's been to get someone that deep, someone who has access and isn't doubling back on us?"

"It's one man?"

Cheng shook her head, saying, "No, I'm not giving that up."

"Chace and Wallace are going to destroy that camp."

"Then you've got to stop them."

"Why in the name of hell should I?"

"We'll lose our man!"

"I don't give a damn about your man," Crocker snarled. "I don't give a damn about your network. There were five separate bombing attempts today, all of them originating from that camp presumably."

"Five attempts! *Attempts*, Paul, that were stopped because we *knew* they were coming."

"Five attempts that could have been prevented altogether if the camp was shut down. The bomb that went off in Cairo killed three, injured fourteen, and four of those aren't likely to make it."

"But it didn't hit the Embassy."

"Which should make the Americans there sleep better tonight, but seven families are going to be mourning—no, wait, *eight*—because the damn thing went off anyway."

"Better that than the alternative."

"And is that alternative better than what happened on the Underground, Angela?" Crocker demanded, furious. "Your man inside, he didn't see *that* coming? Or was it that the CIA didn't think it was worth passing along the intelligence?"

Cheng's reaction was an honest hurt, mixing with disbelief. "We didn't know! Jesus Christ, do you really think we'd have sat on it if we had known it was coming?"

"How the hell did your man miss it, then? If he's as good as all that, how is it that he didn't see it coming?"

"He tried, he told us he tried. We're having a nightmare time running messages with this guy, he's in deep, and he's constantly being watched. There's only so many opportunities he gets to pass along information, and he couldn't warn us—or you—in time!"

"Sounds to me like he's picking and choosing."

"Name me an agent who doesn't, damn you! But it's better than nothing."

"Three hundred and seventy-two dead men and women would argue that point if they could."

Cheng shook her head. "All Chace has to do is lie low, it'll blow over—"

"Are you daft? This doesn't blow over, ever! Even

if the Saudis relent, even if the Government decides *not* to hand her over, she's still buggered. Unless she shuts down the camp, she's an agent who went AWOL, who went rogue, and I'll still have lost my best officer. You put this in motion, Angela, and if you can't control it now, that's your lookout, not mine. I'm getting Chace back, right where she belongs, at the Head of Section, and the way to do that is to remove the Saudis from the equation."

"There's a friendly there, she could end up killing our guy."

"Then you had better signal your guy to get the hell out."

"We can't—aren't you hearing what I'm saying? He contacts us, not the other way around, he's in the middle of the fucking Wadi-as-Sirhan, Paul! There's only so much we can do."

"You didn't give him a microburst transmitter, a receiver? Do you really expect me to believe that?"

Cheng looked, for a moment, almost pathetically defeated. "We did. It stopped working three months ago."

"Oh, fucking brilliant. Fucking brilliant, why hasn't he been resupplied?"

"Well, maybe you could ask Chace to do it," Cheng shot back, "provided she doesn't kill him first."

"I'll take it under advisement."

"This guy is worth gold to us, you've seen it. You do this, it's all down the toilet."

"So you're screwed?"

"That's what I'm telling you."

"I'm sure Chace knows just how you feel."

Cheng fumed at him, then ran a hand through her hair, thinking.

"I could get onto Langley," she said. "Langley gets onto the White House, the White House jumps all over the Israelis, Chace and Wallace, they don't go anywhere."

"No, you can't," Crocker said. "It would require the White House to do a complete volte-face, and for what? A single agent? They want that camp shut down, Angela. At best, they apprehend Chace and hand her to the Saudis, you've still got the same problem."

"You son of a bitch," Cheng said.

"Because I figured it out?" Crocker crushed his cigarette into the bottom of the ashtray. "Because I tried to protect my people? Because you lied to me?"

"I didn't have a choice, don't make it personal."

Crocker laughed. "It's not personal, Angela. It's never been personal, however many gifts you give my daughters for their birthdays."

She exhaled sharply, then fell back, resting in the chair.

"When are they going in?" Cheng asked. "Do you know?"

"No."

"No you don't know, or no you won't say?"

"I don't know. They may be in already, they may go tomorrow, they may never go."

"Fuck."

"If you say so."

"Can you at least get a message to them, can you try to do that? Just let them know there's a friendly, let them know he won't fire on them, that's how he'll identify himself, he'll be unarmed."

"What do I get in exchange?"

Cheng looked sincerely incredulous. "You really *are* a son of a bitch."

"What are you offering?"

Cheng's chin dropped onto her chest, mouth tightening, thinking.

"You want her back in the Pit when all this is over," she said finally. "Langley will push it, we'll smooth any of the feathers that get ruffled."

"No," Crocker said. "Not good enough."

"Jesus Christ, Paul, what do you want?"

"I want it in writing that Chace undertook the covert at the request of CIA London."

Crocker had never seen her look stunned before.

"No way."

"The only way," Crocker said. "It's her job insurance. And mine, for that matter. You come on the chopping block with us, you'll have a vested interest in seeing the blade doesn't fall on any of our necks."

Cheng scowled, then leaned forward, grabbing one of the pens resting on Crocker's desk. He reached into the second drawer on his left, pulled out a pad of paper, handed it to her, then sat back with another cigarette, watching while she wrote. It took her the entirety of his smoke, and when she was finished, she tossed the pen down on the desk and nearly threw the pad at him as well.

Crocker read it over carefully. "You're exonerating the Agency."

"I'm not going to give you a document that could end up with a congressional inquiry, Paul, I don't care how big the pistol is that you hold to my head. I'm taking responsibility for it, that's enough. You, me, Chace, all in it together. Happy now?"

"No. But I'm marginally less unhappy than I was when you came in here."

"And here I am, much more unhappy than I was when I came in here."

"I'll make copies," Crocker said.

"Hold it, hold on a second."

He stopped, halfway to his feet.

"She has to get our man out alive, Paul. That's my condition. I've given you what you want, now I want something, too. She needs to get him out alive and with cover intact."

"You don't ask for much, do you?"

"You've got a hell of a lot of gall, saying that."

Crocker thought about that, then nodded.

"Yes," he said. "I suppose I do."

●

It was past eleven by the time Crocker saw Cheng out of the building, and after leaving her he went straight to the Ops Room. The night staff was on duty, Gary Draper at Duty Ops, Max Fletcher at Coms.

"D-Ops on the floor," Draper announced as Crocker entered.

"Easy," Crocker said. "Max?"

"Sir?"

"We have a direct contact for Noah Landau at Mossad?"

"Checking, sir."

Crocker waited, hands in his pockets, looking at the plasma screen wall. There were two operations running currently, one in Singapore, the other in Accra, both of them run-of-the-mill jobs, missions named Lightbulb and Bookstore, respectively. There was nothing marking Saudi Arabia.

"We have a contact number, yes, sir," Max said. "Two in the morning there, I'm not sure we'll be able to reach him."

"Make the call, then run it through to my office."

"Very good, sir." Max hesitated, then added, "Shall I log it, sir?"

Crocker pretended not to hear him as he left the floor.

•

He caught the phone on the first ring. "D-Ops."

"Noah Landau on the line, sir," Max said.

"Patch him in." Crocker waited for the click, then the line noise to resolve, the slight whining in the background scrambling the conversation. "Mr. Landau?"

"Mr. Crocker." Landau's voice was distorted but understandable. "Very late to be calling."

"I need you to pass on a message to Chace and Wallace," Crocker said. "There's a friendly in the camp, he won't raise arms against them, that's how he'll identify. They need to get him out. Can you pass that along?"

The whining on the line grew louder, then faded before Landau spoke again.

"I'm afraid that won't be possible."

"Why the hell not?"

"Because, Mr. Crocker," Landau said, "they're already there."

44

The helicopter had flown in so low it hadn't actually descended to let Chace and Wallace jump out. As soon as their feet hit the ground, their hands shielding their eyes from the whirling sand spiraling around them, the helicopter banked swiftly away, and for a moment Chace thought the bird would end up nose down on the desert floor. But as she and Wallace ran for cover, dropped to their bellies, their submachine guns in their hands, she heard the sound of the rotors receding to an echo and then to silence.

It was warm, the earth beneath her still holding the heat from the day, but not unpleasantly so. Borovsky had said it would be in the low seventies

Fahrenheit, "good weather for walking," he had told them.

"Want to come along, then?" Wallace had asked, and Borovsky had laughed that annoying laugh of his and shaken his head, saying that he thought the two of them would have more fun without him.

Later, as Chace and Wallace had been kitting up, Wallace had said, "He knows we're shagging."

"It's your fault," Chace said. "You're too loud."

"Right, and you're a churchmouse."

"Oh, so it's bestiality you're after now, is it?"

"I'd say 'moo,' but you might accuse me of calling you a cow."

They'd pulled on their camouflage fatigues, supplied, like all the rest of their kit, by the Israelis. The camo was dark gray, splotched with black, and wouldn't do a damn bit of good for them in daylight, but they weren't planning on spending daylight anywhere they might be spotted. They blacked their faces, checking each other for spots they had missed, and wore black watch caps to hide their hair. The boots Landau had supplied were comfortable and fit well, and he'd even presented them with an extra pair of socks, as requested.

"Anything to help," he'd told them.

•

She'd returned to Tel Aviv via bus, a ride that had taken almost fourteen hours, getting her back to the apartment at six of two in the morning to find Borovsky waiting with Wallace. They'd already heard the news, and Borovsky had once again of-fered a proposal of marriage.

"I drink, I smoke, I swear, I can't cook, I don't do laundry, I won't clean, and I don't like children," Chace told him. "Why marry me?"

"No woman is perfect."

"You've never met my mother," Wallace said.

Chace went to take a shower then, scrubbing the journey and the act from her skin as much as she could, examining her bruises. Her left arm was tender to the touch where she'd taken the baton, but the swelling had finally gone down, and her knee was apparently content for the time being to keep its silence.

She'd been under the spray when Wallace came in, taking a seat on the closed toilet, watching her behind the pebbled glass.

"Borovsky gone, then?" Chace asked.

"Just left."

"Then you should get in here."

So he did, and they made love in the shower, or at least tried to, but the stall was too cramped and the danger of slipping seemed to grow exponentially the more aroused they became. Ultimately, they retired to the bed, taking things slowly, Chace basking in Wallace's touch and attention.

Afterward, lying together, bodies idle but for their hands, Wallace said, "I have a plan."

"Does it include this bed?"

"For the Wadi."

"Oh, that."

"You seem uninterested."

"I'm easily distracted."

"Seems to me I should be the one who's distracted." He propped himself up on his elbow, brushing her hair with his fingers. "Landau's still saying they can't put anyone on the ground, but he's willing to arrange the infil by helicopter."

"Nice of him, considering the favor we're doing for him."

"They're making a drop tonight, equipment, they'll put it down about twelve kilometers west of the camp. Tomorrow night they'll drop us in, twenty kilometers west of the camp. We'll have GPS, move to the cache, load up, close on target."

"Why two drops?"

"Time over target," Wallace said. "We want to limit it as much as possible."

"And what are they dropping?"

Wallace's grin indicated the degree to which he was pleased with himself, and from it Chace concluded he was very pleased indeed.

"Claymores."

"The swords?"

Wallace put his head to her shoulder and nipped at her skin, and she yelped, pushed his head away.

"Mines," Wallace said. "Sixteen of them, four hundred feet of det cord, two timers, one for a backup."

"Daisy chain."

"Exactly."

"You're a clever man, Mr. Wallace."

"I do have my moments," he agreed. "They'll also cache food and water for the exfil."

"So we're going to mine the camp and let it fly?"

"Landau's giving us P90s, suppressed, and I asked for two hundred rounds apiece. We'll set the mines, pull back, wait for the detonation—"

"And shoot the survivors."

"Quick job. Brutal, efficient. Crocker would approve."

"Not of this, he wouldn't."

"Let go of that, that's not yours."

"I disagree. I have staked my claim."

He gently moved her hand away, then wrapped his arms around her, pulling her close, and stayed that way until he fell asleep.

●

Wallace got to his feet slowly, the P90 held ready, and he turned a slow circle in place, checking their immediate perimeter, while Chace used her GPS unit to get a bearing on the cache. The P90s were suppressed, which added roughly a pound to their weight but didn't appreciably affect their handling. The weapons were loaded with fifty rounds; the remaining 150 for each of them with the cache.

In addition to the guns, they each carried a GPS unit and a knife on their person, and that was it. Nothing else was truly needed, at least not yet, and as soon as Chace had the bearing, she rose to her feet and indicated their desired direction. They spread out, putting twenty feet or so between each other, and began walking. They moved as quickly as silence would allow.

There was no moon, but the stars were brilliant

and gave off a surprising amount of light, and she felt better about the fact that they had forgone NVG, relying on their eyes alone. She remembered a story from the SOE days, before the Special Operations Executive had transitioned to become SIS, during the Second World War, when agents had been taught to keep one eye closed during night maneuvers. It was the kind of detail that stayed with you, and she wondered at it, wondered at the way the mind could detach from the action surrounding it.

The terrain was even for the most part, and barren, and she had expected sand and was mildly disappointed that there wasn't much of it to be found. They made good time, and when they reached the cache and found the canister lying on its side, its self-deploying camouflage blanket making it look like nothing more than a large rock, Chace slid back her sleeve to check her watch. Oh-one-fifty-nine.

She stood watch while Wallace broke open the canister, removing the backpacks first, and set about loading them. He divided the claymores evenly, eight for each of them, as well as the det cord and the timers. When he had loaded both backpacks, he dug out the extra magazines for the P90s, handed three of them to Chace, kept the remaining three for himself.

Two hundred rounds apiece, sixteen claymores, Chace mused.

If that wasn't going to be enough to get the job done, she didn't know what more would've.

The backpacks loaded and closed, Wallace reached into the canister again, this time removing two plastic bottles of water, factory sealed, labels removed. He cracked one, drank it down, then closed the bottle and returned it to the canister before getting to his feet and offering the other to Chace. She drank it while he stood watch, then repeated his procedure, putting it back where he'd found it. Inside the canister were another sixteen bottles and six MREs, to be used later, on the exfil.

Getting out was as important as getting in, after all.

The plan, as it stood, had them hitting the camp in the next ninety minutes, returning to the cache before dawn for resupply. After loading up on the food and water, they would strike out to the west, making for the GPS coordinates Borovsky had supplied, across the border with Jordan. It was an eighty-six kilometer hike and would take them the better part of two days to accomplish. Once they reached the lift site, they would wait for pickup, scheduled twice every twenty-four hours, at twenty-two hundred and oh-four hundred.

They had no radios because radios wouldn't do them any good. Who were they going to call but each other?

Chace closed the canister, let the camouflage blanket fall back over it, blurring its lines once more. She hoisted her pack, feeling the thirty-six pounds of landmines on her back, a substantial weight but not an unmanageable one.

Wallace was watching her, and Chace moved her P90 to a low-carry, nodded, and they struck out again, this time for the camp.

Ready to kill.

45

"I told you to take it slowly," Matteen said.

Sinan shot a glare at him, then turned the look on the front right tire of the SUV, deflated and useless.

"Get the spare and the jack," Sinan said.

Matteen sighed, gesturing around them at the expanse of sand. "We can wait until dawn, Sinan. We can sleep in the car."

"I want to get home."

"You wanting to get home is why we have a flat tire in the middle of the desert."

"Fine, I'll do it." Sinan threw his Kalashnikov onto the backseat of the Land Cruiser, went around to the back, opened the hatch. Matteen followed after a moment, grumbling, then reached inside to help him free the spare. They rolled it around the side of the vehicle, loosened the bolts on the flat tire, and then set about raising the car with the jack.

It had taken them far longer to get out of Egypt than it had to get in, and Sinan had been surprised by how swiftly and how viciously the Egyptian authorities had responded to the bombing, for all the effect Nia's death had had. It puzzled him, and it puzzled Matteen, and it was only by Allah's grace, Sinan was sure, that they had not been stopped in the airport in Cairo, where they had boarded the flight south to Hurghada.

Their contact had met them in Port Safaga and put them up for the night, then brought them to the fishing boat that would take them to Duba.

It was in Port Safaga that they learned what had happened to Muhriz el-Sayd, how he had been murdered by the police.

"They take our best from us," Sinan had lamented. "They take our best, again and again, and we make no gains."

"Our gains are not for this world but the next, Sinan," Matteen had answered. "Do not lose your faith."

Sinan hadn't responded, dwelling once more on Nia, telling himself he had done what he had to do, that he had done what was required of him. She hadn't left him a choice.

They'd crossed the Red Sea and made port in Duba, finding the SUV where Abdul Aziz had promised them it would be, the keys in the hands of a local *imam* who fed them and prayed with them before sending them on their way with their rifles once more at their sides. The drive was a long one, and while they made good time on the immaculate and barren highways for the first part of it, as they closed in on the camp the going was slower, and they were required to leave the roads. Before night fell, they stopped and prayed.

"Let's wait until morning, Sinan," Matteen had suggested. "I don't like driving in the dark."

"I want to get back home."

"If we get hung up on a rock or boulder, we'll end up stuck out here and have to walk."

"Allah will not let that happen," Sinan had said simply, and then climbed back behind the wheel of the Land Cruiser.

●

They had the tire changed in only a few minutes, and Sinan's dour mood was only slightly helped by the fact that Matteen didn't say "I told you so."

Once the flat was stowed, along with the tools, Sinan moved to get behind the wheel, but this time Matteen stopped him.

"No, I'll take it for a while."

"I can drive."

"I know you can drive, Sinan, but you're impatient, and we only had the one spare. We'll get there when we get there."

Sinan thought about digging in, being stubborn. Instead, he moved around to the passenger's seat, climbing in, waiting while Matteen got behind the wheel. The engine came back to life without hesitation and the headlights splashed onto the baked earth.

"I just want to go home," Sinan said to no one in particular.

46

It took another hour, because they went much more slowly now. Both Wallace and Chace had agreed that it was unlikely HUM-AA was expecting trouble or that there would be static defenses in place. Certainly, there would be sentries, but they were dealing with a training camp, one where the trainees and the trainers felt secure in their work. The residents were there to learn and to train, their days would be full, their nights dedicated to rest.

But Chace and Wallace weren't going to take any chances.

They climbed down into the actual physical wadi, roughly two kilometers from the camp, picking their way down the sides, cautious with their footfalls, and once at the bottom stopped and took stock. The sides of the wadi rose roughly three meters on either side, and where they had entered was narrow, perhaps only four meters across. The ground beneath their feet was hard earth, cleaned by the rare floods that rushed through it in the spring. Chace saw tire tracks but had no idea how recent they were.

Wallace checked his GPS, showed his findings to Chace, and she nodded, then took the lead, now heading northeast.

After fourteen minutes, the wadi widened considerably and its walls had slowly begun to drop. Another GPS reading put them within five hundred meters, and here they spread out again, Chace to the eastern side of the wadi, Wallace to the western. Chace moved the P90 to her shoulder, made certain the safety was off and the selector was on burst.

They moved very slowly now, listening hard, trying to ignore their own sounds, trying to control their own fear.

With one hundred meters to go, the wadi curved again, and Chace hugged her wall as she followed it around. Over the emptiness, she heard a rustling, the scraping of a foot, and peering the rest of the way, she saw the sentry, Kalashnikov held in one hand, covering his mouth to suppress a yawn.

She looked to Wallace, could barely make him out in the darkness across from her. She held up a finger, hoping he could read the sign, and she saw him return it, then made a circle, then showed him all five fingers. She lowered her hand, went back to watching the sentry, counting seconds.

The time the sentry had left to live.

47

Matteen stopped the car.

"What are you doing?" Sinan demanded.

Matteen grinned at him, opening the door and dropping out of the vehicle. "Relieving myself, if you don't mind."

Sinan groaned inwardly, closed his eyes, wanting nothing more than to be back in the safety and sanity of the camp, where the world was ordered, where doubt could not exist. He remembered Nia's head in his lap, felt a pang of guilt.

Outside the car, he could hear the sound of Matteen passing water.

"Come on."

Matteen climbed back behind the wheel, started

the car once more. He drove carefully and slowly, and when at last they entered the wadi proper, their progress, it seemed, slowed to a crawl.

"It would be faster if we walked," Sinan complained.

"You are too impatient, Sinan. You must learn to take things as they come."

"And what has that gotten us? Patience, what has it brought?" Sinan gestured angrily. "This is holy land, Matteen, and it has been defiled time and time again by those *kufr* who would destroy everything we believe. Patience! Did patience remove the American air bases?"

Matteen just shook his head, concentrating on negotiating the wadi.

"Action," Sinan said. "Action, not patience. We act, that Allah, praise His name, acts through us."

"There is a time for action and a time for planning. The unseen knife cuts cleanest, Sinan, and your way would shout out to all who would hear what it is we do, what it is we are planning."

"They should know! They should know, and they should be afraid!"

"They already are. They live in fear, haven't you seen it? The West awakens every morning, anxious for news, nervous and scared, wondering where we will strike next. That is terror, Sinan. And when they talk about a war against terror, they don't understand that they have already lost, because they are already afraid. And they will never sleep safe again, no matter how many missiles they drop on our camps, no matter how many of our brothers they capture and torture and murder. They fear us already, and thus we have already won. It will just take time for the victory to be complete."

Sinan looked out the window at the rough terrain bathed in the headlights. He could hear the truth in Matteen's words, and it soothed the heat in his blood.

He thought about Nia again, wondered again if she had been afraid. He hoped not; he didn't want her to have entered Paradise afraid.

He wondered if she would be happy to see him when his time came.

48

Chace reached three hundred, uncovered the scope on the P90, raised it again to her shoulder, and settled the crosshairs on the man's chest. She moved her finger onto the trigger, pulling gently, exhaling, and the burst flew, the weapon hissing at the sentry, and through the scope she watched him jerk and topple, and she was moving forward again before he hit the ground. She looked around as she went, scanning, and saw no movement, no light.

She debated about moving the body, then continued past it, thinking it a waste of time.

There were eleven tents, the largest cluster of them centered in the wadi, with camouflage netting draped above them. Smaller tents hugged the walls.

She worked from the eastern wall first, setting down her pack and removing the first claymore, extending its legs, setting it to face the nearest tent, some fifty meters from her, then stripping the end of her det cord with her knife, prepping it before attaching it to the mine.

She repeated the procedure with the remaining seven claymores, placing them roughly twenty-five meters apart, in a gentle semicircle, until the entire line was covered. She returned the pack to her back, its weight now negligible compared to what it had been, then attached the end of her remaining det cord to the daisy chain and quietly worked her way through the center of the camp.

Wallace was already finished and waiting for her with his end of the cord. She stood watch while he prepped the line, joining the segments, and then followed her back the way she had come. Back across the claymores, they stopped again, and Wallace took his timer, fitting it to the recess on the mine nearest the center of Chace's chain. He checked his watch, set the timer, and then showed Chace four fingers.

She checked her watch, noting the time. Oh-three-oh-four, kickoff at oh-three-oh-eight. She slid her sleeve back down, nodded to Wallace.

Wallace pointed at himself, then at the western side of the wadi, then at her, then the eastern.

She nodded again, and they parted. Chace had to sling the P90 to climb out; although the wall was shallow, it was steep, and she needed both hands to get above it.

Once up and out, she scanned the terrain for cover and found an indent in the earth that met with the wadi wall. She rested in it, checked her watch again.

Oh-three-oh-six.

She readied her P90, looked across the wadi, trying to spot Wallace. She didn't see him. She'd have been worried if she had.

She waited, hearing the night, counting down the seconds, waiting for the inevitable. Each claymore held 650 grams of explosive and 700 small steel balls, and when the timer ran down, the whole line would detonate in sequence. At their optimum distance from target, fifty meters, and placed as they had been some twenty-five meters apart, each mine would send its explosive load in overlapping coverage. The steel ball bearings would fly in a sixty-degree arc, covering up to two meters in height, and would tear through the tents as if they weren't there, and tear through the people asleep inside them in much the same way.

For Queen and for country, she told herself.

Then the timer reached zero, the daisy chain detonated, exploding in a sequence of flashing orange and red flowers, spitting steel that tore fabric, flesh, and bone.

49

Sinan jerked awake, thinking at first that the flashes of light were something from a dream. He leaned forward, hands on the dashboard, and the bursts of fire continued in sequence, then vanished behind the wadi wall.

Matteen stopped the car, killed the lights, saying, "Did you see that?"

The heat came rushing back to Sinan, and he reached up, flicking the switch on the dome light so that it wouldn't illuminate the interior of the vehicle as he opened the door. He grabbed his rifle, slipping out, and as soon as the door was open he heard the explosions, but worse, he heard the screams, echoing through the wadi.

"Matteen, quickly!" he hissed, and closed the door, clambering onto the hood of the SUV and then jumping from it onto the wadi wall, holding his rifle with both hands, fitting his finger through the trigger guard. He sprinted low, the Kalashnikov ready, atop the wall of the wadi, stumbling as his pace grew more desperate, driven by the cries of his brothers.

50

There weren't many survivors, but there were enough to keep Chace busy. She hopped her sights from one to the next, squeezing each burst carefully, timing the shots, placing them precisely. She went for center mass, tracking shots where she needed to, one burst for most, two when required.

She reloaded and heard the sounds of the dying, and then heard something else, and whipped around, dropping to her back and bringing the P90 up at the same time, seeing the man twenty feet behind her, his hands folded on his head. All the same, her finger had almost descended on the trigger before she registered what she was seeing, and it took another half a second before the adrenaline coursing through her allowed his words to register.

"Friendly," the man was saying over and over again. "CIA, friendly, CIA."

Chace scrambled to her feet, sprinting toward him, the P90 in one hand. She grabbed his hair and yanked him over onto his back, dropping to a knee and driving the muzzle against his neck. He looked at her with pure alarm, his mouth working inarticulately.

"Friendly," he gabbled. "Friendly, in the name of God, I'm friendly."

"Who the fuck are you?" Chace hissed in return, and she pushed the muzzle harder against his neck.

"Matteen Agha," he said, and his English was accented, vaguely American. "My controller is Dennis Heppler at Langley, Juliet-ought-eight-nine-nine-two, please, I'm a friend, you must believe me."

"Nobody told me that I could find friends here."

The man closed his eyes, whispered, "I am unarmed, I am unarmed, please, you must believe me."

Chace gritted her teeth, the frustration and impatience raging. "Where did you come from, why the hell aren't you in the camp? Did you know we were coming?"

Matteen Agha shook his head, or tried to, saying, "No, we were on our way back, we were in Egypt. There were bombs, I warned Heppler, I told him there were five—"

"We?"

"—of the bombers, we were paired with them to act as their handlers—"

Chace yanked on his hair, hard, trying to silence him. "We?"

"My partner and I—"

The realization was utterly horrifying, and she released her grip on him, trying to get to her feet, turning to look across the wadi, opening her mouth to shout the warning.

Too late.

51

Thirty meters, and Sinan could see it, looking down the short drop, at the place that had been his home.

The tents were shredded, in tatters, and in the starlight that reflected off the desert, he saw his brothers, slain as they had slept. Their blood shone black on the earth, and he heard their sobbing, their pain. He saw survivors, struggling to get their weapons, to get to their feet, to escape the tents, and he saw them twist and fall, one after the other, as if touched by the breath of the Angel of Death.

Sinan looked around, frantic, and he saw the flicker to his left, blue light suppressed, and he heard another of his brothers scream, and he dropped back, still in his crouch, bringing his rifle to his shoulder, trying to circle around behind the shooter. His heart had climbed to his throat, and he tasted a bitterness in his mouth, something acrid, and he felt his hands trembling, his whole body shaking with his rage.

He tried to move slowly, though everything inside him screamed to hurry, telling him the more he delayed, the more his brothers died.

Sinan was perhaps ten feet from the man when he stopped, rolling to his side to reload his weapon, and the man looked up, saw him, and realized what was about to happen.

The man tried to roll, slapping the fresh magazine into place, scrambling to raise the gun and fire.

"Go to hell," Sinan said, and he pulled his trigger, held it down, watched as the muzzle-flash lit the man like a fiery strobe, watched as the man's body rattled and shook as the Kalashnikov tore him to pieces.

52

Chace heard the echo of the shots, saw the muzzle-flash light them a hundred meters away, the man with the rifle, firing and firing and firing, and it wouldn't stop, he wouldn't stop, and she cried out in Tom's agony, saw his arm rise and then fall again. She brought the P90 against her hip, tearing the trigger back, all her control gone. Brass rained around her feet, spent and smoking.

The strobe went off, the man twirling away, and Chace's eyes burned with the memory of light. She heard herself choking, jumped down the wall of the wadi, sprinting its width, her boots pounding the earth almost as hard as her heart, and when she reached the opposite side she scrabbled up it, losing the gun, not caring, pulling herself atop on her knees.

The brutality of his death forced a sob, caught in her throat. There were pieces of him missing, as if torn out by an angry, spoiled child who would rather break his possessions than share them. His eyes and mouth were open, and there was pain and fear in them, and his skin was splashed and painted in his own blood.

The emotion fractured her, stole her mind, too strong and too cruel, far beyond anything she had ever allowed herself to feel. Chace screamed without knowing she was screaming, and she put her hands to him, trying to hold Wallace one more time, trying to feel him warm and alive and hers.

Then the world exploded magnesium-flare red and white, and she came back to herself with blood in her mouth, facedown on wet earth. Disoriented and confused and still lost in the grief, she tried to push herself up. Pain ruptured in her back, sent her flat again, and somehow her mind connected that this was wrong, that she was being hurt, and she snapped her right arm back and up and surprised herself when it connected with bone. She felt another blow, this to her right shoulder, and she realized it had been meant for her head, and that she must have moved out of the way.

She pitched her legs up, to the side, twisting on the ground, and her boots connected with flesh again, not seriously, not enough to do anything but send her assailant back a few steps. She used the momentum to follow through, bringing her legs over and down again, flipping on the ground, getting her feet under her, and again she moved her head just in the nick of time, felt the brush of the Kalashnikov's stock as it stole the watch cap from her head.

Her thought was that it had been Matteen attacking her and that she would kill him for lying, but this wasn't Matteen, it was the other one, the one who had killed Tom. In the fraction she had to see his face, the details burned. He was young, younger than Matteen, and Caucasian, and he was swearing at her, cursing at her, spitting at her, spittle on his lips, swinging the Kalashnikov at her like a club. Blood ran from torn fabric along his left arm, and she wondered that she'd hit him only once, so poorly, and the Kalashnikov was coming at her head again.

She ducked beneath it, sprang up from her haunches, trapping the arm with her right while turning her back into him, driving her left elbow hard into his sternum. He grunted, twisting away, giving her only half the impact, and she felt the blow high on her left side, where her breast joined her ribs, and she screamed louder, yanking him forward, trying to flip him with the trapped arm.

Again, it half-worked, and the man dropped the Kalashnikov, struggling to free his arm as she brought him off the ground, twisting over her in the air, his hand dragging along her neck, pulling her hair, trying to take her down with him. Chace fell into him onto the ground, punched once at his throat, caught the mass of muscle at his shoulder instead. She felt her hair tearing as he pulled her down toward him, his mouth opening, trying to bite her face, and Chace snapped her forehead into his nose, felt the cartilage shatter and melt, and he roared and pounded at her back and side with his free hand, kicking at the earth, rolling them until she was on her back and he was pinning her with his weight.

It was impossible to breathe, agony to breathe, and Chace felt his hand hot on her throat, and something else digging into her skin above her right hip. She reached for it, found the hilt of her knife, and her vision was swimming, and he was over her, and his other hand left her hair, and the world cracked, jumped, as if badly spliced, and she felt wet heat spreading from her nose as he punched her face a second time, then brought that hand to join the first, squeezing the life out of her.

She stabbed him then, felt the blade slide over bone, then sink deep into his side, and the man howled, loud enough that she heard it through the roar of the surf crashing in her ears. Chace yanked the blade toward her, keeping it inside him, with everything she had, feeling it slide through hollow insides, and then she forced it back, in the opposite direction, turning the hilt. His grip on her faltered, and his eyes began to empty, and she turned the blade as if working the throttle of Kittering's motorcycle, ran it down, and felt the eruption of hot blood gushing over her hand.

His grip slipped, and he pitched forward, resting

atop her, and she heard his death rattle in her ear, felt it rustle through her hair.

Chace saw the stars above her blurring, felt her whole body shaking.

It hurt to breathe.

It hurt much more to be alive.

53

She was thinking of a time when she and Wallace had broken into a liquor store because all the pubs in Bath had closed, and they were drunk and wanted something to drink. They'd driven in his Triumph out into the middle of a field and gotten pissed out of their minds, drinking toasts to the memory of Minders past, men with names like Ed Kittering and Brian Butler. They'd been sick drunk and missed work the next day, and Crocker had torn into them for being stupid and foolish, and for, worst of all, being caught on surveillance camera robbing a liquor store in Bath.

Matteen Agha was standing over her, speaking. It took her a few seconds to remember who he was, and even longer to understand what he was asking, but try as she might, she couldn't let go of the knife. He had to pry her fingers away from the hilt before he could topple the dead man from astride her. Then he reached down and took her arms and pulled her to her feet.

"You have exfil, right?" he asked. "You have a pickup?"

Chace couldn't understand him. She knew so many languages, and she couldn't understand what he was saying.

"Where is the pickup?" Matteen insisted. "We need to go."

"Parlez-vous français?" she asked, and it was barely audible, and the pain it caused her throat was as acute as every other in her body and heart.

Matteen helped her sit, propping her against the wadi wall.

"Don't move," he said. "Don't move, don't do anything. I'll be right back."

"Je ne comprend pas," Chace croaked.

Matteen went off, back down the mouth of the wadi.

Chace sat still for most of a minute, then saw her P90 resting in the dirt. She needed two tries to get to her feet, then staggered to the weapon and nearly fell over again when she picked it up. Her fingers fumbled at the flap of her thigh pocket, and it took most of another minute to get out the remaining magazine and replace the empty in the gun.

She heard an engine start, echoing through the wadi.

She pulled herself back up the wadi wall and collapsed again, this time beside Wallace.

She heard the sound of wheels crunching earth, the slow approach of the vehicle beneath her, the headlights splashing fresh illumination. When the light hit Tom, his skin looked as pale as the surface of the moon, his eyes as cold.

A car door opened.

"I have to go now," Chace said to Wallace. "I have to go."

She raised her head and put her lips to his cheek, then pushed herself back along the ground, sliding back down to the wadi floor. She turned, saw Matteen standing beside the open driver's door, and Chace made her way numbly around to the passenger's side, climbed into the seat. Matteen came around and closed her door, then went back to take his place behind the wheel.

Chace fumbled out the GPS unit from her pocket, switched it on, and was amazed that it still worked.

She gave Matteen the bearing, and the car started, and she closed her eyes so that she wouldn't have to look at what she was leaving behind.

54

The SUV had saved them, allowed them to make
the first pickup on the twenty-third, at twenty-two
hundred hours. The bird had appeared out of
nowhere, hugging the Jordanian terrain, set down
just long enough for Chace to pull her battered and
abused self into the back, Matteen following. The
gunner in the back had nothing to say to them as
they took off again, and when they set down at the
base north of Elat, Landau was waiting.

Chace was taken to the base infirmary, where a
brusque doctor gave her an efficient and not unkind
examination, including eighteen stitches along her
scalp, where the first rifle blow had torn away a flap
of skin. He told her that she was lucky her skull

hadn't caved in, and she just looked at him, not feeling lucky about anything much at all. He gave her a shot for the pain, and she was nodding off when Landau returned with two of the heavies she recognized from the safehouse. He told them to take her back to Tel Aviv, and they brought her to another helicopter, and there was another ride, a short one, and she nodded off again while they were in the air, and a third time after they put her in the car.

She honestly had no memory of how she'd ended up in the Tel Aviv Hilton.

●

She awoke in pain, disoriented, and it took her several moments to piece together where she was and how she might have come to be there. When she got out of bed and pulled herself to the bathroom, she saw a plastic shopping bag resting on the closed toilet seat. Inside were clothes, presumably ones that would fit her.

She took a shower and didn't much feel it, even when she made it hot, even when she made it cold.

She dried off and dressed, avoiding looking at herself in the mirror.

●

Landau and Borovsky came to see her for debriefing at nine, and she saw no reason not to tell them everything that had happened, so she did. They listened closely, their faces betraying nothing.

When she was finished, Borovsky asked how she was feeling.

"Dead," she said.

"That will pass," he told her, and laid a pack of Silk Cut on the desk, then excused himself and left the room, leaving Landau behind.

"Where's Matteen?"

"Already gone," Landau said. "CIA was waiting to scoop him up the moment we left the base."

"So he was for real?"

"Apparently. I didn't ask, they wouldn't say anyway, we go on what we know at any given moment, yes?"

Chace nodded, staring out the window at the Mediterranean.

"You should be getting a call shortly," Landau said, rising.

"All right."

"My advice, take some time off. Take some rest."

Chace nodded, not hearing him.

Landau sighed, put a card on the desk beside the pack of Silk Cut. "You call that number if you need anything, you understand, Miss Chace?"

"Sure."

He hesitated, then seemed to acknowledge there was nothing he could say that she wanted to hear. He left the room, shutting the door quietly behind him.

For several minutes, Chace stayed in the chair, staring at the Med. Then she roused herself enough to go to the desk and get the pack of cigarettes and the ashtray. There was a book of matches in the ashtray, and she used them to light the first smoke, then used the ember of the first to light the second, and so on.

She was on her eighth when the telephone rang.

She didn't answer it.

●

She called down to the desk and told them that she wasn't to be disturbed.

She undressed and went back to bed.

When she awoke next, it was early evening, and the message light on the telephone was blinking orange. She took another shower, then used the room service menu to order dinner, which was a bottle of scotch and a Caesar salad.

After lighting a cigarette, she picked up the phone again and called the hotel operator, saying that she would again be accepting calls.

●

The phone rang six minutes later, and she answered it this time, saying, "Yes."

"Tara," Crocker said. "You can come home now."

About the Author

Born in San Francisco, **GREG RUCKA** was raised on the Monterey Peninsula. He is the author of ten novels, including five about Atticus Kodiak, and numerous comic books, including the Eisner Award–winning *Whiteout: Melt*. He lives in Portland, Oregon, with his family.

If you enjoyed Greg Rucka's
A Gentleman's Game,
the first crime novel centering on Minder Tara
Chace, you won't want to miss any of his
bestselling thrillers.
Look for them at your
favorite bookseller's.

And read on for an exciting preview of the
second Queen & Country thriller featuring
Chace . . .

Private

Wars

by
GREG RUCKA

Available now
from Bantam

PRIVATE WARS

GREG RUCKA

AUTHOR OF *A GENTLEMAN'S GAME*

PRIVATE WARS

Preoperational Background
Chace, Tara F.

As far as Tara Chace was concerned, she died in
Saudi Arabia, in Tabuk Province, on the rock-
hard earth of the Wadi-as-Sirhan.

She died when Tom Wallace died, when she
heard the chain of gunshots from the Kalashnikov, saw the spastic strobe of the muzzle-flash
from across the wadi, one man, unnamed and
unknown, lighting the other with gunfire even as
he killed him. There were nights when she still
heard her own howl of anguish, and she knew
the sound for what it was, the little life within
her stealing away into the desert air.

Tom was dead, and as far as Tara Chace was
concerned, she was, too.

She'd been wounded in the Wadi-as-Sirhan, had fought the man who had murdered Tom hand-to-hand. He'd tried to split her skull with the butt of his rifle, and when that had failed, tried to choke her to death with his bare hands. Chace had used her knife, and opened his lungs to the outside air, and at the School they would have called that winning. She might have called it that, too, if she'd felt there was anything left to win.

She was still numb from it all when she came off the plane at Heathrow to discover her Director of Operations, Paul Crocker, waiting for her at the gate itself. It was unheard of for D-Ops to greet a returning agent, and the surprise managed to penetrate the fogginess she now traveled in, and she had cause to wonder at it, but not for long. With Crocker as her escort she avoided Customs, winding through endless switchback corridors and through baggage claim until emerging into the drizzle of an early autumn morning.

Crocker guided her to a waiting Bentley, climbed in beside her, and the driver pulled out as soon as the door closed, and that was when Chace finally understood what was happening, and where she was being taken. Her mission in Saudi Arabia had been entirely unsanctioned, and Chace had gone AWOL to do the job. Even if they did still trust her, she had to be debriefed, and that debriefing would take place away from

London, at a secure facility hidden in the Cotswolds, called The Farm.

The drive was long, and held in silence. Crocker knew better than to try to engage her in conversation, and for her part, Chace was sitting beside a man whose living guts she now hated.

When she'd fled London some ten days earlier, the boys from Box hot on her heels, she'd been a Special Operations Officer in Her Majesty's Secret Intelligence Service. She'd been the Head of the Section, in fact, codenamed Minder One, with two other Minders under her command and tutelage. Along with Minder Two, Nicky Poole, and Minder Three, Chris Lankford, she had provided HMG with covert action capability, as directed and supervised by D-Ops, Paul Crocker. He was their Lord and Master, their protection against vagaries of government and the whims of politicians who saw agents as disposable as Bic pens, as nothing more or less than small cogs in a very large machine.

Stolen documents needed retrieving in Oslo? Send a Minder to get them back and hush the whole thing up. Potential defection in progress in Hong Kong? Send a Minder to evaluate the defector's worth, to then either facilitate the lift, or boomerang the poor bastard back into the PRC as a double-agent. Islamofascist terrorist assembling a dirty bomb in Damascus? Send a Minder to kill the son of a bitch before he can deliver the device to Downing Street.

Tara Chace had left London knowing that she

was one of the best—if not the best—Special Operations Officers working for any intelligence service anywhere in the world today.

She had no idea what she had returned as, but a trip to The Farm made at least one thing clear.

Tara Chace was *not* being welcomed home with open arms.

•

The Farm wasn't, really, though from a distance, if one didn't know what they were looking at or looking for, they could, perhaps, take it as such. From the lane, a single road wended through a gap in the drystone fence, disappearing beyond a wall of trees that concealed cameras and sensors designed to keep people out as much as to keep people in. After another mile came another fence, this one more serious, of metal and chain, guarded by a gatehouse and walking patrols, and past that, one could glimpse the manor house concealed beyond further trees. Into the compound, one found the dormitories, bungalows constructed in the early sixties and that demonstrated all of the architectural grace of the period, lined side-by-side along a paved walkway, surrounded by yet another chain-link fence, this one topped with razor wire.

As far as prisons went, Chace thought that this one wasn't half-bad. Her bungalow was simple and comfortable enough; and when she wasn't being interrogated by the likes of David Kinney and his Inquisitors from Box, or being evaluated by the head SIS psychiatrist, Doctor

Elizabeth Callard, or submitting to yet another physical by yet another physician she'd never met before in her life, she was left alone. She could take walks with an escort, read books from the manor library, exercise in the gym. There were no clocks anywhere she could see, and she was forbidden access to television, radio, newspapers, and the Internet.

The supply of scotch and cigarettes, however, was generous, and Chace availed herself of both.

●

She'd been at The Farm a week when Crocker returned. The Director of Operations came to her bungalow, let in by a guard, to find Chace vomiting into the toilet, and he waited until she was finished, until she had used the sink to rinse out her mouth and slop water onto her face, before saying, "It's time to come back to work."

Chace dried her face on a hand towel, refolded it and replaced it on its bar, before asking, "And what if I don't want to?"

"Of course you want to," Crocker said. "You're a Minder, Tara. You don't know how to be anyone else. You can't be anyone else."

It was what she'd feared the most since arriving at The Farm, the question she'd taken to bed with her every night. Not wondering what would happen if they threw her out on her ear, if they discharged her dishonorably, if they sent her packing. No, that would have made it easy; they would have made the decision for her.

Shunted off with a reminder of the Official Secrets Act and an admonishment to keep her nose clean, she could have left and blamed it all on them, on Crocker and Weldon and Barclay, on politicians and analysts in London and D.C. who felt Tara Chace was a world more trouble than she was worth.

That would have made it so easy.

Instead, her worst fear realized, manifested now by Crocker, telling her that all was forgiven.

Telling her what they both knew.

So she went with him, back to London, and back to work.

●

Six weeks later, she and Minder Two went to Iraq on Operation: Red Panda, to rescue a journalist named Gordon Lenneker who'd been kidnapped off the streets of the Green Zone. Things got bloody.

Things got very bloody.

Perhaps bloodier than they needed to get.

When they returned to London and had been debriefed, Chace was ordered to see Doctor Callard a second time.

"How are you feeling?"

"Fine. Some trouble sleeping, but fine."

"Are you still drinking?"

"I eat, too."

Callard's mouth twitched with a smile, and she scribbled something on the pad resting on the desk in front of her. She asked Chace more questions, and Chace answered them with the requisite evasion. The whole process lasted an hour, and when Chace again descended to the Pit, the basement office she shared with Lankford and Poole, she knew what the Madwoman of the Second Floor would report to D-Ops.

Chace wasn't a fool, and she knew herself well. She was drinking too much and sleeping too little. More often than not she started her mornings by being ill into the toilet. She was sore, and plagued by bad dreams when she could sleep. She was prone to irrational anger and sudden sorrows.

Even if she hadn't been able to read Callard's notes upside down, even if she hadn't seen the words *post-traumatic stress*, Chace would have made the diagnosis herself. Either that, or assumed she was premenstrual, but she'd already missed two periods since Saudi Arabia. That wasn't unique in her life; there had been periods of high stress in the past when she'd missed her cycle more than once.

All the same, she stopped at the Boots nearest her home in Camden on her way back from work that day, just to be certain. She read the instructions on the box, followed them, waited.

And found herself staring at two pink lines, which, according to the instructions, indicated positive.

She left her home, returned to the Boots, bought another test, and repeated the procedure, with the same result.

Two pink lines.

"Bloody fucking hell," she said.

•

The hardcopy of the Minder personnel files—past and present—was held by D-Ops, or more precisely, held in the secure safe in his outer office. Keys to the safe were in the possession of Crocker, the Deputy Chief of Service, Donald Weldon, and the Head of Service, C, known outside of the building as Sir Francis Barclay. Duplicates were stored on the in-house computer network, but access to those files in particular required a password that was altered every twenty-four hours, and even then, only supplied to the aforementioned holders of the keys.

Plus one other person, Kate Cooke, who manned the desk in Crocker's outer office, serving as his Personal Assistant. Not only did she have access to the password, but she had her own set of keys. After worrying the problem all night, it was Kate that Chace finally decided she stood the best chances with. First, they shared minority female status in the Firm; second, they bore a common cross, most clearly embodied in the form of D-Ops, but readily recognizable in the guise of any of the other Department Heads. That Chace was Head of Section for the Minders didn't change this; Minders were considered in SIS to be something of pariahs, more akin to working class thugs than to the more refined agents posted to stations around the world.

Finally, she and Kate had known one another some four years, and, in that time, managed a weak kind of professional friendship, one that began when each entered Vauxhall Cross at the start of the day, and ended when they departed again for home.

All the same, it took Chace some cajoling, and more deft lying, before she was able to get Kate to hand over the file on Wallace, Thomas S. (deceased). She scanned it quickly, and learned that Wallace was survived by his mother, Valerie, and that she lived in a town in Lancashire called Barnoldswick.

•

The following morning, Chace delivered her request for a leave of absence to Crocker, by hand. He read it at his desk, scowling, while she stood opposite him. When he'd finished he lit a cigarette, leaned back in his chair, and glared at her.

"Don't be a damn fool," Crocker said. "You can't possibly keep it."

It was more anger than humiliation that colored Chace's cheeks. Of course Crocker had known. They'd given her a complete work-up at The Farm, they'd have done bloodwork, as well.

Which meant Crocker had sent her to Iraq knowing she was pregnant.

"I am taking a leave of absence." She was more than a little surprised at the sound of her own voice. It was surprisingly calm.

"Is it Tom's?" Crocker demanded. "Is that it?"

"Twelve months," she said.

"You can't do it, Tara, not on your life. You can't have a child and be in the Section, it's not possible."

"Ariel and Sabrina," Chace countered, using the names of Crocker's daughters.

"Jennie." The name of his wife.

"Twelve months' leave. Sir."

"Not on your life."

"Then I quit," Chace said, and walked out.

●

She caught an early train out of King's Cross the next morning, bound for Leeds, riding in a non-smoking carriage that reeked of stale cigarettes. The ride took some two and a half hours, and once in Leeds she changed to a local connection, taking it as far as Skipton, where she hired a car and bought a copy of Lancashire A to Z. She took a room at the Hanover International Hotel, stowed her things, and, famished, ate a late lunch while going over the maps. She went to bed early.

In the still-dark hours the next morning, Chace made the fifteen-minute drive from Skipton to Barnoldswick. She parked the car near the Town Square, and after a seventy-minute reconnoiter, had found four positions ideal for static surveillance of number 17 Moor View Road, the home of Valerie Wallace.

It was light surveillance, the best Chace could manage without giving herself away, the best she could manage working alone. As a result, she was careful, trailing Valerie Wallace at a distance as the older woman went about her business in the town, working at the local charity shop, meeting friends for lunch or tea at this or that house, visiting the local surgery to see her GP. Autumn brought an already cold wind that promised a fiercer chill come winter, and most of the widow Wallace's activities were thus confined to the indoors, which made getting close difficult.

Shortly after midnight on her third day of surveillance, Chace broke into the surgery, curious as to the reason for Wallace's visit. She spent an hour with a penlight in a darkened file office, reading Valerie Wallace's medical history. When she was finished, she replaced everything as she had found it, and managed to relock the door on her way out.

In the afternoon of the sixth day, while Valerie was having her regular luncheon with friends at the tea shop off the Square, Chace picked the lock on the back door of 17 Moor View Road, and worked her way in careful silence through the older woman's home. If her schedule held true to form, Wallace would go from lunch to the local hospice for volunteer work that would stretch until almost the evening, and so Chace took her time. She searched in cabinets and closets, beneath the beds and in drawers, even going so far as to examine the contents of the kitchen, just to gain some insight into the older woman's diet.

In Valerie Wallace's small bedroom, smelling of lavender and laundry soap, Chace discovered a collection of framed photographs carefully arranged atop the dresser. There were pictures of a younger Valerie and, presumably, her late husband. Gordon Samuel Wallace had been a career soldier, and in two of the pictures stood in uniform, looking proud to be wearing it, if vaguely uncomfortable to be photographed while doing so. A third showed Valerie holding a newborn, and the remaining two were of Tom exclusively. One of them mimicked the portrait of his father, perhaps intentionally, wearing the dress uniform of a Royal Marine; the last, more recent, was taken in the sitting room of this very house, the branch of a Christmas tree reaching into the frame as Tom looked out the front window at the moor.

Wedged beneath the last was a folded letter, and Chace freed it, opened it, already knowing what it was.

Dear Mrs. Wallace, It is with great sadness that I must inform you of the passing of your son, Tom, in service to his country. . . .

Chace replaced the letter as she had found it, and departed as silently as she had come.

●

On the tenth day, a freezing November Tuesday, at nine o'clock exactly, Tara Chace knocked on the front door of Valerie Wallace's home.

"My name is Tara Chace," she said. "I worked with Tom."

Valerie Wallace, standing in the half-opened doorway, frowned slightly, squinting up at her. She was a small woman, easily a foot shorter than Chace, with hair more gray than black, and not so much heavy as thickened by age and gravity. She let her frown deepen, and didn't answer.

And Chace found herself at a loss, the speech she'd so carefully rehearsed abruptly gone, disappearing like vapor from her breath. She tried to retrieve it, found only bits and pieces, incoherent and useless.

Valerie Wallace shifted, one hand holding the door, still staring at her.

"We were lovers," Chace finally managed. "Before he died. We were friends and we were lovers, and I'm pregnant, and it's his. It's ours."

She thought it would garner some reaction, at least, if not the words, at least the clumsiness of them. And it did, because, after another second, Valerie Wallace blinked, and then opened the door more fully, inviting her inside.

"Perhaps you'd like to come in for a cup of tea, Tara Chace," Valerie Wallace said. "And you can tell me why you're here."

●

On the twenty-eighth of May, at seventeen past nine in the morning, at Airedale General Hospital in Keighley, with Valerie Wallace holding her hand as she screamed through the final surge of labor, Tara Chace gave birth to a daughter. The baby was healthy, twenty-two inches long, weighing seven pounds, eleven ounces.

She named the child Tamsin.

●

There were nights when, despite exhaustion, Chace found she could not sleep.

Staring out the window that overlooked Valerie

Wallace's well-tended and now fully in bloom garden at Weets Moor, holding Tamsin in her arms as the baby slept, Chace would sit and stare at nothing. She could feel her daughter's heartbeat, the rustle of her breath, the heat of her small body.

And Tara Chace would wonder how she could feel all of that, and still feel nothing at all.